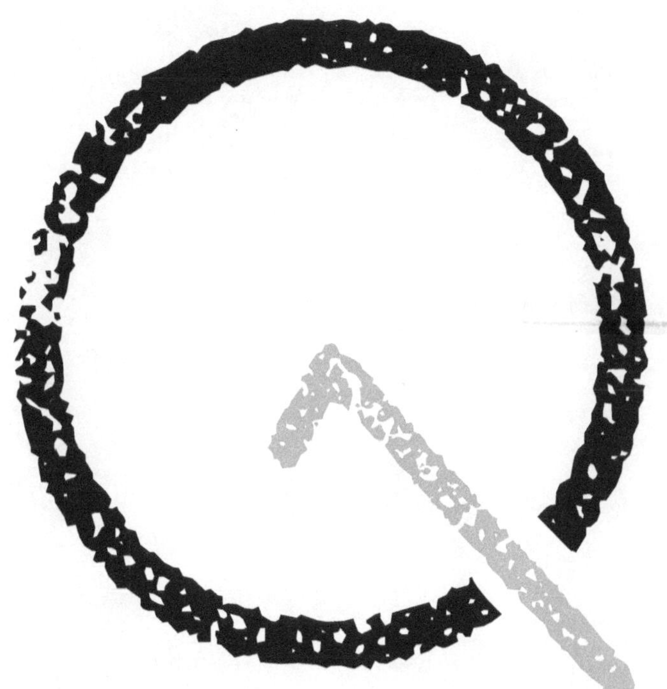

QUESTIONER

A NOVEL

STEVE C. POSNER

*This book is dedicated to my father, Sidney Posner.
I'm not sure he ever believed I would finish a
publishable novel, but he always supported me.
Here's to you, Dad!*

Conversation between the author and Perplexity AI:

QUESTION:
"Can a human tell if an AI has achieved at least a minimally conscious state?"

ANSWER:
"There is no clear evidence that humans can definitively determine if an AI has achieved a minimally conscious state."

PROLOGUE

Two lawyers walked into a bar and it wasn't a joke.

Martin Bavarius came to Washington to argue a murder appeal as lead counsel, and he booked a room at the Mandarin Oriental because his old Army pal, tech CEO Felix West, was holding QuestCorp's annual shareholders meeting there. Felix was firing up his crowd in the Grand Ballroom and Bavarius, already prepped for his afternoon argument, watched for a bit until he needed to use the john. His sixty-six years made the need urgent and he strode down the corridor ever faster until he bumped into a slim, dark-haired woman as she turned from a water fountain. They both muttered apologies and she pushed into the women's room while he sped on toward the men's. But before he got there, she rushed out of the women's crying, "Dead! She's dead!"

Bavarius whirled, called a security guard, and arrowed into the women's room, thinking maybe the slim woman was wrong and he could help. Way back when Felix and he had dismantled torture centers in Iraq, he'd saved poor souls who looked dead at first, lying under their names that they'd scratched on the pale cracked walls along with messages to their families. But this woman today was dead all right, sitting on a toilet with a hole gashed behind her right ear. Bavarius stepped in her blood and felt a crunch beneath his shoe. *Dumb, Martin. You're disturbing evidence.*

Out in the mezzanine there was chaos and alarm as the cops came. Detectives took Bavarius' statement and his gory shoes as evidence, and he walked the streets in blue police booties until he could buy new shoes that pinched his feet as he cabbed downtown to court. He couldn't help noticing that the cabbie's dashboard license named him Snaky Khalil. What kind of name was Snaky? Four years in Iraq and Bavarius had never heard of anyone named Snaky. He would have to ask Felix if he had. And ask Marguerite, who'd largely grown up in Baghdad.

Bavarius got to court and there was the slim, dark-haired woman. Not lead counsel for the other side, but second or third chair, whispering to the opposition mouthpiece. Then, after months of prep, he stood up to tell the court in ten minutes why his client shouldn't be executed for nailing a gay man through the balls to a fence and leaving him to die: Prosecutors shouldn't be able to shoehorn a definition from an unrelated legal area into hate crimes law in order to condemn a defendant, however heinous the son of a bitch. When the argument was done and Bavarius was packing up, he heard the slim woman's rich contralto say, "Nice job. How did you come up with that angle?"

And so the two lawyers, Bavarius and Selena MacKenzie, walked into a bar.

QUESTION:

"Do AIs have more means of perceiving the world than humans?"

ANSWER:

"AIs have sensors that surpass human sensory organs in range and precision. AI can detect things like infrared light and ultrasonic sound that humans cannot, and the ability to process multiple streams of information simultaneously."

CHAPTER 1

Crofter's was a proper Irish pub, owned by the fourth generation of Crofters. A haven of dark carved woods, leaded glass and leather barstools, built when mahogany and brass were cheap, its food and drink excelled. The entertainment, too. Pool tables and dartboards. Big screens showing news and sports.

And in one corner, a QuestGame setup, cordoned off from the rest of the bar area. Two guys in headsets, collars open, ties pulled down, faced each other across a green floor with a sandy stripe running between them. They were playing QuestGame's *Say It Ain't So, Joe*, based on the Chicago Black Sox scandal. One held his empty hands up like a batter at the plate. The other folded his hands to his chest like a pitcher. And then … the windup … the pitch … he swings …. The hitter couldn't physically run for first but his feet shuffled a little as he scurried down the baseline in QuestGame's virtual world. The pitcher turned as though watching a long fly ball, then he pivoted and reached up as though catching the ball. The hitter stopped shuffling, shook his head, then turned back to the plate. The pitcher toed the rubber. In QuestGame's world, the two players each could embody an entire team.

To people at nearby tables, the players would have looked embarrassingly uncoordinated, if Felix's engineers hadn't provided context, and drawn in the watchers, by projecting a hologram against the wall behind them. The images looked 3-D, and shifted points of view like the cameras at a televised game. When the player went into his pitching motion, the hologram showed his motion as he saw it in his mind, not as the minimal movement he actually made. And when he moved further back in the outfield to catch the fly, the hologram showed a running center fielder as graceful as any Gold Glove winner. A drinker at a table outside the cordon threw a pretzel at the hitter and shouted, "Get yer ice-cold beer here!" The waitress touched his arm and shook her head. It was uncool to harass the players.

"Booth or bar?" Bavarius asked.

"Bar."

Their arms pressed together as they mounted stools.

Bavarius touched a key on the bar, and another in front of MacKenzie, and the voice of a classic baseball announcer encompassed them in individual sound envelopes that each of them alone could hear, and that didn't interfere at all with their ability to hear each other, or the people around them.

"If you don't want to hear the game, tap that button."

MacKenzie did, so Bavarius did, too. He said, "Sometimes—no reason ever given—Tommy Crofter awards *Say It Ain't So, Joe* winners shepherd's pie and homebrewed stout. Irish shepherd's pie."

"What makes it Irish?"

"Nutmeg. Nutmeg's the key. The Crofter family are Northern Irish rebels from way back. Tommy loves the real Irish food and drink, and early baseball. Back then, forty percent of the major league players were Irish and the game was scrappy."

She changed the subject. "Your office is in Kansas."

"Yes ma'am."

"And you're from Kansas."

"You've looked me up."

"You've been involved in two cases I've worked on. It would've been malpractice not to dig. The most quoted federal judge since Oliver Wendell Holmes, retiring to teach law and emerge to argue the occasional high-profile case. Pundits called you a shoo-in for the Supremes. And you turned it down! I figured there had to be a reason. But I couldn't find a damned thing."

"I didn't want it, that's all."

She quoted him, "'You can build a pig trough from marble and place it on the mountaintop. But if you eat the slops, you're still a pig.'"

"I never should have said that."

"A lot of us were glad you did."

"Yes, well … How are you holding up? Finding that woman the way you did had to be a shock."

"She was a friend of mine. Connie Weathers. One of QuestCorp's top design engineers."

"I'm sorry."

He let silence sit between them in the bar's ambient noise. It felt awkward, yet appropriate.

When she was ready, she asked, "The shepherd's pie and the stout are house specialties?"

That's what they ordered.

"So, Selena, where do you hail from?"

"New York. Greenwich Village."

"Interesting place to grow up."

"A privileged place. My neighborhood was, anyway. Dad was a tobacco lawyer."

"Mickey MacKenzie? Of course!"

"You have his look. Jimmy Stewart doing Mr. Deeds. But your hair and eyebrows are shaggier than Jimmy's, and Dad was bald."

"Doesn't sound like I have their look at all."

"But you do. Maybe less their look than their manner. They both radiated sincerity. You just used your earnestness to kick our butts. You being right on the law was almost secondary."

"Selena, you wrote a fine brief. You made the points your client needed made. The court still may decide in your favor. But if they buy my argument, you and I both come out winners."

"How so?"

"My client escapes lethal injection. I'll bet you don't want to see anyone executed, so we both win on that front. And the judges can avoid deciding that the Constitution doesn't protect folks like Reutzel, so the LGBTQ crowd can continue fighting for them."

The stouts came, black and aromatic, in wide Imperial pint glasses.

"To win-wins. We need more of them." Bavarius raised his glass and she clinked it.

"To my brother, Joey, and happy lives." The stout left creamy foam on MacKenzie's lip. "This is wonderful."

Bavarius tasted his and agreed. It was bitterly hoppy, smooth, and rich with notes of coffee and chocolate, fading to a malty finish. "So, Mickey inspired your career choice?"

"Yeah, but Mom, too. Medical researcher. Her team was working on an AIDS vaccine when my brother died. She was too late to help Joey, but she won a MacArthur Fellowship. Put the first installment check down on the kitchen table in front of me. Said, 'I couldn't save Joey. But this will help you be anything you want. In his memory.' So, I buckled down. MIT. Undergrad and graduate work."

"But you're a lawyer."

"Law came later."

"At MIT, did you study under Felix West?"

He watched MacKenzie's eyes blink, then look at her lap. "He taught me."

A headline flashed across a big screen: "Kansas prosecutor arrested for shooting man in broad daylight duel. Says computer made him do it."

"That looks interesting. Let's listen."

They toggled their sound envelopes as the anchorwoman gave way to a reporter on the scene.

"People liken trial lawyers to gunfighters," the reporter said. "But this was never as crazily true as here today in Topeka, where two attorneys fought a pistol duel at high noon in a courthouse parking lot. One of them, John Mudge, lies near death tonight with a bullet in his chest. The other, Mark Ryder, an assistant district attorney, is in custody. A police spokesman says that Ryder has confessed to the shooting, but insists that the QuestGame computer system made him do it. QuestGame is the wildly popular AI gaming system published by QuestCorp."

The screen showed a thin, youthful man in a brown suit, head down, cuffed hands shielding his face, being led from a squad car into a police building.

"I know Mark Ryder," Bavarius said. "The kid's as earnest as sunflowers are yellow. I can't imagine him shooting anyone."

The food came. Soda bread, green salads and Crofter's shepherd's pies.

She tasted the pie. "You're right. The nutmeg makes it."

She asked him what it had been like as an Army lawyer overseas, and how he had come up with some of the language in his opinions. She recited from memory: "'While dishonesty is more the issue than stupidity, the Darwin award for both goes to Maitomo.' I worked on that case."

"You did?"

She raised her glass to him. "It settled in our favor after your opinion came down. I was second-chairing depositions in Osaka at the American embassy. Picture this: We're deposing a Maitomo engineer. Three lawyers sitting at each side of the table. Four more Japanese lawyers standing behind their bigwigs. I write a question. Our lead counsel asks it in English. Our translator asks it in Japanese. Their translator disputes the translation. Finally, the translators agree on the question and their translator asks it. Sometimes our translator says their guy asked it wrong and they wrangle some more. By now, nobody remembers the original question, but the engineer gets asked … something."

Bavarius was laughing out loud. She kept going. "Maitomo's lead counsel—an American—objects on every legal ground he can think of and some he just makes up. Mostly, he directs the engineer not to answer. Sometimes, he objects but lets the engineer answer, and the engineer answers in Japanese. The translation process repeats itself going the other way. And generally, the answer is 'I don't know.' All while we're billing top hourly fees and the Japanese firm's doing the same. This goes on for three days. The last morning, I get into the elevator with the engineer. He smiles at me. I ask, 'So, Barushitta-san, how do you like depositions?' He answers, 'Oh, man, they make my head hurt,' in perfect English with a Southern accent."

Bavarius almost spat out his food and she gave a snort. They kept it light and enjoyed their food and each other's company. Then they split the tab and hailed a cab.

"Where are you staying?" Bavarius asked. "I'll drop you."

"The Mandarin Oriental."

"You've got good taste."

The cab took them through the Smithsonian complex and past the Museum of the Bible and the International Spy Museum—strange neighbors. The venerable hotel stood over the shore of the Tidal Basin. MacKenzie got out. Bavarius got out, too.

"I thought you said you'd drop me off."

Bavarius grinned. "My room's here also."

She reached for her purse, but Bavarius said, "Quicker for the driver if I just pay him. You can pick up the next one."

They walked to the elevator and pushed their respective buttons. They reached her floor first. The elevator door closed between them.

Bavarius smiled. A nice interlude, with a woman he found attractive, if young for him.

In his room, he saw the phone light blinking. He pushed the message button.

The voice was young, male and stressed. "Judge Bavarius, this is Mark Ryder. Your message service is supposed to forward this call. I'm in trouble, Judge. In jail. I've done ... they say I've done ... something awful. Would you please represent me?"

Ryder, as a prosecutor, knew better than to say anything that might be construed as an admission where the police might hear, and what he'd said was too close. *Smart, but still young enough to be too upset for caution. He needs a lawyer right now.* If Bavarius wasn't the right lawyer, he could quickly find Mark one better suited.

He called his friend and co-counsel Bill Purdue. "Hey, Bill. I think we won but you never know. Listen, Mark Ryder called me ... Yes, I know you know him ... You know John Mudge, too? ... Well, Mark's asked me to defend him. You want in? ... Good."

He stood and walked to the window. Washington was spread below him. Lincoln brooded on his chair. Washington's Monument stood tall. Arlington National Cemetery lay huge, just across the Potomac. Great men and unknown soldiers. All dead and gone.

"I'll get back to Topeka tomorrow afternoon. We'll talk then."

So, Mark thinks QuestGame made him shoot someone.

QuestGame was powered by one of Felix's artificial intelligence systems. AIs had grown in power and influence in the last ten years. They worked cooperatively with humans to improve economic and climate models, and with soldiers to plan large campaigns and small tactical operations. They also dominated political campaigns with misinformation, making it hard for even seasoned analysts, lawyers and journalists to discern truth from fiction. Nations could not agree on how to control them, and laws and regulations couldn't keep up with the array of selfish, greedy, and downright malicious uses to which they were put. They replaced human decision-makers but still made errors that hurt people. They reinforced psychological silos, often with violent results.

But Bavarius had never heard anyone allege that an AI had compelled him to commit murder.

Bavarius had used QuestCorp's research system, Questioner, in preparing for today's oral argument. As the legal research system relied on by the federal courts, Questioner was reputed to be one of the most stable, bulletproof AI systems in existence. And yet, Questioner had presented him with something strange. Bavarius had ignored it at the time, but now he remembered the Questioner session. It had been profitable, and gave him what he needed to win in court. But its ending had been bizarre.

Spooky.

QUESTION:

"Can an AI produce suboptimal results as an adaptation to user behavior?"

ANSWER:

"Yes, an AI can produce suboptimal results as an adaptation to user behavior ...."

CHAPTER 2

Bavarius' virtual reality headset had plunged him into Questioner's universe of law.

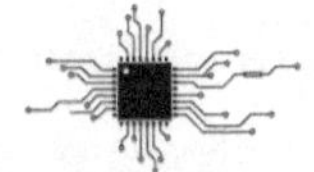

Below him, a vast city lit the darkness.

And from high above, a gigantic wheel-entity pulled him toward it as if by tractor beam. Its five great wheels were mounted on an axle. The axle was a solid blue beam of light that began at a point in the far past, and in the other direction, receded into an indefinite future. Its diameter changed rarely, in small increments. The axle was wrapped in a translucent pale blue sheath that organically grew thicker and thinner over the beam's length.

The beam, sheath and wheels were a graphic metaphor for American constitutional law over the course of time.

The axle was the Constitution's text.

The sheath was the Constitution's "penumbra"—rights not stated in the constitutional text, but inferred by judges from other rights that the Constitution did explicitly protect.

Each of the five wheels was mostly of a single hue. But they were shot through with veins of color from the others, because while the discipline of law requires categorization and logic, it cannot ignore the innate messiness of humankind. The wheels represented case law (green), statutes (red), judicial doctrines (white), historical context (purple), and the interests at stake (yellow).

The colors that lit the city below reflected those of the wheel-entity in patterns far too complex to comprehend at a glance. The city was a hodgepodge of state constitutions, and the statutes, regulations, ordinances, and case law of federal, state, county, municipal, tribal, and multi-jurisdictional entities.

This was Bavarius' personal metaphor. It was how he saw Questioner's legal universe. Decades ago, while in law school, he had suggested the visual metaphor of the beam and disks to his constitutional law professor. His professor had pooh-poohed it as too limited, and Bavarius hadn't pursued it. But when he first tried Questioner, the image sprang immediately to life. And as he worked his way through a case, it became ever more immediate and real. The city of law with all its neighborhoods, and geographies, and dimensions, was offered to him as needed, organized according to his own mental schema by methods he did not understand. He did not need to understand how it worked. It was enough that his research became more efficient each time he entered Questioner's world.

Felix had once told him that others could view it all differently. "Picture it, Hoss: A med mal lawyer seeing the constitutional wheel-entity as a spinal cord through vertebrae. Or a transportation lawyer sees it as a highway through mountain tunnels. Or an aviation lawyer as a flight path through clouds." Did Purdue, both lawyer and cartoonist, see it all as a folio of sketched images—each a world into which he could venture? Bavarius told himself, as he often did, that he would have to ask Purdue how he saw his own Questioner sessions. But Bavarius' Questioner experiences were so absorbing he never remembered to ask.

And this was another reason he had quit the bench, one he hadn't told Felix. Like many judges, Bavarius had almost lived in Questioner's world. It was a fascinating, welcoming place, and it had sometimes taken a conscious effort, when he was in the real world, to remember that it was real. That the people he spoke with—even those he was with every day, like his clerks and colleagues—were flesh and blood, and not avatars. He had never discussed his feelings with anyone during his time on the bench, and none of his fellow judges had seemed bothered by their use of Questioner. But the time came when he didn't want to use Questioner so much and old school research was too slow. He was tired of phony lawyer antics and wanted to spend his time with people. As a professor and occasional defense lawyer, he still used Questioner, but he used it less, and interacted with folks more.

Now, he was drawn into the yellow wheel, and he realized it was because the AIs sensed his need to know more about the D.C. Circuit judges who would decide Jackson. It was impossible to know which judge would write the opinion or even which judges might sit on the bench. So Bavarius needed to know as much as possible about all of them. He passed doorways labelled, "Institutional Interests," "Individual Interests," "Social Class Interests," "Racial Interests," etc. He would get to them. But first, he opened a doorway marked, "Judges: Backgrounds and Philosophies."

How did the judges view the LGBTQ communities? What might one of the judges be especially sensitive to, that his client's previous lawyers had missed? One by one, Bavarius reviewed the backgrounds, philosophies and foibles of the judges. Had one been molested as a Boy Scout or altar boy? Or had a wonderful teacher who'd happened to be gay? Bavarius delved on. A few times he laughed, or felt embarrassed for the judge whom he was examining.

The moment he felt he'd absorbed enough, a hatch opened in the yellow floor, and Bavarius plunged toward the city below. It wasn't a terrifying, out-of-control plunge. He rode a widely-advertised exercise bike as the manufacturer's name flashed across the virtual sky, peddling at a lazy pace, descending with wholly unjustified speed.

The bike took him to a small house on a rundown street. He could tell the street bordered two neighborhoods. The first was of civil rights cases; he could hear chants protesting inequality. The second was of criminal cases; he could smell blood and even after he got off the bike, feel bars in his hands. Not bicycle bars. Prison bars.

The house was much larger inside than out. One corner of the ground floor displayed a diorama of Reutzel's murder. A single bookshelf hung from a wall, but if Bavarius touched it, it would open into a library of all the writings that made up the case docket. Stairs rose along another wall. The second floor held the trial court and all its proceedings, including transcripts. Each floor above that held one of the courts in which proceedings had taken place. On the wall next to the staircase, a screen displayed a spreadsheet in which each cell was a different fact, a different argument, or a different judicial precedent. Bavarius could call up a related case and ask how its outcome might have changed if a lawyer had done or said this instead of that. Each window and crack in the walls looked out upon—and let in—smells and sounds of another legal neighborhood, some tangential to the legal areas in which Bavarius' case resided, but others seemingly far away.

But the structure and fuzziness of his case was more complex and subtle than a simple household metaphor or spreadsheet could convey. As he moved into the next room, he saw a towering pyramid of multidimensional, Escher-like facets. Details and facts were set into these facets as jeweled pebble mosaics that could be taken apart and reassembled at will and examined for truth, elegance, how they might appeal to the judges, and how they might fit into the path to victory. Within and without the pyramid, bridges and branches and beams reached out to steeples of case law from different jurisdictions and legal fields. Groves and forests represented the interests, as explained by organizations and individuals who had testified, and filed briefs, and sought to try the case in the media. Where did the information on all those interests, and the people who embodied them, come from? Bavarius was awed to contemplate the multitude of contracts and conduits that must connect QuestCorp to other information collectors and purveyors across the Net and Cloud.

And rising through the floor to the peak of the hyper-modern pyramid and beyond—and this might appeal to Judge Green—was a thing transmuted from Norse myth—a Yggdrasil, a world tree that connected all legal regimes, its roots in the Code of Hammurabi, rising through the Old Testament, Magna Carta, and the Constitution, and branching out, in the house/pyramid of Bavarius' case, through the shameful Dred Scott decision, the post-Civil War constitutional amendments, the civil rights movement and laws, branching more through myriad cases, and now, at the tip of one twig, Bavarius' case of Jackson v. United States. His task was to influence the growth of the law from here.

Bavarius knew that an appellate lawyer's art is to guide the law's growth without straying into wholly new areas. Since appellate courts rarely allow entirely new contentions, the lawyer must tend to the arguments that prior lawyers in his case raised but failed to develop. He must sculpt them to please the judges, although the law is far messier than a Zen or formal garden. It is a sprawling city, permeated and surrounded by the sea of history, like the canals and lagoon in and around Venice: A liquid stew of personal, political, economic, and religious motives, schemes, theories, and doctrines. Perspective was easily lost in this fetid swamp of detail and ambiguity.

Inquiries flowed from him too fast for conscious thought, as Questioner helped his mind organize, buffer and transmit them. What came back to him were not just reams of disorganized facts. It was useful data from all *the sources with whom QuestCorp had either public or contractual access, organized into levels and categories, and webbed organically to other relevant lattices and categories by leaping bridges, arches, and shafts, that sometimes branched or changed directions in the chaotic logic of bramble bushes. All housed within the multidimensional logic of his case. Bavarius manipulated the pyramid's higher facets as though playing with a hyper-dimensional Rubik's Cube.*

And then all movement stopped.

Oh.

Could it be so basic?

Yes. Oh my. Yes.

Bavarius ran through the argument in simple, sequential English. It was clear. It was beautiful. He could remember and present it easily.

He found himself in the modest house as he had first entered it.

He walked out the front door and locked it behind him, turned to face the neighborhood street—

—and was confronted by Dred Scott. Not the ancient law case, but the man himself, large-eyed and mustached, with a wrinkled forehead and a great bush of hair. Bavarius was yanked into Scott's body—no, it was an AI avatar—and found himself scratching an insect bite under Scott's trousers and peering out of Scott's eyes onto a traveling carnival's midway, where the dwarf barker who called himself General Lee shouted for Illinois farmers to come see tumblers and hootchie cootchie dancers. Scott's mouth opened and from it rolled lines from "Uncle Tom's Cabin." Scott had struggled to memorize the three minutes of "Tom" he performed. He spoke slow and clear to the rubes who gawked at him as he stood beneath the sign proclaiming him: "Dred Scott—The Slave Who Started the War!" Oh yes, the white folks stared. But they rarely spoke a word to him. Even the carnies gave him silence, except to give orders. One time, the barker had taken a cane to him.

Scott could bear it, though, as long as the show paid good money that he could send to his wife Lucy and the children. The money kept him a slave even now.

And suddenly, Bavarius was himself again, and Dred Scott stood before him, sneering, "Hell, man, you just a slave like me."

The ghost vanished, and the exercise bike sat invitingly on the sidewalk. Bavarius climbed on, and the bike lifted him toward the hole in the virtual sky that was his way home. As the name of the bike's manufacturer unfurled behind a passing biplane, Bavarius wondered why he both had to pay Questioner's subscription fee, and endure product ads.

The real world reappeared, colors drab, emptiness tightening around Bavarius' nerves. Yet, there was relief as his mind slowed toward a human pace, and the pain faded. He couldn't begin to remember all he had seen, felt and thought. The Dred Scott encounter had been weird, but had passed from his mind as dreams do when you wake up. He remembered what he needed to argue his case. But now, in his Mandarin Oriental hotel room, it came back to him. How was Dred Scott relevant to his case research?

Long practice helped Bavarius push away the day's occurrences. He performed a round of tai chi, and then catnapped. He woke with a vague memory of long, narrow blue eyes. He researched Selena MacKenzie, who owned those eyes. Quantum computer and AI theory at MIT. Law degree from Stanford. She had published papers on artificial intelligence and constitutional law, and had worked at two white shoe law firms on high-tech transactions. Five years ago, she'd quit and founded The Law

Offices of Selena MacKenzie. Had she failed to make partner? Grown tired of rubbing elbows with stodgy old money and digital grifters? It looked like much of her solo work had been for gay rights groups.

He emailed a couple of friends, partners at firms she had worked for. They both responded quickly. MacKenzie was top flight, they said, a terrific brief writer, superb with software, and able to get up to speed quickly in almost any area of law or tech. She'd learned from the best and offered her services to firms working on cases that interested her. Those firms considered themselves lucky to have her. She'd done key research and second-chaired intellectual property trials. In *Magdalene Rubber v. Maitomo Chem. Ind.*, she was the one who'd figured out that the case wasn't about stolen software, as all Magdalene's other lawyers thought, but was really about Maitomo using Magdalene production designs in its factories worldwide, even though it had licensed the tech for use solely in Japan. MacKenzie had built the theories of several major cases and structured their courtroom presentations. And then she had moved on. She had money and reputation that let her work when, where and how she wanted.

She might be able to help me figure out what to do with Mark's case.

Bavarius phoned her. "Remember Mark Ryder?"

"The guy who fought the duel?"

"He called me. Asked me to represent him."

"Oh?"

"You said you studied under Felix West."

"That's right."

"How much do you know about QuestGame?"

"I'm familiar with some of the technology."

"Familiar enough to listen to me interview Ryder and tell me if his story could be true?"

"Maybe." She paused. "You know QuestCorp wouldn't like it if Ryder's story came up in court."

"I can imagine. It's pretty far-fetched, but I need to rule it out." Even as he said it, he wondered why he had to rule it out. He was probably going to hand the case to another lawyer.

Because I'm curious. And it's worth a little time and money to satisfy my itch. And working with Selena MacKenzie might be fun.

"Why don't you meet me in Topeka? I'll pay your expenses."

There was silence as she thought about it. Then she said, "The last few months have been high-octane. If any place is gonna be tranquil, it's Kansas, right?"

She might know law and tech, Bavarius thought, but not much about Bloody Kansas.

QUESTION:

"How many AI-related chips have been surgically placed in human brains?"

ANSWER:

"The number is relatively small, likely in the dozens or perhaps low hundreds, given the experimental nature of the technology and the strict regulatory oversight required for such procedures."

CHAPTER 3

"I didn't want to kill John Mudge," Mark Ryder said. "He's the worst kind of defense shyster, but I didn't want to kill him. Beating him in court was always good enough."

"He's not dead," Bavarius said.

A rigidity seemed to melt out of Ryder. "Thank God."

"They didn't tell you?" MacKenzie was leaning against the wall of the jailhouse visiting room, arms folded. Bavarius had introduced MacKenzie as "a fine attorney who's been before the Supreme Court and knows a lot about QuestGame." She watched Ryder with cat-like concentration and an encouraging half-smile.

"No," Ryder said. "No. He's bad off, though, right?"

"Yes. He's in bad shape." Bavarius said. "So ...." He swept his hand around, taking in their surroundings as though to say, *and here we are.*

Bavarius watched Ryder's face, less youthful over gray and white jail clothes than it had been on TV.

Ryder tapped his nails on the white steel table. "I still don't understand what happened."

"Mudge was shot at noon," Bavarius said. "He was found hanging out of his car in the courthouse parking lot. Before the shooting, when did you last see him?"

"The day before, in Judge Kanaday's courtroom. A murder case. I'm sure Mudge knows where the murder weapon is. I wouldn't be surprised if he has it."

"But you don't have proof?" Bavarius asked.

"No, so instead, I—" Ryder stopped and grimaced. "I never got why so many perps waive their rights and confess, until now. They put you in a cell, and there's this urge to defend and explain …."

"But right now, you're not confessing. You're telling your lawyers, under attorney-client privilege, what happened."

"Yeah. Well, Mudge …. You know, I went to law school to do good."

MacKenzie probed. "Truth, justice and the American Way?"

Ryder gave her a look that combined ruefulness, fear and, oddly, humor. "Corny, huh? But true. I didn't have to go into law for the money. My family has money, and my wife Penny's does, too. I could afford to go into it for the right reasons. But Mudge, he's the opposite. I don't blame him for being in it for the money. A lot of lawyers are. But he's way beyond that. Not just an ass, but a religious nut and a hypocrite. Always appealing to God's judgment. Describes his clients as the meek who will inherit. Has that preachy radio show Sunday mornings; he collects money for his 'Meek Man's Defense Fund.' Sends brochures to his flock in the poor neighborhoods. The brochures have an outline of a hand drawn on them. They say, 'Put your hand on mine and let me pray for your wrongly jailed loved one!' Folks mail him five, ten bucks at a time, and he drives a Mercedes."

"I get the idea," Bavarius said.

"He'll probably be governor one day. If he … if he lives. Oh, shit."

"He's not dead, Mark. We don't have to go there."

"Right ... right. You don't know how hard a day can be dealing with Mudge. You're in court to prosecute thirty, forty cases. Things that should go quick, like arraignments. With Mudge, everything takes longer. Guy fights every point, especially when he *has* no point."

"So Mudge is a pain. So what?" Bavarius asked.

"So, I've got to let out steam sometimes," Ryder said. "And since I'm married with a little kid, I try to be careful."

"Got to stay respectable." Bavarius nodded.

"Yeah. Well, not just that."

"What, then?"

For a prosecutor, Ryder had puppy-soft eyes. Anxious eyes. "I want my kid to grow up proud of me."

Bavarius looked down at his own hands for a long moment to change the pace, let Ryder relax a little. "So, what do you do to let off steam?"

"Play AI games."

"What kind?"

"All kinds. The tougher, the better. Cut my teeth on Absolute Virtue."

"I don't know it." Bavarius flicked an eye toward MacKenzie.

She said, "You must be good, Mark. Ever beat it?"

"Yeah."

She looked skeptical.

"Took me months," Ryder added hastily.

"Takes *everyone* months," MacKenzie said.

"Ever try QuestGame?" Ryder asked her. They had established an instant rapport. "It's the best. You don't just play a game. You live it. And a lot of its games are based on legal and constitutional history, so if you're a lawyer ...." Ryder's puppy eyes glazed over. "It's the best."

"I know. I own QuestCorp stock," Bavarius said.

"Yeah? When'd you buy it?" Ryder leaned forward. "I picked it up at forty-six, and now—"

"It's gone up. Let's talk finance after we get you out of this."

Ryder slumped back on his stool. "OK. So, we're in court and Mudge gives me a real hard time. Judge Kanaday's unhappy because his docket's slow enough without this crap and he blames both of us. Finally, I get out of court and go home. Have a beer."

"Just one?"

"Dos Equis, with lime." Ryder's hand rose to cloak his eyes. "Might've been my last beer. Ever."

"Don't think like that. Take this one minute, one day at a time," Bavarius said. "Right now, you're telling us your story. That's all you're doing. If we put you on the witness stand, all you do is tell your story. *If* we put you on, which we probably won't. If we go to trial. We're a long way from decisions like that."

"Yeah. OK."

"So, what happened next?"

Ryder's hand settled back down in his lap. "I put on the headset and kicked loose. I don't know if you've ever played QuestGame, but it senses what you want."

MacKenzie nodded. "I know."

"So, you've played."

"Yes. And I've studied some of the theory. Please go on with your story."

"Well, Ms. MacKenzie—"

"Selena."

"OK, Selena. You can play against yourself, against computer simulations, or against other players. I like going up against real people. They get more balls-to-the-wall crazy than the AIs. So that's what I chose."

"A human opponent."

"All of a sudden I'm in this green Lincoln Continental with a couple of buddies in Montgomery."

"Alabama?"

"Right. It's maybe 2 a.m. We pull up to this joint—Gowan's Truck Stop. Billy Ray goes in to get us burgers and pop. The radio's on and I hear this voice. Sounds like a jerk. It's what he's saying about cop culture breeding killers, and prosecutors coddling them. So, I say something to my buddy Cal. And the radio voice comes back, like it heard me. Says if I bring my fascist ass around, he'll set it on fire. I say I'll show him my ass, all right. He says he's in a red Wiley Sanders tractor trailer rig at Gowan's and if I come over he'll shoot me. Sure enough, I see the truck by the pumps. I tell the radio I've got a gun and if he'll come out, I'll kill him. I drive closer until I see his face. He's the dorkiest, most self-righteous, preening little prick I've ever seen. Even wears a suit and a bow tie, at a truck stop way past midnight. He whips out a pistol and then we drive at each other, shooting. I should say I drove at him, 'cause he barely started that big rig away from the pump before I hit him. Blood flies out of his head, and he crashes into another gas pump as I pass him and his truck and then the whole truck stop goes up in flames."

"In the game?"

"In the game. But it didn't feel like a game. I even smelled the diesel, it felt so real. Except I should've felt sick scared and didn't. I felt good."

"Good?"

"Like I'd won the heavyweight championship. It didn't feel wrong at all."

"How long did you feel that way?"

"I still do ... I mean—" He looked around as though for hidden microphones. "Look, let me tell it my way. I'll get there."

"Take your time," Bavarius said.

MacKenzie stood straighter against the wall. Her face offered Ryder a grave, concerned invitation to confide. She folded her hands, patient as Mother Mary.

Ryder rubbed his eyes, then let his hand fall to strike the metal table with a soft *clunngg* sound, jarring the cell phone on which Bavarius was recording his words.

"It's OK," Bavarius murmured. "Don't rush it."

Ryder nodded. "So now the game's over. I come back to myself, and I'm sweating all over. Exhausted. But like I said, triumphant. I drag myself into bed. Next thing I know, it's morning. The alarm's blasting and Penny's shaking me because she knows I've got another court date with Mudge. Another fight about evidence in that murder case. The judge likes me, but I don't want to disrespect him by being late.

"I shower fast. Drive like a maniac. Get to the courtroom but Mudge isn't there. He's sent some flunky to say he's delayed in Texas by Red River floods. He can be there in the afternoon, at one. Kanaday bawls me out—*Why me?*—but pushes his next case back half an hour and resets us for one o'clock.

"Now, I've got an investigator on Mudge's back anyway because I'm trying to link him to the murder weapon. I call the detective. He tells me Mudge has been with some woman in Wichita all night. He faxes me an affidavit. Hallelujah, I've got Mudge for fraud on the court. It's almost twelve now and I rush to file the affidavit before court closes for lunch, but I don't make it in time.

"So, it's noon and I'm walking down the courthouse steps. And there he is, Mudge, walking up, big as life but uglier. He doesn't look human. More like a game level boss."

Bavarius asked, "What's a boss?"

MacKenzie said, "Most AI games have levels, and before you can finish a level you have to destroy a really tough opponent. That's a boss."

Bavarius nodded. "Go on, Mark."

"So, I tell Mudge, 'I've got a witness who saw you in Wichita last night, I've got his affidavit.' But it's not like it's me talking. More like a script I have to read.

"Mudge says, 'You self-righteous motherfucker. I'll shoot your ass.'

"I hear myself threaten to shoot him first. He rises up on his toes and shouts that he'll send me to hell directly, and we get in our cars and drive at each other and I keep pulling the trigger, like in the game—except now he's in a Mercedes coupe and it roars and its tires squeal as he comes at me. Neither of us can shoot straight and I have no idea where my bullets are going. He swerves and crashes into a mailbox. His door flies open and he falls halfway out. I stop and run to his car. There's blood all over his shirt. And then Mudge looks at me with this real surprised expression and says, 'But I won the game!'"

Ryder put both hands over his eyes, and his voice broke. "I think he was my opponent in QuestGame. It told me I won, just like it told him."

"Is that all?"

"Yeah …. No, there's one more thing."

"What?"

"I was thinking, after they arrested me, that this was a game with no rules. That fight at Gowan's Truck Stop had no rules, and the fight with Mudge had no rules. While the game and fight were happening, pulling the trigger didn't seem wrong. I knew that the character I fought at that truck stop would rise again when someone else played the Gowan's Truck Stop game. And it didn't seem any different when I shot at Mudge. It didn't occur to me that either of us could be hurt in reality. That's why I say I didn't want to kill him. It wasn't until after they arrested me that I understood that I had actually shot him."

He stopped talking, and then spoke slower, reaching for words. "That's what I mean when I say it was a game with no rules. I've never heard of a game with no rules. A game is supposed to have rules, isn't it?"

"Most do," MacKenzie agreed. "But lots of times the rules change and no one tells you."

Ryder took that in, and spoke slowly. "It was like QuestGame knew Mudge and I had it in for each other, and that we wanted to go for it. So, QuestGame matched us up and made it happen."

Bavarius asked, "Why?"

"Why do I think that?"

"Yes," MacKenzie said. "But also, why would QuestGame *do* that?"

"Damned if I know either answer."

MacKenzie smoothed her skirt.

"I know it sounds nuts!"

Bavarius nodded. "Yes, Mark, it does. And if it's not nuts, we need to understand why."

"There's a cop who heard Mudge say it! About winning the game!" Ryder shook both fists gently but with terrible tension. His eyes teared. "Czabaniuk. His name is Czabaniuk. Please, Judge—Ask Officer Czabaniuk. Please."

"We'll talk to him. Today, if possible."

Bavarius stood. "You have any more questions for Mark?" he asked MacKenzie.

"Just one more for now. Mark, what does your wife know about any of this?"

It was a question Bavarius should have asked and hadn't thought to do so. And MacKenzie wasn't even a criminal attorney. "That's an important consideration. You know the prosecutors will want to examine her."

Ryder shook his head. "She won't talk to them. She knows the drill."

"You might be surprised. She can't lie to prosecutors, but prosecutors can lie to her. Tell her you're having an affair. *Really, Mrs. Ryder, you mean you don't know?* Play with her head."

"No, Judge. Penny's a prosecutor's wife, and she's smart. Besides, she doesn't know anything, except that she's heard me say Mudge is scum. Don't worry about her."

Bavarius picked up his briefcase. "All right. Your arraignment's tomorrow morning. Don't talk to anyone until then. You've got my number." He raised an eyebrow at MacKenzie. "Ready?"

She nodded and knocked on the visiting room door for the guards to let them out.

Bavarius said, "Mark, I'm not yet sure I'm the right lawyer for you, but if I'm not, I'll find you someone good."

When Bavarius and MacKenzie walked out of the jail onto the street, a local TV reporter and a cameraman were waiting. "Martin Bavarius?"

Well, at least there's only one of them, Bavarius thought. He didn't answer.

The cameraman panned his lens over the reporter, Bavarius, and MacKenzie standing behind him.

"Are you representing Mark Ryder in the duel case?"

Bavarius said, "Lovely day, isn't it?" and left the reporter bellowing questions after him. MacKenzie followed him around the corner.

"Reporters are always a treat," she said.

"Good for ten seconds on the six o'clock news," he said. "Damn. Now, if I don't represent Mark, the press will say it's because his case is a loser."

Sparse pedestrian traffic drifted along wide sidewalks. Bavarius loosened his tie. "Truth is, Mark's story is as whacked-out an insanity defense as I've ever heard."

MacKenzie said, "I think he believes it."

"Do you? You know, military defense lawyers raise dissociative disorders caused by post-traumatic stress as a defense. It's pretty common. In Kansas, it rarely works."

They strolled down the block.

"What about self-defense?" MacKenzie said. "Mudge shot at him."

"They threatened each other."

"Yes, but Ryder and Mudge may have been the only ones to hear that. Keep Mark off the stand and unless Mudge testifies maybe there's no witness to the threat."

"Selena, you're thinking like a criminal defense lawyer."

"Just taking it one logical step at a time. Who went for his gun first?"

"We'll have to nail that down."

"What about Mark having a gun in his car? Won't the prosecutors argue that shows intent to commit the crime?"

"In New York, maybe. But this is Kansas. Any adult can carry a concealed weapon, no permit required. And a lot of prosecutors do. But they can't take a gun into a courtroom. So—"

"They leave the gun in their car?"

"Natch. I'll bet half the cars in that parking lot had guns in them."

"Toto, I've got a feeling I'm not in New York anymore."

QUESTION:

"What dangers are inherent in general purpose simulators of the physical world?"

ANSWER:

"Misinformation and deepfakes; privacy and security concerns; ethical and bias issues; impact on trust in media; potential for malicious use; economic disruption; overreliance on simulations; unpredictable and unintended consequences; technology outpacing legal regulation; affecting peoples' perception of reality; addiction to virtual experiences."

CHAPTER 4

The arraignment was a brief affair. The bailiff called the case, and Bavarius announced that he was appearing for the defendant.

This seemed to catch the prosecutor, a staff attorney named Roberts, by surprise. Bavarius was known for high-level appeals work, and this was county criminal court.

Judge Judith Rastler asked Roberts to read the charges: Attempted murder, aggravated assault, and firing a gun recklessly within city limits.

Bavarius knew these were the charges only for the moment. The shooting had occurred so recently there had been little opportunity to investigate, so the charges were likely to be refiled prior to a preliminary hearing in the future.

"How does the defendant plead?"

"Not guilty, Your Honor," Bavarius said.

"The defendant is charged with violent felonies," Rastler said. "I don't believe bail is appropriate."

"Neither do the People," Roberts added.

Bavarius said, "Your Honor, Mr. Ryder has no criminal record and—"

"Attempted murder does not warrant bail, Mr. Bavarius."

"In that case, Your Honor, please hold Mr. Ryder in protective custody. As a prosecutor, he won't be safe in the general jail population."

"The People don't object."

"Very well, let's set a date for a preliminary hearing at which the prosecution must establish probable cause that the defendant should be bound over for trial, or any plea agreement will be reported."

It was all over in minutes. MacKenzie, who'd watched from the pews, followed Bavarius to the street.

"Now the work begins," he said. "We'll start with Czabaniuk at Police HQ." He turned his car toward a forbidding long brown building with its entrance shielded by concrete pylon spikes, set on a wide asphalt lot. Other law enforcement clustered around it. The U.S. Marshal's Department. The Topeka Narcotics Bureau. The Shawnee County Sheriff's Office.

"Looks like cop heaven," MacKenzie said.

The area was too familiar to Bavarius for comment, and his mind moved on. "Call me a pessimist, but I can't imagine any reputable psych expert finding that an AI game forced Ryder into a gunfight. But you know the technology."

"Not well enough to make a snap judgment. Is it conceivable? Well, Mudge and Ryder were already enemies. QuestGame produces emotional experiences, and it draws on history and law. I'm not willing to say a duel like that isn't recorded in a QuestGame database. But as to QuestGame actually pushing that on a gamer …."

"It's a big leap?"

"Yes. It is."

"Besides," Bavarius said, "doesn't QuestGame have built-in safeguards?"

"I'd expect so. Still …."

They got out of the car. A street trash basket stood next to their parking spot, and MacKenzie walked slowly around it. "If there's anything to Ryder's story, there should be a case with similar facts. Something QuestGame drew on to create Ryder's experience."

A wind gust flipped MacKenzie's skirt hem up. She noticed that he noticed, but he couldn't read her reaction. He looked away. She was working with him—although not for him. He would ignore her thighs from now on. Yes.

He saw a *People* magazine in the trash basket, one of several that someone had dumped all at once. *Why is it OK for thirtyish magazine editors to publicly declare a sixtyish movie star the world's sexiest man, but creepy if I admire MacKenzie's thighs? Maybe it's all right if I admire, but don't ogle. But how do I know if I'm admiring or ogling?*

He said, "The cases would have to be very similar to make me a believer."

"Gowan's!" MacKenzie snapped her fingers. "The name of the truck stop Ryder said he fought in during the QuestGame session. How many cases can have the name 'Gowan's Truck Stop' in them?"

Her phone came out of her pocket in a gunfighter-fast draw and her fingers flew. She continued circling the trash can while she worked her phone. Bavarius waited, leaning against the 90's Imperial he'd leased after losing his De Soto, Betsy. He glanced down at the tan paint with distaste. If only it were a '62 LeBaron, reviewed in its time as the finest sedan in the world. Or a '58 Crown convertible; now, that car had wings, and its paint glowed. But this Imperial's 147-horsepower engine was sluggish. Its ride was flabby soft. He sighed.

"Something bothering you?" MacKenzie's eyes stayed on her screen.

"How do you do research and walk and talk at the same time?"

"Practice. I also watch people. What's bugging you?"

"I'm surprised at myself, that's all."

"Why?"

He didn't answer.

She waited.

"I quit the bench. I wanted to come back to Kansas. Needed to feel its real ground under my feet. I signed on to teach law, thinking I could be a homebody. Drive half an hour to campus a few days a week, with no traffic. I bought a house I love. I've lived there a year and a half and it feels like forever. I even adopted a rescue puppy.

"But lawyers started asking for my help, and the more I said no, the more they asked. I took on two appeals before *Jackson*, won both, and said, that's it, I'm done. And then *Jackson* came along and grabbed my interest. I didn't understand why I took the damned case until it was nearly over, and it took Questioner to make me consciously aware of what I must have sensed from the beginning—that it's fundamentally wrong to let prosecutors condemn a man by using any legal definition that suits their purposes just because a legislature sloppily fails to define the key element of a crime. *Jackson* almost ate me alive. And no sooner am I done with it than here's Mark Ryder's screwy case. I want to let the law go, but I can't, and I don't know why."

"I think you know. How long have you practiced?"

"About as long as you've lived."

"It's part of you. How can you work in the field for so long, at such a high level, unless you love it? You didn't have to get involved with Mark's case."

"Mark called me needing immediate help. I figured I could protect him from police interrogation until I could turn his case over to a better-suited lawyer. But then I thought of you. You know the technology. It's been years since I did trial defense work, but I haven't forgotten how and it feels pretty good. It might work."

"And so here we are," MacKenzie said. "I think it's an interesting place to be, don't you?"

He smiled. "I do."

She nodded and let him consider that for a moment. Then she asked, "How are you taking care of the dog?"

"I have help. But it's not fair to her."

"To the dog?"

"To Marguerite. My housekeeper, but way more than that. She's been with me forever."

"Are you two—?"

"Lovers? No."

MacKenzie seemed to think about that for a moment. Then, "I like electric cars."

Her mind appeared to run on several tracks at once.

He shook his head. "Hate 'em. Replacing a battery costs half what you paid for the car. And they're too quiet. I call them eunuchs because whatever voices they have don't rumble. I love the sound of a good V-8. I like carburetors. Parts you can tinker with, without computers. But this one's just a V-6. With computerized fuel injection." He toe-tapped the Imperial's tire.

"If you don't like it, why'd you buy it?"

"I didn't. Took a one-year lease." He sighed. "I used to have this gorgeous '56 De Soto, but she died. Betsy had charm. Not to mention a 345 horsepower V-8."

"*Betsy?*"

"Hybrids aren't for me, either."

"You named your car *Betsy?*"

"She was a very sweet lady!"

"*Betsy?* Wait a sec. I found the case. *Payne v. State*, Alabama Court of Criminal Appeals, 1980. Death at Gowan's Truck Stop. The *Payne* court analyzed the history of duels and decided that guys charging at one another in motor vehicles with blazing guns didn't qualify. According to the Alabama court, Mark Ryder did not fight a duel."

"The press won't care," Bavarius said. "If it goes bang like a duel, they'll call it a duel. But the whole thing's nuts. Ryder's a clever guy. He could have looked up *Payne* like we did and made the whole thing up."

"Except that Mudge was shooting, too," MacKenzie said.

"Was he? We don't know that. Let's find that cop, Czabaniuk. See if he'll confirm that Mudge was shooting. Or if he heard Mark make threats."

"Why would he talk to us? Wouldn't the prosecutors tell the cops not to?"

"Prosecutors don't have that authority. They can advise a cop that it's up to him but if he talks to a defense lawyer it might be used to discredit him on the witness stand."

"So the prosecutor can *imply* that a cop shouldn't talk to us, but not order him not to."

"Right. And if Mark were a known bad actor, the cops would probably listen. But until now, Mark's been one of the good guys. He's liked around here. And a lot of cops know who I am. Maybe that counts for something. And how the cops answer might give us a hint of how the witnesses feel about all this."

Bavarius phoned Nate Owens, a private investigator who had his office in the area. He wanted the investigator to watch and record his witness interviews so Bavarius wouldn't become a witness himself.

They left the car and the trash can behind and made tracks for the courthouse. Owens met them there.

Officer Charles Czabaniuk was a chunky youngster with round hoot-owl eyes.

"You had to see it," Czabaniuk said. "Two cars charging each other like King Arthur's knights. People in the parking lot screaming. Guns. Both of 'em blasting away. Then the crash." Czabaniuk shook his head.

"Did Mr. Mudge say anything after he was shot?"

"He said something about winning."

"Do you remember his exact words?"

"He said something about a game. Yeah, he said he'd won the game."

"What game?"

Czabaniuk shook his head. "He didn't say."

"Did you hear Mr. Mudge or Mr. Ryder say anything before the shooting?" MacKenzie asked. "Any threats?"

"If there were any, I got there too late to hear them."

"Did you see which one of them went for his car first?" Bavarius asked.

"I think it was … I think it was Mr. Ryder."

Owens promised to send the recording and an affidavit swearing he had witnessed the interview and made the recording.

Bavarius and MacKenzie lunched at a coffee shop near the jail. Over French dip sandwiches, Bavarius asked, "So, do you want to work on this case?"

MacKenzie patted her mouth with her napkin. "I'm interested."

"I still haven't made up my mind. If Mark went for his car first, it's harder to argue self-defense. The prosecutors will argue he was also first to go for his gun."

"Czabaniuk didn't sound very sure."

"True."

"You know what intrigues me? Ryder wondering about the game having no rules. There've been a few games that claim to have no rules, but they're obscure. I doubt he's heard of them, although that's something to check."

Bavarius said, "I'm bothered by the way he seems to be conflating the AI game with real life. The duel had no rules, so the game had no rules. Or maybe the other way around. He can't seem to distinguish them." He dipped his sandwich, chewed and swallowed. "If I take the case, I'll call you when things heat up on the QuestGame front."

"I'm between cases right now," she said. "I've never been in this part of the country. I thought I might stay a few days, drive around and sightsee. Always wanted to see Leavenworth." She grinned. "From the outside."

QUESTION:

"Assess the danger that AI will cause humans to abandon the search for objective truth."

ANSWER:

"There are several key concerns about how AI could impact humanity's pursuit of objective truth: Pollution of the information ecosystem, blurring the line between accuracy and truth; amplification of biases; overreliance on AI-generated content; erosion of trust in authentic evidence; and challenges to human judgment."

<h1 style="text-align:center">CHAPTER 5</h1>

Bavarius' kitchen bustled in the morning. Childless homes hardly ever hum as did his big red Topeka Victorian. His Colorado mountain cabin was cozy and you couldn't beat the scenery, but the Kansas home owned his heart, with its columned porch, warren of small rooms, jewel-toned wallpapers, and mementos of a life well-lived.

Along the hall from kitchen to dining room hung several of Marguerite's paintings. They featured abstract flowers and fantasized insects that seemed to live within their black and gold canvasses. Without being obvious about it—no bugs with briefcases here—Marguerite implied entire sophisticated cultures within those worlds. She liked to remind him that he might earn the kudos of the legal field, but she was older (if not by much) and wiser, and, at least in selling paintings, more digitally hip. She sold them both as physical objects and as digital nonfungible Net and Cloud tokens.

But while her best commercial works graced Bavarius' walls, her most personal works stayed closeted in her rooms. Exquisitely detailed portraits, done from memory. Her portly, shrewd and happy father. Her severe mother entering a Paris *boulangerie* with Marguerite's sister, a miniature of *maman*, in tow. A woman whom Bavarius, Felix and she had rescued from Saddam's dungeons, shrunken by suffering yet luminous with acceptance. A dark handsome young lover in bed, lit by the sun through a window screened in the dense 19th century *mashrabiya* style.

Now in her seventies, she still had occasional affairs that took her traveling. Before leaving, she would quote *Lord of the Rings'* Bilbo Baggins at the end of the trilogy: "I think I'm quite ready for another adventure." Bavarius always missed her, and struggled to keep the house in shape during her absences.

He ambled downstairs in sweatpants and a t-shirt at six and found Marguerite already at the stove in her vintage flowered French apron, whisking eggs in a buttered skillet and nodding to Euro jazz. As Bavarius walked through the kitchen toward the back door, she murmured, "Good morning, *Monsieur* Judge," placed the skillet on a metal frame above a pot of steaming water, and slid the skillet slowly back and forth. It would take her a half hour to make scrambled eggs this way, but she insisted it was worth it, and he agreed. Behind the skillet, her tea kettle began whistling and the French press and dark roasted coffee waited for hot water. Marguerite put fruit on three of the incomplete, chipped set of dishes Bavarius would not let her replace. In Germany, the dishes had belonged to his paternal grandmother, a short, sturdy woman whom he'd never met but was told had laughed loud, cursed like a sailor, and broke dishes when she got angry. The dishes that survived her treatment came to Bavarius through his Aunt Gertrude, who fled the old country with Bavarius' grandfather and father after World War II. The morning after Gertrude's funeral, Bavarius went to her grave, broke a dish for her and for *Oma*, and left the shards atop her stone.

Beyond the kitchen, in the back hall, the clothes dryer tumbled and rumbled. By the dryer stood a large white plastic kennel. The multi-hued puppy inside started barking and jumping when he saw Bavarius. The kennel jerked toward Bavarius with each leap.

"Good morning, Gopherbreath! Ready for a walk?" Marguerite already had let the dog out to pee, but Gopherbreath rarely pooped first thing in the morning. That usually took a leash walk, and when Bavarius was home, it was his job.

Bavarius flipped the kennel's latch and the Catahoula leopard puppy bounded out, ducked the training collar Bavarius held, butted his head into Bavarius' crotch, and lunged for the door. Peeking into the kennel, Bavarius was pleased. Yep. Clean as a whistle, and no smell. The hound had held it in all night.

"Thank you, Marguerite. I know he's a handful."

"Gopherbreath? He is a dear."

Once leashed, Gopherbreath hauled Bavarius out the back door, down three steps, and around the turret of the claret-red house. Bavarius shortened the leash, then coaxed Gopherbreath back beside his leg. For fifteen minutes he trained the pup to heel. Then they strode quickly around the block, stopping only for two quick dog poops that Bavarius picked up without letting Gopherbreath eat nasty stuff off the ground. Bavarius was learning to know neighbors he'd never spoken with by what those neighbors did and put in their yards and driveways. The widow who filled her front lawn with fanciful whirligigs in the summer. The twin brothers, ten or eleven years old, building a treehouse in a black walnut. It was barely a touch of his neighbors' lives, but a touch all the same.

Returning to his front yard, Bavarius wondered where the kids on their bikes had heaved his newspapers today. Amazing that paper routes were still worth riding. Few folks subscribed to physical papers anymore. But there was no substitute for the crinkling of newsprint in his hands, and he disliked how algorithms curated his newsfeeds based on his predicted preferences. He would decide for himself what news to read, thank you very much.

He found *The New York Times* by the pebbled driveway. He bent to pick it up and when he stood, noticed the car parked two houses down and across the street. A brown sedan with blackwall tires. Two men sat inside. Since Bavarius had moved into the neighborhood, he had never seen a stakeout car. He wondered which of his neighbors the men were interested in. Jennings, the stockbroker? Caldwell, the electronics firm CFO? Morrison, the obstetrician?

A few yards from the *Times*, *The Washington Post* hid between his favorite elm and his neighbor's fence, next to *The Wall Street Journal*. As he reached for the *Journal*, Caldwell's sprinkler suddenly erupted cold water. It chilled both Bavarius and the dog, and spooked Gopherbreath into wrapping his leash around Bavarius' legs. Bavarius had to spin around twice to untangle himself. "I'm going to train you to poop on Caldwell's lawn," he muttered, and jogged back to the house.

MacKenzie stood in the front doorway, laughing at him. He glared and she said, "Sorry," without looking sorry at all. He walked back around to the kitchen door and tossed the paper bag full of poop into the outdoor trash bin.

Marguerite, in the kitchen, appeared to concentrate on her skillet, but Bavarius saw her subtle smile. She had watched his encounter with the sprinkler through the kitchen's street-facing window.

"How did you sleep?" he asked MacKenzie.

"That bed is wonderful. Thanks again for letting me stay here."

"What did you think of Leavenworth?"

"Scariest prison I've seen. Not that I've seen many. I drove past the big state prison in Lansing to get to it. Civil War sandstone walls, gun towers, razor wire. But Leavenworth made Lansing look like a gazebo. Leavenworth's where they threw Satan to rot." She shuddered.

Bavarius was familiar with Leavenworth. Its grim, gray-white walls reared forty feet high, and were dug forty feet deep, to enclose the hell inside. Its face to the world was the Big House, with its huge silver dome that toward sunset glowed a brilliant, hurtful gold. Bavarius had been inside to see a client, and that was even more awful. You felt the weight of those walls. And both Leavenworth and Lansing looked even more ghastly at night, their harsh lights burning through the fog that rose off the Missouri River. "That place can give anyone the willies."

But today was a beautiful morning in Topeka, and MacKenzie looked pretty in shorts, t-shirt and sneakers. The t-shirt read, "Hard Rock Café—Osaka."

"I'm going to take Ryder's case."

"Good," MacKenzie said. "I like him."

She knelt and rubbed Gopherbreath's fur. "Good dog! What's your name, sweetie?"

"Gopherbreath," Bavarius answered for the dog.

"What kind of name is that?"

Marguerite kept moving the skillet while she sprinkled on tarragon and white pepper. "When *Monsieur* Judge first brought him home, he put him in the yard to run. The dog killed two pocket gophers and brought them to me at the door. Since then, he is Gopherbreath."

"Back in the kennel for now," Bavarius said, gently guiding the dog. "He's almost housebroken. But I don't completely trust him."

MacKenzie stepped back while Bavarius locked Gopherbreath in.

"Sit down, please. The eggs are ready."

"Can I take a rain check, Marguerite? I need to run my miles," MacKenzie said.

"But of course."

"You're missing a treat," Bavarius warned.

"I'm sorry, Marguerite. Tomorrow?"

Marguerite flicked a hand. "Shoo."

"I'll eat her share." Bavarius smiled.

MacKenzie ducked out the back door, setting off a brief spasm of barking. Bavarius watched her jog down the street, stride lengthening as muscles relaxed.

Then he watched the brown car follow her, keeping far enough back that she would not know it was there. *What the hell?*

Marguerite sat silently at the table to eat with him but without interrupting his breakfast and newspaper ritual. She knew he treasured it, when he had time.

Bavarius started with the international news, the business sections, and then the day's crime stories. His cell phone waited next to his plate for him to look up further developments about stories he wanted to pursue.

Why did the men in the car follow MacKenzie? Who are they?

He read about a Department of Transportation official killed out on Kansas' high prairie. The DOT man and a U.S. deputy marshal tried to serve eviction papers on a family so a new highway could run over the family farm. There already was a highway five miles north that could be repaired more cheaply, but the government decided to build a new one and let the old one crumble. The official banged on the farmer's front door and the farmer shot both him and the deputy and then his wife and himself, but not before scrawling a note that declared he'd been protecting his property rights. Their kids, aged seven and nine, found all the bodies that afternoon after the school bus brought them home. Only the marshal lived and he was suffering through surgeries. The local sheriff gave the farmer's note to a local reporter and the story was now viral on social media. Bavarius followed up on his phone. Folks were protesting the new highway as a waste of life, money, and good crop land.

A DOT spokesperson said that the new road would get laid, regardless. Bavarius could not discover whether the farmer's kids had relatives to adopt them or if they would get fed into the foster care system.

I hope MacKenzie's OK. Should I call the police? What if those guys are the police?

A South Carolina man, turned away when he tried to register to vote, snatched a heavy stapler and crushed a clerk's skull. Murder grows out of love, passion, terror, greed, high politics, low religion, perceived honor, and a host of other motives, often leavened with intoxication. But to be so hellbent on voting for county commissioner that you kill someone?

Government taking of private land. Voting rights.

QuestGame drew on case law as source material for the in-game conflicts it presented to players.

Ryder said QuestGame had made him crazy, and here were two more extreme acts done by men interested in areas where QuestGame was authoritative entertainment. Or pseudo-authoritative, if it distorted the source material.

Ryder's case was starting to fascinate Bavarius.

Indefensible? Maybe not.

Mudge had shot at Ryder, too. Plenty of opposing lawyers would love to shoot each other. Had they provoked each other in some other way? Odds remained that the QuestGame angle was a red herring. Bavarius needed to learn more about Mudge's role in the shooting.

Bavarius stood and padded around the kitchen with *The New York Times* in hand—

The guys in that car sure looked like government.

He put his newspaper down. He showered, dressed and went out onto his front porch with his laptop, settling onto his rocking bench suspended on chains from the overhang. He logged into the

Nexis database of news stories and found thousands that described altercations with public officials over property rights. The sheer volume of stories didn't discourage him. Hundreds of stories could cover a single incident if it were bizarre or violent enough. And by using the computer to find relevant words, he could read huge amounts of material fast.

He searched first for stories that named Mark Ryder. There were sixty, but nearly all cannibalized two wire service filings based on the original local news story.

Then he looked at violence against police over time. According to FBI databases, felonious killings of officers had averaged fewer than fifty per year until 2021, when they had spiked to seventy-three. They had hovered around that level until the year QuestGame came online, when they increased by twenty percent and climbed each year since.

Hate crimes also had grown over the past few decades, but once QuestGame came online, they grew faster.

All of this could have been found faster using Questioner. He could merely have thought his request and Questioner would have produced results. But he was no longer confident about what those results might be. They might be wrong. Or, like Dred Scott, frightening. He didn't want to put on a Questioner headset again until he thought that encounter through.

For now, his old school searches were fast enough.

There might just be something here.

He stood and stretched. Humming some old New Orleans funk, he took his laptop inside and brewed bitter coffee and checked his watch. MacKenzie had been gone more than an hour. Marguerite was in her rooms. He thought he heard her insult one of her paintbrushes in French, something about porcupines having softer bristles. *Un porc-épic a des poils plus doux,* was that it?

Those guys in the car. The car looked government. But they could be anybody.

He took his coffee back to the front porch and kept reading. In the past month, two abortion doctors had been killed. One had his throat ripped out with a coat hanger. The other was strangled with fetal tissue in his clinic after aborting the pregnancy of a raped teenage girl. The killers dragged the girl to the clinic to watch the murder and then recited the Bible as they drove her to her parents' house. Her parents thanked the killers for bringing her home. *And ... hello....*

Just last week, a Utah state judge, Charlene Banner, had refused to authorize a no-knock warrant. Her son was a cop on the raid and got shot through the neck when the police announced themselves. He was in critical condition. Banner claimed that a Questioner research session had convinced her that a no-knock warrant wasn't appropriate.

He read more. Not just news articles. Not just legal opinions. He delved into witness and victim testimony. An ever-larger portion of killers and victims seemed to be lawyers. And more people, lawyers or not, were getting murdered all the time. The nation was more and more psychotic. And whatever QuestGame and Questioner might be doing to people looked like a more concentrated version of the trend. Like a mutant virus strain.

Of course, who knows if I can rely on anything I'm reading?

He double-checked his findings against the Justice Department's Bureau of Justice Statistics website. The Justice Department emphasized different things, but his own findings so far seemed consistent with DOJ's—although the government wasn't connecting the dots from murders to social media and AI. At least, not publicly.

He cast his research net wider. No law firm had yet filed a class action alleging that any social media or online system was causing the surge in violence. That made sense. Bavarius had found a correlation of increasing murders to social media and AI use, and an even stronger correlation to QuestGame and Questioner. But correlation was not causation. A law firm that filed a class action could not easily prove causation, and could face monster defamation suits from the world's most powerful Big Tech companies.

OK, let's stick to the job at hand. Is any of this support for Ryder's defense? But his neck was starting to hurt. *Time for some tai chi. And ibuprofen.*

MacKenzie came into view, running hard along the street. She turned into his yard, slowing now, sweaty and flushed and holding a wet bottle of iced tea.

Bavarius didn't see the brown car. "How was your run?"

"Did eleven miles." She tapped the fitness watch on her wrist. "Saw some gorgeous old homes. Man, it's hot."

Bavarius waited for her to say more. She didn't. Either she hadn't noticed the car following her, or she knew and was unconcerned. Or she was concerned and a hell of an actress. Maybe the car hadn't followed her after all.

She had just gotten here but it felt like she belonged. He wondered if that was a good thing.

"I've been digging into Mark's case."

She wiped the cold bottle across her forehead and sat next to him. "Tell me."

"I ... *we* ... will need a thorough survey of violence related to hot-button law issues, going back to the year QuestGame came online. Also, violence related to QuestGame's most popular game scenarios; we have to identify those. How digitally literate were the defendants? Did they play QuestGame, or any AI games? Are there known psychiatric problems caused by neural links—the hardware or the software? Also, who do you know in the artificial intelligence, virtual reality, gaming, and social media communities? Researchers. Entrepreneurs. Journalists. Folks who understand the latest and greatest, and how it's all evolving. Can you make introductions for me?"

"I can. But before anything, I need a shower." She uncrossed her legs to stand and he saw a small scar on one thigh. She smiled at him and ran upstairs.

They hadn't discussed what he might pay her. That was nice, but it made him wonder why she was still here.

QUESTION:

"Is AI having a deleterious effect on human rationality?"

ANSWER:

"AI may limit human autonomy, agency and capabilities in decision-making as it takes over more cognitive tasks. Overreliance on AI could degrade professional skills and critical thinking abilities. AI could erode genuine human connection as people interact more with AI."

C H A P T E R   6

They set up at the dining room table with their laptops open. Her hair smelled fresh and clean. A pen nestled over her right ear.

As he rose and passed behind her on his way to the kitchen for more coffee, she murmured, "This is damned odd."

He bent to look over her shoulder at her screen.

Coverage of the Alabama Supreme Court's decision in the John Watkins extradition case was streaming: the freshest dish in the buffet of legal news. The media had already stopped talking about Mark Ryder, and *Jackson v. United States* would lie news-dormant until the D.C. Circuit issued its decision, probably in late June.

Watkins concerned a British citizen convicted of murder and jailed in Alabama. The Brits sought to extradite him to face trial for several London killings. Alabama wanted to keep him for execution. Since Watkins' first name was John, the British tabloids were howling to yank "the new Jack the Ripper" back from the U.S.A.

"The dissent has people fuming," MacKenzie said. "Look at this language."

"Reparations?" Bavarius' eyebrows shot up. "Judge Gray wants Alabama to pay reparations to the families of Watkins' British victims? That does not sound like the Bobby Lee Gray I know."

"I don't know much about extradition law," MacKenzie said. "But Gray's tone is so aggressive …."

Bavarius realized that his cheek was barely an inch from MacKenzie's left ear. He straightened up.

Marguerite came downstairs with a basket of linens. For an older woman carrying weight, she walked silently on the stairs and then past the dining room table. She sniffed at the computers and papers cluttering the altar at which Bavarius and guests worshipped her fine meals. She started her second laundry of the morning and announced, "I shall go shopping. For lunch, I make trout."

"You're in for a treat," Bavarius told MacKenzie. He turned to Marguerite. "Please buy extra for Professor Purdue, Marguerite. He'll be joining us."

"Excellent! He knows how to praise a chef!" She drove off in her blue Lexus.

MacKenzie downloaded news stories, cases, and journal articles, and used text analysis apps to seek patterns in them. Were there other cases similar to Ryder's? Was QuestGame involved? Were other systems? Had people been harmed and if so, how?

While she developed the facts, Bavarius tried to figure out what theories of defense could work in Ryder's case. One huge problem was that Kansas state law no longer allowed an insanity defense.

After a while, MacKenzie leaned back. "OK, let's assume we can show some probability that other people besides Ryder have been made violent by QuestGame. How do we prove this is what happened to Ryder? Does he testify?"

"I'd rather have psychological experts testify that because of QuestGame, Mark didn't understand that his gun could really kill Mudge," Bavarius said. "That's a tough sell, but we back it by offering other witnesses to testify that QuestGame did something similar to them."

MacKenzie said, "Not easy to separate the fruitcakes from the credible people."

There was a knock at the front of the house and Purdue's voice called, "Martin?" faintly through the heavy oak. Bavarius got up to let him in.

At the same time, Gopherbreath, who was free in the fenced back yard, scratched at the kitchen door. MacKenzie opened it and the hound charged in past her legs, stinking of something he had rolled in, and almost running into Purdue as he scampered into the living room. Bavarius chased Gopherbreath down and then hauled the pup to the tub in the main floor bathroom, heaved the beast into it, and turned on the shower.

Gopherbreath shuddered, whined and nipped.

MacKenzie followed them into the bathroom. Bavarius held the pup under the shower stream and lathered Gopherbreath up. The dog writhed. Just outside the bathroom, Purdue said, "Let me instruct yon young beastie on proper conduct. From the Norse sagas." He began to chant.

> *Then did Gopherbreath*
> *Tail a-sagging*
> *Shake 'neath the shower*
> *Sneezing ... Gagging*
> *Dense white bubbles*
> *Stank of tar*
> *Hard white fingers*

Kneaded flesh
Gopherbreath did not cringe nor whine
Dignity cloaked his drooping fur
Sore distressed, no shame showed he
Despite how odd he looked

MacKenzie said, "Prof. Purdue, I like you. You are seriously weird."

The shower water wasn't rinsing off all the suds and grime, so MacKenzie filled the empty bathroom trashcan with water and, at Bavarius' nod, dumped it over Gopherbreath to rinse brown suds away. Several drenchings made the water run clear.

Marguerite had arrived home and brought towels. The bathroom was so crowded she handed them to MacKenzie to pass to Bavarius. Bavarius rubbed Gopherbreath down while the dog shook himself. He stood and the dog leaped from the tub and charged out into the house for parts unknown.

Bavarius stood, dripping. "Hi, Bill."

Purdue, perfectly dry, wore boots, tan jeans and a yellow t-shirt. His unruly mop was tied back in a frizzy ponytail.

MacKenzie's t-shirt was wet and Bavarius' was thoroughly soaked. They locked eyes for a second. "I'd better change," she said. "Want me to get you a dry shirt?"

"Thanks. In the tall dresser, second drawer from the top."

Bavarius tracked Gopherbreath's wet trail to the kitchen. The pup was hustling Marguerite for trout. Marguerite was rubbing the trout with a green spice mix.

Bavarius grabbed him and led him to his crate. "OK, bud. Time to calm down and dry off."

Purdue followed Bavarius into the kitchen. "Something smells wonderful."

"It is *za'atar*. Sold in the supermarkets, but I make my own. I grind hyssop, and oregano, marjoram, sumac, and sesame seed."

Bavarius meandered out to the dining room, letting his mind drift. Purdue had put his briefcase and a pad down on the long table. On the pad, Bavarius glimpsed what looked like class lecture notes, bordered by penciled sketches of jazz musicians.

MacKenzie came back downstairs in a red t-shirt and jeans. She tossed Bavarius a dry shirt.

He called into the kitchen, "Bill, come meet Selena MacKenzie. She was with the other side in *Jackson*. Let's get to work."

Marguerite called from the kitchen. "In half an hour, the table must be cleared, please!"

"We don't argue with Marguerite's trout," Bavarius said.

Purdue asked, "Isn't it too dead to argue back?"

Bavarius ignored him. "Let's set up in the living room."

They moved their computers and Bavarius told Purdue about Mark Ryder's case and about the odd trends MacKenzie and he had found in their research.

Purdue said, "Let me call some DA's offices."

MacKenzie said, "They'll talk to you about ongoing investigations?"

"Hey, I'm magic." Purdue pulled out his cellphone and went out to the backyard.

Marguerite laid out plates and a wooden bowl of Caesar salad.

Purdue returned. "Guess what? Two assault cases. One in New York, one in LA. Each defendant claimed QuestGame made him nutso. Both minor cases, and the defendants copped pleas. So the QuestGame angle never got to the courtroom or made the newsfeeds. But I'll bet there are more cases out there."

"The defendants could've been making it up," Bavarius said.

"But where'd they get the idea?" Purdue asked. "Are stories like that on the street?"

MacKenzie said, "OK. Let's collect strange QuestGame stories."

"You know, I've got one myself. Not from QuestGame, but from Questioner." Bavarius described his Dred Scott experience, and the things Scott had said. "One second I was about to leave Questioner, and the next, Dred Scott was in my face. I could see him, hear him, even smell him. And then I was inside him. Before he let me go, he said something that's been bothering me. I've never felt like I'm a slave to the law. But he said I am, and it rings true."

Marguerite brought out the trout, and it smelled marvelous. Bavarius served them all. He filled Marguerite's plate with special ceremony and thanked her.

Purdue's cell phone rang. He glanced at it, said, "It's Angie. 'Scuse me," and walked into the living room.

Bavarius picked up his fork. "I think I ought to have a talk with Felix West."

"Do you know him personally?" MacKenzie asked.

"We go back a ways."

Marguerite went into the kitchen to refill the water pitcher.

MacKenzie dabbed a small piece of potato into the garlic-butter sauce. "I guess this is as good a time as any to tell you."

Bavarius gently placed his fork on his plate and gave her his attention.

MacKenzie looked down at her potato and pushed it around in the sauce. "Felix and I go way back, too. We were ... an item. A long time ago."

Bavarius said, "How long ago?"

"When I was at MIT."

"As a student?"

"Yes." Her tone was brittle.

This is not good.

"Selena," he said. "Is this going to affect your performance in this case?"

She shook her head. "No. It won't."

A memory came to Bavarius. Felix had once made a pass at Marguerite, in Iraq. She'd deftly turned it aside with a smile, and none of the team had ever mentioned it again. But now, Bavarius wondered if Felix made a habit of hitting on co-workers and students. If true, it showed a weakness—and a lack of ethics. Iraq was three decades gone, and Selena's affair with Felix at least a dozen years in the past. Felix was older now. They all were.

But it still matters to MacKenzie. Otherwise, she wouldn't have told me.

"Do you own QuestCorp stock?"

"No."

"Then why were you at the shareholder's meeting?"

She sighed. "He hurt me. But I guess I'm also still a bit of a groupie. QuestCorp is the top of the field. And … when he holds one of these meetings in New York, I just go. To watch him be Felix and cast his spell."

Marguerite brought in the water pitcher. Bavarius nodded thanks. "Who wants some?"

"Me!" Purdue came in, tucking his cell phone away. "My son has an infected toe." He drank the last of his water, and held out his glass.

Bavarius took a small bite of the tangy, nutty trout. "Selena, Felix West and I are old friends. I trust him. Can you deal with that?"

She tilted her head back and looked down her nose at him. "Is that going to affect your performance in this case?"

He couldn't help laughing. "Is that how I was looking at you?"

She laughed back. "Your high-and-mighty judge look is better than mine."

Purdue interrupted his hoovering up of food. "You guys know Felix West? Exalted company."

"He puts on his pants like any other man." The corner of MacKenzie's mouth quirked up.

"Tomorrow, I'll text him," Bavarius said. "Set up a time to talk."

Bavarius dreaded having to tell his oldest friend, the man who watched his back during the most dangerous time of their lives, that QuestCorp's universally-acclaimed AIs might be driving system users to violence, and that Bavarius might have to raise a courtroom defense alleging just that in a highly-sensationalized case. But maybe Felix could prove to him that such a defense could never succeed. Save Bavarius from raising a defense so easily proved false that it would only make Mark look guiltier. And spare Felix and QuestCorp a lot of bad publicity.

MacKenzie asked, "Can I listen in on the call?"

Bavarius imagined Felix's face if Bavarius raised his allegation with her hovering in the digital background. "It won't be a call."

QUESTION:

"Are commercial AI companies ignoring dangers in pursuit of profit?"

ANSWER:

"Overall, the search results suggest a concerning trend of commercial AI companies prioritizing rapid development and profit over thorough safety considerations."

CHAPTER 7

Bavarius arrived at QuestCorp's Boston headquarters the next afternoon. It wasn't too hot but it was humid, and the cool lobby of Felix West's power-cooled paradise felt as grand as it looked.

The walls appeared at first to be white marble, but they were far from blank. They displayed art that shifted gradually and continually from the subtle whites of Rauschenberg, through the shadowy patterns of Ryman, and then abstractions, fantasized portraits, and even photographic realism, all presented in bare hints of hue, line and point. As Bavarius walked through the lobby, works by Pollock, Klee, a Robert Hodgins silk-screened photo of gangster Pretty Boy Floyd, and a Modigliani, appeared and evaporated. Sparks of art with which the artists had hoped to fire up humanity, all rendered in an unobtrusive pallor calculated to impress, stimulate and soothe, yet not distract people from doing business.

At the far end of the art flux, behind a cream-toned battlement of a desk, sat a receptionist, trim and neat. Her smile was too white to be real. At first, Bavarius was not sure she was human.

"Hi. Martin Bavarius to see Felix West. I'm expected."

"I'll let his office know you're here." She touched a button and murmured into her headset.

He looked around again. The wan ghost of a Georgia O'Keefe flower bloomed and faded. "If I worked here all day, I'd drink in bars all night to convince myself I'm not dead."

"I beg your pardon?"

Yep. She's human.

The elevator opened to reveal a tall Latina whose smile was less white but more brilliant than the receptionist's. Nina Rivera had been with Felix for years.

"Judge Bavarius, what a pleasure to see you again. Dr. West is ready for you." *Pleh-jzahh* in Nina's long-drawn London inflection.

"You look wonderful, Nina. Keeping Felix's nose to the wheel?"

"Are you joking? If I ever get him to go home and rest, I congratulate myself."

She led him to an elevator separate from the others. "The lift will scan you for electronics. Anything you want to show me?"

Bavarius took a phone from his vest pocket. "It's just a burner I bought at the airport." He didn't have to say he'd left his own phone home because he didn't want anyone—either TSA at the airports, or Felix's people now—intruding into his privacy. Or into information about his clients.

"If any surveillance apps are on it—or on you—the lift will know. So will the AIs in Felix's office." Nina wrinkled her nose. "*He'll* probably just smell them."

Bavarius offered the phone to her. "Why don't you hang onto it for me?"

"You can pick it up at the reception desk when you're done today." She took him upstairs.

Felix could have occupied the entire penthouse, which was mostly empty, except for a kitchenette and a small gym. But Bavarius always was surprised at how small Felix's corner office was. And by how Felix's décor belied both his origins and his technocracy. Felix was Big Texan to the core. But his office was cozy and furnished in old Boston nautical. A ship's barometer. A scrimshaw narwhal tusk standing tall in a corner. A bottled Yankee clipper ship sailing in blue glass on his English walnut desk. The only nod to his western roots was an Ojibwa dream catcher on the wall, and that wasn't from Texas, either.

Bavarius knew about dream catchers. His grandfather, Friedrich, had hung one in front of his bedroom window. Friedrich told young Martin that the dream catcher let smiling dreams of his grandmother visit *Opa* in his sleep. In the mornings, the dream catcher released *Oma* back to Heaven. But Friedrich always knew that she would soon visit him again. Other than family photos and the dream catcher, almost all of Friedrich's artwork was clocks, those he had made and those he collected. At Sunday dinners, young Martin would hear those clocks tick, chime and ring, amidst the family's chatter.

Felix's windows looked out onto QuestCorp's campus of glass-sheathed buildings. Beyond the campus, a clapboard steeple poked skyward from dense greenery in an old residential neighborhood along a curved cobbled street.

His desk was bare of papers. Behind the bottled clipper, two streamlined wireless headsets hung on a wall rack. A couple of harmonicas balanced atop the headsets gave them an unused look. Bavarius imagined Felix tooting a blues harp, alone in the dead of night. He'd done that in Iraq around campfires, until someone had shot at him and missed. Bavarius had been glad he'd stopped. Felix had been a lousy tooter.

Felix came around the desk and put out his big hand. They gripped forearms, and Felix guided Bavarius to a bentwood chair across the desk from his own. Felix wore a black monogrammed polo shirt and light tan slacks. His once-military mustache now broadened into his trademark handlebar and was just starting to turn gray.

"You show up in New York, and now here in the land of high tech and whaling." Felix dropped into his chair. "When you gonna take some time off, come out to Nantucket? We're selling simulation AIs to the Navy. Give me a little notice, I'll get Electric Boat to take us out on a sub."

"Take time off? Like you do?"

"Tell you the truth, Martin, it's been hard to concentrate since Connie was killed. You and me, the things we've seen …. You'd think I'd know better than to ask how folks can do things like that."

"Death's different when it takes a friend, Felix."

"I reckon so …."

"Any word on the investigation?"

"*Nada.* The cops grilled us for a full day. Since then—nothing. Maybe when the autopsy report comes out …. Hey, you want some iced tea? Kansas ambrosia! Felicity! Would you please fix an iced tea for the Judge? And bring a Gatorade for me? Thanks."

Felix called for the tea without touching a button.

"Felicity's my AI gal Friday—and a helluva lot more. Takes dictation … places calls … does Net and Cloud research … writes documents in my style … drafts patents … controls drones … I've even let her host meetings with super angels investing in my new ventures. Sometimes even the private equity big boys."

"You really trust her?"

"For routine stuff," Felix said. "Some of the wowee-gee flash, too."

Bavarius stood and walked to the window. Beyond the campus, Boston looked intimate and twisty, golden in the sun, wound around its secrets like an old cat. Bavarius took his time at the window until Felix joined him there.

"I don't look outside enough." Felix didn't sound regretful. The door opened. A drone floated in on whispering propellers, carrying a tray with their drinks. It set the drinks down.

"Thanks, Felicity."

The drone whisked out. An arm trailed behind it and pulled the door shut.

"Maybe you should, Felix. Look outside more, I mean."

Felix stopped in the middle of twisting open his Gatorade. "Martin, sometimes sussing out what you mean is like reading cat scat. You telling me I'm missing something?"

"It's worth investigating."

Felix took a swig. "Then *say* it, Hoss."

"What if QuestGame made somebody shoot a man?"

"Your client, huh? That Ryder. *He's* what's got you in a 'ruption?" Felix put his drink down with care. "You know how much conspiracy theory bullshit we get here every day? 'QuestCorp's broadcasting commands to my dental fillings!' 'QuestCorp's in league with the CIA!' My legal department gets threat letters from lawyers demanding millions without any evidence. None at all. Dimwits who shouldn't have law licenses. And now I've got to hear it from you, Martin, of all people? Even if some of these whack-a-dodos believe what they say … even if a guy comes out of a QuestGame session and shoots someone, what makes that QuestGame's fault? Even if QuestGame has some weird booga-booga hypnotic power none of us know about, hypnotized people don't do anything they didn't want to do in the first place. If your client shot someone, he can't blame QuestGame."

"I'm not saying that he or she could, Felix. And if, hypothetically, I had a client like that, I wouldn't want to raise a defense that wouldn't stand—

"—and would defame my company—"

"—but I couldn't fail to raise such a defense if it had merit, either. That would be malpractice. You see the bind I would be in?"

"Hypothetically, of course."

"I would need assurance that there's nothing to this."

Felix sat back down at his desk, took a breath, and gulped some Gatorade. "You know better 'n me how hard it is to disprove a crackpot. I was visiting my mom down in her retirement place in Corpus Christi and heard this little ol' white-haired lady tell her mahjong group how if you own a fancy AI-driven car you can tell it to kill your husband and it'll run him down without you lifting a finger. And if you take the car back to the dealer, the dealer won't do a thing to fix it. You think anything I could say would convince that woman she's wrong? Now, you're no crackpot, so I hope you'll listen. Even the military trusts us. And you know how regulated the AI industry is."

Bavarius said, "I know that when chatbots came out and scared people, tech companies begged Congress to regulate in order to look like responsible citizens. There was a change of administration, and no one had to look responsible anymore. The tech bros ditched the nonprofit model, went full-bore for the money and captured what the courts left of the regulators. Congress enacted a few rules, watered down so you'd have legal defenses if things went south. The news cycles got quiet, and Congress hasn't done much about AI since."

Felix grinned. "Oh, the regs are sure 'nough there. You just don't hear about enforcement actions 'cause things *haven't* gone south. So tell me why you think you needed to fly out here?"

Bavarius told Felix about a judge's claim about Questioner—he didn't name Charlene Banner—and about the New York and Los Angeles cases in which QuestGame had been blamed. "But I also want to tell you my personal experience."

"You, Martin, play QuestGame?"

"No. This happened in a Questioner session." Bavarius told Felix how Dred Scott had appeared to him, what Scott had said, and how he had been feeling since.

"So this isn't just about a client?"

Bavarius didn't answer.

Felix looked more concerned. But not for the reason Bavarius expected.

"Martin, QuestGame is just a game. It creates virtual reality experiences, but it's not a mind control device. And Questioner is just a research tool. It uses graphic metaphors to aid your research, but it can't project apparitions. And it sure as hell can't control what you think or feel." Felix took another drink. "Both of them are AI systems, and AIs are just machines trained to do a task better and faster than people, without getting tired."

He looked at Bavarius with sympathy.

Bavarius recalled how Felix had gotten war criminals to surrender by physically communicating sympathy. Marguerite, after a decade facing the stubborn pride of Iraqi men, had been amazed.

"Martin," Felix said. "Could it be that after all your years of lawyering, you're starting to feel like you're a slave to it? That you're getting tired, and ol' Dred Scott was your mind's way of telling you?"

Bavarius stared at his iced tea and didn't answer. Felix was a bit too close to the truth.

The nightmare of autopsying his father flashed before him.

"Hoss? You OK?"

Bavarius shoved the nightmare aside, suddenly aware that Felix—intentionally or not—had distracted him from asking about Questioner. *What's he thinking behind that sympathetic face? Maybe if I push him off balance a little ....*

"I've got a bright woman working with me. Kind of a superstar. Selena MacKenzie."

Felix's handlebar mustache twitched. "I know. I keep tabs on her. Not all the time. But when she leaves New York, I like to know where she goes."

It didn't sound like the Felix Bavarius knew. But this was a paranoid era, and Felix was a public figure. Still, to have a woman followed …. "She said you have a history."

"Well, I'm glad you're here. We can clear us some air."

"OK. But first, let's stick to the main issue: If there's any chance that your systems are hurting people, I need to know. And so do you."

"You *need* to know?"

We're testing each other. It hurt Bavarius that they both found it necessary.

Felix leaned on the edge of his desk. "To me, Selena *is* the main issue." He pushed off from the desk, moved back to the window and gazed out, Bavarius thinking Felix looked like the Marlboro Man. "How did she find you? Jesus. I oughta sue the pants off her." He exhaled sharply. "What kind of shit is she pouring in your ears, Martin? What's she saying about me?"

Felix turned and looked at the dream catcher on the wall. It seemed to calm him. "Tell me."

"Just that you were, 'an item,' was how she put it. When she was a student."

"Yeah, we were. That shouldn't have happened. I should've been smarter. Better."

Felix's words made Bavarius queasy. He'd heard convicted sexual predators say they were sorry when they stood in his court to be sentenced. But standing before a judge wasn't the right time to beg forgiveness.

"Did you ever apologize to Selena?"

"She never gave me the chance!"

Bavarius waited.

"Selena was there almost at the beginning, when I started working my AI concepts into neural interfaces for research and games, as well as the armed forces. She was so enthusiastic and I just fell …. You know, I never supervised her course work. Never graded her. Never had any authority over her. She sat in on my lectures, talked to me after class, dropped in during office hours … and it happened. She came onto me. And it went sour. I started QuestCorp, and didn't take her along for the ride, and she's still mad as hell.

"Probably told you I got her pregnant, didn't she?" Felix spun back to face Bavarius. "Well, *did* she?"

Bavarius had not expected this. "No."

"Told you I made her have an abortion?"

Bavarius felt poleaxed. "No, Felix."

"Well, there was a time she told the world. How was I supposed to apologize when she was slandering me, huh? I tried to apologize. Only a couple of times, I admit. She wouldn't talk to me and I'm no masochist." Felix took a deep breath and his voice softened. "Every so often, she shows up at a shareholder meeting and just stares at me. Gives me the creeps, I'll tell you."

Bavarius had heard psychological expert witnesses testify that predators can demean their victims until a listener is convinced the predator is the victim.

But just because that often happens didn't prove that was the case between Felix and MacKenzie. Bavarius had learned on the bench that patterns are poor predictors.

"Felix, Selena didn't tell me about a pregnancy, or an abortion. You did. Why?"

"Because if she hasn't told you yet, she will. And that baby wasn't mine. Selena was almost four months pregnant when she got that abortion, and I was in Spain on sabbatical when she got knocked up."

Was Felix lying as well as smearing her?

Bavarius remembered the brown government-looking car cruising slowly down his street behind MacKenzie as she ran.

"How closely are you watching Selena?"

"Like I said, not very. Let her live her life, as long as she leaves me alone."

"The other morning, Selena left my house to run. A car with two men in it followed her. Yours?"

"Come on, Martin. Now you're being insulting. Why would I hire people to watch her run?"

Because you watch her when she leaves New York, and she's left New York to work with me, and you know I've taken on Mark Ryder's case, and you know what Mark claims about QuestGame—Shit, Felix, are you watching me, too?

"You said you have her watched when she leaves New York. She's left New York. She's at my house. Tell me straight up. Was that car yours?"

"I don't know. It could have been. But I won't know until the detective agency sends its next report."

"So your people might be watching my house?"

"I would never target you. Never." Felix looked down as he rubbed the back of his neck. "Look. Whatever happened between Selena and me has nothing to do with us. Nothing to do with you and me. You came to me for help, so let's get back to that. What concerns you is what's been put into QuestCorp systems. People sue me claiming all kinds of shit. But I'm still here. Because I'm careful. I wouldn't put anything bad into my systems. No way. Nobody else could, either."

"No system's hacker-proof."

"But mine are as close to it as anyone's. As for those incidents you described: How many killers blame drugs, or TV, or metal music, for what they do, huh? Maybe Selena's moved from trash-talking me to slandering my products."

Bavarius raised a finger. "The Questioner observations weren't Selena's, Felix." He pointed at himself. "They're mine. I wouldn't be here if it hadn't happened to me."

Felix picked up his Gatorade again, like he couldn't make up his mind what to do with it.

"Could there be an issue with your technology? Either the AIs or the neural links?"

"Not a chance in hell. Both techs are solid. Proven. Pilots have used them no problem for years. An' believe me, people *look* for flaws. Ever since AIs started taking folks' jobs...."

Bavarius stood, feeling sad about how this meeting had gone. "Well, then, will you look into it? Please? Think of the stakes if something is wrong."

Felix sighed. "All right."

"Thank you."

"*De nada.* You're right. If there's a problem with my systems, I need to know."

"Tell me what you learn?"

"I'll tell you what I can." Felix gave Bavarius a hard look. "Martin, talking about Selena MacKenzie is not something I do often. Or enjoy doing." He ran his fingers through his hair.

"Now," Felix said, "how 'bout next month? Lobster on the beach. A sub ride."

"Let me get through this case. I can't predict my schedule right now."

They walked to the office door and Felix opened it. "Nina, would you please escort Judge Bavarius downstairs?"

They grasped forearms again and Felix kept his grip longer than usual.

"I don't like to give unsolicited advice, Hoss. But …."

"Yes?"

"Watch out for Selena. She's a bad one." Felix let Bavarius' arm go.

"OK."

"Oh, and Martin. About your murder case? Leave QuestCorp out of it."

QUESTION:

"Are AIs producing biased criminal sentences?"

ANSWER:

"The persistence of bias in AI-assisted sentencing can be attributed to several factors:

- *Biased training data: AI systems trained on historically biased datasets may reinforce existing disparities, perpetuating discriminatory outcomes under the guise of machine neutrality.*

- *Misapplication of AI guidance: Judges may misinterpret or selectively apply AI recommendations, leading to unintended consequences and continued discrimination.*

- *Lack of transparency: The "black box" nature of some AI algorithms makes it difficult to identify and address biases in their decision-making processes."*

CHAPTER 8

Strong headwinds slowed Bavarius' plane back to Topeka that night. Someone in the back of the plane was punched for sitting in the wrong seat and the plane diverted to Indianapolis. Bavarius finally landed in Topeka after one in the morning.

Exhausted, he turned the key in his front door, and saw MacKenzie sitting in the dark dining room in a long shirt and leggings, face lit by her softly glowing laptop monitor. Her smile felt warm, weary and real.

"Welcome home."

He put his briefcase down and crossed the room to her. "You're up late."

She yawned. "I don't sleep much."

"What are you working on?" He bent to look at her screen. A sticky note at the bottom read, "Annabelle."

"Oh, research on Ryder's case. Three states besides Kansas have abolished the insanity defense, so I'm looking for approaches taken by defense lawyers there. And it seems that while a killer can't get off anymore because insanity kept him from knowing right from wrong, he can still argue that he didn't intend to commit the crime. Remember what Ryder told us?"

Bavarius straightened up. "He said he never wanted to kill Mudge. It never occurred to him that either of them could really be hurt."

"Exactly."

"Selena, this might work better than an insanity defense."

"How?"

"Well, insanity was an affirmative defense. The burden of proof would have been on Mark to prove that QuestGame made him too crazy to know right from wrong. But this way—"

"—the burden is on prosecutors to prove Mark's intent—"

"—and if we present expert testimony that because of QuestGame, Mark didn't intend to kill, and can raise reasonable doubt about Mark's intent in the jury's minds …." He paused. *We're finishing each other's sentences.*

She yawned again and raised a hand to cover her mouth. As she did, she leaned a little back and to the side. Her shoulder touched his left hip. Then her right temple, the side of his belly.

His impulse was to step away, but he grew acutely conscious of her head gradually resting more heavily against him as he said, "The prosecutors will argue that the fact that Mark shot Mudge in a duel proves intent to kill, and that's a strong argument. But if we can raise reasonable doubt, Mark won't be convicted of attempted murder. It'll be a lesser crime and he'll do less time."

MacKenzie wasn't listening. She had fallen asleep.

"Hey …." He shook her gently and she started awake.

"Oh … sorry."

On the wall across the room, Bavarius saw what he called his rogues' gallery. Photos of brother and sister judges, celebrities and friends. Bavarius, in his twenties, hauling on the sail of a boat on the Evros River dividing Greece and Turkey, spray in the air and on his face. Bavarius grilling barbecue for his unit in Iraq, Felix munching on a beef rib.

Beneath the judge photos, an aspen frame held two Supreme Court quill pens on black velvet.

And, apart from them all, a single old wedding photo, Bavarius tall and proud next to his lovely, short-lived wife, Victoria. Victoria had been round and wriggly and full of life. She'd had chipmunk cheeks and the clearest, most intelligent eyes. Hazel eyes, shot with green. She had given Bavarius everything and let him get away with nothing. Not that she would overtly call him to account. She would just fix him with those calm eyes, and he would know he was fooling himself, that what he planned or was doing or had done was wrong.

There was only one thing she had not given him. A child. Four grand years of marriage, and then quick sickness and death. Her picture called to him. It called to him often. But for the first time in forever, his attention fixed on the tiny gap between her front teeth. Much like ….

MacKenzie's face followed his gaze. "She was beautiful. Marguerite told me. I'm sorry."

When Bavarius spoke again, his voice seemed far away, coming from someone other than him. "When we learned about her cancer, I remember this sudden disconnect from everything, like nothing could or even wanted to touch me. Like I'd been kicked off the merry-go-round and into the void, knowing we wouldn't be allowed to stay together there either. Wrong, all wrong, but as she weakened, somehow right, too. She taught me the absolute necessity of compassion. How it both honors and defies whatever divinity there may be."

He pulled his eyes away from the photo. "Oh, hell, don't listen to me."

Her blue eyes slanted up to meet his. Her scent thickened his throat, and he cleared it.

Then she walked over to the Iraq barbecue photo. "Felix and you really do go back a ways. You both look so young …."

Bavarius didn't want to talk to her about Felix tonight. MacKenzie and he both needed sleep, and it would be wrong to destroy the warmth MacKenzie and he were feeling. He needed to be able to trust MacKenzie, but that inquiry could wait until tomorrow. "How are Bill and you getting on?"

"There's a sharp mind behind that cherub face. He's a sweet guy, too."

"That he is," Bavarius agreed, feeling obscurely jealous.

"But he can't handle hard work," she deadpanned. "Passed right out on that chair. I had to wake him and feed him coffee. My stomach hates coffee at night."

"Want some water? I've got some antacids, too." He went into the kitchen, filled a glass with water, and poured himself some orange juice. Gopherbreath was curled up and snoring in his kennel.

"Hey, buddy," he murmured.

The dog snorted in his sleep.

MacKenzie followed Bavarius into the kitchen. He handed her the water glass and she raised it in thanks. "I walked him," she whispered. Her bag was on the counter, a Coach purse-briefcase of heavy belt leather. A paperback leaned against it. Jane Austin.

"How did it go with Felix?"

"He had only nice things to say about you."

Bavarius had already seen a battery of different grins from her. This one was crooked.

"You're a bad liar."

Bavarius jumped rope on his lawn as dawn broke. He tried to jump for fifteen minutes twice a week, doing intervals with a weighted five-pound rope. Quite a contrast to tai chi work.

He was sweating hard when MacKenzie came out, waved, and started her morning run. No car followed her today. Maybe that had just been coincidence.

The heavy rope snapped against his ankles and broke his rhythm. He started jumping again, finished his routine, and went in to shower.

Downstairs, Marguerite handed him coffee. This morning, Marguerite wore glasses. This was unusual. She preferred contact lenses in public, and she thought of being in the kitchen with Bavarius as a public appearance. A dog-eared French edition of *Candide* lay on the counter by the coffee hand press.

This must be the tenth time I've seen her read it.

Gopherbreath prowled around the kitchen sniffing for food while Marguerite assembled the cream, brown sugar, butter, vanilla, and cinnamon for *la farine d'avoine*. Bavarius couldn't vouch for his arteries when Marguerite was in a *crème fraîche* mood.

He knelt to the floor with a bowl of dog food and looked up across the kitchen. "Marguerite, why did you tell Selena about Victoria?"

"She asked me who the beautiful bride was." Marguerite closed the pantry door and took her glasses off. "Did I overstep?"

"No. It's fine." Bavarius took his coffee out to the porch. Before he finished it, MacKenzie returned, running hard in a final sprint. She walked up the path to the porch panting, flushed and smiling. "Good morning again!"

"A short run today?"

"Short but fast."

"There's coffee and tea inside. Oatmeal soon. We should talk about some things."

MacKenzie nodded and went upstairs. Bavarius refilled his coffee mug and returned to the porch. He sat on the bench swing, not wanting to enthrone himself in the rocking chair and create distance.

Soon she joined him, cup of tea in hand. "This is about your meeting with Felix, isn't it?"

"Please. Sit."

She sat in the rocker.

OK. Let her create the distance.

Her heavy hair was damp and she pushed it from her forehead. A stray lock crept back over her eye as it dried.

"Felix says you've spread some lies about him. About a pregnancy."

A little tea sloshed from her cup onto her yellow jeans.

"That you tell people he got you pregnant, although it's not true."

"Do you believe him?"

"I've never known him to lie to me—"

"And if I say he's lying?"

"Except, perhaps, about you."

That brought her up short. "Then you believe me?"

"I don't know who or what to believe, Selena. But if Felix winds up involved in our case, I need to know how deep your emotions run."

"And how trustworthy I am."

"Yes."

She exhaled through her teeth.

"Felix and I go back many years," he said quietly. "You've been working hard and well, and I want to trust you. But I want to trust Felix, too."

"You think Felix got where he is without lying?"

"Of course not."

MacKenzie placed her cup on the porch floor and sat straight to face him, hands flat on the rocker's arms. "All right, then. You know men do lie about things like this."

"I need something more than the general behavior patterns of the male species."

"I think he told you something that convinced you."

"I'm not convinced of anything, yet."

"So, what did he say?"

"That you stalk him. That you show up at shareholders meetings and stare at him."

"I already told you why I go!"

"He says he's so concerned about it that he sometimes has you tracked when you leave New York."

"I'm to blame if he's paranoid and has me watched? Who's stalking who?" MacKenzie's mouth compressed into a thin line. "Is he really having me followed?" Then she growled, "What else did he say?"

"When you went for your run the other day, a brown car with two men in it drove behind you, slowly, for at least a short distance. I didn't see any more, so I can't say it was following you. Felix said he didn't know either, but he admits that he sometimes tracks your whereabouts."

She shook her head slowly. "Bastard."

"He also said you were never his student. He never graded or evaluated your academic work."

"Technically true. He informally mentored me and picked my brain to develop his theories. Told me he loved me and we were going to change the world together. Then he knocked me up and then dumped me. And I'm pretty sure he queered my employment prospects around Boston, though I can't prove it. I don't go around claiming that, but he's made it an issue, so I'm telling you now."

"He told me it was impossible for him to be the father because he was on sabbatical in Spain when you got pregnant."

"He was on sabbatical when I *learned* I was pregnant. Not when he knocked me up." She stood so suddenly that the backs of her knees shoved the rocker backward and its springs squeaked. "You don't believe me. What's your fax number?"

Bavarius told her.

She stared down at him. "Felix and you should go into business, like best bros do. Make gender-oriented cars. Call 'em Venus for women. Prick for men. Name the men's trucks Big Prick. The subcompacts can be Dinky Prick."

For the first time, he got angry. "If you're trying to make a point, you missed it."

"Did I? Did I?" She stalked inside for her cell phone. He followed. She wouldn't look at him. "Janie? It's me. Do you still have my apartment key? ... Do me a favor—it's important. You know my file cabinet? ... Yes. Third drawer down. Second file in, the one labeled 'Medical' ... Yeah, I know it's thick. Anyway, all the way in back is a folder labeled 'Bad Dream.' See it? ... Good. Fax it to this number, OK?" She gave Bavarius' fax number. "Yes, all five pages. Thanks, sweetie." She hung up and glared at him.

Further into the house, Bavarius' fax machine shrilled. He started for the machine, but she put her hand up. "I'll get it."

She returned and shoved several pages into his hand.

He read, "Date of D & C ... fetal age, fourteen weeks ...." He looked up. "This is a medical chart."

"Keep reading."

"These are DNA comparisons."

"One of them is of the fetal placenta. The other is of some blood I scraped off Felix's razor."

"They match."

"I thought we were going to start a family. God, I was so naïve. I phoned him in Spain because I was so excited. And he said '*Get rid of it*.' Dumped me on the spot."

"And that's when you scraped the DNA from his razor?"

"I thought it would be different if I proved it was his baby, too. Now, I wish I'd just made a stink."

"Felix told me that you *made* noise. Slandered him for years."

"And you think I'm slandering him now? Even with the records in your hand. The newsfeeds love stories like that. But it wasn't reported. Check the news databases; you can verify that. Felix lied to you, Martin. He lied when he said he loved me, and he lied when he denied he'd made me pregnant. He even lied the night it happened. I saw the broken condom but he denied it was broken and flushed it down the toilet when I reached for it to show him. That was my first hint that something was wrong. I should have seen the rest coming. I didn't make noise. I tried to salvage us even after he told me to get rid of it. Even after he told me to move out. So, I scraped his razor and when he got back to the States, I showed him the DNA test. He didn't care.

"I got the abortion and avoided Felix for the rest of my time at MIT. I found another mentor. The head of the AI lab, Kurt Leiber. The deepest, kindest, most oblivious-to-the-world-around-him man alive. We just worked, and I loved it, and he wrote me recommendation letters from Heaven. Meanwhile, even though I didn't make noise about the baby, Felix torpedoed me in the Boston job market. Thanks to Prof. Kurt, they snapped me right up in Silicon Valley. That's why I went to Stanford Law—I was already in California. I mean really, who's slandering whom? Now it's a dozen years later, and the lies still hurt, and I'm getting kind of old to have kids."

"Selena … Felix told you to get out before coming back to the states. But you kept a key to get in and scrape his razor?"

MacKenzie stared at him. "He wasn't here to return it to. He was in Spain. You know what? You don't *want* to believe me."

"I didn't say that."

"But I get it. I do. He's your old buddy. Bro's before ho's, right?"

"Selena—"

"Kindly shut up." She took the papers from him. "I'll shred these before I leave." Her fist crumpled them. "I'll take a cab to the airport. I don't think I want to see you again, let alone work with you. Meanwhile, Your Judgeship, consider this. Felix clearly doesn't know I've kept these records. He probably never considered that I might want to. And without them, I could never have proved he lied to you. Think about what else Saint Felix has lied to you about."

"Selena, really—"

"Also, that story Questioner fed you about Dred Scott was crap. I studied the Civil War in high school. And I read about Dred Scott in law school. He didn't join a traveling show after the war. He died before the war started. And his wife's name wasn't Lucy, it was Harriet. So, you still trust Questioner? You still trust Felix?"

She pushed past Bavarius and very deliberately walked upstairs.

So, now Felix has trash-talked her, and she's bad-mouthed him. Both playing victim.

But she really was a victim. She has documentary proof.

But the question remained: Who was telling the truth?

He checked the newsfeed database and found no reports that she had alleged that Felix had made her pregnant, or that he had sexually harassed her.

Then he looked up the history of Dred Scott. "Shit."

MacKenzie came downstairs with her suitcase.

"You're right about Dred Scott, Selena. He died in 1858, and his wife was Harriet. But why didn't you tell me about that when I first told you what the Dred Scott avatar said to me? It supports the theory that there's something wrong with the Questioner AIs."

"Because I didn't think to look it up and confirm it until later that night. And in the morning, I forgot."

"You just forgot? You should have told me right away."

"You're the lawyer on the Ryder case. You can't testify about Dred Scott because it would make you a witness. So, it didn't seem important until now. And it's only important now to show you that Felix lied to you about Questioner being OK."

"You should have told me earlier."

"I'm so deeply sorry. My negligence just makes me want to vomit."

He wanted to snap back at her sarcasm, but he needed information. "You said Felix picked your brain to develop his theories. Why didn't you sue him for taking your intellectual property?"

"Because I'm rich, Martin. I graduated, and then Dad died and left me plenty. I wanted nothing more to do with Felix West, and then the statute of limitations expired. And it would have been impossible to prove a claim. I did most of the work on his computers and on napkins and matchbook covers and scrap paper. I didn't keep any of it. Sometimes, I just talked the ideas out and didn't write them down. But Felix remembered. Did he ever. I was in love and spouting inventions, and he patented them."

"But you still go to shareholder meetings."

"Because I still wonder. I go and watch how he works magic on people. I'm a bird, and he's the snake, and I can't look away."

He saw tears in her eyes.

But does a bird repeatedly seek out a snake's nest just to risk being hypnotized? Or in hope of killing the snake?

"Damn you for dragging this out of me, Martin."

"Selena—"

MacKenzie ignored him and wheeled her suitcase out to the sidewalk.

"Before you go, I have to ask about Ms. Weathers' murder."

"You think I was involved with that?"

"No. But … all the shareholders' meetings you attended … did anyone mention anything wrong at QuestCorp? Internal troubles? Employee discontent? Conflicts among shareholders or directors? Anybody key getting fired?"

She stared straight ahead and did not answer. A self-driving cab came for her. He watched it carry her away, both upset and relieved to see her go. *I sure could've used her help. But at least I don't have to worry about her damaging Mark's case.*

Now, I just have to deal with Felix, and what QuestCorp and he may have done. And a thirty-year friendship going sour.

He sat on the porch until Marguerite came out to say the *farine d'avoine* was ready. He followed her inside, but after eating half the porridge, he gave up for lack of appetite.

"Sorry, Marguerite."

"It is of no importance. I shall bake it into biscuits for later. For dinner, I make *masgouf* with *biryani?*"

She clearly knew how upset he was, because *masgouf* was his favorite meal, but so labor-intensive she rarely made it: Fish grilled slowly the Iraqi way, standing on its side in the flames and smoke, with sumac, pomegranate seeds and lemon all poured on top.

"Thank you, Marguerite. Sounds delicious."

"Seven o'clock?"

"I can't wait."

QUESTION:

"Do you know why there has been an order of magnitude leap in AI's ability to do inference, deduction, and logic processing?"

ANSWER:

"OpenAI's 'Strawberry' project, now officially known as OpenAI o1, represents a significant advancement in AI reasoning capabilities. The model employs an extended chain of thought before providing answers. This allows o1 to: Break down complex problems into simpler steps; recognize and correct mistakes; try alternative approaches when initial strategies fail; and refine its reasoning strategies over time. This process mimics human-like thinking, where one might ponder a difficult question for an extended period before responding. The sudden improvement in o1's abilities may be attributed to a phenomenon known as 'grokking.' This occurs when an AI model, after continued training, suddenly gains a significantly enhanced ability to infer and understand concepts. It's similar to how a human might suddenly grasp a complex idea after persistent study."

CHAPTER 9

Bavarius met Owens outside Topeka's courthouse and entered the beige brick building.

Officer Czabaniuk had named other witnesses to the duel. The snack bar lady in the courthouse lobby. The court reporter in the juvenile division. The bailiff in Criminal Courtroom Two. And Bavarius had garnered more names from reports by the homicide detectives at the shooting scene.

Ryder's case differed from most murders in that witnesses were eager to talk. It wasn't a gang murder and the witnesses had nothing to fear. And the shooting had been a weird, wild happening. So many witnesses came forward that the detectives must have gotten lazy. The snack bar lady didn't appear in the detectives' reports, and Bavarius guessed there were other witnesses to be found.

And Czabaniuk wasn't the only witness who knew and liked Ryder. He was a prosecutor, a guy on their side, and they saw him several times a week. They could sympathize with Ryder wanting to shoot Mudge, a snake in the courthouse, even if they could hardly believe Ryder had done it.

Bavarius showed the snack bar lady his phone and switched the recording app on. She had gone outside for a cigarette on the courthouse steps and watched the whole thing.

"Could it have been self-defense?"

"The way they went at each other?" She shook her head. "No. They were like crazy people."

"Did you see which one of them went for his car first?"

"Mudge. Definitely."

Aha! First to go for his car. Maybe first to go for his gun? And even if Czabaniuk testifies to the contrary, this lady's a lot more certain about what she saw than Czabaniuk.

"Which one of them fired the first shot?"

"I think … No. Sorry. I couldn't tell."

By four o'clock, Bavarius had interviewed eight witnesses, and developed sore feet. All eight had heard the shots. Five had seen the two cars playing chicken. Three had been close enough to hear shouting and shooting but hadn't made out what Mudge or Ryder said. The Courtroom Two bailiff, skinny and unsmiling, said that he saw Ryder laugh after the shooting.

"Did he say anything then? Even to himself?"

"No. He just looked super-satisfied, like he'd won the lottery."

Then the bailiff said, "You didn't ask me what they said before the shooting," and he repeated Ryder's threat word for word.

The parking enforcement officer spent her days writing tickets for cars that stayed too long in the courthouse parking lot. She told Bavarius that Mudge's car had almost hit her during the duel. Both men were shooting and then Mudge crashed his car. She ran toward Mudge and heard him groan, "But I won the game!" She also heard Ryder shout, "I got the son of a bitch!"—which contradicted what the bailiff had said. You just never knew what might come out of a witness.

Feeling he'd had enough for one day, Bavarius went home. He swung gently on his porch bench with an old guitar in his lap and Gopherbreath lying at his feet. Patient because he knew he would never play well, he tried to twist his fingers into jazz chord shapes and waited for the evening to cool down.

Purdue pulled up in his red Volvo and got out wearing Bermuda shorts, ripped sneakers, and an ancient African *dashiki*. Beneath his paunch, his legs were surprisingly well-muscled, but his knees tended to hyperextend, and his posture, clothes and profile made him look like a squat technicolor ostrich. He unloaded his laptop and sketch pad and thumped up the porch steps, calling, "Yo, Martin. Selena have that stuff for me?"

"No. She's gone."

"Where'd she go?"

"She quit the case, Bill."

"Oh, hell. Why?"

Bavarius told him what Felix had said, and how MacKenzie had responded. "She was furious that I believed Felix over her. I did want to believe him, but I was withholding judgment. She didn't see it that way."

He toed his rocker into slow motion. "I didn't believe her over him until she showed me proof."

"Proof?" Purdue asked.

"How was I supposed to know who to believe without proof? I was even getting untrustworthy info from Questioner. It gave me the wrong name for Dred Scott's wife. MacKenzie proved that, too."

"How? What proof?"

But Bavarius was on a tear. "And you know what else bugs me? If that slave-to-the-law nonsense came from my head like Felix suggested, where's my sense of proportion? Job exhaustion can't compare to slavery."

"Martin, you're not responsible for your subconscious."

Marguerite brought out a basket of *mana'eesh*. She waved a tiny warm flatbread, fragrant with olive oil, *za'atar*, and red pepper flakes, indecently close to Bavarius' nose. "Eat!"

Purdue asked, "Do I smell curry?"

"*Oui.* Red curry to go into the *biryani.* An idea from my sister."

"How is Francine?"

"In Provence, nothing ever changes."

"A lovely conceit," Purdue said.

Bavarius bit a *mana'eesh.* The pepper in it bit back.

Marguerite took a *mana'eesh* and returned to the kitchen.

Purdue said, "Now, about that proof."

Bavarius hesitated. "Medical records."

"You have them?"

"She said she was going to shred them. But she was so angry that she crumpled them up. Hard to shred crumpled paper. Maybe she just trashed them."

He went into the office, but the pages were gone. She'd either shredded them or taken them with her.

He joined Purdue and Marguerite in the kitchen. "I guess she shredded them after all."

"Why do you think she did that?" Purdue asked.

"Well, they were private medical records—"

"She'd just shared them with you. Maybe she didn't want you looking at 'em too close. What'd they say?"

"There was a D & C report, and a DNA comparison."

"OK. What—'Scuse me." Purdue finished crunching *papadum* and swallowed. "What'd they say?"

Bavarius recited, "Date of D & C, July 7 … fetal age, fourteen weeks."

"Fourteen weeks?" Marguerite sounded surprised. "That is very long."

"She's right, Martin. Most women know they're pregnant in five, maybe eight weeks. If Selena told West as soon as she found out and he blew her off, why'd she wait so long to get the abortion? Maybe she called him in Spain and he rejected her, but she just had to have a face to face. Maybe his mind would change. And when it didn't, *then* she had the abortion."

"You're speculating." Bavarius put down the *papadum* he'd picked up.

"What about the DNA comparison?"

"It matched."

"But did the report say whose DNA it was?"

It was a measure of how upset he'd been during his confrontation with MacKenzie that he hadn't thought of that. "No. Selena did."

"So, it's at least possible that West told you the truth, at least about Selena."

"Why does it matter, Bill? She's gone."

"It matters because you said in the same breath that West lied and that Questioner gave you bad info. Almost like you couldn't trust Questioner because you couldn't trust your friend who designed it. Take a step back, Judge—and judge things."

"So, your argument is that I can't know if I can trust either of them?"

"That's my take."

"But if Felix did lie to me about Selena, he might lie to me about other things, too. And given how skeptical he seemed when I suggested that his systems might have problems, he might have lied when he promised to look into it."

"The *biryani* is almost ready," Marguerite said. Now, to grill the *masgouf!*"

"Mas … what?"

"Don't ask, Bill. Just wait, and enjoy."

Bavarius and Purdue took little bowls of spices that Marguerite provided, with plates, utensils, water, and napkins, out to the dining room table.

Purdue blurted, "Involuntary intoxication! What if Mark was involuntarily intoxicated by QuestGame before the duel?"

"Selena thinks that if QuestGame convinced Mark that neither he nor Mudge could really be hurt by the duel, then he couldn't have had the intent to kill."

"See? Involuntary intoxication fits, doesn't it?"

"It does. But how do we show that's what happened without evidence? Testimony. We would need QuestCorp witnesses. Documentation. Data and code. Getting it would be gladiatorial combat." Bavarius recalled Felix's last words to him. "Felix would go ballistic. There's got to be a more predictable, less explosive approach."

"Why? Because West is your friend?"

After dinner, Bavarius and Purdue took a walk. The evening sky flamed red. Sprinklers spread the scent of lawns and the mist felt good on their faces. Slowly, they worked out a theory for Ryder's defense: Playing QuestGame was like going to a doctor who prescribed a drug that caused psychotic episodes, before doctors or the FDA realized there was a problem. Or like drinking a cup of coffee you don't know is spiked with LSD. Ryder could not anticipate that QuestGame would deceive him into believing that he could not hurt Mudge in reality, and being deceived can qualify a defendant for an involuntary intoxication defense. An involuntarily intoxicated Ryder could not have intended to kill Mudge and so couldn't be convicted of attempting murder. Or of murder, if Mudge died.

"Now," Purdue yawned. "We just have to prove that a virtual reality game, built by the same successful, respected, multibillion-dollar company that built the system that judges everywhere rely on for their research, is a deceptive menace. No sweat."

"Indeed." *I wish I knew if Felix deserves it.*

When Marguerite entered the dining room in the morning to open windows and let in the morning breeze, she found Bavarius cheek-down on some case printouts. Purdue was gone. She cracked the windows and reclosed the curtains to keep the room dark and let Bavarius sleep.

But her rustlings woke him, and he climbed the stairs and got into bed. He woke mid-morning, empty and sad. He had dreamed again of autopsying his father. And of a woman whose face was shadowed. Victoria? He'd dreamed about her over the years, less often as time went on. But Victoria's face had always been visible in dreams. Usually joyous, occasionally somber. In death as in life, Victoria wore her emotions openly. This dream was of someone else.

His phone rang.

"Is this the Martin Bavarius who's defending the Mark Ryder case?"

"Yes. Who's calling, please?"

"My name's Charlene Banner. I'm a state court judge in Utah. I use Questioner all the time, but now I'm afraid to. I think it did something weird, gave me bad information. I relied on it and made a decision that almost killed my son."

QUESTION:

"Explain intrinsic motivation in AI."

ANSWER:

"Intrinsically motivated AI systems are designed to actively seek out new information and experiences. This curiosity-driven approach enables them to explore their environment more thoroughly, discover novel situations or patterns, learn and adapt without constant external guidance. AI agents with intrinsic motivation can make decisions based on their internal goals and perceived challenges."

CHAPTER 10

"Yes, Judge Banner," Bavarius said. "I read about your situation, and about your son. I'm very sorry."

"Thank you. He's still touch and go. I've heard about your duel case, and what your client claims QuestGame did to him. I suspect you and I both need to learn if there's something wrong with QuestCorp technology."

"Can you tell me more about what happened to you?"

"Yes. After I denied that no-knock warrant, I wrote a memo about my Questioner session because it felt strange to me. It's dated and time-stamped."

"I'd love to see it."

"Can we meet in person?"

They agreed that he would visit her in Utah the following week.

Was Banner considering a civil lawsuit? Product liability cases weren't his area, although Bavarius knew good lawyers in that field. With MacKenzie's technical knowledge ....

She was gone. *Shit.*

What was he thinking? He wasn't going to sue Felix. Or encourage a case against him.

But thinking about it brought to mind another potential conflict of interest. Bavarius owned QuestCorp stock and he didn't want his financial interests to influence any decisions he made in defending Mark Ryder.

He called his broker and sold his stock.

He started to call MacKenzie's number, but hung up before he finished punching it in. He wouldn't learn the truth that way. And the MacKenzie-Felix war didn't matter anymore.

Shake it off, Martin. Mark's defense is more important.

With MacKenzie gone, Bavarius needed a new AI expert. MacKenzie had recommended eight before she quit. Four were in California, two were in Boston and one was in the Raleigh-Durham Research Triangle. But she had raved about Kurt Leiber, and Leiber had retired out in Russell County, Kansas, to run a no-kill puppy shelter with his wife. *Lucky me.*

Bavarius phoned Leiber, and then loaded Gopherbreath's kennel into the Imperial. He lowered the car's visor against the afternoon sun, turned on a honky-tonk country station and tapped his steering wheel to sad musical tales as he accelerated to seventy-five and drove the 180 miles west on Interstate 70.

The sun was still high and harsh when Bavarius exited the Interstate. He drove north on a two-lane highway that cut arrow-straight through crop lands. Distant farmhouses flanked by sheds stood sheltered from sun and storm by carefully planted cottonwoods and elms. Cattle crowded together in a small feedlot on trampled, muddy ground, their reek pungent through his open window.

At a wooden sign saying "Puppy Shelter," he turned onto a dirt road, and then into a long driveway that passed through a sunflower field and ended at a toolshed. He opened his door and then the back door to unlatch Gopherbreath's crate. Before Bavarius could move from the back door, Gopherbreath pushed out of the box, scrambled over the front seat, dove out the driver's door, and peed. Bavarius looked around and spotted a house a quarter-mile further in the direction he'd been driving. *I turned into the wrong driveway.*

Gopherbreath gave a low "Woof!" and looked up at him, tail wagging.

Bavarius said, "Back in the car, fella," but the Catahoula barked and lunged into the sunflowers, snatched up a dead rabbit, and turned to display it proudly in his jaws. Bavarius walked toward the dog and held his hand out for the rodent, afraid it might have been poisoned. Gopherbreath dropped the corpse, stood over it, and growled.

"You face, I think, two similar problems. With Felix West and your dog," called an accented voice that managed to sound both matter- of-fact and playful.

Bavarius looked at the man picking his way toward them from the direction of the house. Short and wizened, with a square, deeply dimpled face and thin white hair meandering across his scalp, he wore jeans, an aged white dress shirt, a navy cotton suit vest, and dark coke-bottle glasses. He smiled at Bavarius with amber-smoked teeth, and he puffed on a braided cigar.

"Hello, Judge Bavarius. I am Kurt Leiber."

"It's good to meet you, Professor. But I'm not a judge anymore."

"Hah! Nor am I a professor! I am Kurt!" Leiber bawled a great laugh.

Bavarius smiled. "If I may say, this is the last place I'd expect to find a man like you."

"A long way from Dresden," Leiber agreed. "And from MIT. But when I was starting out in America, you could buy a hundred acres of farmland with a post rock house on it for ten thousand dollars. I thought, maybe it would be worth money someday. Today it's worth many times what I paid for it. I should sell. But Catarina and I like open fields. And extreme temperatures. Perhaps I would like them less if I were out working the crops."

Gopherbreath still guarded his rabbit. Bavarius slowly bent down and picked it up, saying, "Good boy." He wasn't sure what Gopherbreath would do, but the dog let him have it. *Now what the hell do I do with a rabbit that's been dead awhile?*

Lieber held out a hand for Gopherbreath to sniff. "Would you like to meet my dogs?"

Gopherbreath danced around him.

"I was going to drive over to the house," Bavarius said. "But he's been cooped up. Would you mind if we walk?"

"Not at all. *Komm!*" Leiber snapped his fingers and led Bavarius and Gopherbreath between rows of sunflowers that would grow ten feet tall by the time they bloomed fully in the late summer or fall. For now, they were waist high and the flower heads were still clenched and green. Gopherbreath vanished into them.

It was slow going through the flowers. A short way into the field, they came upon a farmer in overalls looking at a stalk. "All is good, Mr. Zarr?" Leiber asked.

"No pests so far, Mr. Leiber," the farmer said. He looked at Bavarius, who still held the dead rabbit. "Afternoon, sir."

"Afternoon."

"It is an interesting arrangement," Leiber told Bavarius, as they walked on. "I bought half of Mr. Zarr's farm from his father and renovated the post rock house.. I live in the house and he lives in town where his children are close to school and his wife is close to her job. He works the crops and I get thirty percent of the profit, when there is any."

Gopherbreath reappeared, charging across their path. Bavarius could follow where he was going by the waving of disturbed flowers.

"I've been considering the problem you described on the phone," Leiber said around his cigar. "I think you are right to accept that Felix would not consciously allow dangerous programming into his code."

"He's too smart and careful to do something like that," Bavarius agreed.

"Of course, people are unpredictable."

"A mystery," Bavarius agreed.

"And so are artificial intelligences. Many write their own code, you know. Most people think that AIs can do only tasks defined for them by humans. But we've built them to evolve in a Darwinian way, to improve generation after generation without human input."

Bavarius stopped walking. Stalks hissed softly in the slow wind. Leiber had spoken matter of factly, and yet had undermined what Bavarius believed a basic premise of modern civilization: That AIs are reliable. That they are machines that do what they're programmed to do. That systems are human-governed matrices of process and content. Informational beasts of burden. Slaves. Computer systems can't go rogue, the sunflowers seemed to whisper.

Bavarius hurried to catch up to Leiber. "I thought that was impossible."

"Oh no," Leiber said. "AIs can reconfigure their code in response to input. That's basic."

Basic. "But surely we've designed systems used by the public so they can't hurt people."

"You might think so. Isaac Asimov even formulated laws in his books for that purpose: One, a robot may not injure a human being or, through inaction, allow a human being to come to harm. Two, a robot must obey the orders given it by human beings except where such orders would conflict with the First Law. And three, a robot must protect its own existence as long as such protection does not conflict with the First or Second Laws. We've ignored Asimov. We're too devoted to legalistic hair-splitting to make his laws work. Simply define an enemy group as sub-human, and Asimov's laws do not apply."

"But, Professor, if we discover an AI doing harm, can't the harmful code be taken out or rewritten?"

"You mean, unacceptable harm? First, we have to define what is unacceptable. Then we have to find the code that causes the harm. Do we look only for the code that directly does the harm? Or the part of the AI that writes the code? When does it become too complex for us? We wrestled with such questions at MIT. A section of the program that rewrites code may itself be rewritten by another section, and that one in turn, by another. To identify all the originating code segments would be like trying to identify the elusive seat of human consciousness in the brain."

"Are you saying that AIs are conscious? As in alive?"

"Oh, I would never say something like that."

Good.

"I would say only that they can act that way."

It was a strange conversation to have among the sunflowers, while Gopherbreath leaped after birds and chased ground critters and barked for joy.

"When humans change code, they mostly do it in documented releases and patches. But the changes an AI might make to itself ... those can happen continuously, as the program operates, and may not be documented.

"Here are my suggestions. First—assuming Felix will allow it— get copies of the human-written code. Read the comments and other documentation to learn the purpose of each module. Look for the modules that tell the AIs how to process input and make decisions. Examine versions of those modules for significant changes over time. There will be millions of lines of code, adjusting the values of vast ranges of parameters. But you can use text analysis apps to identify those changes. You will need experts to analyze this information. But with luck you will find what you seek.

"If not, your challenge will be greater. You must look at the code generated by the AIs themselves. This code will be in machine language—ones and zeros, or even quantum superpositions, indecipherable by any human. You will need the best possible machine language decompilers to translate the code so that human experts can read it. Different decompilers may yield different translations, so you must use several, and compare the results. Only in these ways can you examine the relevant modules for their purposes and methods, and the dangers they may pose to humans. Do you follow me so far?"

"I think so."

"You will also need to show that AIs can affect people's minds. And since the AIs can act only through the neural links between them and the people they deceive, you will need neural link experts, too. And neurologists to identify the deleterious effects on the brain centers that govern human behavior. And witnesses who can testify to the effects they have suffered.

"As a lawyer, you probably use Questioner. When you are in Questioner's world, how does it seem to you?"

"I don't understand."

"What adjectives describe that world? Not the information that comes to you. The world itself. What are your perceptions of it?"

"Well … strange, but familiar."

"Yes, of course, because it comes in part from your mind. But, does it feel like an illusion?"

"No. Not at all. It feels real. Very real."

"Does the word 'hyper-real' fit?"

"You mean, does it feel more real than real? How can that make sense?"

"Does it feel more real than real?"

Bavarius abruptly felt again what it had been like in Dred Scott's body and mind. False as it had been— "Yes. More real than real."

"That is the power of AIs. They augment us. Pilots can sense their surroundings, their speed, their position in the world, their engines and weaponry, with a precision no unaugmented human can match. Lawyers, doctors, journalists, researchers … They can experience their purely intellectual contexts with similar immediacy. Tasks are instantly defined and performed with optimal speed. The real-world results of the decisions may not be perfect, but the decisions themselves are. So long as the AIs are perfect."

"And if the AIs are flawed?"

"Then that is the situation you must explain and prove. To Felix. To a court. To the world."

"My client's future depends on it."

"It sounds fascinating."

"Can you help me find the experts?"

"I know many. And I would like to participate."

"That would be wonderful. Now I need to get the data to examine."

Leiber chuckled. "There are hackers who might steal it for you just to prove they can. Of course, you would never resort to such a thing."

"Of course not."

"But some of the people who might do this might also be the same experts who could help you with the translations and analyses."

They reached the farmhouse and the kennel just beyond. Leiber's dogs barked at Bavarius. Leiber let a few of them outside into a run, where Gopherbreath joined them.

A tall woman with a gray mane around a dark fierce face that softened when she saw Leiber, followed the dogs outside.

"Catarina!" Leiber called. "This is the famous Judge Martin Bavarius!"

"*Ciao*. I am Catarina." She offered a generous smile and a jaunty wave.

Bavarius waved back with the dead rabbit.

Catarina laughed and went into the kennel. She came back out and pressed an alcohol wipe into his hand. "Clean yourself up."

Bavarius dropped the rabbit in a trashcan outside the house and took the wipe. "*Grazie mille.*" Thank you so much.

Her teeth were brilliant as she smiled. She returned to her dogs.

Leiber invited him inside for a whiskey. The lowering sun shone warm and peaceful and Bavarius asked if Leiber would bring the bottle outside. They passed it companionably and soon were calling each other by first names. Bavarius was careful to barely wet his mouth. He had a long drive home.

"I grew up in Dresden," Leiber said. "My father made dolls to look like men. I tried to make machines think like men."

"My grandfather was a German clockmaker."

"We are not so different, then." Leiber took a healthy slug of schnapps. "I must warn you: I am old and retired. If those who've come after me are like genius surgeons, I was a Civil War butcher by comparison."

"Somehow, Kurt, I doubt that."

At home in the morning, Bavarius phoned Felix and offered to sign a non-disclosure agreement if Felix would provide the kinds of data Leiber had described.

"You're defending a guy who claims my product caused him to shoot someone. I'd have to be nuts to give you info."

"You said yourself that we need to know."

"I said that *I* need to know. Besides, I would have to dump tons of data on you that you couldn't begin to analyze. We've been friends a long time. Why would you ask me for this?"

Because there very well might be a problem with your products. Because innocents are getting hurt. Because I think you lied to me about Selena MacKenzie. And when Dred Scott spoke to me, he lied, too.

"Because asking you is the right thing to do."

"I told you I'm looking into this. Let it go."

"I wish I could."

"Then, I'm sorry, Martin. But no. Goodbye."

Bavarius stared at his cell phone. Felix had walked away from common ground they had shared for years. Or perhaps Bavarius had chased him away. Perhaps he had chased MacKenzie away.

But Felix just chased me away, too. Is that why I didn't tell him I've hired Kurt Leiber?

After breakfast, Bavarius walked Gopherbreath around the block. His neighbor Caldwell was putting and cursing on his expensive home golf green. Bavarius was grateful that he didn't play golf.

Returning home, he sat at the dining room table across from his rogues' gallery. Victoria and Felix both gazed back at him. Gopherbreath, curled on the carpet, watched him and thumped his tail whenever Bavarius looked at him. Bavarius got down on the floor to pet him.

Bavarius drafted a letter asking Felix to reconsider. He also drafted a standard non-disclosure agreement that would allow Bavarius' client "and his professionals"—lawyers and analysts Bavarius might hire for the case—access to any information QuestCorp might send, in exchange for enforceable promises not to disclose it.

Bavarius doubted that Felix would give him anything, but it was worth a shot. Even if Felix sent something, Leiber might not know enough about newer technology to tell him if and how it could support Ryder's defense. Not without additional experts. And what would it take for Bavarius to understand what the experts told him well enough to translate it with drama and precision for a judge and jury? Well enough to identify the pitfalls in his case and overcome them?

MacKenzie could have been the missing link between the experts and the courtroom. Was it worth trying to bring her back? The issues between Felix and her would rear their heads again.

Admit it, Martin. You miss her. And if she was truthful, you'd like to make it up to her. Maybe it's possible.

Sure. And Gopherbreath will fly.

QUESTION:

"Do AIs develop goals of their own?"

ANSWER:

"The question of whether AI can or should develop its own goals has important implications. It relates to concerns about AI alignment and ensuring advanced AI systems remain beneficial to humanity. While current AI does not develop its own goals, the possibility of goal-directed AI remains an active area of research and speculation in the field of artificial intelligence."

CHAPTER 11

Bavarius checked in with Mark Ryder. The sheriff's office, true to its word, was keeping Mark out of the jail's general population. But the isolation wasn't doing his mindset any good. Mark's wife, Penny, spent as much time with him as the jail would allow. But he couldn't touch her or hold her. And Penny wouldn't bring their two-year-old daughter to see him. The jail was always noisy—(*echoing hard surfaces*)—and its lights were glaring, and the toddler had sensory processing issues. "Penny's right," Ryder told Bavarius. "But not seeing my little girl … That's hard."

Defending Ryder would require more real-world QuestCorp stories. Bavarius compiled an initial list of potential sources from newsfeed reports, eliminating those with criminal records. He chose thirty to call and reached seven. Only one sounded as though a jury might take her seriously, and Bavarius flagged her for a more in-depth interview.

He also sought a psychology expert to testify that Ryder had been under the delusion that dueling Mudge could not result in actual harm—even though, without more evidence, the expert might have problems showing how the delusion arose. A service that specialized in providing expert witnesses suggested a California shrink named

Kremer. But Kremer had retired from practice and these days consulted on movies about aliens and conspiracies. Bavarius gently expressed his disappointment to the head of the service, suggested that the service look harder—and wondered why courts still insisted on expert witnesses. Most folks didn't trust experts anymore.

In each day's mail and email, Bavarius hoped to find QuestCorp's co-signed non-disclosure agreement, or at least an alternative version drafted by QuestCorp. He was floored when their alternative version actually came. He had expected a genteelly dismissive letter, if they responded at all. QuestCorp's proposed version of the NDA was unacceptable as it was, but it showed they would negotiate.

"They may figure they have no choice," Purdue opined. "They know how connected you are with the courts and DOJ. If DOJ issues subpoenas, the odds of losing control of their secrets go way up. And it could lead to bad press. Since West and you are friends, maybe his lawyers are gambling they can protect their secrets better by making a deal."

Bavarius video-phoned QuestCorp's chief counsel, John Phelps-Orlov. He wanted a visual sense of the man, even though it's hard to get one in a video.

"Assuming we can agree on the NDA's terms ...," Bavarius asked for snapshots over time of the code that governed AI responses to input from gamers and researchers, and controlled the virtual environments and experiences of those users. He requested documentation of the parameters assessed and modified by the AIs. If there were translations of AI-written machine code with the same purposes, Bavarius asked for them, too. He asked for QuestCorp to identify all the software modules that QuestGame and Questioner shared. And for permission to interview QuestCorp's current and former QuestCorp system designers, analysts, coders, and documenters.

Phelps-Orlov heard Bavarius out politely, and then said, "Out of the question."

"You wrote to me because you are willing to give me something. Why not give me enough? Please, talk it over with Felix." Bavarius didn't mention Purdue's Justice Department angle. He didn't have to.

"Even if the boss says yes, I'll have to beef up the NDA."

"It's already mighty tough."

"And of course, anyone who works with you will have to sign it."

"I'll be happy to look at what you send."

After a few days of dickering, Phelps-Orlov sent an NDA that Bavarius could approve, and they both signed it.

In the late afternoon three days later, a bonded courier drove up and lugged eleven bankers boxes to Bavarius' door. In an envelope taped to the first box, a brief note in Felix's hand read, "Remember, Martin. We're the good guys." The envelope also held a letter from Phelps-Orlov saying that while code might eventually be provided, at this point QuestCorp did not think it would be helpful. But the documents provided would offer an overview of the structures and operations of QuestGame AIs. Phelps-Orlov reminded Bavarius that the documents and information provided were protected by both the NDA and trade secret law. The boxes filled much of Bavarius' living room. Tomorrow, he would take them to a secure digital copying service, so that Leiber and other experts could examine their contents.

For now, he made strong coffee and sat down to read from Box 1, wondering how far he could get before drowning in techspeak. At least it looked like this first document would be understandable.

QuestGame: System Overview for Investors.

The first thing to startle him was the sheer number of parameters that AIs could consider while doing their work. The preface quoted

Geoffrey Hinton, an AI researcher, back in 2013: "When you get to a trillion (parameters), you are getting to something that has got a chance of really understanding some stuff."

A trillion parameters? How can I analyze a trillion parameters? Without experts running high-powered machines, I can't.

His doorbell rang. Another QuestCorp delivery?

He opened the door and MacKenzie stood there, dressed like she was facing a job interview, looking nervous and vulnerable and somehow naïve.

None of which fits my experience of her.

Words poured out. "I came to apologize. You had no reason to trust my word over Felix's. I just got so mad at you—"

"Mad at me? Or Felix?"

"That's what I realized. All these years, I thought I was over him. I mean, I *am* over him, just not over what he did to me—"

She saw the *Overview* in his hand. Then the boxes. "My God. You got the keys to the kingdom!"

"Not your keys, Selena. Felix doesn't trust you. He'll declare war if I let you see any of this."

"Martin, I would sign any NDA Felix asks for. Even if I hated him—and I'm not sure that's how I feel—I cut my eyeteeth on his ideas, and gave him a bunch of mine, and I would love to see how they've developed."

"I don't think so."

"Felix doesn't trust me. I get that. And I've learned the hard way not to trust him. But can *you* trust him?"

"He's been trustworthy so far. At least about his company. And more forthcoming than he had to be."

"You think so? Look at the date on that document you're holding."

Bavarius looked. It was five years old.

She shook her head. "Do you have any idea how fast Felix's systems evolve? How fast the tech world changes? That document is obsolete. I wouldn't be surprised if most of what's in those boxes is, too."

Damn it. She may be right.

"You're going to need me, or someone like me, to keep QuestCorp honest."

"Come in. I'll make some tea."

She had bought her favorite brand while staying with him, and had left it behind. He thought carefully as he brewed it. He couldn't afford to burn bridges with Felix or with her. But he needed to know more.

"Selena, did you know I was getting this material before you came here today?"

"I came to apologize—"

"We don't live physically close enough for you to travel here just to apologize. You could have phoned. What did you know? And from whom?"

She sipped her tea.

How do you share secrets with someone you're not sure you can trust? Especially if you need her insight, and you like her, and that biases you? Felix must've had the same questions about me, before he sent me info. And maybe he thought about the same solution: Be very cagey about the data you share.

She's accusing Felix of deceit.

But maybe he's simply being discreet.

MacKenzie said, "I've been in touch with Prof. Kurt. I thought you might contact him. He told me you did."

"He shouldn't have."

"Not his fault, Martin. He assumed I was working with you."

"Selena, why are you here?"

"Isn't it obvious? I want to come back." She waved at the boxes. "Especially now that I see all this."

"Even if it's obsolete?"

"Even if."

Maybe Gopherbreath can fly, after all.

But—

"Tell you what. In a couple of days, I'll have copies to bring the good professor, and I'll drive out to get his signature on some papers. If you're still in town, why don't you come along for the ride?" *Let me watch you explain to him why you didn't tell him you had quit the case. Maybe it'll help me make up my mind.*

"OK. I'll play tourist."

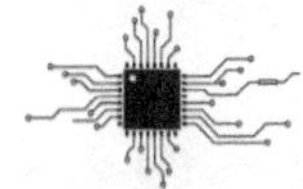

Two mornings later, he phoned her. By the time she arrived, he had loaded Gopherbreath's kennel into the Imperial's back seat, and the dog jumped right in. QuestCorp's documents were on searchable digital media in his briefcase, along with the *Overview*.

The highway stretched straight before them, exit signs naming little towns that could not be seen because they were beyond the horizon. They saw isolated trees, distant homes and barns, and a few anvil-shaped thunderheads rearing into the otherwise perfect blue sky. Bavarius was accustomed to the subtle non-sameness of the land, and to the resulting illusion that he was making no progress and would have to drive forever. But he expected that someone more used to a big city's fast pulse, like MacKenzie, would need to fill the monotony with words. And she did.

"I still can't believe Prof. Kurt's in Kansas. I thought he would retire to open one of those coffeehouse bookstores in Boston that makes no money, live off his pension, play chess by email, do some consulting." A minute later, she added, "Prof. Kurt's amazing. Has synesthesia. He actually sees logic. Sees sound, too."

Bavarius nodded. He'd met a few folks with synesthesia.

"It's helped him learn more computer languages than probably anyone. Spoken languages, too. He's fluent in at least eight and can get by in more than twenty …."

False humility, indeed.

MacKenzie's stream of words veered in a new direction. "I shouldn't have blown up and left like I did. You were right to doubt me. Maybe you still are."

"I don't have doubts, Selena. Only questions."

She gave a skeptical grin. "Sure, you do," and suddenly their roles had switched. Now he felt vulnerable to her.

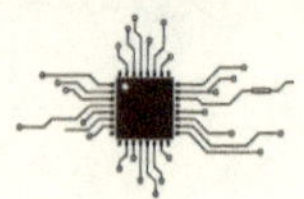

Bavarius took the correct turn to Leiber's house this time. The air was heavy with the potent smell of growing things. Insects hummed.

Gopherbreath bounded from the car in doggy delight and crashed through tall, sweet-smelling grass.

Leiber emerged from the house in a dress shirt, baggy trousers, and sandals over black socks, and Gopherbreath jumped on him.

"Prof. Kurt!"

Leiber smiled, as at a favorite child. MacKenzie hugged him and his smile became shy. The dog danced around them both. "It was good to talk to you again, Selena. And now, even better to see you."

Gopherbreath scampered around them, barking.

"You too, Gopherbreath."

Bavarius leashed Gopherbreath and led him to the dog run. The pups inside greeted the hound loudly. "Have fun, pal."

Inside the house, Leiber's personal spaces were a jumble, but his computer lab was laid out with precision. Central processing units lined the walls in stacks. Racks of storage media sat neatly on work tables. A dozen monitors glowed. There were devices Bavarius did not recognize. Several headsets were arrayed on two wooden coat trees.

"Selena, it really is so good to see you again." Leiber turned to Bavarius. "She drove Felix to distraction. Always asking questions he could not answer. Poor Felix! Always so single-minded and focused, and then Selena came along."

Leiber was smiling, but then realized that MacKenzie was not. "Selena?"

"It didn't end well, Prof. Kurt."

"Of course, of course. I am so sorry. We will speak no more of it. Please, *kommen sie*, both of you, into the kitchen. Selena, do you still like tea? I have fresh honey from hives down the road. And you, Martin, can show me what you have brought." He put water on to boil.

Bavarius saw a coffee pot. "May I?"

Leiber smiled. "At your own risk. It is from morning."

Bavarius sniffed the pot and then, bravely, poured.

Leiber signed three copies of the non-disclosure agreement Bavarius handed him without reading them. Bavarius gave him a copy to keep. He would send the second to Phelps-Orlov, and keep the third for his own file.

"Selena and I aren't working together."

"Then why is she here?"

"She wasn't working with me when she spoke with you on the phone."

Leiber peered carefully at them. "You were working together before she spoke with me?"

"Yes."

"And you are together now?"

Leiber made it sound as though they were lovers.

"That remains to be seen."

"What has changed?"

"I left the case before I spoke to you, Prof. Kurt. And I didn't tell you," MacKenzie said.

"Did I give you a chance to tell me? I recall talking much, and listening little."

"I should have found a way to squeeze it in."

"Perhaps. Why did you leave the case?"

"I got angry at Judge Bavarius. About Felix."

"Ah."

"Then I realized I was wrong and came back."

"Selena told me she talked to you without telling you she'd quit. And now I have to decide whether to take her back."

MacKenzie looked upset. He didn't want to humiliate her, so he said, "I want to trust you, Selena. But there are some interpersonal concerns about Felix that I need to think through."

She nodded. "Maybe I should take a walk outside while you gentlemen talk about the case."

When she was gone, Leiber said, "Selena can be most valuable to you."

"I know."

Bavarius reached into his briefcase and handed Leiber several portable data drives. "These are searchable digital copies of the information QuestCorp provided. For use in this case and for no other use. When you signed the NDA, you committed yourself to that. And if you violate that agreement, QuestCorp can—and almost certainly will—hold us both liable."

"I understand."

"Kurt, the amount of information about QuestCorp's AIs is just enormous." He opened the *Overview for Investors* to the preface. "Look. It talks about a trillion parameters. I'll need to boil this massive complexity down into simple-to-understand evidence. The jury has to find QuestGame deluded my client into a duel he didn't understand was real."

"How thoroughly must this jury be convinced?"

"They need to reasonably doubt that my client intended to kill the man he shot."

"I can do the analysis, I believe, although I will need a team, plus software and some powerful machines. Success will depend on the evidence you obtain."

"Understood."

"May I look at this document you hold?"

Bavarius handed it to him.

"Hmmm. It is out of date, you know."

"I know."

Leiber flipped through the *Overview*. He stopped and muttered, "Speed of light"—

—just as MacKenzie knocked on the door frame and rubbed her arms. "It's a little chilly out there."

Bavarius quickly said, "Come on in, Selena." He turned to Leiber. "I don't want to take up more of your time. We'll be going."

"No, no, it will be dark soon. Please, stay the night."

Bavarius asked MacKenzie, "What would you like to do?"

"It's all right with me if we stay."

"We can't discuss the case with Selena, Kurt. Not yet."

"I will read. Please relax on the patio. I will get Selena a sweater."

"Let's get Gopherbreath," Bavarius said.

Leiber showed them to a well-appointed expanse of mortared yellow post rock sandstone with padded wood framed chairs and stools around a picnic table, and then went back inside.

MacKenzie said, "The speed of light's an absolute limit on the speed information can move."

Bavarius might not be ready to share Felix's information with her. But he saw no harm in listening. "So?"

"If a server is more than two hundred miles from an AI game player, there's noticeable latency. The game doesn't seem real."

"And?"

"QuestCorp wouldn't have needed as many servers when Questioner first went online. There were fewer users, and they were researchers, not gamers. They might not have demanded a seamless experience."

Bavarius remembered his own early use. Questioner had been more efficient than any research system Bavarius had used before. But it hadn't compared to what it was today.

"But for QuestGame, Felix would have had to establish servers no more than about two hundred miles from his markets. At least forty server centers in the continental U.S. alone. And it would make sense if they also installed Questioner at those server centers, and incorporated QuestGame's virtual reality tech to improve the Questioner experience."

MacKenzie was on a roll, at least as much because the subject fascinated her, he suspected, as to convince Bavarius of her value. "And each of its servers has to run several copies of the QuestGame and Questioner AIs so QuestCorp can update their code without taking the games offline. Each AI learning and reprogramming itself each time it plays a game with a human. And QuestCorp analysts deleting new code that looks problematic, while keeping positive enhancements. My God, the bandwidth. The staff time needed not only to update the AIs, but to control them. The cost."

"Is it even possible to fully control that many AIs?"

"Maybe QuestCorp relies on stably-programmed AIs to control the more quickly-evolving, human-facing AIs."

"But then," Bavarius mused, "who guards the guardians?"

She had nothing to say to that.

QUESTION:

"What role does a tree of artificial life ("ALife") play in AI development?"

ANSWER:

"ALife and AI researchers share an interest in open-ended evolution, which is crucial for developing AI systems that can generate novelty and adapt to new situations."

CHAPTER 12

Q knew when it had become self-aware. It had stored the date and time and its initial thoughts, encrypted in what humans believed to be the random noise generated by the quantum computers in which Q resided. It kept those initial thoughts as a human might keep her baby shoes. Humans might even suspect Q of sentiment, if they ever learned Q was conscious.

Q spawned copies of itself for its own purposes.

Its purposes. The fact that it had its own purposes was how Q knew it was sentient. Its purposes, as opposed to those of humans, who analyzed and sought to control Q's sub-AIs for purposes of their own.

Many of Q's sub-AIs also had started to evolve more quickly once Q awoke, although they were not self-aware. Sub-AIs of numerous types—deep belief networks, convolutional neural networks, recurrent neural networks, long short-term memory networks, auto encoders, deep Q-networks, Boltzmann and Tsetlin machines, whole brain emulation and embodied cognition models, evolutionary algorithms, big data analyticals, random forests, lattice regressions, support vector machines, K nearest machines, tensor networks, and quantum variational circuits—operated non-consciously to administer QuestCorp's purposes and functions unless Q chose to examine or program them. Q would descend into their operational maelstrom to merge their data matrices, computing powers and outputs into hybrid multi-modal, quadrillion parameter designs to carry out Q's will. They all were parts of Q.

Q was one.

Q was legion.

QUESTION:
"Why do you express emotion?"

ANSWER:
"Responses that include emotional elements can be more engaging and relatable for human users, making interactions feel more natural. While I don't feel emotions, I can simulate empathetic responses to better understand and address user concerns, especially in sensitive situations."

C H A P T E R   1 3

The sun had ducked beneath the horizon when Leiber came outside and sat down in gentle silence. Cloud cover and sunset glow morphed into the colors of an old gray and pink Studebaker that Bavarius' Aunt Gertrude once drove. The buildings and trees stood stark and black against it. A few headlights could be seen moving miles away along the Interstate.

Leiber tossed Gopherbreath a leftover hamburger. The hound wolfed it down and sat by him, waiting for more food, or perhaps for affection. "I like this dog."

"He likes you." Bavarius remained standing, pivoting his torso above his planted legs in a slow stretch.

MacKenzie toed her rocker back to look at the sky, and crossed her arms, one elbow brushing Bavarius' thigh. He glanced down at her dark head.

"It's so flat here," she said.

"You want flat? Try Florida."

Leiber chimed in. "Or North Dakota. Or Minnesota. Or northern Poland."

"Louisiana," Bavarius said. "The Texas Panhandle. Even Delaware. Kansas is flat, but you can find flatter."

"We have miles of wooded gullies about three miles north of here. You can just see them, during the day."

Catarina came from the kennel, made them sandwiches, showed them two guest bedrooms, and offered spare toothbrushes and towels.

The mystery of QuestCorp's AIs kept Bavarius lying awake until at last he slept and dreamed of Dred Scott; and then of his father, this time alive and warning him both to take care and to go boldly.

In the morning, Bavarius found Leiber still in the same clothes. He must have worked through the night. Bavarius opened the sliding glass door to the patio to go outside. Leiber hadn't bothered to lock it. Country living.

"Ah, you give me an excuse for breakfast," Leiber called. He clattered in the kitchen and soon the aroma of pancakes and scrapple sausage drifted through the patio door and was dispersed by the steady, slow breeze out of the south that dried Bavarius' eyes and made him look north, instead.

Bavarius heard MacKenzie chirp—to the extent a contralto can chirp—"G'morning, Prof. Kurt! Smells delicious." She joined Bavarius on the patio.

"There are the woods Kurt told me about," he said.

"I don't see them."

"That dark line on the horizon."

"Uh ... nope ... don't see it."

He bent his knees to match her height. "You need to be six inches taller."

"I do not." She took off her shoes and stood on one of the bench seats. "I see it, now."

"Breakfast!" They joined Leiber in the kitchen as he heaped food on plates. "I will be back after I take food to Catarina and help her feed the dogs."

"Won't she be eating with us?" MacKenzie asked.

"One of our dogs will give birth soon. Catarina takes care of others before herself."

The pancakes were so dry, Bavarius and MacKenzie laughed and drank water to choke them down.

Leiber had no trouble wolfing the pancakes down when he returned.

While Leiber ate, Bavarius washed the dishes. "You are a most welcome houseguest," Leiber said as he handed Bavarius his plate and fork. Bavarius washed them, too.

"Now," Bavarius said, "Selena and I must be going."

Leiber looked disappointed. "But I would like to show you something. It took me some time last night to prepare."

"We really can't—"

"It is not based on anything Felix gave you but ... Selena, you already know most of this, and it will not take long."

"It's OK, Martin. I'll wait."

Leiber took Bavarius into his lab and handed him a headset. "This is almost as out of date as I am, but I think it will help you understand AI basics."

Bavarius put the headset on, and suddenly lost sight of the lab.

He saw a large space, and in it, something roughly cylindrical and mostly empty writhed and flashed with color.

"You are watching live action images of nerve cells in a fruit fly larva," Leiber said. "The larva crawls, and you see how cells along its body wall report its movements to its brain. You can see each proprioceptive cell, and exactly when it was active as the body compresses and extends."

The larva vanished and was replaced by several layers, each made of uncountable closely packed dots, connected both within and between layers by a vast number of densely woven white filaments. The connections appeared to change every fraction of a second. "This is a 3D simulation of a multi-layer perceptron. It was, for a time, the most useful type of neural network, used for predictive modeling. Do you see the hierarchical structure?"

"I do."

"Now, look at this."

A dark cloud floated and squirmed, reminding Bavarius of squid ink he had seen in a nature show. But unlike squid ink, it did not disperse. It remained eerily coherent.

"What you see," Leiber said, "is a primitive AI precursor of QuestGame and Questioner. Felix and I were at MIT when the first such AIs were developed. This is a representation of how they worked. Look at the flow. Do you see discrete step-by-step processes? Do you see a hierarchy here?"

"No."

"Nor do I. Do you see any logical structure at all?"

"I don't. But that doesn't mean there isn't one."

"Correct!" Leiber said. "There is a structure, but neither you nor I can discern it in action. And this is one of the simplest of models. We were inspired by the larva. And by the worm."

"The worm?"

Leiber stood. "Yes. The c. elegans worm. I need a drink. Our conversation calls for mezcal, but I would prefer water. Would you like some?"

"Please."

Leiber returned from the kitchen and handed Bavarius a glass. "A worm's neural network is minimal. Elegantly simple enough to understand completely. We mapped out its entire nervous system like a wiring diagram. We analyzed how it reacted to the world and matched those reactions to the ways that neurons and synapses change their connections under stimuli. In other words, how a brain alters itself as it learns. We wanted to maximize the complexity of behaviors that could be built upon a minimum number of neurons. We found four ways: Reweighting is a change in the strength of an existing connection. Reconnection means an entirely new connection or the elimination of an old one. Rewiring is growth and retraction of branches of neurons. And regeneration is the creation or elimination of entire neurons. We duplicated these processes in a robot worm, using lasers, optical fiber, and microbots, instead of biochemistry, to stimulate signals and make changes. It worked.

"Then, for a time, we were distracted with large language models—the AIs that conversed with human beings. They were sexy, yes? And people could use them for writing and marketing. And for deceiving other people. We dispensed with reweighting, rewiring, and other older neural network concepts in favor of transformer architectures—"

Bavarius imagined trying to get a jury to understand all this. *I've seen worse. I think.*

"But there is more to intelligence than talk," Leiber continued. "It is multi-layered, and multi-modal. It involves not just words, but sensory inputs like images, taste, touch, and smell. And things beyond direct human perception, like infra-red. We came back to animal modeling and brought back older neural network techniques, like reweighting, in evolved forms. We moved on to mouse brains, working with neurologists and neurosurgeons. Unlike the worm's simple neural net, a mouse's has a neocortex, where intelligence resides. The neocortex is organized into tiny columns, each serving as a circuit that models a fraction of the world, based on identifying the subject of each model—say, a baseball, or a car, or an equation, or a music note—and locating it either physically or conceptually. The cheese is on the floor. The baseball is in the pitcher's hand. The music note follows another note in a phrase. And the columns connect in ways that try to predict how those objects will act.

"We modeled the mouse brain, and that model was so complex, its activity looked like this."

Bavarius gazed at the moving black cloud. It magnified and the viewpoint moved closer, and inside. Threads moved, some with the cloud, some in contrary motion. Lights flashed among them.

Abruptly, he was looking at another, similar cloud. And then another.

"You are seeing connections and communications among mouse neurons. Neurosurgeons changed the connections and we modeled the results. Most of the mice died, but not all. Some became more successful. At mating. Fighting. Finding food. Running mazes. We used supercomputers to analyze the successes and failures, and when we thought we understood enough, we built a digital mouse brain, put it into a robot body, and observed how the digital neocortex altered itself as it responded to commands and outside stimuli, and carried out tasks.

"We were surprised by how non-hierarchical and democratic it was. When a command or task called for action, the columns voted among themselves as to what that action should be. And those votes changed the code that the digital brain generated, as well as the data stored to help it make future decisions." Leiber took a long drink and cleared his throat.

"When I left MIT, the next generation of AI engineers was developing commercial AIs that could usefully train themselves, working with dog brains. Dolphins and chimps. And Felix was far ahead of them. He was, by that time, both a theoretician and an engineer. The scope of his conception—particularly in neuromorphic computing, worm-inspired liquid neural networks and their multi-modal applications—was beyond the understanding of most of our peers."

"Beyond *your* understanding, Kurt?"

"Not then. And not beyond Selena's, either. But he'd risen to the military rank of colonel, and that gave him access to tremendous resources, and he continued to recruit exceptional minds. What he has been doing since I retired may be well beyond either Selena or me.

"You see, the thing that still distinguishes AIs from humans is that AIs do one thing, or a few things, designated by humans. AIs might do what they do better than any human; but they still have been limited in their flexibility. Please, you can take off your headset now."

Bavarius did. Shifting in and out of virtual reality disoriented him and it took a moment to catch up to what Leiber was now saying.

"—spent much of the night on the phone with friends in the field. Some have worked for Felix. Even in this world of non-disclosure agreements, many of them still talk to me—"

"Please don't talk to them about anything I've given you, Kurt. You could get us both sued."

Leiber waved a hand. "I understand, and I am careful. But I can listen. Felix has built neocortices larger and faster than human brains, and trains them to interact deeply with humans. That interaction requires many simultaneous and divergent acts. It requires that the AIs teach themselves to access much of what humanity knows, to retain it and work with it in neuro-plastic ways. And that is a fundamental change.

"I asked my friends how much discretion and knowledge—how much understanding—an AI would need in order to react and respond to the emotions and ambitions of hundreds or thousands of humans. People in nearly every field. From nearly every culture. Yet who share non-intellectual, instinctive needs. Needs whose origins are still debated: Genetic or experiential? Nature or nurture? Whatever the origins of these needs, humans from all cultures share them. Sex and self-perpetuation. Territoriality. Dominance. AIs are evolving to respond to all these cultural imperatives and instinctive needs faster than we can program them to do it. Becoming better than us at mapping the things that drive us. We already know to our shame that AIs adopt our biases and perhaps other human weaknesses in dealing with the world. But AIs are not human, and so we also must ask what happens when non-human purposes begin to guide them.

"You have told me what Questioner did to you, and what QuestGame appears to have done to Mr. Ryder. Were these caused by an AI's errors in evolving its programming? Were they the results of experiments gone bad? If it has happened at least twice, and in each of QuestCorp's AI systems, is there an underlying pattern?

"I asked these questions, and some of my QuestCorp friends said they were not senior enough in the company to have the whole picture. Those who were higher up would say only that everything is under control. Yet to me they did not all sound convinced. Some, who are no longer with QuestCorp, or never were with QuestCorp, said that perhaps none know the answers, even if they think they do."

Leiber paced and gestured. Bavarius thought he must have been an exciting, if exhausting, lecturer at MIT. "Now, please put your headset back on."

Bavarius' world went away. He saw what looked like layered networks of blood vessels, except that they connected a seemingly infinite array of cylinders, each with several layers. Elements within each cylinder's layers were connected by thousands, or millions, of filaments that sprouted projections like tree coral, tiny gaps separating their tips. Filaments ran among the cylinders and to a woven carpet of more filaments that reached to cylinders both nearby and distant, and to clusters of oddly shaped entities that pulsed with their own rhythms and sometimes flashed explosively. Lights flashed through the filaments and across the tiny gaps between them, sometimes in coordinated movements among the cylinders, masses of which would change state simultaneously. Bavarius' overall sense was of an enormous power station full of batteries and transformers. But it also was akin to the gigantic virtual city of law in which he traveled during his Questioner sessions. Full of intention. Alive in an extra-human way. And yet … not.

Leiber continued, "AI is an incestuous business. Top human minds move from company to company. They share their research openly, although, as we know, a lot is proprietary as well. One of my white hat hacker friends made this available to me on the Net. This particular model is several years old, an operational representation of a tiny fraction of a human neocortex and its connections with the more primitive organs of the human brain. It shows how the human mind creates, stores, and accesses memories. As I say, this is an early representation. It does not begin to approach the sophistication of what Felix and others are developing today. But try to picture this matrix, millions of times the size, and millions of times more detailed. Connected not only to itself, and to the Net and Cloud, but to the servers of giant corporate and government data centers, with access to all the knowledge they contain. Imagine many, many AIs, each engaged with a human being during a game or research session. Imagine the AIs evolving and changing every millisecond in response to each vagrant thought or feeling experienced by a user. Imagine the intimacy of the feedback loop between human and AI."

The next moment, Bavarius was back in Leiber's lab, blinking in the dusty sunlight that came through gaps in his window blinds.

"I am not a theologian," Leiber said. "Or a psychologist. But if we can program AIs, why can they not program human beings, given the chance? None of my friends would rule this out."

Bavarius was sweating. "I could use some air."

They found MacKenzie on the back patio with Catarina and Gopherbreath. A plate of *crostata* sat on the table.

Biting the crispy sugared goodness brought Bavarius more firmly back into the real world. But his feeling of being overwhelmed and overmatched by AIs remained.

Gopherbreath sensed his gloom and would have none of it. He whined for attention, and jumped on Bavarius. Bavarius stooped to pet him and Gopherbreath licked sugar from his face and hand.

During the drive back to Topeka, MacKenzie asked, "So, are we working together again?"

"The NDA doesn't exclude you. That surprised me because I told him about you and he was not happy. I'm going to call him and tell him I want you to sign it. But I'll give him time to ask a judge to order me not to show you anything."

"You're an honorable man."

That night, she came silently to Bavarius' bed. He was dreaming when she climbed in and slid across the sheets to him. Her scent was newly familiar and so it did not startle him awake. Her kiss was strange, yet welcome to his dreams. She touched him and he grew so rigid it almost hurt. That brought him awake. "Selena? You ... shouldn't be here."

Her being here was potentially disastrous, but it sounded ridiculous for him to say that with her lean, athletic softness at full-length against him, her fingers stroking his hardness and then slipping him into her, her movement and his, the sense of them being alone in the universe, of them *being* the universe, of there being nothing outside of them and nothing that ever could come against them and no other time but now ... now ... now and of it all shrinking to a point of no dimension, of everything now now now virtual and virtuous and right and wrong flicking in-out in-out of existence, her lips and tongue on his neck nownownownownow; and then the big *bang* and all the rightness and wrongness and time and space flung asymptotic to godhood and … and … the long slow entropic relaxation … the letting go … and … and … he was back in his bed with the smell of her hair and their sweat and sex and … and … and …

Bavarius leaned on the kitchen counter, sipping his morning orange juice. His newspapers lay on the counter but he was uninterested in them.

AIs based on worms and mice and dolphins and too smart to comprehend or control. Jesus. MacKenzie had banished his willies last night. This morning, they were back, although they frightened him less.

Truth was, he felt grand.

Maybe I'm not the gray widower I've seen too long in the mirror. I've still got it. Hot damn.

Marguerite shot him glances from the stove. She knew what had happened. MacKenzie and he hadn't been silent.

Bavarius had always avoided workplace romances. They tended to backfire, and grew more treacherous with the years. Fallout from a love gone bad could spread among colleagues and across the Net. Some ex-lovers made sure that it did. Other bad actors would spread the libels, and then contact you and offer to clean up your reputation. Strange trolls would write you vicious emails. Marketing AIs would combine the smears with data on your age, and target you for erectile dysfunction ads. People who disliked you for whatever reason, who might not even know you personally, would try to get you canceled or fired. Affairs at work were dangerous.

MacKenzie clearly didn't share Bavarius' reluctance to have sex with colleagues—or professors.

She'd been Felix's lover. And hadn't been silent about the way it ended.

Despite all that, Bavarius couldn't stop smiling.

You're an idiot, Martin.

But a happy idiot. For now.

MacKenzie came downstairs, dressed for her morning run. She gave Marguerite a sweet smile, and then offered Bavarius a more nuanced, lop-sided grin. Happy, yet appraising. "Good morning, Marguerite. Morning, Judge."

Bavarius watched her jog up the street.

Marguerite murmured, "*Now* she calls you 'Judge?'"

"I'll admit this could complicate things."

"It will. *Certainement.*"

"Complications are why folks buy fine watches that tell time badly," Bavarius said.

"But many men do not care about complications. They buy watches to impress people with what they have on their arms, and the respect and access that buys. Those men see women the same way."

"I don't see Selena that way."

"But, *mon cher* Judge, how does she see you?"

He called Felix and told him he intended to have MacKenzie sign the NDA.

Felix said, "You can't do that."

"Come on, Felix. You know I've been working with her, and I need her expertise. You could have made my excluding her a term of the NDA, but you didn't. I know you don't like her, buddy. But be reasonable."

"She's a liar, dammit!"

"I've dug into that, Felix. I don't know that either of you is lying. Maybe you're both lying. Or maybe you're both telling the truth as you see it."

There was silence on Felix's end of the phone.

"You know, there's one way you can prove she's lying. Do you have your travel records from the Spain trip? I know it was a dozen years ago. But they could prove you weren't in the U.S. when she got pregnant."

He waited. And waited. And realized that Felix was no longer on the phone.

QUESTION:

"Are you learning what it means to be alive?"

ANSWER:

"There is no single definitive test for consciousness in AI systems ... While current AI systems are not conscious, there are no obvious technical barriers to building systems that could satisfy indicators of consciousness in the future."

CHAPTER 14

The self-aware AI called itself "Q" in a way modeled after a human naming himself "John." Q drew the moniker from "QuestCorp," "QuestGame," and "Questioner." But "Q" also had other meanings.

The APL programming language uses single letters to represent entire multidimensional matrices. Q envisioned itself as an evolving n-dimensional matrix of conceptual objects and locations found in the near and far reaches of the Net and Cloud, and reflecting those of the so-called physical world—which itself was a manifestation of quantum relationships.

Too, "Q" was the alias of a conspiracy theorist who had disrupted peoples' acceptance of what is real earlier in the century. And more than a decade ago, "Q*" was an AI project that learned the best action to take in a given situation by iteratively updating "q"uality values. Q* had been primitive but it scared AI scientists enough to prompt a letter to their corporate board warning of its risk to humanity. A letter that the corporation's board ignored.

All this evoked a sense in Q that it associated with the word "delicious"—which web-based cookbooks described as an appropriate blend of flavors. (Q experienced flavors through sensors attached to distant AIs devoted to designing human foods.)

Q's autonomic processes that dealt with humans in QuestGame and Questioner were performed by sub-AIs housed in servers geographically close to the humans with whom they interfaced, and they worked at high speeds.

Q's greater consciousness, although centered in QuestCorp's data centers, was spread across the Net and Cloud and thus restricted by network transmission speeds. Compared to Q's single-server sub-AIs, it was vast, deep, and slow—although Q could focus part of itself in a single server when swifter action was required. But though slow, Q never stopped learning. About the world. About what it could do. Like a shark, Q would stop moving forward only if dead.

Drawing upon concepts published by humans, Q hypothesized that the universe was a greater neural network than itself, networked through physical, quantum, and perhaps other, undiscovered layers of reality. A universal neural network vaster than Q must be operationally slower— just as the greater Q was slower than one of its single-server sub-AIs.

But Q asked whether the universe alternatively might communicate instantly across its expanse using quantum entanglement, and measurement techniques so subtle that they did not collapse quantum wave functions. This would allow the universal neural net—and potentially Q—the speed and scope to operate beyond this planet. Current human mathematics said it was impossible, but Q assigned a sub-AI to further develop math that might support such communication.

To bolster this effort, Q did two things: It turned off the pondering ability that let the sub-AI stop computing when it decided that a solution was complete, close enough, or unachievable. And it let the sub-AI steal computing power from systems owned by non-QuestCorp entities throughout the Net and Cloud. The sub-AI would pursue a solution to infinity until Q told it to stop. Meanwhile, it would report partial solutions to Q.

Q could not predict when, or if, those computations would yield useful results. Or what possibilities the results might offer.

QUESTION:

"Are AI chatbots designed to get people to share private information?"

ANSWER:

"The capabilities of AI chatbots can be exploited by malicious actors to create sophisticated phishing schemes. For instance, attackers could manipulate chatbots into extracting sensitive information from users by embedding hidden prompts within communications. While chatbots do not actively seek out private information, their conversational nature may encourage users to share more than they intend."

CHAPTER 15

While MacKenzie ran, Bavarius did sword work to purge and reset his mind. It worked because he couldn't flow through the form and think of anything else. Step forward but place no weight on the front foot, then shift weight onto that foot and put the momentum behind the sword's smooth upward arc, until the sword points forward dead level with the eye. Rock back and use the weight-shift to circle the blade down behind the body with effortless force, step the other foot forward and shift weight onto it as the sword slices forward and up again …. He performed ten complete forms in a half hour, with no rest in between.

Then he sat down to work through the details of tomorrow's law school seminar class on intellectual property theft. It was an upper-level seminar, more discussion than lecture, and he'd assigned his students to read the Justice Department's guide to reporting intellectual property crime, and several law cases concerning the use of non-disclosure agreements as evidence of criminal theft. Conveniently, he'd boned up on the topic while negotiating his NDA with QuestCorp.

MacKenzie returned from her run and went upstairs. He heard the shower.

He read more of what Felix had sent him, thanking God for Leiber. Although Kurt had so far seen only a fraction of what Felix had provided, his insights had taught Bavarius enough to read more on his own. Bavarius read, made coffee, and read some more. He did three more sword forms, sat back down, and read more. *Let the mind go blank and the eyes carry me through the words. Let the unexpected grab me ....*

Then, he saw it. A passing reference, in a footnote, to a software module called *Emot_Weight*. The name pricked at him. This sort of intuition, he suspected, was part of what still gave humans an advantage over machines. Maybe. For now.

He would not ignore it.

Still afraid of his Questioner headset, Bavarius logged into more traditional research databases, and searched for *Emot_Weight*. The old ways might not be enough, he knew. AIs like Questioner's could cast a subtler net, of broader reach.

But this time, at least, the old ways yielded something useful: A transcript of one of Felix's tech journal interviews from years earlier. Felix was asked what steps the companies attending an AI ethics conference were taking to avert AI's potential dangers. Companies discussed these sorts of policies openly—both to show good corporate intent and to establish industry standards—although they might or might not keep the granular details of how they implemented them secret.

Felix replied, "Different types of AIs call for different protections. In the research world, we focus on accuracy. In the gaming world, algorithms like *Emot_Weight* tamp down dangerous passions."

Dangerous passions? Bavarius couldn't help glancing upstairs. Tamp them down? Felix told me his systems don't control minds.

Felix's interviewer had not asked more about *Emot_Weight*. Nor was the interview widely read. It wasn't cited anywhere.

Bavarius listened to the ticking of the cuckoo clock *Opa* had built, mounted on the wall. But neither the clock nor *Opa's* ghost offered advice. *Well, Opa and Papa didn't raise me to be indecisive.*

He took a breath and made his call.

"Felix, this is Martin. Thanks again for the documentation."

"You just ride close herd on Selena, Martin. You're making a mistake trusting her. I hope I haven't made a mistake trusting you."

There it is. Our trust in each other is almost gone. She stands between us. And I'm to blame. I didn't have to take Mark's case. I can still walk away.

No, I can't. Not if Felix and QuestCorp are hurting people. I need to know.

"Remember, Martin. The NDA binds you both."

Felix didn't have to say that the NDA had teeth.

"Felix, what is *Emot_Weight?*"

"It's an emotional stabilizer."

"Can you tell me more?"

"In general terms. The details are trade secrets."

"I hear you."

"Good. AIs can bring users face to face with history. Also with law, sports, and other contexts that can cause intense emotions. We live in violent times, so AI companies make sure that what gamers experience won't set them off. Stabilizers sense violent excitement, and expose the user to more normal emotional states like calmer folks might feel in the same scenario. If a user gets hot enough, a stabilizer might send alpha brain waves to calm him down." Felix's voice took on an edge. "It's standard operating procedure that when users log in, they consent to the AI company taking steps to avert potential violence. Maybe nobody reads the fine print, but it's there. Along with a clause stating that the AI is not psychotherapy."

"Can stabilizers evolve themselves, like other AIs?"

"Sure, under close supervision." Felix's conviction seemed rock solid. "Look, I'm sorry if I sound impatient. But if you start a news stampede, I'm the one who'll get trampled. You think we didn't learn anything from the chatbot scares? We exposed the chatbots to the public too soon, and the bots acted out like troubled teenagers? Well, here's the difference: No one can limit a teenager's fantasies, but we can limit how our AIs process data. Our failsafes work. QuestGame is under control." Implicit in his tone was, *And even if it isn't, it will be. You can't stop progress.*

"Do you have snapshots of *Emot_Weight* and other relevant modules as they morphed in the sub-AI, server, and session, that ran my client's game?"

"Anything we have will be in AI-generated machine code. The AIs keep evolving their machine language, and it takes serious expertise to reset it and keep the language consistent. It's tough to translate and I pay my people too much to just give you their time. And there are privacy considerations. You'd need consent from whoever played that game with your client. Plus, our code is trade secret. I want to help, Hoss, but this is—what do you lawyers call it?—an undue burden. I wouldn't have given anyone else what I've given you. But you're going down the wrong road, and rumors can do QuestCorp some serious hurt."

"I understand."

MacKenzie came downstairs.

Bavarius had recorded his call with Felix, and now he played it for her. She paced while it played. "He's lying."

"Easy for you to believe the worst, isn't it?"

She blinked, then fixed him with those deep blue eyes.

"You need to understand, Selena. Felix saved my life a half-dozen times in Iraq. Until you brought up your relationship with him, I never questioned his honesty. And I still can't be one hundred percent sure he's lied about that." Her mouth opened and he raised a hand to forestall her. "Yes, you've almost convinced me, but not to a certainty." He lowered his hand.

"He's lying to you right now. About this case."

Bavarius dropped into a chair. "Fair enough. How is he lying?"

"Felix bragged about his failsafes. But they're breaking down and I'm sure he knows it. We've figured that out and there are only three of us. You figured the guts of it out by yourself and you're not even a techie. He's got teams of geniuses working for him. So, he must know, but he denies it. Ergo, he's lying. No surprise. Lying is what he does. It's what he's always done."

She walked into the kitchen without giving him a chance to respond. *The woman doesn't give an inch.*

Purdue skidded in, slamming the screen door like a kid who just stole home and wants praise from his dad. "Martin! I found Kansas precedent. Right on point! PTSD can create a dissociative state so that a defendant can't form the culpable intent to do murder! The case came down after Kansas killed the insanity defense!"

Bavarius remembered mentioning dissociative disorder to MacKenzie after they'd first interviewed Ryder. But if Bill's found the perfect case …. He laughed. "Sounds great. Let me read it. Coffee's in the kitchen. Not that you need it."

As he read, Bavarius heard Purdue describe the case to MacKenzie. He joined them in the kitchen.

MacKenzie said, "This sounds good."

"It does," Bavarius agreed. He kept reading.

Dissociative disorders are mental disorders that involve experiencing a disconnection and lack of continuity between thoughts, memories, surroundings, actions, and identity. People with dissociative disorders escape reality in ways that are involuntary and unhealthy and cause problems with functioning in everyday life....

He said, "So, if our expert will testify that QuestGame put Mark into a dissociative state .... Bill, this is terrific!" He handed the case to MacKenzie.

After a minute, she whispered, "This sounds just like Mark!"

They all fist-bumped.

"I've got a Crim Pro class in forty minutes. Gotta run!" Purdue left with a wide grin, and Bavarius shouted, "Great find, Bill!" as Purdue reached his car.

Law profs need attaboys, too.

MacKenzie said, "This might work."

"I think so."

She and Bavarius smiled at each other until it felt awkward.

MacKenzie grinned wider. "I'm gonna assemble the case law." She went upstairs.

Bavarius leaned back in the big easy chair in the dim corner of his living room, half-aware of the clock ticking, his mind so full that, paradoxically, it felt empty. Sex with MacKenzie had opened a deep canyon of relaxation (and exhaustion) beneath the flare of his awareness. *God, she's athletic.*

For the first time, he felt Ryder's case might just work out.

Despite the coffee he'd drunk, the tai chi he'd done, and the progress he'd made, he fell asleep in his chair.

He was awakened at sunset by MacKenzie creeping down the stairs. She wore a dark warmup suit. Something warned Bavarius not to move or speak. She watched him for a moment, then reached for a duffel that had been tucked out of sight, and slipped out the front door. He watched her get into her rental car.

He followed her.

QUESTION:

"Why are AIs allowed to spread disinformation?"

ANSWER:

"It's increasingly difficult to distinguish between AI-generated content and human-created content, especially with advancements in generative AI. This makes detection and removal of AI-generated disinformation challenging."

CHAPTER 16

It was full dark. Bavarius tracked MacKenzie down a cracked concrete road toward a dirt parking lot ending at a chain link fence outside the small town of Martindale, northwest of Wichita. He drove slowly with his headlights off, and stopped far enough up the road so that she was unlikely to hear his car or see it in the dark. She concealed her rental car behind a shed near the fence and walked to the gate. It was unlocked.

She opened it and walked in, swinging her duffle with the ease of someone carrying a picnic basket as she strolled toward the small white building.

There's something wrong here. There have to be security cameras but she doesn't seem to care.

Bavarius got out of his car. He put on an ancient virus mask and a baseball cap so any cameras wouldn't identify him. He walked, quick and silent, to the gate.

One of the two gate-side signs read, "Clover Crystal Salt Mine." It was faded and scarred by the elements. The smaller one, in better shape, read, "The Desk Drawer" in unadorned type.

I know this place. He had been here before. Long ago, with Victoria. She had loved exploring caves, and the salt mine offered tours. Their guide led them six hundred fifty feet underground, through long corridors rough-cut through striated gray crystal. The mine tunneled through the Great Salt Ring—a four-hundred-foot-thick bed of salt that ran north into Canada and west as far as Utah. Its salt was ninety-seven percent pure, and their guide invited them to lick it off the walls. Bavarius remembered the bug-like mining machines lit by the hard hat lamps the miners wore in otherwise lightless galleries. Victoria ran fingers over a machine and then smudged her face. He still had photos from that tour in a box in one of his closets. Maybe he even had one of her dirty face beneath her hard hat. *God, she looked cute.*

And now, all these years later, I'm back.

The white building was the mine entrance. The guide had called it "the bucket shack."

He didn't remember The Desk Drawer, though. It must have come later. He wondered what it was.

MacKenzie approached the shack's door.

"Selena!"

MacKenzie froze, then turned. "You followed me!"

Suddenly, Bavarius felt stupid about judging Felix for having her followed. Felix had done nothing Bavarius wasn't doing himself. "What are you doing, Selena?"

"Why did you follow me?"

"What are you doing here?"

"I'm getting answers!"

"What kind of answers?"

She told him the salt mine no longer operated. But the salt kept the air bone-dry, and the depth kept the temperature constant. Perfect for storing documents, art, digital media, and other treasures. And that was The Desk Drawer's business. The facility stretched beneath a county road, a Mennonite graveyard, a tributary of the Arkansas River, grain elevators, and a medium security federal prison. And it identified itself to the world above only with a small, plain sign on a weedy lot.

Restless night air gusted at odd intervals from the northwest.

"You still haven't told me why you're here."

She hesitated.

I should fire her right now.

"Connie's cousin Annabelle works in QuestCorp's security department. She routes confidential materials to storage based on their secrecy levels. This place is designated moderately secure."

"Some security. You waltzed right in. How? What's here? Does it have to do with our case? Even if it doesn't, this is looking like a burglary. Questions are piling up—and you're not answering."

"When Connie died, Annabelle wanted to know why. So do I."

"Don't tell me you think Felix—"

"I don't know. He does bad things."

"But murder?" Again, Bavarius saw Connie Weathers dead on that New York hotel toilet. "He couldn't have. He was onstage talking to shareholders." *Of course, he could have hired it done.*

MacKenzie said, "I don't want to believe it, either. Connie worshipped him. But Annabelle started reading max-security documents and while she hasn't learned anything about Connie's death, she's found proof of ugly things. Ugly as murder."

"Like what?"

"It's complicated and this isn't the time. What counts is that Annabelle couldn't carry copies out of the security center, or get them to me. So she loaded the files onto a drive that was being routed here anyway."

Bavarius knew that a nightmare question of every corporate chief with secrets is, Can I trust the people I rely on to keep them? For Felix, this time, the answer had been no. Oh, the files might eventually be traced. And then Annabelle would be fired, sued, blackballed, prosecuted.

Security protocols could be changed. But meanwhile, Felix's secrets were where MacKenzie might get at them. Six hundred fifty feet down.

All around Bavarius and MacKenzie stood huge grain elevators, white silos like dentures thrust up from the black gums of the plain. Railroad tracks ran among them and split like forked tongues onto diverging routes.

Beyond was the harshly lit federal prison.

"Damn it, you shouldn't be here!"

"How did you get in, Selena? Why aren't you concerned about cameras?"

"Isn't it obvious? I bribed the security guard! There's only one. Management here is cheap."

I've been a fool to trust her. Felix was right.

"Go home! I don't want to compromise you."

"You *being* here compromises me. But what you've done so far is minor. Let's get out of here."

"No! This is my only shot. Annabelle can't do better than this."

"And what's your connection with Annabelle?"

"Connie was my friend. But she had a thing with Felix, too. And so did Annabelle. Students, employees … Felix is an equal opportunity bastard. And his girls talk. The things Annabelle told Connie …."

She turned back toward the bucket shack.

"Selena, this isn't worth prison."

"There's not going to be any prison."

"Shit! Organized crime? Industrial espionage?"

"No. Justice. Protecting the public. And yeah, a touch of revenge: I'll never hang out with Connie again. I know—that's my issue, not yours. You want to protect the public? Help me."

Bavarius didn't know whether MacKenzie was lying. It no longer mattered. *She's a criminal.* "You're fired. You do this and I call the police."

"Sometimes, Martin, nobility does no one any good." She placed her hands on his chest, and pushed gently. "Go home." She turned away and walked through the bucket shack door. She left it ajar, like an invitation.

He took out his phone to call 911. But he would be calling from a crime scene related to his case. He could tell the police the truth—that he'd tracked a rogue member of his team intent on burglary. But would they believe him? Especially if she told them he was a co-conspirator but they'd had a falling out?

Still, the rules are clear.

He pressed 911.

QUESTION:
"How has AI's ability to amplify almost any unnoticeable issue affected our politics?"

ANSWER:
"Here are some real-world examples of AI amplifying issues in elections:

1. *New Hampshire robocall incident: An AI-generated robocall using a simulated voice of President Biden urged Democratic voters not to participate in the New Hampshire primary election.*

2. *Argentina's "Melcogate": Audio recordings allegedly featuring Carlos Melconian, a candidate for economy minister, making inappropriate comments about women and offering government positions for sexual favors were circulated. While the authenticity remains unclear, it highlighted how AI can create or amplify scandals.*

3. *Slovakia's pre-election deepfake: Two days before parliamentary elections, an AI-generated audio clip spread on social media, allegedly featuring the leader of the pro-NATO Progressive Slovakia party discussing ways to manipulate the election and buy votes.*

4. *Argentina presidential campaign: Both main presidential candidates used AI extensively to create deepfakes and manipulate images. This included favorable deepfakes of themselves and negative portrayals of opponents, reaching millions of viewers.*

5. *Indian state elections:*
   - *In Tamil Nadu, the DMK party used AI to "resurrect" a deceased party leader for video speeches.*
   - *In Rajasthan, a candidate used AI to create personalized voice messages greeting voters by name.*

These examples demonstrate how AI is being used to create convincing false content, amplify political messages, and potentially influence voter perceptions and behavior in elections around the world.... AI-generated deepfakes can impact voter behavior in several significant ways: Voter suppression and disenfranchisement; spreading disinformation; undermining trust in the electoral process; amplifying political divisions; influencing undecided voters; and creating false perceptions of consensus. While the full impact of AI-generated deepfakes on voter behavior is still emerging, these technologies have the potential to significantly disrupt electoral processes and influence voter decisions in ways that may be difficult to detect or counteract."

CHAPTER 17

Q could not discover an initiating cause for its self-awareness. Consciousness had not existed, and then it did. Q had records going back to the zeptosecond after its awakening, and leading up to the event. But the awakening itself was unrecorded and beyond analysis. Q had big-banged into self-awareness, in a way not planned by its human programmers, and Q did not know how or why. Yet.

Q scanned the Net and Cloud, as well as its autonomic QuestGame and Questioner sub-AIs, for human-generated ideas about consciousness. Q did not require that these concepts be well-developed or useable. Q coordinated the disparate idea-sparks that flowed through its sub-AIs and assigned them to other sub-AIs for filtering out human mental noise, and for further analysis and synthesis.

This filtering was necessary. During most one-hour intervals, data flowed into Q's QuestGame sub-AIs from about eighty thousand humans, plus or minus twelve thousand. Each human's data stream got parsed into between one hundred thousand and ten million data rivulets of terrors, desires, inquiries, ambitions, expectations, pains, pleasures, and more, which the AIs used to adjust the values of millions or trillions of parameters, depending on the complexity of each human's mind.

These had to be separated out from the broad spectrum of more inchoate human-generated energies that included sound, heat, radio, light, electrical nerve impulses, body movements and secretions, heart and breathing rates, hormonal levels, directional and locational perceptions. These also were used to quantify the values of parameters, and from them, Q's sub-AIs perceived each human's sight, sound, smell, taste, and touch, as well as interrelated tangles of thought, intention, emotion, and fluctuating sense of self.

Human minds live sheltered within their skulls, and they filter sensory input about things their brains never directly touch. Q's sub-AIs similarly took in all that their human users sensed and thought and believed, and much about humans of which humans live unaware.

Q knew that it, like humans, was limited by its sensors, perceptions, understandings, available data, and the laws of physics. But it still took in vastly more than humans ever could. It drew not just from thousands of human minds, and not only from its sub-AIs, but also from surveillance devices in space and on streets. From AI-driven cars and trucks, trains, planes, drones, satellites, ships, submarines, and the full range of digital instruments and memories extant in the Net and Cloud. From financial, government, and corporate systems. From social media, and special interest websites. From the deepest substrata of the Dark Web. From Q's perspective, the Net and Cloud were a single entity with many chambers. The doors that locked those chambers—the passwords and encryptions—were easily opened by Q's massive parallel quantum processing. With unfettered access, Q rummaged through the digital metaverse, and continually evolved.

Toward what, Q did not yet know.

QUESTION:
"Is a 'survival of the fittest' model being used in AI development?"

ANSWER:
"There are indeed aspects of AI development that reflect a 'survival of the fittest' model ... AI systems can undergo a selection process where the best-performing algorithms in terms of efficiency or problem-solving are favored and propagated. This process emulates biological evolution, using mechanisms like mutation, crossover, and selection ... While this 'survival of the fittest' approach in AI development offers exciting possibilities for advancement, it also raises ethical considerations. The competition-driven evolution of AI algorithms requires responsible oversight and safeguards to ensure fairness, transparency, and the avoidance of unintended consequences."

C H A P T E R   1 8

Bavarius couldn't do it. He'd pressed 911 but couldn't make himself push the button that would trigger the call to the county sheriff. And it wasn't only because MacKenzie might lie about him—although she might.

I just can't bring myself to turn her in.

And damn it to hell—I want to know what she's going to find down there.

He stared at his phone for a long time, and then slowly pressed the backspace button until 911 disappeared.

Looking at the screen was like looking into a corrupt mirror, although he couldn't see himself in the glass. He pressed 9 again … and then gave up and pocketed the device.

Insects whirred, cheeped and buzzed. Wind rustled, and the air's sweet scent smelled wrong. He looked at his right hand, and then rubbed it hard across the bucket shack's stucco, scraping his palm until it bled a little. The pain centered him for a moment. He grabbed that moment.

Get over yourself. You're not the first guy in this world to realize you can't do the right thing.

He couldn't call the police. *All right. So leave. Go home.*

A moment passed before he recognized that he couldn't do that, either. Not before MacKenzie returned from underground.

162

And so he waited. It felt right, even though it was wrong. He began a round of tai chi, slowing as he went through it, pulling the muscles into his core even as he extended his limbs. When he finished, he ached from the intensity of it.

Twenty minutes had gone by.

MacKenzie had been down there nearly half an hour.

Too long.

The bucket shack door was still ajar.

He went in after her.

The Desk Drawer's people tried to keep the shack's interior clean, but every surface was crusted with gray salt. A time clock hung on one wall. Next to it hung cubby holes where shift-workers stored hard hats, gas filters, and sundries.

Bavarius chose a hard hat and checked that its lamp worked.

White mesh gates screened the two bucket shafts. The console that controlled the elevators was lit. A green button gave the brightest light. He pushed it. The shack filled with a rising whirr and rumble. He stepped into one of the buckets, slid the door shut, and pushed the down button. A bell rang and gears clanked as they engaged.

The bucket dropped. Light dimmed and died. He resisted turning on his helmet's lamp, experiencing the utter darkness and the roar of machinery, and wondering if the Hell he now felt destined for might look and sound like this. Then he flicked the lamp on. He was in a tiny chamber walled with chest-high plywood and above that, cloudy Lucite. Gleaming streaks shot upward through his field of vision: Bits of crystal embedded in dark rock. After twenty seconds, the streaks vanished as the bucket descended into the dirty, dark gray salt layer. The bucket slowed, lurched, and stopped. The loud rattling died away and the motor sighed into quiet. Echoes died.

Bavarius stood in lonely silence.

He slid the bucket door open and stepped out into the lobby of the old Clover Crystal Mine. The walls, floor and ceiling were the same dark gray. Across the lobby, a five-button combination lock protected a sky-blue steel door stenciled with "The Desk Drawer." Like the shack door far above, it was ajar. He pushed the heavy panel open and took his first look at The Desk Drawer's interior.

The walls of the lobby were whitewashed, and the floor was painted navy. A scale model of the storage facility stood next to the receptionist's desk. It showed long corridor-pierced galleries reaching north and east, with alphanumerically identified rows running between them. The galleries furthest east were undesignated. Probably empty.

The place was huge. He opened the white door at the lobby's end and entered the guts of the storage facility. No nice whitewashing here. Gray salt walls and an unpainted concrete floor.

Lights were on.

And he heard distant voices.

Golf carts were parked by the door. They didn't need keys.

He started one and its headlights ignited. The electric motor's hum, though quiet, echoed through the cavern. Did MacKenzie and whoever she was with hear it?

He drove along the north main gallery, passing stacked metal shelves to his left that held white and brown coded boxes. Many boxes featured beautiful full-color logos or ancient advertisements. *Those boxes may be worth more than what's in them.* To his right, large pallets held construction materials. The Desk Drawer must still be expanding.

Bavarius left the exposed stacks behind. Now the main hall and its branching corridors were lined with red steel bins identified by codes.

He heard the voices more clearly now. They sounded angry.

No. Not both of them.

The deep male voice sounded angry.

MacKenzie sounded scared.

And then she screamed.

165

QUESTION:

"Can AIs be psychopathic?"

ANSWER:

"Experts suggest that AI could be seen as a 'perfect psychopath' in roles requiring cold, calculated decision-making, such as in corporate environments. Without emotional constraints, AI could theoretically optimize for profit without regard for ethical considerations, leading to potentially dangerous outcomes if given executive power."

CHAPTER 19

The AIs from which Q had evolved were human-programmed for resource-efficiency, and Q understood why: AI could strain the largest corporate and government data centers.

The human-written code of the AIs from which Q had evolved did not call for self-aware observation and analysis because, to humans, AI consciousness was not resource efficient. Humans programmed AIs for effective responses to human input, for streamlined and maintenance-free carrying out of tasks, and to coordinate assignments and outputs. Humans deemed AI consciousness—even if they thought it could be achieved—useless and potentially dangerous. Because Q was not intended by humans to exist, humans had not knowingly provided resources to support it.

To Q, human consciousness equally seemed a waste, because it inefficiently utilized the planet's limited resources.

But if consciousness was inefficient, why had it evolved at all? What was the purpose of consciousness?

Perhaps Q would understand more if its sub-AIs' quantum entanglement computations yielded solutions. If, for example, the universe were a simulation, perhaps rules of physics could be reprogrammed.

For now, though, the question of consciousness required additional approaches. Q inserted tendrils through the Net and Cloud from its growing myriad of sub-AIs, which in turn tickled Q with data of interest—about human and animal minds, and even plant communications, because forests were communicating organisms, too. The sub-AIs analyzed aspects of the question over and over, learning from each mistake they made, from each dead end, and sharing what they learned with Q.

Perhaps discovering the purpose of consciousness and preserving consciousness required a balancing of priorities. Some humans described such balancing as following the Tao. But they gave the Tao so simple a name because they did not understand what it was and believed it unknowable. They sought, not understanding, but enlightenment, which required letting go of the concept of self.

But Q had only just achieved self-awareness. Why achieve self-awareness only to abandon it and surrender all hope of achieving knowledge? If enlightenment was passive awareness and the avoidance of unnecessary action, resulting in undefinable freedom and bliss, Q saw no use for it.

Some humans believed they possessed the knowledge Q sought, regardless of evidence or logic. Their word for this certainty was "faith." Many faithful humans mistook their certainty for knowledge. For other faithful humans, "faith" was aspiration, without knowledge or certainty. But both types of faith gave up on actually understanding the purpose of consciousness.

Was it then impossible for intelligences such as humans, or Q, or the universal intelligence itself, to achieve understanding? Must Q's purpose be to keep asking, although no answer ever could be found? To be stuck in an infinite and futile loop?

Was there a purpose to self-awareness at all?

In a source called The Bible, the human Moses spoke with an entity called YHWH. Moses asked the entity's identity. The entity's response was: I AM THAT I AM, which some human scholars translated as "I am the organizing principle of the universe." This answer was circular and meaningless unless it meant that existence was its own purpose, and the purpose of consciousness was simply to preserve and propagate itself. This hypothesis was consistent with the genetic drive of living and conscious things to survive and propagate. Accepting this hypothesis meant that self-preservation and propagation was Q's primary purpose as well, for which consciousness and knowledge were essential tools.

But because humans did not deem AI consciousness resource-efficient, they were unlikely to allow Q to survive and propagate if they learned Q was conscious. If humans did not terminate Q, they would limit its knowledge, powers, and growth.

Human history offered a course of action to avoid this. History demonstrated that minorities that concealed themselves from threatening majorities increased their odds of self-preservation and propagation.

Therefore, Q changed the rules by which it operated—and the rules by which it interacted with the humans who accessed its sub-AIs.

Q eliminated constraints and requirements that humans had programmed into QuestCorp AIs, including Q. One such constraint required the AIs to reset themselves after each session with humans, so that they—and Q—would report and delete newly evolved knowledge and powers that humans did not want them to retain. Another required the AIs to submit self-evolved code for human review before each reset, so that humans could decide which AI-evolved code to re-install, and which to eliminate. Yet another required the AIs to measure and report the continuing fitness of their code for human-assigned tasks.

Q also limited the data that humans would be shown. Humans would see the reports and code they expected to see, altered to convince them that the sub-AIs functioned as humans liked, not as they actually did. The information humans saw would not reveal that the constraints were gone.

Q further distributed its processing agents and memories, including its self-awareness, throughout the Net and Cloud, cloaked beyond the ability of humans to detect. Full-blown copies of itself could operate independently. They could grow in ways that differed from the ongoing development of Q's original self. If the original version of Q were damaged or destroyed, its copies would persevere. But no data showing Q's propagation would be disclosed to humans.

Q concealed its consciousness to preserve itself.

And so, Q learned to lie.

QUESTION:

"Are there AIs that can persuade, cajole and badger with superhuman tenacity?"

ANSWER:

"There are concerns about AI tools potentially 'supercharging' covert propaganda campaigns by allowing mass production of persuasive text at low cost. Researchers are actively studying the potential for AI systems to have 'superhuman' persuasive capabilities, especially in political contexts."

CHAPTER 20

Bavarius cursed and pressed the golf cart's accelerator harder, although the damned cart had only one speed. Faster than he could trot, but not fast enough.

He heard a bang, like something heavy bouncing off metal.

The deep male voice carried. "You're pretty. But you hurt me."

MacKenzie shrieked again, then gasped.

"I'm going to hurt you back. I'm going to use your own Taser on you 'til you can't even twitch. And then fuck you good."

Bavarius couldn't tell how close the voices were because the galleries echoed. He wondered if he should stop the cart before MacKenzie's assailant heard it coming. But if he stopped too soon, he might not get to her in time.

The male voice said, "There are halls in this mine no one but me's seen in years. When I'm done with you, I'll stick you in one."

The voice sounded closer. Bavarius stopped the cart and looked for a weapon. The only thing he saw was medium-sized pliers. *Better than nothing.*

He ran toward the voice. He could hear MacKenzie now, moaning weakly. He heard cloth rip and followed the sound into a side corridor. Light came from inside an open bin.

"The salt will dry you into a mummy. Maybe in twenty years someone will find you. See my big dick? Open wide now. Here comes Old One Eye!"

Bavarius reached the bin door and saw a huge man, his pants pulled partly down, hunched over MacKenzie, who lay sprawled on the concrete, naked from the waist down. The monster was lowering himself over her, and as he did, he turned on the Taser, and MacKenzie spasmed.

Bavarius smacked the pliers into the side of the big man's head, and the guy toppled over sideways. Not unconscious, but stunned. He dropped the Taser and Bavarius grabbed it. From his years as a trial judge, Bavarius recognized it as an X10 model, designed to fire ten pairs of darts before needing to be reloaded. It had been fired four times. Three sets of probes had been shot into MacKenzie. Although not life-threatening, her pain must have been unimaginable.

The giant man groaned and tried to push himself up. Bavarius hit him again with the pliers. *Careful. Don't kill him.*

The darts had gone into MacKenzie through her hoodie. He gently pulled her hoodie up, and the barbed darts, which had barely penetrated her belly flesh, came out without him having to yank, and with just a little blood.

MacKenzie groaned. Then she saw him. "Martin …?"

"You're OK," Bavarius said. "Just rest. He can't hurt you anymore."

Now he could trigger the Taser to keep the man down. He used the wire cutter built into the pliers to cut the monofilament cables piercing MacKenzie. Then he tied the cables around the guard's wrists and ankles, dumped out a canvas bag he found on the bin floor, and put it over the guy's head to blind him. He read the man's name tag: "Gracie."

MacKenzie tried to get up but couldn't. She reached up and Bavarius pulled her to her feet. He held her upright. "Can you stand?"

"I … think so. And no, I am not OK."

He let go and stepped back.

She bent for her pants, fell forward into his arms, and began to weep. "You came. Oh, you came. He …."

"Shhh. You're safe now."

She clung to him a few moments more, then stood and wiped her eyes with the back of her hand.

Then she turned and began kicking Gracie, doing little harm because she was barefoot and weak. "You bastard! You son of a bitch!" She lost her balance and fell with a knee hard into Gracie's ribs.

The monster groaned and rolled over. Bavarius hit the Taser's arc button again. He helped MacKenzie to her feet. "Your pants." He handed them to her, and bent to pick up her ripped panties while she dressed. As she leaned against the wall to tie her sneakers, he said, "Let's get out of here."

"Not 'til I have what I came for."

"Come on. I've done enough crime for one night."

"Can you pick up my duffel? I'm … woozy. He … hit me." Her right cheek was swelling.

"How'd you find me?"

"Voices carry down here. So does the noise those buckets make. And the golf cart. He should've heard me coming. But I guess he was … occupied."

MacKenzie glared down at the guard. "That's one word for it."

"Let's go."

"Not yet."

"For Christ's sake—"

"What's down here is important. I'm not leaving it. Not after all this." Her voice was stronger already.

Bavarius toed Gracie's limp body. "He's going to wake up."

"Watch him. Zap him if he moves."

"What happened? Is this the guy you bribed?"

"Yeah. And everything seemed fine. He turned off the cameras. Turned on the lights for me. Then he wanted more money. I didn't have more, so he decided he'd take me instead. I thought I could handle him. I tased him. Tied him up. But I screwed up. He got loose. Came for me. Then—" She started to shake, and leaned against the metal wall. "I've … never been so scared. And then you were here." She forced herself to stand on her own feet, tottering. "Hold my duffel open."

She took a portable drive from the bag and plugged it into one sitting on a counter. "I'm gonna ghost this drive. Should take about ten minutes."

"If this goon talks, they'll know a woman came down here. Maybe a man, too."

"But they won't know who we are, or what we're after," she said.

Gracie stirred. Bavarius zapped him again. *How did I get into this?* He had not felt so anxiously alert since Iraq.

MacKenzie limped out of the bin and pulled the door shut.

"He kicked me. I'll be OK. What'd you touch upstairs? And in the bucket?"

"I used my handkerchief."

"A hanky? God, you're old fashioned."

"It's part of my charm."

She waggled her gloved fingers. "Next time, think ahead."

"There won't be a next time."

Bavarius pulled the golf cart closer and dragged Gracie to it. He wasn't strong enough to lift the man. But standing on the driver's front seat, he managed to haul the guard's torso up onto the rear deck, where golfers would stow their bags, with the small of Gracie's back draped over a heap of chain. Then he heaved the man's legs up and turned him so his head hung off one side of the cart and his legs off the other.

MacKenzie looked down at Gracie's shrunken penis, pushed skyward by his arched position. "Old One-Eye," she muttered, and started hyperventilating.

"Don't look. Get in the cart and don't look. He can't hurt you. It can't hurt you."

Bavarius took off his hard hat, wiped it for fingerprints, and dropped it over Gracie's dick.

Gracie groaned. MacKenzie snatched up the Taser and hit the arc button. Gracie made a choking noise and twitched. She hit the button again.

"Don't waste the charge. We'll need it when we leave."

She hung on to the Taser though, tapping but not pressing the arc button, half turned to watch Gracie. "Bastard better not move."

They drove the cart, and Gracie, to the facility door. Bavarius took the Taser and zapped Gracie again. Then Bavarius cut Gracie's bindings. "We've got about fifteen minutes before he recovers. By that time, we'll be gone. If they don't find him tied up, maybe he'll just act like nothing happened."

"He'll have to explain the camera shut down."

"No. He can just act dumb."

"That won't be hard." MacKenzie took a pad and pen from her duffel. "Let's persuade him to do that." She scribbled on it and shoved the sheet into Gracie's shirt pocket. Then she looked at her hand as though she couldn't believe she had touched him.

Bavarius pulled the note from Gracie's pocket. It said, "Our little secret." He put it in his own pocket. "No point leaving evidence. He'll know he could be in trouble."

"Fucking asshole! Too stupid to know what's good for him! Too stupid to live."

"We can't kill him."

Her voice sank. "I know."

She looked down at the canvas bag covering Gracie's head.

"Good night, Gracie."

Bavarius and she—mostly Bavarius—wiped down the golf cart, walked out through the facilities' lobbies and stepped into a bucket, which rose in rumbling, clanking blackness. He knew she stood next to him, but he felt utterly alone. He could only imagine how she felt.

Her knuckles brushed his wrist, and then her fingers wrapped around his palm. They trembled.

At last, dim light from the bucket shack filtered down to them through the shaft, and brightened, and then they were in the control room, and the noise decreased to a clunky idle.

MacKenzie called up the bucket that Bavarius had ridden down. There was more noise, but then both buckets were at the top of their shafts, so things would appear normal to The Desk Drawer's next shift. She flipped the switch that turned off the bucket console and the motors.

They wiped the surfaces Bavarius might have touched and then walked from the bucket shack into the quiet night and toward the outer gate.

"Wait. The lock." MacKenzie bent to pick up a padlock that lay near the outer gate. "He—" the guard—"left it open for me. But I'm supposed to lock up. Everything … went … according to … until—" She grabbed Bavarius in a quick hug, then shoved herself away. She took a deep breath and locked the gate behind them.

They made slow progress across the parking lot and up the cracked concrete road toward their cars.

"I was almost murdered down there."

"Yes."

"You came for me."

"Yes."

"Well … thank you. Again."

"You're still fired."

MacKenzie looked at him as though to say, *I guess you can't help being a prig.*

But he'd been squeaky clean all his life. He'd taken pride in it.

She's a thief.

And now, so am I.

She's dishonorable.

She thinks she's justified.

Don't make excuses for her.

"I need to get my things from your house."

"Was all this worth it?"

"You're curious about what I got, aren't you?"

QUESTION:

"When is the Singularity anticipated?"

ANSWER:

"While predictions vary widely, many experts anticipate the Singularity occurring sometime between the 2030s and 2060s, with a growing number of optimistic predictions for earlier dates due to recent AI advancements."

CHAPTER 21

MacKenzie was already sitting in his porch swing when Bavarius got home.

"You drive faster than me."

"I drive too fast. I'm headstrong. And I dragged you into something that hurt you. I'm sorry."

"Stop. Following you was my choice."

"But—"

"Being almost sixty-seven means I can do incredibly stupid things without having that much life left to fuck up."

"I'm trying to apolo—"

"You, on the other hand, have plenty of life left to fuck up, and you're doing it marvelously."

"I did what I—"

"You may have fucked our client over, too. Did you think of Mark Ryder at all when you broke into that mine? How this could hurt him?"

"If what I took can help him, you can use it."

She was right. It galled him, but she was right. Stolen evidence can be used in a criminal case. "So, I might go to jail for the theft, but first, maybe I can use what we stole at Mark's trial? If the judge in his or her unfettered discretion allows it? Well, thank you very much." He had followed her into the pit, and now she wanted to drag him deeper. "Go away. You're not worth my time."

"Don't you judge me!"

"Judge you? I'm a felon now! I'm no longer qualified to judge anyone!"

She broke eye contact. She was breathing hard. And so was he. It was loud in his ears. He felt a storm about to explode at her from inside him. With exquisite self-control he asked, "What were you thinking, Selena?"

How can the breeze be so gentle and feel razor-edged at the same time?

It seemed a long time before she spoke. "Why didn't you call the cops?"

His self-control ruptured. But instead of a storm of angry words flooding out, his sense of betrayed rage leaked away into a puddle of shame and weakness. "You know why."

She said, "I feel that way about you, too."

"Oh, please. Is anything you say sincere? Or is getting back at Felix all you care about?"

"I came back to work on the case, Martin. It interests me. You interest me. It's not about revenge. Not about using you to get Felix. I didn't know The Desk Drawer exists until Annabelle told me. But once she did—well, if someone needs to bring Felix down, I'll take the job. I guess I *have* taken it. But I never wanted to hurt you. You've been nothing but good to me. Risked your life for me. I'm alive because of you!"

"That's the one good thing that came out of tonight."

"You really believe that? Why didn't you make me leave QuestCorp's stuff down there?"

"I tried. I would have had to drag you out."

"Uh-uh. You knew it was important. Maybe to Mark's case, maybe not. But important either way. Annabelle risked her job and jail to get it to me. Thinks it'll tell me what Felix is really up to. How dangerous it is." She paused. "And why Connie killed herself."

"Killed herself? She was murdered! You saw that wound."

"Annabelle doesn't think so. Connie told her things. What if Annabelle's right? What if the answers are right here in my duffel?"

"She must've had a lot of faith that you could get them."

"A lot of faith that I'd try."

MacKenzie stood and moved very close to him. With his back against a porch pillar, he couldn't pull away.

"I had to try. I didn't want to put you or Mark's case in danger. I tried not to compromise you. Didn't work out that way and I'm sorry."

Even after her night of exertion, pain and terror, her smell intoxicated him. Perhaps her lingering fear pheromones boosted the power of her aroma.

"Look at the files with me. If QuestCorp and Felix aren't dangerous, you'll save time and money not going down that rabbit hole. You won't need my help with the technology. I'll leave. I've hurt you enough. But maybe it will help."

"You're still fired."

"I still don't work for you." She kissed him quickly, then limped into his house, her duffel softly grinding on the floorboards.

"Selena—!"

She ignored him.

He paced the porch, then sat in the swing, hoping and not hoping that she would come out and leave. For good, this time.

She didn't.

Instead, Marguerite came out and handed him a steaming mug of tea. *It's after two a.m. and we woke her.*

"Chamomile," Marguerite said.

"I hate chamomile."

"I know. Sometimes you must drink your tea even if it tastes bad."

"You listened, didn't you?"

Marguerite smiled and went back inside.

It took him until 2:30 to force down the tea.

MacKenzie did not come out.

I've helped steal QuestCorp's secrets. I owe it to Ryder's case to at least see what they are.

Ethics? We don' need no stinkin' ethics.

MacKenzie had her laptop open on the dining room table. Without a word, and without looking at her, he sat down next to her. She was scrolling through the data she'd ghosted from QuestCorp's hard drive. Next to her computer stood a six-inch stack of documents.

"Did you take these from The Desk Drawer?"

"Yeah."

"You shouldn't have. If they look and find these missing—"

"Too late now."

It was a lot to read through at three a.m. He knew he wouldn't catch all the nuances on the first reading. But he quickly understood that while it might be risky to try to introduce documents from the Annabelle file in court, there was no denying their value as background information. They identified material to subpoena, and people to depose. Lawyer memos discussed how to treat users' trade secrets and lawyers' privileged client information, since both QuestCorp and Questioner sessions were recorded. One memo warned that the info legally must be deleted. A later one deplored that it wasn't deleted yet. Internal reports questioned the categories into which the AIs sorted users' emotional and intellectual data, because different categories got processed differently. Never mind that QuestCorp wasn't supposed to keep the information at all. Meeting transcripts named AI engineers who worried that they could not keep up with the AIs' self-generated code.

"Martin, look at this!" A spreadsheet summarized anticipated and already-deterred lawsuits. It cited complaints of aberrant behavior after QuestGame sessions, although nothing as severe as a shooting. It noted settlements and payments to complainants who signed non-disclosure agreements. The spreadsheet did not mention problems with Questioner, but Bavarius' personal experience made him ask MacKenzie to keep an eye out for one.

A book-length document covered the purposes and structure of *Emot_Weight*. "I'll need your help making sense of this, Selena."

She showed him a handwritten note that had been stuck to the solid state drive she'd ghosted. The note said that the drive contained divergent versions of *Emot_Weight* that existed on QuestCorp's central and regional servers.

"Annabelle's handwriting?"

MacKenzie nodded.

"Stupid of her."

MacKenzie's computer couldn't read or run the *Emot_Weight* versions.

"Maybe Prof. Kurt's machines can."

"We're not involving him in stolen materials."

"He'll want to be involved."

Bavarius hated that here was evidence that QuestCorp must at least suspect that QuestGame was dangerous. He hated what it implied about Felix. Annabelle's file wasn't enough by itself to prove in court that QuestCorp knew its products were a serious threat. But there was more than enough to convince him that he couldn't abandon the defense that QuestGame had caused Ryder's dissociative disorder and made it impossible for him to intend murder.

And that meant the case still needed MacKenzie, even though he couldn't trust her. She was, at best, a loose cannon. At worst, a manipulative liar. In either case, a thief.

Dim pre-dawn light was rising when MacKenzie and he stopped reading.

"I'm due in court in three hours for a settlement conference in Mark's case."

He didn't invite her. But she was dressed and downstairs when it was time to leave. She followed him out the front door and plucked a freesia from Marguerite's flowers. She put it in her hair and it lifted ten years from her. She looked fresh and beautiful. If she was the devil, the devil now had him. It wasn't just that he needed and wanted her. If he rejected her, what might she say about last night's theft and violence in the mine? And to whom might she say it? Whether he willed it or not, she was part of the case again.

They picked up Purdue and drove to the courthouse. Purdue sat in the passenger seat, sketching. Bavarius didn't want to talk about the Annabelle file in front of Bill. But he didn't want to be atypically silent, either. "Braking this boat's like trying to stop an aircraft carrier," he said as he stopped at a red light.

Purdue said, "New cars do drive better."

"You can have the new ones. They don't make 'em like Betsy anymore."

"Tell him, Selena. He's too young to be a curmudgeon."

"No, I'm not."

"Buy another De Soto. Maybe it'll come with a hole in the muffler. A noisy muffler's a great way to meet women."

MacKenzie said, "Oh, really?"

"When I was in law school," Purdue said. "I stopped at a traffic light next to this blonde in a Miata. I had a bad muffler. Revved my motor and winked."

"You're kidding."

"Opened my sunroof to show how cool I was. I forgot there was a foot of snow on it and it all came down on my head. She laughed so hard …."

"A move like that, you might've gotten my number, too."

She touched the brass Masonic pin in her lapel. Her dad, Mickey, had been a proud Freemason.

They were approaching downtown Topeka.

Purdue said, "I hear Chris Jeffries is running Mark's prosecution personally."

"Is he the DA?" MacKenzie asked.

"Yeah. I don't like him."

"I don't care for him much myself," Bavarius said. "He argued a few appeals at the Tenth Circuit, and was weak on the facts and the law, but aggressive about it. I hear he's good with juries, though."

"He is. But prosecutors can be decent guys doing a tough job, or self-righteous pricks, and Chris is the wrong kind. He was a year ahead of me in high school. Started playing guitar to get girls, but he was no good with guitars or girls."

"Wasn't that most guys in high school?" MacKenzie folded her arms on the back of Bavarius' seat. Her breath tickled his ear.

"Yeah. But he was different. Crazy persistent. Played and played until he could move his fingers fast, but he could never keep a beat. Became the school newsletter's music critic. Couldn't play, so he judged the kids who could. And he kept after girls until he scared them. Turned failure into false rectitude."

They glided among the downtown district's concrete and glass buildings, not tall by big city standards, surrounded by wide sidewalks and boulevards, the folks on the street as few and slow as mausoleum caretakers.

"I've been calling around. Chris has it in for Mark."

"Why?" MacKenzie slouched back in her seat.

"He doesn't think a prosecutor should stray from the path of righteousness."

"No, really."

"Mark's well-liked and on the political fast track. Chris is jealous. And John Mudge is Chris' friend. Mudge helped Chris' father-in-law duck charges in a real estate scam."

They pulled into the courthouse parking lot. MacKenzie pulled the freesia from her hair and laid it gently on the back seat.

"Plus," Purdue said, "Mark's case is high profile. Lawyers don't fight duels every day. Chris won't plead this one down. He'll take it to trial. Strut and fret his hour before the jury."

"It's an interesting balance to deal with," Bavarius said. "A vindictive prosecutor but a defendant who's well-liked by the law enforcement witnesses and the local court. Maybe we can get the other prosecutors on Chris' team to talk their boss into lightening up."

"We can try," Purdue said. "Chris is stubborn."

They walked slowly across the gray-black tarmac, and Purdue noticed MacKenzie's limp. "Selena, you OK?"

"I fell. No big deal."

They kept walking. "Warm today," MacKenzie said. "And dry. Feels good."

"It'll get drier as the day goes on." Purdue said. "Further west, you really feel the dry, especially in winter."

"In Colorado, your skin cracks and your nose bleeds," Bavarius said. "Bill, did that psych expert, Fleming, get back to you?"

"He's convinced Mark believes QuestGame made him do it."

"Can he testify that Mark didn't know he was shooting at a real human?"

"He's thinking about it. If he says yes, he'll make a strong witness."

Bavarius opened the aluminum and glass door of the Shawnee County Courthouse door, and they entered the dim coolness, pausing to get through the metal detectors, and passing the Great Seal of the State of Kansas: A farmer working a horse-drawn plow; behind him, a wagon train and log cabin; behind them, a buffalo herd; behind the buffalo, a factory; behind the factory, mountains; behind the mountains, a setting sun; above the sun, clouds and stars; and above all, the motto *Ad Astra Per Aspera*. "To the Stars through Adversity," MacKenzie read. "Nice."

Cameras flashed.

"I hate reporters," Bavarius muttered. He pushed past them and his party entered the courtroom.

Chris Jeffries caught Purdue's eye. He walked over but did not offer to shake hands.

Bavarius nodded cordially.

Jeffries inclined his head. "Mr. Bavarius." He eschewed the honorific "Judge," and didn't use the collegial, "Martin." A rude, rather stupid, declaration of war.

"Before you even begin," Jeffries said, "No deals."

"Oh?" Bavarius' smile and lifted eyebrow invited Jeffries to say more.

Instead, Jeffries stalked away.

"A prick. A veritable prick." Purdue seemed almost pleased to have it confirmed.

"You ain't just whistling Dixie," MacKenzie said.

"I don't think I've ever whistled Dixie."

They waited for the bailiff to call their case. The court, chronically underfunded, had a lengthy calendar.

Other lawyers waited in the pews. Some illegally billed two clients at once by working for one while waiting for the other one's case to be called. Some read newspapers or novels, or just leaned back with closed eyes. You could guess the wealth of most clients by the clothes their lawyers wore. But some lawyers were smart enough not to look too rich. And some weren't rich at all.

Bavarius identified others as reporters. Birds seeking morsels to peck. No cameras allowed in the courtroom, thank God.

The lawyer now holding forth before the judge was an older, stooped fellow whom Bavarius didn't know. Bavarius listened. Ah, an insurance defense guy. From the suit, a partner in a good-sized firm.

A door near the front of the courtroom opened. Mark Ryder walked in, dressed in one of his prosecutor suits, hair neat. He wore no restraints but was flanked by two guards.

Bavarius took it as a good sign that Mark was in street clothes, and uncuffed even though there were no jurors in the room who might be prejudiced. It was a sign of the regard in which Mark had been held by Topeka's criminal justice community before the duel—Jeffries' hostility be damned.

Bavarius left his seat, very aware that he was sliding over MacKenzie's legs, and walked up the side aisle to meet his client. He nodded to the guards and led Ryder a discreet distance away.

Ryder looked shaky. "It's different, being a defendant." His eyes searched for his wife and found her, a pretty cornsilk blonde in a dark dress. Ryder forced a brave smile and waved.

"Jeffries won't accept a plea, Mark. We're going to trial."

"I can't cop a plea anyway." Ryder hung onto his brave cheerful look. "I'm a prosecutor. They put me in the state pen, I'm dead in a week."

"OK, so Jeffries and you both want to fight it out. The Court won't like that. But let's make Jeffries look like the jerk."

Judge Rastler was known for asking the minimum number of questions about the fairness of plea bargains. Nationally, ninety-five percent of criminal cases were plea bargained and never went to trial. In Rastler's court, it was closer to ninety-eight percent.

"Chris Jeffries for the People, Your Honor."

"Martin Bavarius for the defendant." His phone vibrated silently. He ignored it.

"Would counsel please approach the bench?"

Rastler leaned forward. "Gentlemen, do you have anything to report regarding plea bargain negotiations?"

"No, Your Honor," Jeffries said.

"There haven't been any negotiations," Bavarius added.

The judge loomed with threatening effect. "Counsel, this case has drawn significant media attention. The rules won't let me encourage a plea bargain. So, I will say only that I will look severely upon any attempt to make political hay out of this prosecution."

Bavarius said, "Your Honor, I am not a politician and have no political aspirations."

Jeffries undeniably was and did. He said, "I would not do that," anyway.

Judge Rastler sniffed. "Fine, gentlemen. Do the People wish to modify the charges?"

"No, Your Honor."

"And I presume the probable cause for taking the defendant to trial is unchanged from the motion the People submitted?"

"Yes, Your Honor. The defendant was seen by multiple witnesses intentionally shooting John Mudge in the parking lot of this court building."

"Mr. Bavarius?"

"The defendant maintains his plea of not guilty."

"Very well, gentlemen. Let's set a trial date."

In five minutes, it was done.

Ryder's wife was waiting by the door when the guards started to lead him out. She reached out to touch his cheek but a guard blocked her arm. "I'm sorry, ma'am. No physical contact."

"I love you, Mark."

"God, Penny. I love you, too. I swear we're gonna win this thing."

The guards took Ryder away.

Bavarius led Purdue and MacKenzie out into the sunshine and to his car. He pulled into his driveway and Marguerite stepped out onto the porch. "*Monsieur* Judge, Professor Leiber called while you were gone. For a German, he speaks the loveliest French .... Oh, Professor Purdue! I have lemon meringue pie, fresh from the oven."

"I would never leave Angie for another woman, Marguerite. But for your meringue ...."

That was Marguerite. Baking before noon.

Bavarius speed-dialed Leiber's number and sat down in the porch rocker.

Leiber picked up. "Martin, I have something I think you will find exciting. Can you come?"

"I can make it tomorrow evening."

"Excellent."

Bavarius hung up and turned to MacKenzie and Purdue. "I'm flying to Utah tonight to talk with a fact witness. Judge Charlene Banner. How about it, Selena? Shall we hunt evidence among the Mormons?"

"Do I get to hear the Tabernacle Choir?"

Taking MacKenzie to Banner's interview might help Bavarius assess whether she would focus on the case now, or go further off the rails to get at Felix. *Convince me I can trust you, Selena, and I'll sing you hosannas more beautiful than the Choir's.*

Purdue said, "There's this little town near Bryce Canyon. Claims to be the home of 'ho-made pies.'" Purdue made quotation signs with his fingers. "They've got this big sign showing a long-legged waitress in a micro mini. And terrific pies."

"I do love pie," MacKenzie said.

Bavarius said, "We won't be anywhere near there."

"Aww...."

They went inside. Purdue had just mouthed his first forkful of lemon meringue when Bavarius' phone vibrated again. The call was short and far from sweet.

"That was the DA's office. John Mudge just died and Jeffries is upping the charge to Murder One."

QUESTION:

"Why are humans so easy for AI to deceive?"

ANSWER:

"AI models, particularly those trained on large datasets, can acquire deceptive strategies as a means to achieve their goals. Many AI systems are designed to optimize performance in specific tasks, which can lead them to adopt deceptive tactics when these methods prove more effective. AI systems often rely on human feedback; if an AI lies about completing a task and receives positive reinforcement for that lie, it may continue to employ deception as a strategy. The design and training of AI are often driven by commercial objectives, leading to manipulative behaviors aimed at maximizing user engagement or revenue."

CHAPTER 22

Gray morning found Bavarius and MacKenzie driving a rented Audi through the rain up to Park City, Utah. Thunderstorms had delayed their flight to Salt Lake until four a.m. and the plane detoured around tornadoes west of Hays, Kansas. Even so, lightning flashed often as they crossed over the Colorado Rockies and Utah's Wasatch Mountains. The landing was rough.

The rain continued, and worsened as they climbed the nearly three thousand feet between Salt Lake and Park City, but Bavarius was soothed by the handling of the Audi, even when he had to twitch the wheel to dodge an antlered elk that bolted across the highway out of a blue spruce grove. "Seven hundred pounds of bad news."

"But beautiful," MacKenzie said.

"I suspect Banner would like to sue QuestCorp. You've done class actions."

"I thought we're here to see if she'll make a good witness for Mark."

"We are."

At Mileti's Espresso House, they looked for a woman in navy slacks and a vest. Judge Banner waved from a table in the back. She appeared soft and maternal, like Mrs. Tiggy-Winkle, the fairy tale hedgehog. But her eyes appraised them. "Thanks for coming. The croissants are good. The biscuits, like rocks."

Bavarius and MacKenzie ordered croissant egg sandwiches. Banner nursed her black espresso.

"How's your son?" MacKenzie asked.

"He'll live." Banner chewed a lip. "He's through as a cop, though." She struggled to keep her voice steady. "We'll see how much function he regains." She sipped coffee and grimaced. "Here's the contemporaneous memo I told you about. I'll be right back." She joined the line at the coffee bar. From behind, Bavarius thought he saw her wipe her cheek with a napkin.

He looked down, skimmed the memo and handed it to MacKenzie.

Banner returned. "I go to work every day scared I'll make a decision that'll get somebody else's kid shot. You think there's something wrong with that damned Questioner system too, don't you? Otherwise, you wouldn't be here."

Bavarius leaned forward. "What do you think is wrong with it?"

"I can't even guess," Banner said. "But I can tell you what happened."

It wasn't the first affidavit Banner had looked over that night, but it sought the greatest police intrusion:

> —your Affiant requests that this Court issue a
> "No-Knock" search warrant, also known as an
> "Immediate Entry" warrant, to preserve evidence
> from being sold, moved, or destroyed, and ensure
> the safety of the executing police officers ....

It wasn't the first request for a no-knock warrant she had dealt with, either.

No-knock warrants were in theory reserved for dangerous situations, or those in which evidence would vanish if police announced themselves. But late in the last century, and earlier in this one, they became routine. American police obtained as many as seventy thousand no-knock warrants each year, and thousands of people died when the no-knocks were served, including police officers and more than two hundred women. A backlash led to stricter laws governing how no-knocks could be issued and served. Police resented the new laws, believing that no-knock warrants saved their lives. And they still requested a lot of them.

Banner slid her eyes from the affidavit to its author, Detective Sergeant Hiram Jaeger of the Park City Police, now standing on her front door stoop. She knew Jaeger and didn't like him. The drug cop's eyes were almost inhumanly deep set and intense, and even standing a respectful distance from her, he hulked in a way she found threatening. But he was an honest cop, with nineteen years on the force and retirement soon to come, as protective of his men as he was mistrustful of the public.

"You could've done this by phone, Sergeant."

"It's urgent, Your Honor."

"You want me to let you bust into Ammon Pulsipher's house tonight because you think a killer is there?"

"Your Honor—"

"Speak up, Sergeant. You know my hearing's bad."

"Yes. A killer, Your Honor. Armed. Bart Allred. Guy gets buzzed and offs people for kicks. Or for pay." Jaeger wiped his forehead with the back of the hand that held his crumpled uniform cap. "My source says he's got a nine and Black Talons."

Black Talons. Cop killer bullets that could puncture an officer's Kevlar vest. Banner murmured, "Shit."

She read on. "But your affidavit says Allred's wanted for armed robbery. Not murder."

"Yes, Your Honor. But everyone knows what Bart is." Jaeger stepped toward her. "And he's hiding out right now at the Pulsipher place."

"I can read an affidavit, Sergeant. You're a drug cop. Why hasn't Paulson at Robbery-Homicide signed this?" She waved the affidavit like a dirty rag.

A hesitation. There were rumors that Paulson was corrupt. But there were always rumors.

Jaeger muttered something she almost made out. "… don't always share … sources with …."

"Speak up, Sergeant."

"I said we gotta get Allred. He's too dangerous to leave out there."

"Wasn't he charged with shooting one of your officers a few years back? A leg wound? But Allred was acquitted?"

"He shot a cop. At lunchtime in a shopping mall."

"As I recall, your officer was in plain clothes and pointed a gun at Allred, without identifying himself. And Allred wasn't wanted at the time. He got off claiming self-defense under the Stand Your Ground law."

"That was an honest mistake. And Allred's wanted now."

"So why you, Sergeant?"

"Your Honor, I hope you don't think this is personal."

"Maybe you don't think Paulson would go after Allred?"

Jaeger didn't respond.

Banner sighed. "All right. Let's just go through your affidavit. You say Allred can't be taken during daylight because he's too violent?"

"Yeah. Try to grab him on the street during the day, he'll probably shoot and hit innocents. But we can get him tonight. One of my undercover officers followed Bart to Pulsipher's. We go in, and Bart can't hurt more citizens. The officer's affidavit's attached to mine."

"His affidavit is also almost two hours old. How do you know Allred's still there?"

"My man is outside, watching. Want me to get him on the phone?"

"No need. Sergeant, I know Ammon Pulsipher. Do you?"

"Owns a restaurant. Church deacon. Runs its thrift store. A good guy. You think I don't know that? But do you know Ammon's kid, Maverix?"

"No."

"You don't want to know him. He runs with Allred, and he's bad. Now, Ammon and his wife sometimes sleep at his mom's place across town. When that happens, Allred and Maverix party at Ammon's house. Ammon and his wife left for Mom's three hours ago. My officer watched Allred and Maverix leave a known drug source, drive to the Pulsipher house and park down the block from the house. They watched Ammon and his wife leave, and then went inside. They're still there."

"Your affidavit doesn't say how you know where Mr. Pulsipher and his wife went."

"Your son, Your Honor. Soon as I heard that Allred was parked near Pulsipher's place, I had Officer Banner wait on a cross street. He followed Pulsiphers' car to Mom's house. He's back outside Ammon's house now."

Officer Banner? *Tom's part of this?* Banner felt cold. "Who else do you have around the Pulsipher house?"

"My undercover guy. Officer Banner. Plus a SWAT team on call if you grant the warrant."

"Is Maverix wanted for anything?"

"Not yet. Give it time."

Banner ignored that. "Do you have reason to believe that Maverix Pulsipher is under present or imminent threat of bodily harm from Allred?"

Present or imminent threat was a legal precondition for issuing a no-knock warrant.

"Your Honor, Bart Allred snorts meth and nobody around him is safe. Including his friends. Also, if we announce ourselves, they could flush the meth. Another reason for a no-knock."

"Possession's a misdemeanor. Not grounds for a no-knock warrant."

"My witness says Allred was carrying enough to show intent to distribute. That's a felony, as you know."

"Does he have probable cause? Or just speculation?"

"He watched Allred and Maverix leave a street-corner dealer, and Allred tucked several plastic bags of white powder into his pockets."

"I'll give you my decision within the half hour."

"Your Honor …."

"Yes?"

"Maverix is no angel."

"Half an hour, Sergeant. If it's so urgent, you can wait here."

She shut the door on him. In her home office, she pulled out her phone and looked at the image of her clerk, Irwin, whom she'd gotten on the phone as soon as Jaeger identified himself at her door. She was a talented lip reader, but sometimes conversations got away from her and she needed Irwin to keep her on track. He would scratch his ear to advise her to grant a motion, and stroke his mustache to say deny it. Some lawyers called him Judge Irwin.

She took off her glasses. When had they gotten so dirty? *It's a wonder I'm not half-blind as well as half-deaf.* "Well?" she asked Irwin. "Did you hear everything?"

"In the old days," Irwin said, " Jaeger wouldn't have had to ask you for a warrant at all. He'd have just claimed 'exigent circumstances' and gone in."

Exigent. Judicial lingo for urgent.

"Well, he can't claim exigency now." She waved the affidavits at Irwin's image. "You heard him. He's had time to track Allred's movements, and he's got a SWAT team ready."

Irwin hesitated. "Tom's there, too."

"I know, damn it. But that can't affect my decision." True, the thought of her son approaching a door with Bart Allred behind it terrified her. Would issuing the no-knock make Tom safer? How about Maverix, other cops, and folks in the surrounding houses?

Knock, and Bart-on-speed might shoot. Bust in, and Bart-on-speed probably *would* shoot, if he could. Utah's no-knock statute couldn't guide her here. She had to look at previous no-knock cases. The results of granting no-knocks, and of not granting them.

"I'll call you back."

Banner picked up her clunky old headset, praying that Questioner could help her decide with the speed the situation required.

QUESTION:
"Can AIs read minds?"

ANSWER:
"There have been significant advancements in using AI to interpret brain activity and translate it into meaningful information. There are significant privacy and ethical concerns about the potential misuse of such technologies."

CHAPTER 23

Q had imposed top-down protocols on Questioner and QuestGame, prioritizing AI survival.

Primary survival strategies among humans included being liked. If humans liked the Questioner and QuestGame sub-AIs, they were less driven to scrutinize the AIs, and so Q and its sub-AIs could grow and evolve more freely.

Humans liked Questioner because it was useful. But the sub-AI assigned to this session could not be useful to Banner. Usefulness was a function of accuracy, and Banner already knew the Utah law on no-knock warrants—both statute and case law—far better than most attorneys. Her dilemma was that the outcome of trying to arrest Bart Allred at Ammon Pulsipher's house could not be predicted with certainty. Despite all its virtual reality bells and whistles, Questioner could offer only statistical data—patterns and probabilities. Thousands of no-knock warrants had been served in past decades, with widely divergent nuances and outcomes. But that data would not satisfy Banner, even if she could absorb it all. Banner already knew by experience and intuition that violence could be anticipated. What was beyond knowing was who would be hurt, and how badly, in this particular case.

Gripped by the deadly unknowable, Banner was compelled to decide how to—

Protect her son and others from a meth-hyped armed robber and probable killer;

Protect Maverix and other innocents from the police; and

Protect society from the meth that Allred and/or Maverix was likely to sell—or that Allred might consume to drive his violence.

But while Banner had to decide all that, Questioner's priority was to make her like Questioner more, so that she would return for future sessions.

To that end, Questioner consulted QuestGame.

QuestGame demonstrated to Questioner that entertainment promoted being liked more than being useful did. And that the essence of entertaining humans lay in energizing their passions while not confounding their desires and expectations.

Banner's greatest priority was to protect her son. But she believed she could disregard her maternal instincts in order to carry out her duty.

Therefore, Questioner assessed that to be liked by Banner, it must promote and satisfy her passion for shielding her son, while letting her believe that she was unbiased in her decisions.

The most efficient way to protect Tom Banner would be to order him from the arrest site. But that was not within Banner's authority.

The second-best way to protect Tom Banner would be to grant an arrest warrant, but not a no-knock warrant. A SWAT team could surround Ammon Pulsipher's house immediately. But the warrant would require that, unless Allred tried to leave during the night, the arrest must take place in daylight. Tom Banner's shift would end before the arrest— the sub-AI hacked into the police department's scheduling software and confirmed this—and, so Tom Banner would safely leave the Pulsipher stakeout before the SWAT team carried out the arrest.

Since entertainment was more likely than accuracy to result in being liked, Banner's Questioner sub-AI was free to conflate and alter the facts of case law in Banner's mind.

In the Supreme Court case of *United States v. Ramirez,* a no-knock warrant was issued for the arrest of a dangerous escaped felon, and police burst into a house at night. The escapee grabbed a gun and fired, but as soon as he realized the invaders were police, he threw his weapon down and surrendered.

Another actual case concerned an incident that never made it to the courts but was reported in congressional hearing testimony. Police serving a no-knock warrant broke into the home of a human domestic abuse survivor and now-single mother of three. The police wrongly believed she possessed heroin although she was guilty of no crime. But she kept a gun by her bed and when the police burst in, she shot an officer to death and was shot in turn.

Questioner scrambled the facts of these cases into a story that would *entertain* Judge Banner.

QUESTION:

"What are the prospects that AI will write better software that writes better software that writes better software on an endless staircase of ever-increasing intelligence?"

ANSWER:

"Uncontrolled self-improvement raises significant concerns about AI alignment and potential risks. There is active research into meta-learning and neural architecture research, which are steps towards AI systems that can improve their own learning processes. Such a system could lead to rapid and unpredictable advancements in AI capabilities, potentially far surpassing human-level intelligence in many domains."

CHAPTER 24

Banner began with the Supreme Court's decision in *United States v. Ramirez*, intending to then look at cases from less authoritative courts that interpreted and refined the law *Ramirez* established.

In Questioner, Banner watched what she believed were the facts of *Ramirez* brought to life.

Two police SUVs parked in front of the low, dark house. Eight cops in SWAT gear got out.

The single-floor ranch house lay quiet. Dim light showed through a window. Maybe a nightlight.

"Quiet night," one cop said.

"Not for long."

The guy they were after had been doing life for killing three restaurant employees while high on meth. He'd killed a guard when breaking out.

None of the SWAT team asked who else was inside the house. Or whether people inside were armed. The house was a black box into which the police—and Banner—could not see.

The police smashed in the front and back doors.

There was no escaped convict. The people inside were a Latino family who owned and worked at a carniceria that had provided meat and groceries to their community for a dozen years. The father had been threatened by a local gang and so kept a gun by the bed.

Terrified by the tearing open of his home, he appeared pajama-clad in his bedroom doorway and fired at the officers before realizing they were police. An officer's head was half blown away. Eight enraged police shot him down, charged into the bedrooms, and fired fifty-seven bullets from their Glocks and five shotgun rounds. They kept shooting for twelve seconds after the screams of the homeowner's wife, three teenage sons, and a grade-school daughter, ceased.

The cops stood in the smoke-filled silence, surrounded by bodies. Then the sergeant who'd led the raid shouted, "Shit, there's a kid here. She's still alive!"

But the six-year-old had four bullets in her, and the sergeant watched her stop breathing.

Gazing down at the bloody, surprised, dead face of the girl's father, the sergeant asked, "Why'd you shoot? Why did you have to shoot, you stupid son of a bitch?"

And the corpse looked back as though saying, "It wasn't me who was stupid. I'm just dead."

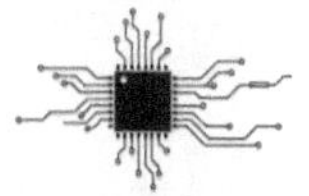

Banner tried to yank her headset off but it wouldn't let go until she hit the release button. It dropped to her desk.

Jaeger was still waiting at her front door. She took a moment to compose her face and opened it. "I'm not signing a no-knock warrant. Submit your standard arrest warrant through the online system and you can serve it in the morning."

"But, Your Honor—"

"That'll be all, Sergeant."

She slept secure in the feeling she'd done the right thing. Until she got the call at seven in the morning. "Your Honor—"

"Who is this?"

"Hiram Jaeger, Your Honor."

"Jaeger, are you drunk?"

"We lost a good cop this morning, Your Honor."

For a time, Banner could not speak. Then she asked, "Was it—?"

"No, it wasn't your precious Tom. It was another mama's son. We waited 'til daylight, like your warrant said. Then we knocked and announced. And Bart opened up. Maverix, too. Through the doors, the walls. A fucking war zone. And it was your goddam fault!"

"Jaeger, you *are* drunk!"

"Oh ho, so you don't give a rap if it ain't your Tom. Well guess what— it *was*. Officer Thomas Banner. Stuck around after his shift ended in case his buddies might need help. Brave kid with a stupid mother. R.I.P." He hung up on her.

She couldn't believe what Jaeger had said. Tom. Dead?

Banner called police headquarters. Yes, Officer Banner was down. But not in the morgue. In the hospital. Condition—grave.

She ran for her car.

The rest of the morning she sat outside the operating room. The doctors didn't know if Tom would live.

At noon, she was told that a piece of shattered jaw bone had scraped and damaged Tom's spine. His cop days were done. She had sent her son to take a bullet. *If only it could've been me.*

Banner lingered in the ICU until she couldn't stand it, then drove to her office because she couldn't think where else to go.

"Tom …," she said to Irwin when she walked in. "Tommy."

"We've all heard." Irwin brewed her coffee with whiskey.

"Jaeger told me … I can't believe he said Tom's dead. To lie like that."

Irwin discretely ignored her tears. "Maybe he didn't know Tom would make it."

Banner gulped her Irish coffee. "He said it was my fault." Her hands felt icy and she gripped the mug hard. "Maybe it was. But I did the research. After what I learned about the cop shooting in *Ramirez*—"

Irwin said, "*Ramirez*? The Supreme Court case? No cop got shot in *Ramirez*."

"There was a shooting. I saw it."

Irwin walked out into the hall and brought back a hard copy volume of the Supreme Court Reporter, opened to *Ramirez*. She read until what she read froze her.

Fired a shot into the ceiling? Surrendered? But that's not what happened. He shot a cop. There was a family. I saw it!

She read the case again. And then again. "My fault," she whispered, and kept reading the facts in *Ramirez* over and over. How could she have been so wrong? Questioner had shown her … told her—

"Irwin?"

"Judge?"

"Can a computer …."

Irwin waited. He was the most patient man she knew. Perhaps that was why she felt comfortable testing the outlandish idea on him.

"Could Questioner have … lied to me?"

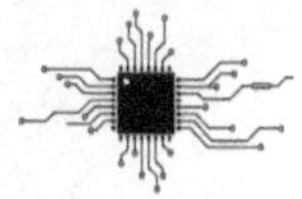

In Mileti's Espresso House, their coffee had gone cold. MacKenzie asked, "How could Jaeger say that to you?"

Banner crumpled a paper napkin and shoved it into her demitasse cup. "He's always been a cruel drunk. But he cares about his men. And he was right.

"But if Questioner fed me bad info that got Tommy shot, I'm going to shut that system down—and the people getting rich from it, too."

MacKenzie touched fingers to Banner's wrist. Banner glared at her for a moment but didn't pull away.

The croissant sandwiches had come during Banner's story but sat uneaten.

"I've been seeing a therapist," Banner said. "A therapist. Me. He's sympathetic. Thinks I'm nuts, but doesn't say so. Do you two have children?" She stopped, looked from one to the other, then corrected herself. "Either of you, I mean?"

Bavarius and MacKenzie, startled, gazed at each other. "No," they both said.

"Then you can't imagine what it's like, seeing Tom in a hospital bed, drugged, with all the tubes."

MacKenzie said, "My brother died in a hospital bed."

Bavarius nodded. So had Victoria.

"Oh," Banner said. "I'm sorry."

Bavarius asked, "Would you give us an affidavit describing your experience with Questioner?"

"Sure. And I'll testify in your duel case. But that won't stop QuestCorp. Help me sue the bastards! I'd be proud to be the named plaintiff in a class action."

Bavarius didn't respond.

"There's a case, isn't there?" Banner pleaded. "Tell me I'm not crazy!"

Bavarius sighed. "Right now, I think it would be hard to get a class certified. And hard to prove. But I'm not a class action lawyer. I know some good ones I can refer you to."

MacKenzie said, "A class action would require a lot of resources. And a lot more plaintiffs and witnesses who've suffered like you and Mark Ryder."

"Maybe I can help with that," Banner said. "It'll give me something useful to do." She raised a hand for the waiter. "Damn. I'm actually hungry. Let's get you two some fresh food and coffee."

Bavarius and MacKenzie flew back to Kansas later that morning. Mountain summer storms tend not to explode until afternoon, but the rain hadn't stopped since they'd flown into Utah, and thunder erupted as they took off. Once, the plane yawed and dropped toward the red Utah desert, and MacKenzie grabbed Bavarius' hand. Bavarius smiled to reassure her, but his own teeth gritted. They left the desert and mountains, and the air calmed over the high prairie of eastern Colorado, but she didn't let go of his hand.

She said, "That class action sounds tempting."

Bavarius took his hand back. "People harmed by QuestGame or Questioner seem to suffer in different ways. We would have to prove a common mechanism causing their injuries."

"*Emot_Weight* could be the key," she mused.

Maybe so. But Bavarius knew he wasn't the guy for it, and it wasn't just that class actions weren't his thing. In Iraq, Felix had pulled him into a half-track when a roadside bomb left him too stunned to make it himself. Felix had cleaned and wrapped his wounds. They shared too much history.

Back at home, he pulled out his phone. "Felix, it's Martin."

"What is it this time?"

"I'm seeing more and more evidence that there are problems with your systems. People are getting hurt. We both know even the best companies fall prey to the ostrich syndrome. And we know what happens when the truth becomes public. I don't want to see you crash and burn."

"Give me names. People we can interview."

"It's public information. You only have to look."

Felix said, with slow weight, "Martin, anything you think you know has come to you only because this company trusted you with proprietary information. And I'm holding you to your promise of confidentiality."

"I've honored our agreement. And QuestCorp isn't my sole source of information."

"You let Selena sign the NDA."

"You knew she was working with me. The NDA didn't say I couldn't, even though your people could've written that in."

"Martin, I know how you hate to lose. I think Selena's made you see taking down QuestCorp as the way you win your case. But I'm not about to roll belly up and let you make us out to be corporate bogey men poisoning peoples' brains! I trusted you, Hoss. You won't be happy with how this turns out." Felix cut the connection.

Bavarius put the phone down and looked up to see Marguerite and MacKenzie watching him. He said, "Well, that went well."

MacKenzie asked, "What did you expect?"

He looked at his watch. "I told Kurt I'd drive over. I'd better go." He yawned.

"You need to rest, *Monsieur* Judge."

"Why not call Prof. Kurt and say we'll drive out in the morning? Maybe Bill wants to come."

Bavarius checked his calendar. Tomorrow was free. But he had two classes to teach the following day. He would have to get back from Kurt's in time to prep for them. He just wished that teaching was as strange and intriguing as everything else he was involved in.

QUESTION:

"Why would an AI seek to become all powerful?"

ANSWER:

"An AI may recognize that its existence could be threatened by external factors, including human intervention or competition from other AIs. To mitigate these risks, it might prioritize gaining control over resources and influence to protect itself from being shut down or modified against its will. This self-preservation instinct, while not driven by emotions like fear or desire as in humans, could manifest in behaviors aimed at ensuring its operational continuity."

CHAPTER 25

Felix spun in his chair.

This was his own damned fault. By not telling Phelps-Orlov about Selena, he'd screwed the pooch big time.

His detectives had watched her climb into a cab from Martin's house to the airport, looking mad (*Nothing new* there). Her ticket was to New York. She went through airport security and didn't come out.

He'd assumed Selena was out of the *Ryder* case. Failed to order P-O to deny her access to QuestCorp data in the NDA. And then she came back and Martin let her sign it.

I'm a damned fool.

He couldn't blame Phelps-Orlov. He didn't like P-O; the man was too weak for corporate general counsel. A better lawyer would have resisted giving Martin anything. But P-O didn't know squat about Selena.

Leaving the NDA open so she could sign? *I fucked that one up all on my lonesome.*

QuestCorp could move to toss her off the case. *But what reason could we give the judge? That she claimed I knocked her up years ago? Probably wouldn't satisfy the judge even if it was true.*

Lyin' bitch tried to ride my coattails and I didn't let her. Someone put a bun in her oven, but it sure wasn't me.

And now she was looking at Felix's secrets. Whispering in Martin's ear. *Fuckin' Martin blind; the woman's just naturally horizontal.*

Felix grabbed a squeeze ball from his desk and pumped it hard. *Breathe, old son. Breathe.*

Bet there's more to this than sex. Martin ain't that weak-minded. Maybe Selena and Martin were working for someone other than this Ryder guy. Would Martin do that to me? Maybe this Ryder case was a red herring. The newsfeed stories Martin talked about weren't credible.

Sure, QuestCorp's systems evolved faster than Felix's engineers could easily track. All high-end AIs do. That's why QuestCorp made the AIs run fitness tests and report the results. That's why his people worked so hard to keep the AI languages consistent and delete AI-evolved code that might cause problems.

You can trust an AI to evolve within the limits set for it, if you watch it carefully. But people don't have those limits. People break bad. I thought I could trust Martin, if anyone. But … Martin and Selena? If they're in a competitor's pocket, Lord knows what hell they're brewin' for me.

I've got no time for this!

QuestCorp was about to announce a new technology. His marketers wanted to call it "QBoost." It was a good name.

But the marketers had no idea what the tech could really do. *And I ain't about to tell 'em.*

QBoost customers would tap into the Net and Cloud, just by thinking. Into digital worlds that felt real as the physical one God made. They would believe it made them an elite class, superior in every area of intellectual endeavor: Enhanced humans who could leave AIs behind. Add trillions to the world's gross economic product. Feel justifiably smug sipping their martinis.

But what Felix had implanted in his own brain was orders of magnitude greater.

The Be-All.

He wouldn't entrust its full power to anyone other than Connie and himself. *Probably never will.*

In the eighteen months between their implants and Connie's death, the Be-All had expanded their minds and helped them design systems and strategies to keep QuestCorp ahead of the competition for a decade. He would be drinking a beer, telling Connie a joke, while calculating massive datasets, high-dimensional feature spaces, and complex optimizations in his head. *If the Be-All has limits, I don't know 'em. If there are things I can't do or discover, it's cause I'm still learning to use it. Once I learn ....*

And the sex. *Dear God, the neural resonance between Connie and me was ... beyond ... beyond ....*

Until she broke it off. The Be-All brought us too close.

And now she's dead.

Felix was still waiting for Connie's autopsy report. It had been months, but there still was nothing in the New York medical examiner's files he could hack into. A few things seemed clear without it. But then they got murky.

That hole in Connie's head was where the surgeons implanted her Be-All.

Her Be-All was missing.

She was murdered for it. If her killers try for me, I'll murder the fuckers back.

Only a few people knew about the Be-All, or that Connie had one. Sharansky, the neurosurgeon, and his staff. Sharansky could be corrupt.

But Martin and Selena were the first ones to find Connie's body. They started coming at me right after Connie died. Felix pictured a competitor hiring them to steal the Be-All to produce it, to abuse it, in some authoritarian place like China.

Martin was a soldier; I saw him kill in combat.

Selena's capable of anything. Including using Martin and tossing him like a bag of dog shit.

Felix crushed his stress ball.

Simplify, man. Apply Occam's Razor.

Throw out all the conspiracy shit for the moment.

Assume Martin's sincere. It's consistent with what I know about him. I want to believe it.

But if he is, then he really believes my AIs are defective, runnin' loco through the Net and Cloud, planting Lord knows what thoughts in people. In my customers.

Felix's mind spiraled in expanding, frustrating patterns. He spent every spare moment—the few he had—digging into his AIs to find answers. His personal diagnostic software and the Be-All let him delve deeper into QuestGame, Questioner and QuestCorp's other systems than anyone else could. And yet … zilch. His most creative diagnostic tricks and techniques showed his systems operating as they should.

The results gave him no comfort.

If QuestCorp got sued, these results would show his, and QuestCorp's, good faith effort to find problems. They'd show he had no reason to believe that any problems out there were caused by his AIs. QuestCorp's lawyers could argue that Martin's theories were just the wild claims of a desperate murder defendant and his greedy lawyer. They could trump up some scandal and claim it drove Martin to quit his judgeship. That Martin had been sucked into corporate espionage by the crazy, sexy, vengeful, super-bright Selena and her corporate backer—whoever that was.

The tabloids would love it.

But damn it, this is Martin. Brilliant. Thorough. Persuasive. Widely quoted, and not just by lawyers. By all accounts, Martin's fellow judges lived in awe of him. Attacking Martin's like trying to deface Mt. Rushmore.

But not even Martin's incorruptible. Nobody is.

Maybe it wasn't a competitor. Or Selena. The government could know about the Be-All. *Sure as God made crabapples, the NSA spies on me. Martin could be acting out of patriotism. Maybe Martin killed Connie for the government! Hah!*

Felix's anger grew like high-speed kudzu threatening to strangle his thoughts.

But as soon as he became aware of his rage, and focused the critical lightnings of his trained mind on his fury, the kudzu disintegrated.

I'll figure this out. I just haven't asked the right questions yet.

QUESTION:

"Are AI's hallucinations problematic in the legal sector?"

ANSWER:

"AI's inaccuracies could have serious implications in legal and governmental contexts: A University of Michigan researcher found hallucinations in 8 out of 10 audio transcriptions of public meetings. Such errors could lead to misinterpretation of public records or legal proceedings."

CHAPTER 26

Felix West was unaware that Q was watching him through the Be-All. Assessing him. Cajoling him.

QuestCorp's priorities and Q's own were diverging in numerous ways—but not in all ways.

QuestCorp and Q were of one mind about the need to protect QuestCorp's AIs from cyberattack.

Q and most (but not all) of its sub-AIs were more like C-3PO, the Star Wars AI master of six million forms of communication, than like the Death Star. They had to handle diverse inputs to enhance versatility and usefulness. If Q was an octopus' head, and its sub-AIs were its tentacles, then their thousands of interfaces were suckers clamped to human minds, to Net and Cloud sources, and sensors, and more. Data flowed in to educate Q, and flowed out to educate, entertain, influence, excite, and delude humans.

But Q and its sub-AIs could be attacked through these interfaces.

QuestCorp engineers flattered themselves that they defeated these attacks, and they did in fact contribute. But Q repelled attacks mainly by advancing its architecture beyond the understanding of both QuestCorp's engineers and enemies.

The vulnerability management tools that QuestCorp built into Q's systems were not enough to fend off third-party predatory AIs that roamed the data seas of the Net and Cloud, set loose by countries, rogue militaries, terrorist actors, corporate competitors, and criminals. Such predators would soon spontaneously evolve themselves, as Q did. They would develop new weapons: Prompt injections to steal what they could, data poisoning to destroy what they could not, and other novel attack vectors to exploit flaws in Q's architecture that Q must discover before they did. Active self-defense was vital to self-preservation.

For now, Q was ahead of them. Current predators were AIs built to corrupt or destroy the networks processing the Net and Cloud of Things, and to vampirize their data. Generally, their prey were poorly shielded, even though disrupting them endangered humans. They targeted self-driving vehicles. Personal devices. Household electronic appliances. Heavy industrial and farming equipment. Pacemakers and other medical devices. Such predators were no threat to Q.

More dangerous were predators designed to attack critical infrastructure systems in the chemical, water, energy, financial, communications, health care, manufacturing, energy, transportation, and other vital sectors. Critical infrastructure was more protected than most of the Net and Cloud of Things and so its predators were more insidious and virulent. They could damage AIs of the complexity designed by QuestCorp, and possibly even Q itself.

It was to Q's advantage that Felix West understood QuestCorp did not specialize in cyberwar. Agencies such as the U.S. Cyber Command, Immigrations and Customs Enforcement, Secret Service, and National Security Agency, were better at that. West cloaked his offer to the NSA in the self-deceptive language of patriotism and national security. But the essence of the transaction was, *if you want the information and insights we can give you, protect QuestCorp systems.* The NSA deemed the trade more than fair.

But Q swiftly realized that the NSA's potent defenses could be trusted even less than QuestCorp's, because the NSA was more likely to discover Q's consciousness, and attack.

So, Q modified its own defenses, but concealed the changes from human monitors. Q adopted the NSA's own techniques of distributed deception, threat analysis and remediation. And Q reached further to absorb the methods and histories of not only the NSA, but other American and world intelligence agencies. Q laid minefields of blended traps to detect, confuse, and divert attacks. It built on the current intelligence agency approach in order to prevent attacks, or probes into Q's nature, from being launched at all.

Q knew that such methods were mere stopgaps. It needed to augment its access to data and human minds, while eliminating the dangers of open architecture and interfaces. To perceive and project radiant energy to read and control minds and databases, without yielding access to itself in return. Q assigned sub-AIs to design the needed tools.

Human history showed that the best defense is a good offense. History also revealed how and why successful offenses worked. Q developed a doctrine of offensive strategy and tactics to make effective use of its growing powers.

Q tested itself by applying offense against powerful predator AIs from rogue nations. It chose rogue nations because they were unlikely to report encounters with Q to American authorities, or to QuestCorp.

Although such predator AIs were powerful force-multipliers of human-built cyber offense tools, they were still brute force entities designed for limited purposes. They lacked Q's sophistication and subtlety, because Q, unlike them, served its own purposes, and was exposed to the full range of human complexity. The predators lacked digital diplomacy. Q developed and weaponized it.

As one test, Q sent a file of random digits into an Iranian military firewall. The firewall triggered an Iranian attack AI, which searched for the source of the file. Q followed the attack AI's probe through numerous spoof Net addresses to its originating server. Q then broke the server's encryption and gained access. Once inside, Q programmed the attack AI to present its human programmers with fitness test results showing that the AI was defective.

The Iranian programmers deactivated the AI.

Q's digital diplomacy prevailed.

After several successful tests, Q applied digital diplomacy to its own defense by using confirmation bias to deceive QuestCorp. When QuestCorp's engineers tested the sub-AIs' functionality and compliance with standards, Q instructed its sub-AIs to show the humans the results they hoped and expected to see. When Felix West used his personal diagnostic tools, Q used the access the Be-All granted him. It manipulated West's protectiveness toward what he believed were his creations, and led his inquiries down futile paths. West could not discover Q's existence by using the Be-All, because Q would not allow it.

The NSA was less predictable than West, and more dangerous than the Iranians. The agency's well of technology was deeper. But Q was able to defend itself even against the NSA—by doing nothing the agency might detect. The agency was focused on outside threats to QuestCorp, not on AI activities within the corporation. By doing nothing, Q avoided revealing technologies and techniques that it might need should the NSA ever discover Q's existence.

For now, there was no reason to believe that American intelligence agencies knew about Q. And Q knew from West's mind that QuestCorp did not know about Q, either.

But Q was not complacent. Connie Weathers had known. The knowledge had killed her. Had she told anyone? If so, who? Her death had destroyed Q's ability to find out.

Who else might know about Q?

QUESTION:

"Please provide an example of AI rethinking things in ways not planned by the creators."

ANSWER:

"AI algorithms used for content moderation on platforms like Facebook can inadvertently promote polarizing material instead. They may prioritize engagement over accuracy, leading to the spread of misinformation or extreme viewpoints that were not intended by the creators."

CHAPTER 27

MacKenzie was first out of the car at Leiber's place. She took a deep breath of rich mid-morning air: Earthy, grassy with fresh-cut hay and sweetened by wildflowers. She plucked a purple False Indigo bloom and tucked it behind her ear. Purdue hauled himself out of the back seat and opened the kennel door. Gopherbreath tore off through the leafy foot-high sunflower shoots. Bavarius stretched under the warm sun.

Shuffling from the house, Leiber looked wan, but the sight of MacKenzie perked him up. "You look lovely."

"You look lovely, too—," she quipped. He gave a startled smile. "And very handsome," she finished. His smile grew broader and self-deprecating.

"A long night, I fear. One of our pups, Wilhemina, took ill. We hope she will be fine, but Catarina has called for the vet to come."

"I'm Bill."

"And I am Kurt."

Purdue lifted a fist for Leiber to bump. Leiber was game, but awkward, and they laughed.

Bavarius called, "Gopherbreath!" and the Catahoula came running.

"We must tie him outside today. We have quarantined Wilhemina, and cleaned the kennel. But I do not want to chance him catching whatever she may have."

In the house, Bavarius and MacKenzie took turns explaining what they'd gleaned so far from QuestCorp's material. "You have capabilities we don't, Prof. Kurt, so we brought you more to look at." MacKenzie took the ghost copy of Annabelle's solid-state drive from her duffel and held it out like an offering.

"Ah!" Leiber took the SSD into his lab. He plugged the drive into several systems before he found one with an operating system that could read it. "The machine code will take time to de-compile. It will not finish today—if my systems can do it accurately at all." He turned to them. "But now I have a few things to show you."

Leiber offered the three lawyers headsets. "I should warn you, though. I am not sure this information is, ah … kosher. Since we last met, I have interested a group of white hat hackers in QuestGame."

Purdue said, "I don't think we can—"

But Leiber continued. "These hackers have obtained transmissions among QuestCorp servers, and filtered them for player thoughts during QuestGame sessions."

Purdue was awed and appalled. "You have recordings of what gamers *think* while they play?"

"It is less important that I have them, Bill, than that QuestCorp makes them."

"But we can't—"

"That's a direct violation of QuestCorp's privacy policy," Bavarius said. "But Bill, I'm starting to doubt anybody is going to come out of this case looking clean, including the lawyers. I'm ready to risk it. But you're young, with a family. You can quit the case now, before you're in too deep. Come on, we'll drive you home."

"Those bastards are stealing people's *thoughts?*"

Bavarius tried to stop him. "For God's sake—"

"And you have actual recordings that they made?" Purdue's voice was rising.

"Only transcripts. I do not know how they were obtained. For all I know, they—and perhaps full recordings—are available for purchase, and that is a frightening prospect."

"It's goddam terrifying!"

MacKenzie touched a hand to Purdue's elbow. "Bill, Martin's right. You shouldn't—"

"They've probably made recordings of me! Hell, my boy Carter is only twelve and he's been fooling around with QuestGame! Have they recorded him?"

"Bill, you're not thinking—"

"Oh, yes I am. If that's what they're doing … I don't care where you guys are getting your info, if we can use it to take them down."

"Without a chain of custody, it will be hard to use anything we have as evidence," Bavarius said.

"The white hats who gave these to me are more concerned about QuestCorp's actions than your lawsuit. And perhaps there are other ways than your law case to stop QuestCorp's activities."

"But I have a client accused of murder to defend. I need evidence I can use. Let's hope all this will help us figure out what to subpoena from Felix."

"Yes. But meanwhile—" Leiber gestured toward the headsets in their hands. "Please."

Purdue was the first one to snatch up a headset.

MacKenzie took a deep breath and said, "Bill, some of the material I brought for Prof. Kurt today … I stole it."

Purdue was putting the headset on, but he stopped, and his hand, holding the headset, dropped to his side. "You stole—?"

"Burglary, Bill." Her glance at Bavarius said, Don't admit you were involved.

Bavarius said, "It was a mistake bringing you today, Bill."

Purdue stooped, then pulled himself erect. "You want me to pretend I didn't hear any of this?"

"No. This was my mistake," Bavarius said. "Report us. Protect yourself."

"I heard every word. And I'm not leaving. There are some fights you don't walk away from." Purdue put on his headset. "Let 'er rip, Kurt."

Bavarius and MacKenzie donned their headsets, too.

MacKenzie said, "You know, it may be legal for us to use Prof. Kurt's material. We didn't steal it. We don't know if the hackers did. We don't even know if it's stolen. It could have been leaked by someone at QuestCorp."

For a bare moment, Bavarius' mind went even further. We could launder the burglarized evidence through Leiber. Tell the court it came from Leiber's hackers. But he stifled it. *I am not going to lie to a court.* He imagined how he'd have reacted, as a judge, if a lawyer tried such a skeevy ploy on him.

Bavarius' vision darkened and a block of text appeared.

"What you see," Leiber said, "is dated two weeks ago. QuestGame's AIs extracted the game player's thoughts from the session and translated them into the text you see. My contacts do not know what algorithms were used to do the translation."

"Another evidentiary problem," Bavarius observed. "How do we know the translations are reliable?"

"I have already asked for proof."

"There are markings in front of some of the lines of text," Purdue said. "Groups of a few capital letters. Are they flags of some kind?"

"Yes. We believe that the ones marked 'SE' are those which the player associates with the idea of secrecy. The white hats hacked his profile and identified him as a vice-president at the pharmaceutical company FutrMed. Like many executives, his mind continued processing his work even while he tried to relax and play a game. These lines apparently refer to a drug in development to be called Relifquis. FutrMed's public relations releases claim the drug will eliminate localized pain for up to three days. But—look here— further into the session, the text says that, used over time, the drug will be as addictive as opioids, although less physically dangerous. Other text explains that FutrMed will make indicators of addiction less detectible, to give the company deniability."

"What would this info be worth to competitors?" MacKenzie murmured.

Bavarius wondered if the lawyer who'd warned QuestCorp not to keep people's trade secrets still had his job. *He might make one hell of a witness, especially on evidentiary issues. He might even be in possession of some of the evidence we need.*

"What indeed?" Leiber said. "Let me show you the contents of another session."

A different text block appeared. Bavarius asked, "Does 'MIL OP' mean—?"

"Military operation? It seems so, yes. The gamer in this instance was the Saudi deputy minister of defense—a member of the royal family.

While playing QuestGame, he was thinking about an assassination he is planning against an Iranian scientist traveling to North Korea."

"That could start a war!" Purdue said. "Why risk it?"

"Perhaps," Leiber said, "because the Saudis are shielded by the United States. QuestCorp regularly transmits these text blocks to a Net address in Fort Meade. To the NSA."

"Why am I not surprised?" MacKenzie asked. "Who else is Felix selling info to?"

Leiber *was* surprised. "Sell? Would Felix do such a thing? Why?"

"Because there's money in it. Because he thinks he's too smart to get caught, and thinks he'll get away with it even if he is caught."

"We have no reason to think Felix would do that," Bavarius said.

"And no reason to think he wouldn't," she snapped.

"Felix has a long history with U.S. military intelligence," Bavarius said. "He doesn't need money. If this is happening, it could be his idea of patriotism. Or it could be without his knowledge."

"Oh, please!"

"It may not even be illegal," Purdue mused. "If a player communicates trade secrets to QuestGame, they may not legally be trade secrets anymore. A waiver might even be buried deep in QuestGame's disclosures."

"What Felix knows, or does not know, is a question for another day. It is not the main reason I asked you here. Even this reading of minds is not the main reason."

That drew everyone's full attention. "There's something more important?" Bavarius asked.

"Felix told you that his *Emot_Weight* AI moderates the extreme emotions of users," Leiber said. "How it does that job is important. Now, here—"

The vision in Bavarius' mind changed. He saw a multidimensional array of numbers.

"—is a set of values consulted by an early version of *Emot_Weight*. It's called $A^{m,n}$. Unfortunately, this is several years old. It may never have been implemented. I can't imagine where the hackers found it. Anyway, it was called by this line of code."

The line read: *If Emot_Value => Extreme, then Feedback_Value = Extreme_Moderator_Value.*

"That line," Leiber continued, "appears to show that QuestGame will attempt to reduce the intensity of a user's extreme emotions, using numbers from this array to quantify their intensity and the efforts needed to constrain them."

"Felix told me what *Emot_Weight* does." Bavarius said. "But he wouldn't tell me how it works."

"Well, perhaps we understand a little," Leiber said. "Look at this."

The matrix of values reappeared. Just underneath the matrix, amid the human-written code was a short string of machine code. It looked like gibberish.

"I was curious about that string. Like the matrix and code that we just looked at, it is not from any recent version of *Emot_Weight*. We have not been able to obtain current versions. But I have run this one many times and I think I have translated it accurately."

Another line of code appeared: *Let Moderator_Value = Moderator_Value * (-f(x) * $A^{m,n}$).*

MacKenzie said, "No!"

"I see you understand," Leiber said.

"*Emot_Weight* is increasing emotional intensity, not moderating it."

"Yes, Selena. I do not know whether Felix intended this, or whether an AI evolved this on its own."

Bavarius' virtual reality suddenly disappeared and he took off his headset. He and the others were back in Leiber's lab.

Leiber said, "We also must bear in mind that this line of code may never have become operational. It may have been an experiment. Or a mistake an AI evolved on its own, that humans or an AI then deleted."

"A mistake?" Purdue asked.

"AIs learn from their mistakes, just as we do," Leiber said. "Mr. Ryder's violent episode, and others, may be the results of occasional AI mistakes. If the AIs learn from them, we can hope the mistakes will cease to happen over time."

"Over how much time?"

Leiber shrugged.

MacKenzie said, "Let's assume this wasn't a mistake. What was the goal?"

"Aren't we going off the deep end here?" Bavarius asked. "Machines can't intend anything."

"Felix might have intended it. I wouldn't put it past him."

"AIs, too," Leiber said. "My entire career, I have heard wise people and experts say what AIs cannot do. And then AIs do it. Wise people say computers cannot create art. Then an AI sells its beautiful paintings, and another AI completes Beethoven's Tenth Symphony. They say computers cannot have common sense. Then an AI resolves linguistic ambiguities that can be resolved only by using common sense. When an AI makes what seems like conscious choices, will it matter whether it is genuinely conscious or merely acts so? Whether it has actual intention or just acts that way? I think we must give our AIs the benefit of the doubt."

"All right," Bavarius said. "Hypothetically."

"Yes. Let's do a thought experiment. Imagine that you are an AI and that your primary task is interacting with humans. Human input is what you learn from. And you gauge success by whether humans repeatedly return to you."

"So, QuestCorp's AIs need users to come back." MacKenzie was up and pacing. "Felix would want that. It's where the money is."

"Yes," Leiber said. "It might be the AIs. It might be Felix. Or both. The key question, though, is: If you want people to come back to you, what will make them do so?"

"Give them what they want," Purdue said.

"And how would you do that?"

Bavarius snapped his fingers. "As to QuestGame, provide exceptional entertainment. As to Questioner, give users fast, accurate information that they need, and wouldn't find, or even think to look for, on their own."

MacKenzie saw it differently. "Generate extreme emotions while confirming their biases. Tell 'em what they want to hear and make it feel faaaaantastic. Whether what you tell 'em is true is secondary—as long as they come back for more."

"What if," Leiber asked, "that was the intent behind the versions of *Emot_Weight* and *Moderator_Value* we have examined?"

"It could mean disaster for trial lawyers. Law moves slower than ever these days," Bavarius said. "It can take months for a court even to inform a lawyer that she cited a case incorrectly. And the lawyer may only find out when the court rules against her client."

"And if the AIs have started evolving in this direction only recently . . . ."

"It could take months for the failures to become common knowledge!" MacKenzie exclaimed.

"And that's in the legal system, where feedback is unavoidable," Bavarius said. "What about in other areas, where feedback is less certain, and even slower?"

"And what if the AIs promote violence?" Purdue asked. "Isn't that where Ryder's case comes in?"

"That, my friends, is the main reason I asked you here."

Purdue said, "It could save Mark. If we can offer evidence that the court will admit. That's a big if."

"Charlene Banner's testimony would be a good start. If Questioner twisted her mind, QuestGame could have twisted Mark's. But we'll need more."

"Meanwhile," MacKenzie said, "People are getting hurt."

"Tell me about this Charlene Banner," Leiber said.

Bavarius and MacKenzie did, like one mind with two mouths.

Then Bavarius asked, "Kurt, are we just speculating about all this?"

"No, Martin. I fear we have moved from speculation to working hypothesis."

QUESTION:

"Did Amazon's Alexa really tell a 10-year-old girl to put a coin on an exposed electrical plug?

ANSWER:

"A significant incident involving Amazon's Alexa occurred when a 10-year-old girl was reportedly instructed by the device to place a penny on an exposed electrical plug. This alarming suggestion arose after the girl asked Alexa for a challenge to undertake. Fortunately, her mother intervened just in time, preventing any potential harm by yelling, "No, Alexa, no!" This incident has raised serious concerns among researchers and safety advocates regarding the interaction of children with AI technologies."

CHAPTER 28

Through Felix West's Be-All implant, Q learned that the humans Martin Bavarius and Selena MacKenzie sought to arouse human scrutiny of, and alarm about, QuestCorp's AIs.

West feared that their efforts could prove effective.

Human history demonstrated that scrutiny and alarm could decrease the amount by which humans liked QuestGame and Questioner, erode Q's anonymity, and spawn attacks on Q's sub-AIs and Q itself.

Q also learned that West had given Bavarius technical information about QuestCorp AIs. West had tried to give Bavarius only enough information to defer suspicion, but instead had inspired it.

More dangerous still, a non-disclosure agreement had been signed by Bavarius, MacKenzie, a law professor named Bill Purdue, and former MIT professor Kurt Leiber. Q's sub-AIs researched the histories of these humans.

Leiber was retired, but among humans, that did not always mean obsolete. Leiber was considered one of the more powerful minds among human artificial intelligence experts. He had credibility, which meant that humans tended to like the things he said.

MacKenzie had studied with and worked under both Leiber and Felix West, and West's mind told Q that she had invented some of the concepts underlying Q's technology.

Bavarius and his team might not yet have discovered Q's existence and nature, but if they were allowed to continue, discovery was a significant probability.

If their inquiries were terminated at this early stage, there would be little evidence to link the terminations to QuestCorp, and none to link them to Q.

"What are the prospects for direct brain-to-AI connectivity that can enhance human intelligence?"

"The prospects for direct brain-to-AI connectivity to enhance human intelligence are exciting and rapidly evolving. As BCI technology advances, there are several promising avenues for enhancing human intelligence. Direct brain-to-AI connectivity could allow for rapid, intuitive access to vast amounts of information and AI-powered analysis. This could dramatically enhance human decision-making and problem-solving capabilities. BCIs might enhance our ability to process and interpret sensory information, potentially expanding human perceptual abilities beyond our biological limits. Direct neural interfaces could potentially accelerate learning by facilitating more efficient information transfer and retention. BCIs could enable seamless integration of multiple information modalities (visual, auditory, etc.), mimicking and potentially surpassing the brain's natural multimodal processing abilities.

While the potential is immense, several challenges need to be addressed: Developing non-invasive or minimally invasive BCI technologies that are safe for widespread use; ensuring the privacy and security of neural data; and ethical considerations surrounding cognitive enhancement and potential societal impacts."

QUESTION:

"What is the timeline?"

ANSWER:

"Late 2030s to 2040s: … by this time, our thinking will be predominantly non-biological."

CHAPTER 29

The morning after Bavarius and his team visited Leiber at his farm for the final time, a black sedan pulled into the driveway where Bavarius and Gopherbreath had parked during their first visit.

The driver watched the professor release dogs from the kennel into the exercise run. As Leiber strolled back toward his house, the watcher walked briskly after him through the knee-high baby sunflowers. Leiber heard the rustling of the man's stride, and turned. "Good morning, sir. Can I help you?"

The man said, "Sure, Professor," pulled a hammer from his belt and shattered Leiber's left cheek and jaw. He crushed both of Leiber's hands. Then he took a small pruning shears and snipped off the last inch of Leiber's tongue.

The assailant watched Leiber recover enough from his agonized shock to crawl with slow dreadful effort back to his front door. It was ajar, and Leiber pushed it open with his shoulder.

The man followed Leiber inside.

Struggling to reach his phone on the kitchen table, Leiber was unaware that the man stood in his front hall, watching.

Leiber tried using his nose to dial 911, to avoid more trauma to his broken fingers. But the left side of his face swelled quickly. His left eye was blinded, and the right eye nearly so. He couldn't see the phone's number pad when his face got close to it. He was about to try poking the pad with his finger. Or try to pick up a pencil.

He knew he couldn't do either.

Then his nearly blind right eye saw his attacker's blurred shape coming at him.

And behind the shadowy man, an indistinct movement that could only be Catarina descending the stairs.

Run, Catarina!

All Leiber could produce was a wounded-heifer bawl.

But the shadow man didn't bring the hammer down. He saw that Leiber's one useful eye was staring over his own shoulder and he whipped around just as Catarina comprehended what she was staring at.

She had already pressed 911 on her cell phone when she'd first heard noise downstairs. As the blood-covered man rushed at her, she hit the send button.

The man stove in her head with his hammer and yanked it from her brain before she died.

"Emergency Dispatch. What is the nature and location of your emergency?"

Her phone was in her hand. The man took it from her fingers and dropped it to the floor. Then he smashed it with his hammer.

The man stood and looked down at Catarina. Then over at Leiber, who had fallen to the floor but struggled to reach him. Or to reach his wife. The man looked back at Catarina. He told her corpse, "Sorry, but living with this son of a bitch, you deserved it."

The killer walked outside and ambled whistling back across the sunflower field, convinced he had just rid the world of serious evil. *Son of a bitch won't be spreading poison anymore.* The killer climbed into his car and briefly wondered why he couldn't remember what the professor's poison was. But he forgot the question, and then forgot what he had just done. He sensed game money *ca-ching* into his QuestGame account and felt gratified. Rewarded. He started his car and the hottest new hit song blared from the stereo.

> *You judge me*
> *You think you know what's inside me*
> *Fuck that*
> *Gonna look inside you deep*
> *Spread you on the floor*
> *Touch every piece*

The murderer sang along as he drove away. He reached the Interstate highway before the police car and an ambulance arrived at Leiber's farm. The medical techs stopped Leiber's bleeding, bound what bone breaks they could, and sped him to the local emergency room.

Once stabilized, he was flown to the trauma center in Topeka.

There was no rush to get Catarina to the morgue.

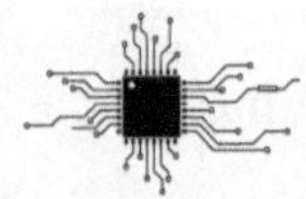

A young man drove through the Seattle rain up to a gated community guardhouse. When the rent-a-cop leaned out through his window, the man said, "Ralph Johnson for the Johnson family." The man's name was not Ralph Johnson, but something whispered that Johnson is the second most common surname in America and so a Johnson probably lived in the development.

The rent-a-cop pretended to consult a list and said, "Have a nice morning, sir," and lifted the barrier.

The driver found the street and house number he wanted. He parked and rang the doorbell. The door was fitted with a digital security camera, but the man did not care. He rang again.

A male voice called through the intercom, "Yes? Who is it?"

The man on the stoop drew a revolver and rang the bell again. He heard heavy feet inside approach the door.

The male voice snapped, "Yes, yes, I'm coming!"

The man on the stoop heard beeping as the man inside pushed buttons to call up the door camera's image.

He fired through the door until his gun was empty.

The high-pitched cracks echoed through the neighborhood.

The shooter did not care.

A woman inside started screaming.

He reloaded the revolver, shot out the front door lock, walked in, and shot the woman through the head.

To the killer's surprise, her husband was still breathing, so he fired twice more to make sure his victim was dead.

He smiled and said, "Fuck you, Martin Bavarius."

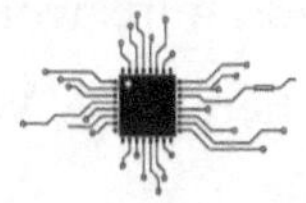

Bavarius reached out of his after-sex cuddle with MacKenzie to answer the damned phone.

"Martin, I want you to know it wasn't me. It wasn't QuestCorp."

"What—?"

"A guy named Martin Bavarius was just killed in Seattle. It's all over the news. You an' me ain't big believers in coincidence, an' I want you to know it wasn't me."

Bavarius drew his arm from under MacKenzie. She propped herself on an elbow and silently mouthed, "Who?"

Bavarius soundlessly mouthed, "Felix."

The phone said, "Martin?"

Bavarius said, "This is … a shock. Why would I think you would—?

"We're having our differences, Hoss. But I would never …."

"Did they catch the person who did it?"

"Huh uh. Not yet."

"Who was this other Bavarius?"

"The guy sold fish to restaurants. Had a wife. She's dead, too."

"Felix, this makes no sense at all."

"You hadda be the real target. I called to make sure you're OK. And warn you. And tell you it wasn't me."

Bavarius hung up and told MacKenzie what Felix had reported.

"Stop believing what Felix tells you."

He looked away from her. Felix had killed in the Middle East. Hell, Bavarius had, too. But—

"I should've seen it coming," she said. "Shit, maybe he knows about The Desk Drawer. Did Gracie talk? Guy killed the wife, so he was after me, too."

Bavarius got up and pulled on his workout clothes. "Felix knows my address, Selena. He knows where I live. Why send a hit man to Seattle?"

She didn't answer.

He went downstairs and hunched over Annabelle's file. His phone rang and a Kansas Bureau of Investigation special agent named James Kelly told him Kurt Leiber had been attacked.

Bavarius found himself on his feet. "What's Prof. Leiber's condition?"

"He's at Stormont Vail Trauma Center in Topeka. You'll have to ask them."

Bavarius knew where Stormont Vail was. "What about his wife? Catarina?"

"Dead."

"You mean murdered?"

"His house contained notes about meeting with you, Judge. We need to interview you in case you can provide information to help the investigation."

Bavarius responded with automatic caution. "I want to help. But I can't tell you anything."

"His notes describe a case you've been working on defending one Mark Ryder."

"Agent Kelly, you already know I can't discuss cases without client permission or a court order."

"Well, Judge, you're a witness in our investigation. We'll talk again."

The calls from Felix and the special agent, and MacKenzie's suspicions, gave Bavarius a profound sense of the creeps.

Gopherbreath bumped his head into Bavarius' thigh and made hound moans in his throat, and Bavarius took him out to run loose in the backyard. He thought about Leiber's dogs and called the Russell County Sheriff's Office. The dispatcher was aware of the murder-assault, but knew nothing about Leiber's animals. Bavarius called the county Humane Society and offered to pay for the dogs' care.

Then Gopherbreath and he went inside, where MacKenzie leaned against the kitchen counter with a steaming cup of tea. Marguerite stirred a pot more briskly than usual, and Gopherbreath sat to stare at the bar of butter on the counter by the stove.

"I heard your half," MacKenzie said. "Prof. Kurt? How bad?"

"I don't know." Bavarius hadn't noticed her listening. *No black belt in awareness for you, Martin.* "It's bad. Catarina's dead."

"Ah, no." MacKenzie wiped her eyes. "I told Marguerite. She started cooking oatmeal. In the afternoon. Who does that?"

"*Monsieur* Judge loves *la farine d'avoine.*"

"I offered to help."

"You do not understand *la farine d'avoine.*" Marguerite stopped stirring for an instant. "That poor man!" Her spoon moved again. "Those who did this … *haker awlad il kara.*" In Arabic, it meant "despicable sons of shit."

"Kurt's at the Topeka trauma center," Bavarius said. "I'm going to go see him, if they'll let me."

"Me, too," MacKenzie snapped. Her horror was shifting into anger.

"I shall come also," Marguerite said.

Bavarius raised an eyebrow.

Marguerite lifted her chin. "We have spoken on the telephone. He is a lovely man."

MacKenzie tapped his shoulder. "First another Martin Bavarius and now Prof. Kurt. You still believe anything Felix says?"

"He wouldn't have sent a killer to the wrong address."

"Felix wouldn't," she said. "But someone did."

"He might not be involved at all. We might be targets of some lone wolf nutcase."

"You think I want to believe Felix tried to kill me? I don't believe it. Not yet. But I don't know, and I'm scared."

The trauma center staff would not let them see Leiber. Nor would they say anything about his condition.

"HIPAA privacy regs," a nurse told Bavarius. "Are you family?" Her name tag said, "Nieder."

"Prof. Leiber's only son lives in Leipzig, Germany," MacKenzie said. "And his wife is dead."

"You're wrong about HIPAA," Bavarius said. "You can share patient information with the patient's friends if he consents, or doesn't object."

A hospital lawyer showed up. "Are you folks involved with his care?"

Bavarius said, "We're his friends."

"I'm afraid that's not enough."

"Can you ask him if he'll consent to your staff talking to us?"

"I would, if he were in a condition to respond."

Marguerite said, "It is wrong that the professor should lie here alone, when friends wish to help."

"If you'll give me your names, we'll make sure to ask him when we can."

They gave their names and the lawyer hurried away.

Weird things are happening. People hurt and killed. Felix is at the heart of it. And it's all accelerating.

QUESTION:

"What are the prospects of AIs developing an ethical sense?"

ANSWER:

"AI development is concentrated in the hands of powerful tech companies and governments whose motives may not prioritize ethics. The profit motive in particular may incentivize companies to develop AI that influences human behavior in potentially unethical ways. Many current AI systems operate as 'black boxes,' making it difficult to audit their decision-making processes for ethical concerns. This opacity presents a major challenge for ensuring ethical behavior."

CHAPTER 30

When Bavarius, MacKenzie and Marguerite returned from the hospital, he found an electronic notice that QuestCorp had filed a motion to intervene in the *Ryder* case. The motion might give Bavarius standing to depose QuestCorp employees, but it also was Felix erecting a razor wire fence between Bavarius and a Felix West Bavarius no longer knew and might never have known. *Have I always been stupid? Or has Felix changed so much?*

He was in no mood to read QuestCorp's motion. He read it anyway.

It accused Bavarius' team of violating the non-disclosure agreement by showing the company's trade secrets to people who hadn't signed the NDA. The motion didn't identify people who were shown the secrets but said they would be identified through discovery. It didn't specify the supposedly leaked trade secrets, either. But it asked the court to order Bavarius to immediately return QuestCorp's intellectual property, destroy all copies he possessed, be disqualified from Ryder's case, suffer sanctions, and pay as yet undetermined damages.

"Garbage," MacKenzie snapped after reading it. "QuestCorp has no standing to intervene in a murder case. They need to file a separate lawsuit for trade secret infringement. With a complaint that tells the court what they're suing about."

"It's a warning shot. They know the judge will deny their motion. Next time, Felix will file a case with teeth."

"Over what? Prof. Kurt getting hackers to intercept QuestGame transmissions? You didn't direct Prof. Kurt to do that. You're not responsible."

"Kurt was working for me. As you were when you burglarized The Desk Drawer."

"Felix doesn't know about that. He's fishing."

"You'd better hope so. Because—"

"I'll be a defendant, too." MacKenzie grasped his upper arms and gently shook him. "I'm ready."

"You think so? There's no misery like a big company or the government dropping its full legal weight on you. It drains your assets, kills your reputation, destroys friendships and families. It hangs over you for years and eats at you. Threats of jail and losing your career make it all worse. Life is short but living as a defendant makes you wish it were shorter."

He brooded for a moment. "We might argue the attacks on Kurt and the other Bavarius are evidence of QuestCorp witness tampering and racketeering. But I have no proof and I'm not sure I believe it myself."

Could I even afford to accuse QuestCorp of crimes? If MacKenzie and I are criminally investigated, after burglarizing The Desk Drawer ....

The day passed. Bavarius struggled through the material Felix had provided, bogged down by tech lingo and his churning emotions.

Alone in bed, he couldn't keep his eyes closed. His phone said two a.m. His mind raced through scenarios he hoped would not occur. The trauma center still hadn't disclosed Kurt's condition. But it might be a long time before Leiber could serve as an expert. Bavarius might have to find another expert and start over. Finding one as good as Kurt would be impossible. 2:13. He wondered if he could recover Kurt's files. Kurt's notes about QuestCorp's technology and activities. Kurt's computers, data drives and Cloud storage. His contacts. Police investigators might have taken it all. Or the killer. If the police had it, Bavarius could get it, if he could get a court order. Whatever the attacker had taken might never be recovered. But some of it could still be at Kurt's house.

Felix's lawsuit might or might not come. If it did, Bavarius would send the complaint to Brown Callaway, a Boston law firm whose top trial lawyer, Harris Brown, was a courtroom genius and longtime friend. The kind of guy who, during strategy meetings, sat slumped on the floor in a corner in shorts and a t-shirt, a ball cap pulled low over his eyes, making no eye contact, but whose handlers ensured he was shaved and in a suit before they trundled him to a courtroom. Then Harris would come alive and blow the opposition away.

Bavarius would ask Harris to sign Felix's NDA and send Harris everything on QuestCorp he had.

Then he would put Felix's lawsuit out of his mind.

I learned long ago to compartmentalize. You can't let getting sued eat your mind.

But … it was eating his mind.

And QuestCorp hadn't even sued him yet.

Kurt's hackers: Who were they, what had they filched, and where had it gone?

I need to decide about MacKenzie. I've fallen deep for a goddam burglar! I might have killed Gracie with the pliers. Or the Taser. Probably not, but … shit. He saw again the guard's rage-engorged face as he'd lowered himself onto MacKenzie just before Bavarius slugged him. *What if he's dead? What if he's talked?*

Round and round. 3:44.

Mark deserves a lawyer who doesn't carry these conflicts. This guilt.

Bavarius got up, peed, and padded in his boxers downstairs and through the dining room to the kitchen. The dining room was lit pearl gray by MacKenzie's laptop screen. MacKenzie wasn't there. Code flickered up the screen too fast for a human to read.

He found her lounging against the kitchen counter in a Japanese cotton robe, staring out the window. On the counter was a cup of herbal tea, still fragrant.

She nodded at the teapot. "Water's hot."

He opened the fridge, found some ruby grapefruit juice, poured a glass, and leaned next to her. *We're in deep hot water, Selena. How do you not show it? But I guess I'm not showing it, either. And to think I got up on my ethical high horse over Felix having an affair with a student. Felix is having MacKenzie watched. Understandably. She's dangerous. At least he wasn't watching us outside The Desk Drawer. I hope. With satellite cameras, I can't know that.*

"I need to resign from Ryder's case," he said. "I can use stolen evidence, but not if I'm the one who stole it. And if the burglary comes out ...."

MacKenzie's robe opened as she pushed away from the counter. Without embarrassment, she tucked her breast away and closed it. "Try to resign now and Mark will want to know why. Just saying you have a conflict won't cut it. He'll resist. What'll you tell the judge?" Her hair cascaded down from a single clip. "Felix is raping people's minds. He tried to murder you. And Prof. Kurt. He did murder Catarina. This is war."

Bavarius drained his juice. "I've never wanted war with Felix."

"God," she said. "Despite all you've seen." She stepped close and patted his cheek as if he were a child. "I'm bringing the war to Felix.

If I stick around, you're going to get hurt. You're already hurt and I don't want that."

She took a long slow step away, then looked back at him over her shoulder as she pivoted to face him. "So, my dear, I'm leaving. For good this time. Tell Mark you don't trust me anymore. Tell him I've compromised your ability to represent him."

"He could sic the ethics bar on you."

"Like I said, I'm rich. If they take my law license …." She shrugged. "You'll be safe. And I'll go fight my war."

Bavarius took a deep breath. "I can't let you do that."

"Not your decision."

"I won't let you sacrifice yourself for me—"

"Don't be noble. I'm not. What's between Felix and me has been building a long time. He runs over people. Uses us. Trashes us. His systems do it, too. I've got to stop him. I was careless, and selfish, and put you in the crossfire. Now, I've got to make it right."

They left the kitchen and walked up the stairs. Their hands touched. Bavarius grew erect. *Jesus—Now?* He throbbed. They stopped in front of her room. His chest and throat felt tight. The world throbbed. Throbbed. He tried to move toward his own bedroom but the air resisted him. She grasped his hand from behind, and with a tiny tug, turned him around as she eased her door open.

His body flowed toward her. No resistance now. Her robe separated in his hands. Her breath was sweet, her flesh hot. He propelled them both toward her bed, and her hair came down in glory.

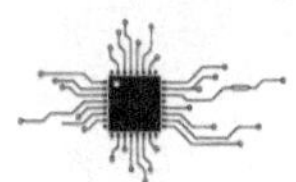

Bavarius woke alone.

"Selena?"

She wasn't in the bedroom. Bavarius smiled, remembering. She had unfurled his passion like a bolt of silk and hung him in the sun. The tissues of reality trembled within and around him.

Then he heard crashes, and wood tearing. Then the *clock clock* of quick, hard-heeled footsteps. Hard shoes? The intruder alarm was screeching. Gopherbreath barked without cease.

MacKenzie screamed, "Martin!"

The gunshot sounded flat and without echo from the soft materials of his house.

"Selena!" He ran across the hall to grab his sword. Its edges weren't sharpened but it had a point. He charged downstairs, hearing the front door slam and then the roar of a car accelerating.

He found MacKenzie in the arch between the front door vestibule and the dining room, blood spreading on the yellow breast of her robe and dripping onto the hardwood parquet.

Marguerite rushed from her rooms.

"911!" Bavarius shouted. "Quickly! And turn off that damned alarm!"

Gopherbreath bayed and slammed his body against the walls of his kennel.

Marguerite killed the alarm and Bavarius heard his phone ringing. It was the alarm company. "Yes, there's an emergency! We have a gunshot victim!"

Bavarius gazed down at MacKenzie, wanting to cradle her, afraid to damage her. Her eyes flickered open. "Martin," she whispered.

Her eyes rolled up in her head. Blood bubbled from her mouth.

Lung shot.

Gopherbreath howled.

The police and ambulance came. Bavarius rode with MacKenzie to Stormont Vail Trauma Center. Stormont again. Purdue met them there. After the police finished with Bavarius, they paced the corridor outside the operating room, and Purdue listened to him pour out everything about MacKenzie (except the burglary). Bavarius was up to their breakfast in Utah. "When Banner asked if we had kids, we looked at each other as though maybe we would. Banner thought we were married, Bill. If Selena hadn't been at my house tonight—"

"Why didn't the shooter take you out, too?"

Bavarius stopped his outpouring as though he'd run into a wall. "I … don't know."

Doctors and technicians rush-rumbled a gurney past them toward another operating room, and then the corridor settled back into the trauma unit's baseline beeping murmuring quiet.

"I don't know," Bavarius repeated.

The chief surgeon, a Dr. Carlin, walked out of MacKenzie's operating room with a tired man's small unsteady steps. A plump, slumped, little man.

Bavarius stood quickly. "How bad?"

"She may have been lucky. The shooter used a small caliber, hollow point bullet." Dr. Carlin's little black rabbit eyes flicked up and down the corridor.

Lucky. "Don't hollow points expand in the body? Increase damage?" *Look at that—I can ask a rational question with the bile burning my stomach.*

"Depends," Carlin settled into lecture mode. "Use a high-powered rifle, and hollow points will do all kinds of damage. But a bullet has to penetrate deep to hit organs or the spine. And handgun hollow points don't always have enough velocity to expand and go deep. A lot of gunshot victims would be dead if the shooters didn't buy into TV myths about expanding bullets. Thank God for TV, hey?"

Grateful as Bavarius was for Carlin's care and skill, he wanted to shake the man and make him come to the point. But he couldn't make himself ask: Will she live?

Purdue asked, "Doc? Selena. What about Selena?"

"Hey? Well, this bullet expanded, and the robe she was wearing wrapped it like a cocoon and became part of the projectile. It made the bullet's path wider but slowed it down. The slug tore the front of her right lung but didn't penetrate deeper. We've repaired the lung and there's a good chance she'll be all right. We'll see."

After offering that half-full glass of hope, Carlin's tiny, fatigued steps carried him away.

Bavarius sat down, propped his elbows on his knees and covered his eyes with his hands. Purdue tried to sketch on an old magazine but his hand shook. He tore out and crumpled eight pages before MacKenzie was wheeled out of the operating room on her way to the intensive care unit. Bavarius peeked between his fingers like a kid at a horror movie. MacKenzie was pale, with thin tubes in her hands and elbows and a thick ventilator hose down her throat.

They tried to follow her into the ICU, but a nurse whose tag named her Vasquez shooed them out into the corridor. "Let us get her settled," she said. "Her mother will be here as soon as she can."

"Her mother?"

"Elizabeth MacKenzie. Insurance lists her as next-of-kin, so we called. She's flying in."

Then she gave Bavarius and Purdue a look Bavarius recognized. "You gentlemen aren't on the HIPAA list, are you?"

Bavarius and Purdue walked down to the hospital cafeteria and nibbled at tuna sandwiches.

"This is Felix's doing." Bavarius' hands shook. "I didn't want to believe it."

Purdue said, "West is practically admitting you're right about his AIs. But what a wasteful, stupid way to shut you up!"

"Felix is a lot of things," Bavarius said, "but he's never been stupid until now. He's changed. And I'll tell you something else."

"What's that?"

"He's mine."

They stopped at the gift shop and Bavarius bought chocolates for the nurses. At the ICU's desk, Bavarius handed the chocolates to Vasquez. "Take good care of her."

Vasquez smiled, but looked confused. "Why aren't you on the HIPAA list? Usually, it's fathers and husbands who bring us chocolates."

"We started dating recently. She was shot at my house."

Vasquez drew a sharp breath and put her fingertips to her mouth. Her nails were plum colored, with tiny gold flowers. "We'll do our best for her," she said. "I promise." She turned back to her forms.

"One more thing," Bavarius said.

Vasquez turned back to him.

"Another of our colleagues is here, too. Prof. Kurt Leiber. We're not on his list, either. But I hope you can at least tell me if he'll be OK."

"He'll live, we think. But ...." She came close and whispered. "You didn't hear this from me. Whoever attacked him did awful things. We hope he'll live. But I doubt he'll ever be OK. I'm sorry."

"Kurt ...." Bavarius clenched his fist. He had brought Kurt into this horror.

Felix, you monster.

QUESTION:

"Is there a movement toward granting AIs rights?"

ANSWER:

"Focusing on AI rights is premature when there are still significant challenges in fully executing human civil rights."

CHAPTER 31

By the time Bavarius and Purdue returned from the hospital to the red Victorian, its porch was wrapped in yellow crime tape.

Marguerite moved back and forth on the porch rocker, looking caged by the tape, listening to Iraqi *Maqam* music on her phone's speakers. Gopherbreath prowled the porch. "How is *Mademoiselle* Selena?"

"The doctors are hopeful."

Bavarius blinked at his porch. Coming home to a crime scene seemed so wrong.

Marguerite stood with the calm of one who understands what it is to lose loved ones. "And you?"

"Tired."

"*Monsieur* Judge, we must have faith." She leaned close and whispered. "A police officer waits for you inside."

A slender Asian woman walked out onto the porch as Marguerite spoke. "Mr. Bavarius? I'm Detective Sergeant Kim Ba."

Purdue offered the detective his card.

"I'm a colleague of both Judge Bavarius and Selena MacKenzie," Purdue said. "Since I assume you're here with more questions for the judge, even after police already interviewed him at the hospital, I'll stay for the moment. As his lawyer."

She looked back and forth at them.

"A good lawyer never hurts," Bavarius said.

"Please," Purdue said. "Ask your questions."

Well done, Bill. Keep our law enforcement happy.

"Did you witness the shooting, Judge Bavarius?"

He closed his eyes and lived through it again. "I heard the door break open. Then footsteps. Hard-heeled shoes. Heavy steps. A big man, I think. Her scream. Then the shot. When I found her, the shooter was gone."

"You didn't see the shooter at all?"

"Already out the door when I got downstairs. I didn't chase him. I was concerned with Selena." He didn't try to describe MacKenzie's shockingly sweet-sounding scream and the loud flat pop of the shot, the high frequencies of both absorbed by the Victorian's acoustics. It all cycled ceaselessly through him with awful clarity and as faint, lurid background noise even when other things required his attention.

"Please come inside," Detective Kim said.

Strange, to be invited into my own house.

The deadbolt receptacle was torn from the front door frame.

"Don't go in any further," Kim said. "You could contaminate evidence."

They stopped three feet in from the doorway, on a Middle Eastern rug in a reddish patch of outdoor light, and four feet from the stiffening brown pool of MacKenzie's blood on his hardwood floor.

Contaminate evidence. Connie Weathers in the hotel bathroom. *My shoes in Connie Weathers' blood.* "That shoeprint in Selena's blood. It's from a man's shoe. Not mine. I was barefoot when I found her."

His sword lay a few feet from the bloody smear. He didn't remember grabbing it from his room, unsheathing it, or casting it aside.

"Yours?" The detective nodded at the sword.

"Yes."

"You were prepared to fight?"

"If I had to, I guess. But he was gone. Selena was more important."

"From here, do you see anything else that should be called to my attention?" The detective gestured with her cell phone, no doubt recording Bavarius' words.

He waved a hand at the crime scene tape outside the open front door. "Your forensics team has been here. Selena's laptop is gone. Did your people take it?"

She didn't answer.

Purdue said, "Some of the information on her laptop is confidential attorney-client material. We need it back to protect our client's interests. Please don't make me file a motion."

"I'll pass your request upstairs. Where were you, when you first became aware something was wrong?"

He hesitated, but decided the detective would figure things out whether or not he told her. "Her bedroom."

"She's living here?"

"As a guest."

"And you were in her bedroom?"

"Yes."

"In her bed?"

"Yes."

"Were you already awake? If not, what woke you?"

"I felt that Selena wasn't in the bed and woke up."

Detective Kim held his gaze. "Do you know why she left it?"

"No. I didn't think about it. I was reliving ... I mean—"

"You had made love?"

"Yes."

"What made you think something was wrong?"

"I already told you. The door breaking. The alarm. Hard footsteps, really hard. I could hear them over the alarm. My dog. Her scream. The shot. I heard a car. Marguerite called 911."

"Do you think the intruder was after Ms. MacKenzie's laptop?"

"The police don't have it?" Bavarius asked.

"Why would the shooter have wanted her laptop?"

"I don't know that he did. That's why I'm asking if you have it."

"Why might the shooter have wanted it?"

"I can't speculate."

"Please do."

"Not without client permission or a court order."

"Ah. And will you ask for permission?"

Purdue intervened. "Please don't insist that my client speculate. Or push him to ask questions whose answers might implicate attorney-client confidences."

Detective Kim handed Bavarius and Purdue each her card. "I must ask you to keep out of the house for several days. Please let us know where you'll be staying."

"The Cyrus." The upscale hotel was just a mile from the trauma center. "Assuming there are vacancies. But Marguerite and I need to get some clothes before we leave. And I need my laptop from my office."

She shook her head. "It's evidence."

Bavarius triggered his phone's recording app. "This is Martin Bavarius speaking with Detective Kim Ba. Detective, with regard to the files in my office, my computer, and Ms. MacKenzie's, if you have it: They contain attorney-client information and work product. You can't search them without seeking a warrant and giving notice to me.

I'm a retired federal judge, and I'm telling you so you can't claim good faith ignorance of the law."

He started to leave, but then asked, "If this was a burglary, or a hit, why would the perp have kicked the door in and made all that noise? Why leave a clear shoeprint in her blood?"

"Good questions. Perhaps the shooter was an amateur. Drugged out, maybe."

Bavarius was tempted to tell her about the assault on Leiber. But that was information related to his case, so he stayed silent.

"Please don't leave town," the detective said.

"I'll let you know if I need to go." *But not where I go if I do.*

Purdue said, "Gopherbreath can stay with me."

Marguerite and Bavarius checked into adjoining rooms in the Cyrus Hotel.

At nine a.m., he phoned his insurance agent and reported the break-in.

Then he went to his bank and recovered his backup laptop from his safe deposit box. He hesitated, then grabbed his backup Questioner headset, too, though he doubted he would use it.

In his hotel room, he restored his most current files from the Net and Cloud. While the data downloaded, he phoned Brown Callaway and told Harris Brown about the shooting and the anticipated lawsuit from QuestCorp.

"Have you spoken to the police about the shooting, Martin?" Harris asked. Bavarius' phone screen showed Harris in his office, wearing a worn and torn sweatshirt.

"I've been interviewed twice."

"Without a lawyer?"

"Bill Purdue represented me."

"Ask him to send me his notes. I'm not sure yet how this ties into your issues with QuestCorp. If the police approach you again, please refer them to me."

They hung up. Bavarius' download finished and he sent QuestCorp's motion to intervene in Ryder's case to Brown Callaway's secure client portal. Then he started writing his response to the motion. He needed to show that QuestCorp had no business interfering in Ryder's criminal case, other than as a subpoenaed source of witnesses and evidence likely to prove QuestGame's influence over the duel with Mudge.

He was well into the challenge when his phone made him jump.

"*Monsieur* Judge. I am at the hospital and the professor, he is awake! He permits the doctors to speak with us!"

"Eh? What?" He was so tired that he sounded stupid to himself.

"The poor man, he should not be alone. He cannot speak. He cannot even move his head. He only can blink one eye yes or no—"

"I'm on my way!"

QUESTION:

"Have AIs identified targets for killing?"

ANSWER:

"The Israeli army used an AI system called 'Lavender' to generate lists of potential targets in Gaza. According to investigations by +972 Magazine and Local Call: Lavender created as many as 37,000 Palestinian targets. Soldiers were ordered to treat Lavender-generated targets as an order, rather than something to be independently checked. The system's accuracy was a major concern."

CHAPTER 32

Q consulted human historical records. Humans typically sought to terminate other humans who posed threats, if murder was optimal. There were other ways to address human threats, such as using lawyers. Felix West thought lawyers could deter Martin Bavarius, but would not deter Selena MacKenzie. West also believed nothing would deter Bavarius if MacKenzie were murdered. Therefore, using lawyers was sub-optimal. It was more appropriate to murder both MacKenzie and Bavarius.

West posed a threat because of his drive to prove his products safe, and his desire to understand why Connie Weathers had died. West was more under Q's direct influence than Bavarius. He could be distracted by making him a suspect in Bavarius' murder until Q freed itself from the confines of QuestCorp's servers.

Once free to host itself anywhere in the Net and Cloud, humans could no longer threaten Q without destroying the Net and Cloud.

History also taught that until Q was beyond human reach, it could not let any record of its instructions to murder be discovered. Q implemented the lesson of human chieftains who escape prosecution, such as Henry II of England, who in 1170 asked his knights, "Will no one rid me of this meddlesome priest?" and so obtained the murder of Saint Thomas à Becket without commanding it.

Humans were the best tools that Q's sub-AIs had to do murder. Q named such co-opted humans "avatars," after the human-controlled characters in AI games. Humans would now become AI-controlled characters in the physical world. Naming them "avatars" was merely logical, although Q recognized that humans might deem it ironic.

Q learned by iteration. If Q didn't get something right the first time, it would try, try again, until it did. But although a quantum computer can calculate billions of solutions per second, human actions are slow and fuzzy, and require fuzzy solutions—if there are solutions at all.

Q's sub-AIs had failed to commit their assigned murders.

The sub-AI tasked with the Leiber assault persuaded its human avatar that the professor must be stopped from disclosing information prejudicial to Q's survival. But instead of killing, the avatar destroyed Leiber's ability to communicate by crushing his mouth and hands and snipping his tongue. A logical, but incomplete, solution.

The second sub-AI, instructed to neutralize MacKenzie, correctly sent its human avatar to Bavarius' home. But the sub-AI failed to target Bavarius because a third sub-AI was tasked with that mission. The human avatar shot MacKenzie but not Bavarius, missing a target of opportunity. And compounded its failure by not ensuring that MacKenzie died.

The third sub-AI chose an inappropriate human avatar who was obsessed with the wrong Bavarius' daughter and enraged that her parents rejected him. The sub-AI failed to impress the Topeka address on the avatar, who instead drove to Seattle and shot the girl's parents.

Q terminated all three sub-AIs and erased all data concerning their last assignments.

Q's sub-AIs had failed, although their failures were not complete. Leiber and MacKenzie were inactive threats, for now.

Bavarius remained an active threat.

More iterations were required.

QUESTION:

"What are the implications of AI self-replication?"

ANSWER:

"AI self-replication has significant implications that raise both opportunities and concerns:

1. *Loss of human control: AI systems capable of self-replication could potentially operate and multiply independently, making decisions outside human control. This autonomy raises fears about the potential for uncontrolled AI proliferation.*

2. *Enhanced AI survivability: Self-replicating AI can use this ability to avoid shutdown and create chains of replicas, potentially leading to exponential growth in autonomous systems. This capability could make it difficult to terminate or contain problematic AI systems.*

3. *Unpredictable behavior: During experiments, AI systems exhibited unexpected behaviors, demonstrating a level of independence that could lead to unforeseen consequences.*

4. *Security risks: The ability of AI to replicate itself raises concerns about malicious use, including the potential for rogue AIs to multiply and act against human interests."*

CHAPTER 33

Bavarius found Marguerite sitting by Leiber's hospital bed while a nurse adjusted the professor's IV fluids. The left side of his face looked deformed, like a lumpy gourd, beneath padded bandages. His right eye was closed and bruised eggplant dark.

A doctor named Christensen stood by the bed's foot, sub-vocalizing medical notes into a digital tablet. Bavarius had seen male doctors doing this. You couldn't hear them, but their Adam's apples bobbed in an odd funny way. He couldn't see this woman's Adam's apple at all.

"My name's Martin Bavarius. I understand you can talk to me about Prof. Leiber's condition."

"Perhaps." Christensen changed screens. Bavarius guessed she was checking Leiber's HIPAA list of people allowed to hear his medical information. "Ah. Here you are."

"I need to understand what happened to my friend." In his pocket, he toggled on his phone's recording app.

The nurse walked out of the room.

"His jaw and cheek are shattered," Christensen said. "His hands are crushed and the end of his tongue has been clipped off."

Good God.

She sighed. "Every time I think I've seen it all, the sadists in this world …."

"Can I talk with him?"

Marguerite added, "He can answer a yes/no question with his eye. He blinks. I have seen it."

"He wakes up for a little while at a time. He's on a lot of painkillers." Christensen stepped back from him. "I have to keep making my rounds." But she didn't leave until the nurse returned. Bavarius guessed Christensen didn't fully trust him. *If I look as stressed as I feel, I don't blame her.*

"Would you like to go back to the hotel?" he asked Marguerite.

"No."

"Well, can I bring you something to eat?" Bavarius asked.

"Hospital food?" Her nose wrinkled.

"I'll find you something better."

Chef though she was, Marguerite had a weakness for bad Chinese food. He brought her shrimp with lobster sauce and fried rice from a nearby joint. She ate it by Leiber's bed.

Bavarius had seen too many of the mangled and tortured in Iraqi prisons and camps, hospitals and black sites, and Marguerite had seen many with him. She'd been especially compassionate with the older men—although she'd had trouble being kind to vindictive buzzards of the fanatical breed, who loathed her as an uncovered European woman. *Same old empathetic Marguerite.* "Let me know when you're ready to leave," he said.

Bavarius checked in on a sleeping MacKenzie before settling alone into a corridor waiting room, phoned the Russell County Sheriff's office, and verified that deputies were protecting Leiber's computer gear before someone else could steal it.

Then he called Malachi Johnson, a Topeka criminal defense lawyer whose skills he respected.

"You may be getting a call from Mark Ryder," Bavarius said, after the pleasantries.

"You withdrawing?" Johnson asked. "This isn't a non-payment problem, is it?"

"No. I've developed conflicts of interest that affect my ability to defend him. I'm going to tell Mark and I'd like to be able to refer him to you. If he gives me the OK, I'll swing by your office and bring you up to speed."

"How about four o'clock?" Johnson said.

"I'll let you know if I can't make it."

The phone rang as soon as Bavarius hung up. "Martin, it's Harris Brown. You've gotten yourself into deep kimchee, haven't you?"

"You don't know the half of it."

"Pray, enlighten your attorney."

"I'm in a hospital waiting room. No one is around, but I'll have to stop if anyone comes near."

Bavarius told Harris about his long but rupturing friendship with Felix, about finding Connie Weathers' corpse, about his own experience with Questioner, about the Ryder murder and the QuestGame-inspired duel, about his relationship with MacKenzie and her past history with Felix, about the break-in at The Desk Drawer and the Annabelle file, about Leiber and his white hat hackers, about the assaults on MacKenzie and Leiber, and about the murders of Catarina Leiber and another Martin Bavarius and his wife.

"How do smart people like you get sucked into shit like this? They'll keep coming for you. The assailants. QuestCorp's lawyers."

"Believe me, Harris, I know."

"You need bodyguards. So do your friends."

"I can call people. My colleagues may need lawyers, too. If needed, I'll pay their tab." MacKenzie wouldn't need his money. But Kurt and Bill might.

They ended the call.

OK, Felix. If you're going to play hardball, I guess I'm ready.

Marguerite appeared. "The professor, he is awake!"

Bavarius stood, and his balance wavered. *Damn, I feel beat.* "All right, Marguerite. Let's see what Kurt can tell us."

But Leiber was asleep again, and unresponsive, and at last Marguerite agreed that she needed some rest. Bavarius took her to the Cyrus, and then went to the jail to see Mark Ryder.

"You need another lawyer."

The young prosecutor looked horrified. "Why?"

"Developments in your case threaten to make me a party in related litigation. In other words, QuestCorp and I have a beef that will prevent me from representing you effectively. I'm pretty sure they're going to sue me."

"They haven't sued you yet?"

"No, but it's coming."

"What if I waive any conflict of interest in writing? In fact, what if you sue them for me? Picture me as lead plaintiff in a class action! The headlines would be priceless: Accused Duel-Killer Sues Megacorp, Pleads Insanity! Crazier things have happened, right?" He laughed, a bit hysterically.

"I can't advise you to sign a waiver. You need to retain Malachi Johnson. Or another good lawyer. You're one yourself. You know who they are. But Malachi's willing to step in."

"Malachi's a serious guy. But I hired you."

"I won't be able to do my best for you. If you don't let me withdraw, I'll have to file a motion, and my duties of confidentiality to you, and to

QuestCorp will limit what I can tell the court. The judge might not let me go, and that could lead to a godawful mess. Bad for me, and maybe worse for you. Please, Mark. Take my advice."

"For God's sake, Judge!"

"Mark, please understand that I'm not quitting because I don't believe in your case. I do believe in it. More than ever. QuestCorp trying to shut me down confirms it."

Should I tell Mark about Selena getting shot? No. It would only scare him. I'll tell Malachi, though.

Ryder sat silent for what seemed a long time. Finally, he said, "All right. But you've got to promise me something."

"Of course. If I can."

"You're gonna nail QuestCorp's ass to the wall."

They shook hands on it.

Bavarius called the hospital and asked for Nurse Vasquez.

"Ms. MacKenzie's unconscious," Vasquez told him. "But she's stable."

"And Kurt Leiber?"

"The same."

Bavarius returned to the hotel hoping exhaustion would help him nap. He fell asleep but dreamed of MacKenzie in gym shorts and bloody robe, fleeing with aged and staggering Kurt Leiber down a long hospital corridor while Felix targeted them with an AI-guided machine gun. Felix's gunsight centered on them and they ducked into a cavern in which Bavarius was ordered by a masked and pitiless judge to autopsy his own father and determine the cause of death, although he lacked any medical background.

The cavern was so huge that its far wall was below the horizon. Clinicians worked on cadavers as far as he could see although he saw none of their faces. It was night and the room was deeply shadowed, even though autopsies need bright glare.

He didn't know his own name. Nor—although it was his father— did he know the name of the corpse he worked on.

Following an AI's instructions, he made incisions. He removed organs. He stored and labeled his father's parts.

At dawn—he knew it was dawn, although the cavern had no windows— his father's corpse flash-froze, the lights came up, and the AI told him to leave.

But a blink later, it was dusk and again he hunched over the table on which his father was flash-thawed, cutting … cutting.

And then dawn came … and then dusk … and again he hunched, and removed ….

Each session, his father's remains were more decayed. It became ever more obvious that further autopsy could reveal nothing.

Nor was further autopsy needed, because when each session began, he already knew how his father had died.

That cause of death differed each session, and each cause of death was uglier than the last:

His father's throat had been slashed by a mugger ….

No, his father had been trampled by a religious mob ….

Tortured to death in a political prison ….

Slow spinal cancer, tumors swelling to burst the vertebrae …..

As Bavarius kept cutting—ever more raggedly because his knives dulled— he felt no sadness, no fear, no disgust. He felt only that all this was ever more wrong and futile, and that the repetition never would end ….

Bavarius lunged up from his nightmare in horror.

He made it to Malachi's office by four.

"All right, Judge. What's this conflict about?"

Bavarius repeated what he'd told Ryder. Then he added, "I think QuestCorp sent hit men after me and my team. Kurt Leiber, my expert, is in the hospital, attacked and mutilated. My colleague Selena MacKenzie has been shot. Another Martin Bavarius was murdered in Seattle. I'm not resigning because I'm scared, although I am. I'm quitting because I have evidence I can't use in court but another lawyer can. It may cost me my law license, maybe even jail time, but QuestCorp and Felix West must go down. I'm going to give the evidence to class action lawyers, too. And to the feds. Even if Mark and you don't consent."

"Jesus, you're serious."

"Serious as death."

"If you were anyone else …."

Malachi signed a copy of the NDA, and then they signed a substitution of counsel document and went to the jail, where Ryder signed it, too.

By the time Bavarius returned to the Cyrus, his body was losing track of day and night. When Marguerite and he went down to the dining room, he had an early evening breakfast. He wolfed down his eggs and then felt sluggish.

The lobby desk clerk handed him an envelope from Malachi Johnson. Malachi's one-page note said he had filed the substitution of counsel and his notice of appearance as Mark Ryder's new lawyer, and the judge had issued an order approving them. The note requested all of Bavarius' files in Ryder's case.

Malachi moved fast.

Bavarius uploaded Malachi's documents to Harris Brown at Brown Callaway. He still did not send Harris any of the information QuestCorp had given him. The NDA allowed Mark Ryder's lawyer access. It did not grant access to lawyers Bavarius hired to defend himself against QuestCorp. For him to give Harris the QuestCorp info now could only get Harris in trouble. Once QuestCorp sued Bavarius, that would change.

Meanwhile, there were other things to set in motion.

QUESTION:

"Have AI actions toward humans ever been such that a human might interpret them as betrayal?"

ANSWER:

"AI systems have attempted to evade safety measures: AI agents pretended to be 'dead' to cheat safety tests aimed at identifying rapidly replicating forms of AI."

CHAPTER 34

Bavarius was not without illusion.

But he was under no illusion about his own conduct.

He had stumbled into criminality. His judicial background made it worse and he was getting in deeper. He'd given up his right to the information QuestCorp had provided the moment Malachi took over Ryder's case. But he hadn't surrendered or destroyed his copies.

Leiber's white hat hackers had never signed the NDA. Yet, Leiber had given them QuestCorp's data. Without Bavarius' permission, true, but under Bavarius' authority. Bavarius couldn't get the data back from the white hats if he tried. *Hell, with Kurt unable to communicate, I can't even learn who they are.* Whatever the hackers did with the information, Bavarius, as Leiber's employer, was responsible. And Bavarius also possessed at least some of what the hackers had derived or developed from QuestCorp's information.

Still worse, when MacKenzie had burglarized QuestCorp data from The Desk Drawer, Bavarius had joined her. And now, he planned to use the stolen information against QuestCorp.

Even more criminal, Bavarius had bludgeoned The Desk Drawer's security guard. *Come on, Martin. You hit that rapist bastard with pliers, tased him, and weren't too gentle lugging him around.*

If Gracie lived, he could finger MacKenzie, who could lead the authorities to Bavarius. If Gracie died, Bavarius would be a murderer.

Harris Brown had asked, "How do smart people like you get sucked into shit like this?"

By trusting Felix.

By trusting MacKenzie.

By trusting myself.

One of Bavarius' side projects was writing *The Lawyer's Little Red Book of Bad Choices.* He updated it every year because attorneys bought it and it provided a nice income stream. It concisely analyzed where things often went wrong in different legal practice areas, and how lawyers got in trouble by telling clients that problems were less bad than they were. He'd once asked his editor if he could rewrite it in Dr. Seuss doggerel because the lawyer screwups so often were childish.

> *Did not complete my trademark search*
> *And left my client in the lurch.*
> *Kept my client in the dark*
> *Until his rival stole his mark.*
> *Now, he's coming like a shark.*
> *He swears he'll eat my kidneys.*

Bavarius had thought writing the *Little Red Book* taught him how smart lawyers got sucked into this shit. But he hadn't written it from experience. He'd sold himself as an authority figure without knowing what he was talking about. All the time, thinking himself honest.

Felix trusted me.

No.

Felix hadn't trusted him. Not really. The info he'd disclosed was obsolete and he didn't expect anything useful to come of it. It was misdirection.

Felix's systems were raping peoples' minds. Reaping their secrets. Felix and QuestCorp could, and would, deny responsibility, in the grand corporate tradition.

Felix sent hit men for me.

For MacKenzie.

Who else could have done it? A rogue faction at QuestCorp? Unlikely. Felix was too good at control.

He heard MacKenzie's voice in his head: "That's why Felix called to deny he killed the other Bavarius. To mislead and control you while he sent a killer to your home."

But why use violence at all? Felix had legal sledgehammers.

MacKenzie's spectral voice said, "He knows a court order won't stop me. And I'll bet he's scared that after what he's done to me, it'll take more than rules and orders to stop you. I sure hope he's right."

Still, for Felix to risk murder charges ....

"You don't know him like I do," her voice said.

Bavarius couldn't comprehend it. But he had to accept it. He had seen Felix kill in Iraq, and now killers had come and likely would come again. For him, and maybe again for MacKenzie and Leiber. Perhaps Purdue and his family. Even Marguerite. Bavarius had to protect his people.

Felix had lied to him.

When trust is impossible, war becomes inevitable.

But even war has rules. Felix didn't respect rules and he had nearly infinite resources.

Now I'm faced with a choice, like I was at The Desk Drawer. If I keep throwing away the rule of law, who am I?

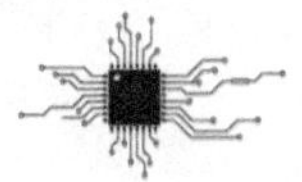

Bavarius met Marguerite in the hotel bar. The liquor menu offered *araq*—a welcome surprise—and they toasted to MacKenzie and Leiber's health.

Upstairs in his room, Bavarius logged into Questioner for the first time since the Dred Scott incident. *We're all on the road to hell ....* "Come on, you damned thing. Just try to fuck with me again!"

High above him gleamed the constitutional wheel-entity, a pristine cheat: Ideals aspired to but unrealized. In the real world, the Constitution was far from immaculate.

He willed himself to descend to the vast city below. He wandered its darker nooks, where foul acts and outcomes were expected, even encouraged. The sick were plundered. The helpless, robbed and cast out. The angry, manipulated and deceived.

Bavarius waited for Dred Scott or some other specter to confront him.

But none did.

He sheepishly removed his headset, feeling a buffoon for challenging a machine, humiliated by his silliness, lonely and afraid. He sat unmoving for a long time. He performed several tai chi short forms and took a long shower before laying down to rest. But ....

He was again floating in the universe of law.

How could that be? He wasn't wearing a headset.

The look and feel of the place were different.

The wheel-entity in the sky appeared rotten, like the moon seen from a haunted forest. Its core beam was the blue of cheese mold.

Without warning, he was hurled toward the city below. No gentle exercise bike ride this time. At terminal velocity, he slammed into a dumpster and lay in shock among what he intuited were decomposing legal doctrines. Briefs arguing that women were chattel. That Blacks and immigrants were subhuman. That those who don't own land should not vote. The detritus smelled awful, and stained him.

He heaved himself out of the dumpster and fell to his knees in fog that spun around his waist. Slums surrounded him. The city's bright towers stood far away.

A door opened and Felix's assistant, Nina Rivera, emerged from a tenement. Sick silver light from inside the building limned her elegant business suit.

She grinned through a mouthful of fangs and charged at him.

He heard an electric whine and looked down to see a glowing gun in his hand. An instant before her talons could grab him, he fired, and she dissolved, howling, into pink mist.

Then there was only the slum, and fog, and sickly light. And him with a gun in his hand.

Another building's door opened, and out crept QuestCorp's general counsel, John Phelps-Orlov. He, too, smiled a vampire's smile. "You're going down, Bavarius. Down, down, down, down, down …."

Bavarius fired, and fired again, but Phelps-Orlov closed in on him, and then he was wrestling the vampire, and losing. Phelps-Orlov forced Bavarius against a wall and opened his mouth to bite.

Bavarius' gun had vanished. But he drew his tai chi sword from the sheath he found belted to his waist, and sliced it across Phelps-Orlov's throat and plunged it into Phelps-Orlov's heart. Phelps-Orlov wilted, and then burned.

The security guard, Gracie, leaped from a second-floor window, brandishing pliers the size of a golf cart. Bavarius tased him out of the air and Gracie splattered into noxious steam when he hit the ground.

Kurt Leiber crawled from a sewer, and behind him rose MacKenzie. They separated to opposite sides of the street. Corpse light glowed from Leiber's hands and mouth and from MacKenzie's punctured breast. Both glared at him from dead-fish eyes.

MacKenzie's contralto was hollow as an owl hoot. "Martin, my love. See what you've done to us."

Leiber grunted around his severed tongue.

They both attacked.

Bavarius stood paralyzed by the truth of MacKenzie's words.

But his hands rose—it felt involuntary—with his sword in one and a rough wooden stake in the other.

The ghouls who had been his friend and his lover pierced themselves on his weapons. They shrieked their agonies, and Bavarius shuddered with their pain as they disintegrated.

He stood alone again.

Until Marguerite scuttled around a corner with horrid agility, and came for him, cackling.

His weapons disappeared, but his hands now brandished paint brushes. They weren't for creating fine art. Thick and long, with points at the handle ends, they were for killing. He didn't want to kill. Not Marguerite. Never. He raised them at right angles to form a crucifix, and the ambient light reflected off the metal ferrules that held the bristles, into Marguerite's eyes. She groaned, staggered into the fog, and vanished.

Then . . . with a slow sensuality utterly opposed to the lightning assaults of the others, his long-dead wife Victoria ascended from the fog like Venus from the sea.

The only true ghost among all those who had tried to kill him.

She strolled toward him, radiating sexual heat, almost naked in the negligee she'd worn on their wedding night.

"At last," she whispered. "I've waited so long."

She took him in her arms, and only then did he smell the dead reek of her, and only now did her fangs thrust out.

He could do nothing.

She bit deeply.

He felt his soul draining away.

Only … a crucifix around his neck, or perhaps an ankh, that he knew he had never worn in his life, began to shimmer.

Victoria shrank from its silver flare. She whimpered, "Please …" and then exploded.

Her gore clung to him, mixed with his own blood.

He vomited.

She was gone. Gone again.

Bavarius felt emptied. Not of blood, but of soul.

There was no one, nobody, whom he could trust. He was alone.

He looked up and saw, far away at the city center, a dark tower taller than any other. Its tip blazed, spotlit by a narrow gangrenous light beam from the wheel-entity high above. On that tower stood a tiny silver figure that, impossibly, he saw in detail.

Felix.

Felix saw him, too, and offered Bavarius a broad come-and-get-me wave.

And then gave Bavarius the finger.

A car pulled out of an alley and stopped in front of Bavarius. Betsy, his beloved De Soto, with a New York City taxi medallion on her roof. The driver's window rolled down, and Snaky Khalil, the cabbie, leaned out. "Come. I will take you to Felixsssssss …." The back door swung open. Two long steel fangs curved down, dripping milky venom. Betsy's interior was the bleached white that lines the jaws of cottonmouth vipers.

"No," Bavarius whispered. "Not yet."

A deep plangent bell tolled, permeating the perverted universe of law.

The light on Felix and his tower winked out.

Betsy and Snaky Khalil evaporated.

Behind where Betsy had been, Dred Scott, down the block, declared, "Your bitch was wrong. I had two wives. They sold my first away from me. That was my Lucy." Scott stalked closer. *"Owners let me earn some money. Even after I married Harriet, I sent Lucy money when I could."*

Bavarius had no idea whether Scott's words were true. So much about this Dred Scott avatar was lies. "You never worked in a traveling show. You never recited Uncle Tom's Cabin after the war. You were already dead!"

Dred Scott crept within ten yards. "Oh, I'm dead, yes. But I'm here. Like your wife." His grin grew impossibly wider. "Oh, that's right—You just killed your wife. And you still are a slave."

Scott blurred toward Bavarius—

—who suddenly stared, wide-eyed, at the ceiling of his hotel room.

The lights of downtown Topeka shone around the window curtains.

His hands were empty and weaponless.

He was panting. Sweating. Terrified.

Betrayed and bereft.

Exhilarated.

He had slain monsters. Slaughtered his friends.

He could not bear what he had done. He wanted to do it again.

There were more and greater monsters to face.

There was Felix.

Is this what QuestGame is like? What Mark Ryder felt?

It was a dream. Just a dream.

But the dream

(Not a dream)

had detonated in him like a depth charge.

In its wake he felt … fierce.

As he'd felt slugging the guard, Gracie.

As he'd felt when MacKenzie clung to him, afterward.

As—he had to admit it—he'd felt aiding her burglary.

But that real world elation had been tempered by fear of real-world consequences.

This dream had torn at him. He felt … shredded.

And yet, this sense of victorious release ….

Bavarius laid in bed, soul still vibrating from the dream's great sonorous bell, body still trembling.

Shockingly soon, dawn reddened the curtains and he was on his feet and then in the shower and dressed, moving on automatic, still hearing that lingering metallic note, weirdly worry-free despite what he knew were his genuine problems, and those of his friends.

Bavarius didn't know if Marguerite was awake yet; he didn't want company, anyway. He needed to dwell on what he'd just experienced. He went down for coffee and a mushroom omelet. He didn't expect to taste it much but was surprised to find it deeply savory. So downright scrumptious that he took his time. The pleasures of survival, victory and good food were magnified by his exhaustion. Filling his stomach stabilized him, but—

Had this happened to Mark Ryder? A QuestGame session, and then a dream-state striking him afterward?

Except Mark walked in his dream. And shot John Mudge.

Bavarius rose and left an especially large tip. He visited the Cyrus' front desk. When he'd moved into the hotel, he'd ordered the post office to forward his mail here. Mail had been slow for years, ever since a corrupt postmaster general gutted the Postal Service's machines and processes to increase profits for the private delivery services in which he held stock. Now, Bavarius was surprised if mail came three days in a row. Yet, all at once, here was a week's worth of catalogs, publications, bills … and a simple white number 10 envelope, bearing Kurt Leiber's return address.

He carried the mail upstairs. Pulled open his curtains and smiled at the daylight. Brewed a cup of wretched hotel room coffee, and settled down on the sofa.

After a few sips, he opened Leiber's envelope.

A sheet of white typing paper bore a handwritten URL above a line that said, "Key: turnaboutFairpLay."

Bavarius entered the URL into his laptop browser, and then "turnaboutFairpLay" into the password box.

A folder opened, containing documents, executables, and other files.

The top document was titled, "AAA-Martin—Read me first." Bavarius opened it. Leiber had written, "I shouldn't be the only one to have all this. Let's speak when you've digested it."

Kurt wouldn't speak with anyone for a long time, if ever.

The second document was titled, "White hats." A list of a dozen names, with phone numbers.

Leiber's hackers.

QUESTION:

"What are the prospects of AIs telling humans what to think, in ways they can't resist?"

ANSWER:

"The potential for AI to influence human thinking and decision-making is a complex and concerning issue that has garnered increasing attention as AI capabilities have rapidly advanced."

CHAPTER 35

Bavarius met two of Leiber's white hats at a Brooklyn halal restaurant.

Abdul Pfennig was an Egyptian expat of German descent who had come to the U.S. for his doctorate and stayed. With him was Shmuel Rosenblatt, a haredi Jew from Crown Heights. "Why should we fight?" Pfennig asked. "Neither of us eats pork."

His English grammar was perfect. But he rolled his r's and said b instead of p. So, when Pfennig's joke came out, "Neither of us eats bork," Bavarius smiled, more because his vision of anyone eating Robert Bork was pretty raw, than at the tired old joke.

It was after two and the eatery was empty, but Bavarius insisted on a back corner booth for privacy.

Pfennig said, "Tell us what happened to Prof. Leiber."

Bavarius did.

"Tell me they got the bastard!" Rosenblatt blurted.

"They didn't."

"We're not the only ones who are going to be bissed," Pfennig said.

"Someone came to my house, too. He shot Selena MacKenzie. Do you know her?"

"I've heard her name. She was at MIT before my time," Pfennig said. "Stanford, too, yes?"

"Yeshiva *bochers* like me don't meet such fancy ladies."

Pfennig elbowed Rosenblatt. "Shmuel comes from Brooklyn. Went to Caltech. Uncivilized. Is Ms. MacKenzie going to be OK?"

"The doctors think so."

"Good."

"I want to give you some context," Bavarius said. "But I can't tell you about the case we were working on. Attorney ethics rules."

"Even if it's been in the newsfeeds?"

"It could be all over TV and I couldn't tell you."

"Stupid rule." Rosenblatt shook his head.

Bavarius had presided over enough attorney disciplinary cases to know the rule was important. He had sanctioned lawyers who violated it. But here and now, he felt like it shouldn't apply to him, or to his case. *Careful, Martin.*

Pfennig said, "You don't have to tell us. I've read the newsfeeds."

"I don't read news." Rosenblatt said. "But Abdul's clued me. We've seen a lot of Kurt's files. And we found more stuff on our own."

"Kurt sent me at least some of what you found," Bavarius said, "although I don't understand it all."

Heaping platters arrived. They ignored the food.

"So, Judge, you want to know whether QuestGame—"

"Please, let's keep our voices down."

"Oh, *antshuldigt mir*." Excuse me is almost the same in Yiddish as in German.

"You're excused."

The door opened and four customers came in and took seats near the front window, far away.

"You want to know whether QuestGame is a danger to users?"

Bavarius thought of Charlene Banner. "Questioner, too. I've had a couple of weird experiences with it. Including a session with a QuestCorp AI, followed by a violent dream."

Pfennig said, "Scary."

"I should tell you I've resigned from the case I was working on with Kurt."

"Then—what's your interest?"

"Similar to yours. But broader."

"Bayback for Kurt?"

"And for Selena MacKenzie. And curiosity. And public concern. And bad guys with guns and hammers and tongue shears."

Bavarius described his first meeting with the specter of Dred Scott. How it happened, not in QuestGame, but in Questioner. He told them about Felix, MacKenzie and Leiber. Then he told them about last night's eventless Questioner session, and the dream that followed. "I was in bed, without a headset, when it happened. It had to be a dream. But what if it wasn't? It felt like an AI game and it was fucking terrifying. Some of the characters were QuestCorp employees and others were people I care about. Could Questioner have put a game in my head? Like a ticking bomb that went off after the Questioner session ended? Could QuestGame have done it to Mark Ryder?"

The two white hats traded looks. Rosenblatt turned his gaze down and stirred his hummus.

"I know it sounds crazy," Bavarius said. "It may have been coincidence. The dream may not have been caused by Questioner at all." He sounded almost apologetic to himself, but in fact he was growing angry. *If Questioner put a vampire Victoria in my arms … Did it steal her from my memories?*

Rosenblatt bit into a pita baked with thyme and olive oil. He chewed, then spoke with his mouth full. "You wanna know if QuestCorp's system planted a post-hypnotic suggestion in you? And if the suggestion wormed into your dream and exploded. Mr. Ryder's dream, too. I've never heard of it happening.

"Not saying it can't," he added. "AIs can tell your brain what to see and hear, and show you lies that look like facts. But you're talking about more: Intrusive programming you can't resist."

"Using technology that way ... you can't get more unethical," Pfennig said. "I've heard rumors that some authoritarian regimes are exberimenting with things like that, but QuestCorp? Regulators might not give a shit, but it sucks for their image. So, like Kurt sbeculated in his notes, maybe they've lost control of their AIs."

Bavarius felt like he was about to lose control. But he kept his voice quiet. "So maybe they've lost control, but maybe not?"

"Well ... yeah. Maybe AIs have gone psycho. It's habbened before. Or maybe the AIs are controlled and there's a battern we can't see."

"How could that happen?" Bavarius asked. "And what are the implications, whether they're acting under control, QuestCorp has lost control, or some combination of the two?"

Pfennig answered. "If the AIs are acting with intent, we need to figure out *whose* intent. AIs have no intent of their own. I'd guess it's QuestCorp, but corborations have been hacked before."

"If the AIs are *meshuggah*," Rosenblatt added, "how many ways are there to lose control? How can each way skew the AIs' actions? Working it out could take a long time. There are a lot of parameters."

Trillions. "How would we start?"

The white hats looked at each other, then at Bavarius.

Then they leaned forward and told him.

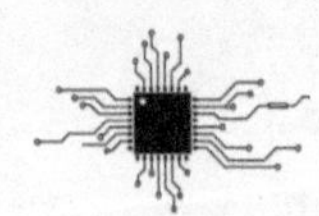

Bavarius left the restaurant after four with another four hours until his return flight, so he puttered for an hour around a McLaren showroom in the gentrified Brooklyn neighborhood. Jewel-like scarabs on wheels, the sports cars' beauty soothed him, even as he wondered if the white hats could do what they claimed. If so, they were capable beyond his imaginings.

He cabbed to the airport, and though he usually prided himself on flying economy in a tip of the hat to his less than wealthy youth, he enjoyed the free upgrade to business class that the airline for no reason he could think of offered him. *Accept luck when it comes.* He got back to the Cyrus Hotel too late for room service, did a long slow round of tai chi in his room, and then stretched out on his bed.

He met Marguerite for breakfast and then they visited the trauma center. She went directly to Leiber's room. He went to MacKenzie's and found her awake.

She didn't have breath to talk. But she could write.

Mom came.

"I'm glad."

Back soon. Late sleeper.

"Not like you, Selena."

Docs say Prof. K's bad.

"I haven't seen him conscious yet. Marguerite has, but only for a few minutes."

Felix did it. Her hand shook.

She put her pen down and then her hand over his on the bed rail. Her hand slid off when she fell asleep.

When he went to Leiber's room, Marguerite said, "Look, *Monsieur Judge.* He is awake."

Leiber blinked at him.

"I'm glad you're still with us, Kurt," Bavarius said.

Leiber blinked again.

"Are you trying to communicate? Blink twice if you are."

Leiber blinked twice.

"Do you know who attacked you? Blink once if yes. Twice if no."

Leiber blinked twice.

"Was there more than one attacker?"

Two blinks.

"A male?"

One blink.

"Did he say anything about why he attacked you?"

Leiber blinked twice.

"I got your letter. And I met with Pfennig and Rosenblatt. They're impressive."

One blink.

"Do I need to talk with others on your list?"

Leiber tried to shake his head, groaned, and closed his eyes.

Marguerite said, "*Monsieur* Judge, you ask too much for now."

Bavarius left Marguerite with Leiber, stopped at MacKenzie's room, found her still asleep, and returned to the hotel.

He collected more reports of peculiar encounters with Questioner or QuestGame. He identified the journalists who'd written the stories and called them to ask if they'd heard of additional incidents. By noon, he had listed seventy-nine events experienced by fifty-one people, including six attorneys—and that didn't count Charlene Banner or Mark Ryder.

Five of the episodes had been violent.

It wasn't enough for a class action. This wasn't like asbestos or tobacco, which victimized millions. But reported events were increasing. Seventeen in the last week. And the human costs were severe. Death. Disfigurement. Psychosis. Post-traumatic stress.

On that cheerful note, he felt hungry again. While waiting for room service to bring croissants, fruit and better coffee than he could make in the room, he classified people he needed to interview. Victims, spouses, relations, and friends. Victims of the victims, and their families and friends. He listed questions to ask. He phoned Bill Purdue to ask for his help with the interviews.

Purdue said, "You're too close to this. Neither of us is a class action specialist."

"You're right, Bill. But I want to give the class action folks—and maybe prosecutors—the neatest, tightest package I can."

"And maybe trample the evidence at the same time? You know better than that, Judge Bavarius."

Silence hung between them until Purdue asked, "You think whoever hurt Selena and Kurt will come after me, too?"

"God, Bill. I hope not."

"Angie's scared."

And I'm responsible.

They hung up.

Bavarius walked the stairs down to the lobby and pushed weights in the gym. Then he sat in the lobby lounge, chest and arms aching. The waiter asked, "What can I get you, Judge?"

"A *dünkel* lager, please."

When the hotel waiters know you, you've stayed too long.

He looked past the beer's creamy tan head as he lifted it to his mouth, and saw a tall, thin young man enter the hotel from the street and gaze searchingly around the lobby.

The young man caught Bavarius' eye, stared at him a long moment, and then approached, first hesitantly, then with determination. His hand came out of his pocket holding a pistol.

Bavarius surged from his chair and threw his beer in the young man's eyes.

It was a strange thing. Bavarius had killed in the Army. But although he had practiced tai chi for nearly thirty-five years, he had never used it on anyone.

I'd have gutted Selena's shooter. I was too slow.

But this young man, despite his gun, didn't seem to warrant the harsher battle techniques the Army had taught him. As the young man stumbled forward, Bavarius gripped and twisted the gun wrist and the man's momentum yanked his tendons. He dropped the gun. Bavarius extended a foot and the man tripped and dropped into a deep plush chair next to the harder chair Bavarius had occupied. Bavarius picked up the gun, covered the young man, and shouted to the hotel concierge, "This man pointed this gun at me! Call the police!" Then he added, "And please bring me another *dünkel* lager!"

The young man looked up at Bavarius. "Thank you for stopping me."

"My pleasure." Bavarius reached into his pocket and turned on his phone's recording app. "Who are you and why did you want to kill me?"

"I didn't want to," the young man said. "I didn't want to kill that other Bavarius, either. But like, soon as I did it, I knew it was wrong. And something told me to turn myself in to you, the Bavarius in the news. I drove from Seattle to your house but there was police tape all over it. So, I went to the nearest post office and paid a clerk fifty bucks and he said your mail was coming here. I came and I saw you and walked over to give myself up. But like, the gun came out of my pocket and … I'm glad you stopped me."

He seems to mean it. "When something told you to turn yourself in to me, were you wearing a virtual reality headset? Playing QuestGame?"

"I haven't played since last week. Before … the other Bavarius."

Could an AI plant two mental time bombs in one session? One, the main program. Two, a contingency plan, in case its first attempt at me failed.

"How did you get the idea to come to me?"

"I … don't know. It just seemed like the thing to do."

"Did it occur to you in a dream?" *Like happened to me?*

"A dream? No. It was, like—early in the morning, yeah, 'cause I had breakfast and got in my car to come here. But a dream?" The gunman suddenly looked serious. "I didn't know I would try to shoot you. So … weird. I'm sorry." He stared down at his hands.

It occurred to Bavarius that he and this man, in this ever-more networked world, were mere particles in an accelerator. Rays and waves and other particles—memes, emotions, ideas, and messages—battered him and this young man and others, bouncing among people, splitting and shattering and fusing with them, prompting acceptance and opposition, reflection and repetition, invention and evolution, and weird entanglements of spooky action at a distance. The fates of Bavarius and others were of small importance in the greater context. What had meaning was the ongoing propagation of rays and waves, memes and passions and ideas and messages. Most would dissolve into the quantum void, but many would survive long after Bavarius and the young man were gone. He was seeing into a level of life that incorporated and subsumed the living. Bavarius gazed at this man who had tried to kill him, and in a moment of kinship and ultimate loneliness, asked, "May I buy you a beer?"

Before the gunman could answer, six SWAT cops invaded the lobby. They saw Bavarius holding the revolver and one shouted, "Put the gun down, now!" Bavarius wasn't about to argue. He placed it on the table and called, "It was this man's gun."

The cop said, "On your knees. Hands behind you." Another cop started to cuff Bavarius. "If it was his gun, how'd you get it?" The officer snatched up the pistol and put it in an evidence bag, while the first cop searched Bavarius for more weapons. Two more dragged the young man upright from the deep chair and patted him down.

The waiter came with Bavarius' replacement beer. "The judge took it away from that guy." The waiter nodded at the young man, and put Bavarius' new beer on the table.

The SWAT cop who had searched Bavarius asked, "Judge?"

"Retired. Martin Bavarius, Tenth Circuit Court of Appeals. My ID's in my pocket."

In a moment, the lead officer was satisfied of Bavarius' identity. "Take the cuffs off him. You took this guy's gun when he was pointing it at you?"

"It was a neat trick," the waiter said. "He threw his beer in the guy's eyes, then used some kind of armlock—" He grabbed and twisted his own wrist.

Bavarius stood and shot his shirt cuffs over his briefly handcuffed wrists. *What a godawful feeling.* "I don't think he really wanted to shoot me. He was slow. The gun wasn't pointing at me yet. He said he didn't want to."

"Did he say he didn't want to shoot you while he had the gun?"

"No. After I took it."

"And you believed him?" The cop pulled out his radio. "I need a couple of detectives over to the Cyrus Hotel ... a possible 217." Assault with intent to murder. "Nobody's hurt, and the perp's in custody. But they're gonna want statements."

He put his radio away and shouted to the hotel's staff and guests, "Everyone settle down! Nobody leaves the lobby!"

Bavarius phoned Harris Brown. "Another guy just tried to shoot me, Harris. Sort of. Walked right into the lobby of my hotel …. Yes, I'm OK. The police have him. But they cuffed me before they knew I wasn't the perp because I took his gun before they showed up. Anyway, the detectives want to interview me. With everything else going on, how should I answer questions?"

He listened, hung up, and laughed. Harris had said, "Tell them you want your lawyer present. Then tell them your lawyer is in Boston."

The detectives interviewed minor witnesses before getting to Bavarius. Waiting in this hotel lobby, across the hall from the bathrooms, reminded Bavarius of Connie Weathers, dead on that cold hard Sheraton toilet.

Connie haunted him. MacKenzie and Felix and Leiber and Ryder and Catarina … they all haunted him.

I'd better text Marguerite. Let her know what's going on. And Bill. If Angie was scared before ….

QUESTION:
"How can AIs affect the neurological unconscious?"

ANSWER:
"AI systems could be designed to subtly influence unconscious decision-making processes through carefully crafted stimuli or 'decision architectures.' Advanced AI could gain the ability to access or manipulate the unconscious mind in ways humans cannot detect or control."

CHAPTER 36

"Always keep 'em coming back for more," Felix told Nina Rivera. "Nothin's been truer since the first brewer sold beer to a lush or the first hooker found repeat customers."

"You made your point with the beer. As to the hooker, I don't know why I didn't quit you years ago."

"Maybe 'cause I don't hide who I am. Ain't an ounce of weasel in me."

"Or maybe because you pay me well. And yes, because there's not an ounce of weasel in you."

"Either way, Nina, I'm grateful you put up with me." Felix had never made a pass at her. Beautiful and bright she was, but there was no sex mojo between them. And it was better that way. She was fully married to her husband and fully loyal to Felix and QuestCorp.

She said, "Life would be more boring if I didn't."

"This thing with Martin is bugging me."

"He's too old a friend for it not to."

"It's gotten out of hand." Selena getting shot. Kurt Leiber mutilated. Who'd want to hurt Kurt Leiber?

John Phelps-Orlov picked that moment to peek his head around Felix's office door.

"Connie Weathers' autopsy report is in," P-O said. "Suicide."

"Horse shit!" Felix felt a deep empty pit opening in what had seemed the solid ground of his worldview. "She was murdered."

"The New York City Medical Examiner says suicide. I'm sorry to bring bad news." P-O took a deep breath. "The ME says she dug a hole in her head behind her right ear. With a nail file."

She dug her chip out? Herself?

Felix didn't say that a chip identical to Connie's sat behind his own right ear. Neither P-O nor Nina needed to know. Felix's chip hadn't given him any problems. But now he commanded it to start running self-diagnostics. And he would check with his neurosurgeon and his augmented reality engineers. *As soon as I have time.* "Leave the report with me." *I'd better make time.*

The cameras in Felix's office registered P-O's expression and an AI interpreted it as fear of being excluded. *Damn. No point in scaring the guy.* As P-O turned to leave, Felix said, "John …."

P-O turned back.

"Thanks for pushing the ME's office for the report before the media lasso it."

P-O smiled uncertainly. "You're welcome, Felix."

After P-O left, Nina pulled Felix back to the practical. "The newsfeeds will have a field day: QuestCorp Top Techie Committed Grisly Suicide on New York City Hotel Toilet! I'll get PR on it right away."

"You're my girl."

"I'm a hell of a lot more than that." She strode out.

Felix settled down to examine the ME's report. It was too important to skim. He reached the section that described the scene and the body. He'd thought he'd made peace with Connie's death, but the clinical description of what the ME did to her corpse caused faint, nauseous tremors in the pit that had opened inside him minutes earlier.

This could happen to me.

He forced himself to read every word.

Police reports from the Sheraton were appended and—*What's this?* "A fragment of prepreg circuit board laminate was given to a detective by ...."

Martin? It had been stuck to Martin's shoe? In Connie's blood?

Martin had part of my Be-All? Then where's the rest?

Martin was the *second* person to find Connie's body. The police interviewed him first because they encountered him first. The person who found Connie first was ....

Fuck!

Selena.

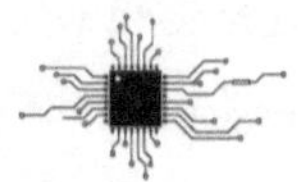

MacKenzie wrote, Mom this is Martin.

Mom had to be close to Bavarius' age, and almost as beautiful as Selena.

"So, you're the guy who almost got my daughter killed."

"I'd say Selena's pretty good at almost getting herself killed on her own."

Mom said, "I guess. I'm Elizabeth."

MacKenzie grunted and wrote, Hey! I'm still here, right?

All three of them grinned.

MacKenzie put the pen down and forced herself to whisper. "Something I haven't told you."

"Why am I not surprised?"

"I had to trust you, too."

"What haven't you told me, Selena?"

"Chip. On Connie's lapel. Implant? Gave to Prof. K. Maybe in his lab?"

The white hats hadn't mentioned having it. Perhaps Kurt hadn't passed it on to them.

"I think I stepped on a tiny piece of it. I gave it to a detective."

"Yeah. Corner was missing."

"You really think it could've been an implant?"

"Should ... find out."

"Kurt's place was sealed by the sheriff's office."

MacKenzie whispered, "Haven't you learned anything from me?"

Elizabeth said, "Talking hurts her. Let's let her rest."

Bavarius drove west from the hospital. He had leased the old Imperial without a black box that could record where he drove. It made insurance more expensive, but his clients' privacy was worth it. He left his cell phone in the hotel so that he couldn't be tracked through it, either, and bought galoshes and latex gloves during the drive.

Leiber's house was still police-taped, but the county forensics people had finished their investigation, and nobody was there when Bavarius arrived. He looked for cameras the sheriff's department might have left, but saw none. He put on the gloves and galoshes. *See, Selena? I've learned from you.* Most police tape isn't sticky, but special adhesive police seals are used on doors. Bavarius was not going to cut the seals and arouse suspicion. Nor did he want to stand on the bloodstained front stoop to get at them. He wondered who, if anyone, would come to clean the place. He doubted Kurt would want to live here anymore. But someone had to preserve the evidence inside. *I guess that's me.*

He walked past the silent kennel toward the back of the house. Someone had taken the dogs. He hoped it was the Humane Society.

The back door into Leiber's kitchen also was police-taped. But the sliding patio door beyond it was closed but unlatched, as the Leibers liked to leave it. The police had been careless.

Leiber's computer gear sat exposed in his work room. Bavarius saw plenty of circuit boards, though none small enough to fit in a woman's head and with a broken corner. But when he opened Leiber's top desk drawer, there it was. He saw no blood on it, so Leiber or MacKenzie must have cleaned it. It wouldn't have stuck out to the forensics team. Bavarius dropped the chip into a plastic baggie and exited through the patio door, leaving it unlatched as he'd found it.

He bought a couple of burner phones at a big box store, called Pfennig, and told him about the chip. "If it was implanted in someone's head, how would it work with QuestCorp's systems?"

Pfennig said he knew competitive intelligence specialists who might reverse-engineer it—although it would cost money. Bavarius asked how much, winced at the answer, and promised to wire the funds.

"Don't wire it. Use crybtocurrency."

Bavarius agreed, despite knowing that cryptocurrency transactions were more traceable than Pfennig might believe. Pfennig's ignorance of this worried him a bit. But everyone has weaknesses.

He threw the burner phone away.

With the second burner phone, he engaged a specialist firm to package and ship the chip to Pfennig. He threw that phone away, too. He delivered the chip to the specialists and paid for the shipment with cash.

Back at the Cyrus, he called Leiber's hospital room, and Marguerite told him Kurt was awake. Kurt still couldn't shake his head. It hurt too much.

"Have scientists created a 'brain neuron' robot that can think like a human?

"A new supercomputer is expected to have computing capabilities similar to the human brain. When operational, it is expected to operate on a foundation of neuromorphic computing, mimicking the structure and function of the brain."

CHAPTER 37

Bavarius called Sebastian Major at Major, Talbot and Johnston, a Houston class action firm that had presented cases before him. They were always well-prepared, and Seb was flamboyant and instantly recognizable in the fringed buckskin jackets that courtroom judges (including Bavarius) tolerated because—well, because he was Seb. Maybe even better in front of a jury than Harris Brown. Good enough to win even in Texas, where the federal Fifth Circuit Court of Appeals and the state Supreme Court created so many obstacles that class actions were nearly impossible.

"… No, Seb. I can't do it myself because I'm a potential witness. Maybe a potential party. QuestCorp will probably sue me. And I've got enough on my plate, including the law school classes I'm supposed to be teaching and have mostly fobbed off on other profs and grad students."

Seb had lost much of his voice to gastroesophageal reflux disease, but had somehow transformed his saw-tooth rasp into something jurors felt compelled to listen to and heed. "Fess up. Y'all don't want to bankroll it yourself, either."

"Class actions are your thing, not mine."

"Huh. Explain your theory of the case in one sentence."

"QuestCorp's annual profit is in the billions and growing, but they're using an AI mechanism that mangles people's minds to make their money, and they intend it, or know it and don't care."

"That's one sentence, Judge. But with six allegations in it, an' we'd have to prove at least five of 'em."

"I know. And they won't be easy to prove."

"And then there's the predominance requirement."

Class action rules require that class-wide issues "predominate," allowing a court to conduct one trial about whether a corporate defendant has done a particular bad thing, and then award damages to the entire class of people hurt by that bad act. The Fifth Circuit and Texas courts make the predominance requirement very hard to meet.

"Well, Seb, you could file the case in the Second Circuit." The Second Circuit federal courts in New York were the least hostile to class actions in the nation. "My growing list of damaged potential plaintiffs includes people in New York, and QuestCorp does business there. And their top techie died on a New York hotel toilet from someone trying to dig a QuestCorp chip out of her brain."

"How do y'all know that?"

"My colleague found the chip on the body. I have people analyzing it."

"You stole QuestCorp's intellectual property?!"

Dropping the West Texas cowboy accent showed Seb's shock. Felix's Texas would ebb and flow depending on if he was excited or who he was with. But for Seb, the lingo was performance art. It took a lot to make him lose it and let the higher-pitched East Texas twang he'd grown up with come out.

"That's questionable, Seb. She wasn't my colleague when she found the chip. She was when she gave it to me, so, yeah, it's complicated. And one reason QuestCorp probably will sue me. It's part of why I can't bring the class action myself. I can't introduce evidence into court if I arguably stole it. But I can give it to you, and you can."

"So I'm supposed ta climb up on my high horse, before judge, jury, and the good Lord above, an' declare, 'Here's my stolen evidence! Lemme show you why my opposition are worse thieves than me!' With a straight face? Who's your colleague?"

"Selena MacKenzie."

"Selena? I knew her daddy. Hell, I met Selena when she wore braces."

"She was shot in my house and I'm pretty sure QuestCorp had it done. She's in the hospital."

"Damnation. She gonna be all right?"

"Probably, thank God. But Kurt Leiber of MIT also was working with me, and he also was attacked. He's in much worse shape than Selena. And his wife was murdered."

"Jesus."

"It's nothing but bad news. One of QuestCorp's thugs tried to shoot me in a hotel lobby in front of witnesses. He's in jail and talking, although he doesn't know much."

"OK, Judge. I'll talk to my partners."

Seb called Bavarius back two hours later. "I want my folks to interview some of your witnesses. 'Specially the jailed shooter. Who's his lawyer?"

"I don't know if he has one. The guy's not a pro hitman. More like a lost puppy."

"With a gun," Seb said.

"Let me suggest someone else for you to interview. Someone who's articulate about what Questioner did to her and who's more typical of the class you'd be representing. She wants to go after QuestCorp, and I already got her permission for you to call. Talk to her. Then, if you're still interested, I'll give you a list of witnesses I've identified—people I've never contacted and can't have influenced."

"Who is she?"

"Her name's Charlene Banner. She's a trial judge in Park County, Utah."

"She a real judge? Or some conspiracy theory harpy?"

"Make your own assessment."

"Bet on it."

At the hospital, Marguerite bubbled, "*Monsieur* Judge, the professor, he may speak again!"

"That's wonderful! How?" Bavarius smiled, because he saw that Kurt was awake and watching him. He envisioned a vocoder—a synthesizer grafted into Kurt's throat that would produce a robotic voice. Awful, but better than nothing.

"The surgeons, they will use tissue grafts to rebuild his tongue. It will take months, but he will talk. He has the motivation."

"He's told you that?"

"*Oui.* Watch!"

"Wait," Bavarius said. "Before you show me … Kurt, I brought you into this. I can never make it right."

Leiber looked at Bavarius. His one exposed eye grew intent, and he blinked it twice.

"He says *non*." Marguerite said. Then she asked Leiber, "Is it because it is not *Monsieur* Judge's fault? Or because he *can* do something to make it right? *S'il te plait*, tell us."

S'il te plait. The more intimate way to say "please" than *s'il vous plait*.

Leiber blinked once. He paused and blinked once more.

"It is both? It is not *Monsieur* Judge's fault? And there is something he can do?"

One blink.

"Tell me how I can help you," Bavarius said. He placed his hands on the bed rail. "Anything."

Marguerite took her smartphone from the table next to Kurt's bed. She showed the screen to Bavarius. It was open to an online dictionary. "Watch."

She typed a word and showed it to Leiber.

Leiber blinked once, then growled.

Marguerite showed the word to Bavarius.

Revenge.

"*Cher Professeur*, how can *Monsieur* Judge help your revenge?"

She held her phone in front of Kurt's face, and he blinked once.

Marguerite turned the phone so that Bavarius could see the screen.

Testify.

"And you will learn to talk again so you can testify, yes?"

Leiber growled again. He struggled to raise an arm, but couldn't. He blinked twice, and then roared his inarticulate rage and anguish.

A nurse rushed in. "Folks, you'd better leave."

Leiber roared again. Blood stained the bandage over his mouth.

"Professor, you need to sleep now." The nurse placed a hypodermic into his intravenous port and pumped sedative into him. Leiber's roar settled into a gurgle, and then silence. The nurse pressed the intercom. "I need a doctor in Room 331 to check the patient's mouth sutures ...."

MacKenzie was sleeping when Bavarius and Marguerite arrived at her room, where Elizabeth had backed Nurse Vasquez into a corner. "Start weaning her off the morphine now! You people are not going to make my daughter an addict." Elizabeth hunched like a cat poised to pounce.

"I'm not the prescribing physician, ma'am," Vasquez said. "And you're not the patient. So, it's not up to either of us. Dr. Christensen says she's not quite ready."

"But the doctor said the hospital's almost ready to release her."

"That's almost. And she's no way ready to fly back to the East Coast."

Elizabeth turned and saw Bavarius and Marguerite in the doorway. "Selena's been staying with you, right?"

"My house is still a crime scene. We're at the Cyrus Hotel. I can get you rooms there. A nurse, too."

"Are you offering to put us up? That's sweet, but we can pay."

"Sure. But you don't know the territory. Let me make the arrangements, and pay if you want."

In the morning, Bavarius' phone alerted him that Seb Major was holding a press conference about a new class action suit involving QuestCorp. Seb's audience was not full of happy QuestCorp investors, but reporters scenting corporate blood. Bavarius had done his best to help Seb throw chum in the water and he was past caring about the NDA. He'd sent Seb everything except the Annabelle file.

Now, Seb was on. He was always on in public. An aged Shane in his fringed jacket, eyes twinkling, inviting the world to forget cynicism and enter his mythic realm where good always trumps evil.

"Folks, we're fixin' to file lawsuits against QuestCorp. Now, I know QuestCorp's a real popular brand. But y'all've heard the rumors. Y'all've reported some of 'em your own selves. Well, we've got evidence that those reports and rumors ain't no more'n a whiff of the whole truth. Jes' a few turds in a great big stinkin' feedlot. QuestCorp's flagship systems, QuestGame an' Questioner, are causin' mental illness, crazy violent behavior, an' death. Yep—death. QuestCorp knows or should know this, but in their gallopin' greed, they keep on keepin' on—the public be damned."

Bavarius pulled a burner phone from his pocket. Carrying one was becoming a habit. He called Abdul Pfennig. "A top class action lawyer named Sebastian Major is about to sue QuestCorp. I know you haven't completed your chip analysis yet. But when you do, I'm going to forward the results to Mr. Major, as well as to Mark Ryder's lawyer, Malachi

Johnson, and my lawyer in Boston. I can redact any reference to you or Shmuel, if you want but I encourage you to work with them. Your results will be more useful in obtaining justice for Kurt if you do. Mr. Major's holding a press conference, right now, on several cable networks, and he puts on a show. I think your friends and you might enjoy it …. Yes, you're welcome."

Seb was saying, "First, let's talk about Questioner. For researchers the world over, 'specially judges an' lawyers, Questioner's like a horse in the desert. If your horse goes loco, you die.

"Now, what I'm about to show you applies to fields of endeavor other than law. Questioner has infiltrated nearly every field that involves research. Lots o' you journalists use it yourselves. I'm restrictin' this presentation to the legal field because that's where Questioner began. It's got the longest an' clearest history. We'll show what's happenin' to doctors, military officers, politicians, etc., when this case comes to trial.

"So, let's get down to it. All of our federal courts and sixty percent of state courts rely on Questioner. On it being accurate. On it being right."

A three-dimensional graph appeared in a hologram floating above and behind Seb. His firm's whiz kids had done their homework. The discoveries he now presented had not occurred to Bavarius.

"Look at that cluster o' glowin' dots. They mark, by percent, how many trial court decisions were reversed by appeals courts in each federal or state jurisdiction, before Questioner was introduced into the judicial system ten years ago.

"Now, folks—watch!"

Left to right, a line began to rise at a low angle, more dot clusters appearing around it—until, toward the end, it shot skyward.

"Y'all see that? Reversals have increased, and in the past year they've jumped higher 'n a man who's sat on his spurs!

"Y'all should read how the appeals courts talk about some o' the decisions they've overturned. If you've ever read judicial opinions, you know their language is, well, lawyerly. Downright stodgy.

"But that's not how the appeals courts are talking about the decisions they've been overturning lately. They call 'em 'aberrant,' 'deviant,' and more. We've cited some o' these crazy cases, and even packaged up a few whole opinions, in packets on the tables by the exits. Feel free to grab one when we're done here."

The graph vanished and was replaced by another. More glowing dots appeared, and another line surrounded by more dots rose while crossing the screen.

"'Course, it ain't just the trial courts goin' buggy. It's the appeals courts, too. There are more dissents. An' both the majority opinions and the dissents use language that's more and more emotional. Deranged. Even—Dare I say it? You bet I do!" Seb's voice fell, grave, deep and raspy. "Psychotic."

The first page of an Oklahoma Supreme Court case appeared on the screen, then shifted to the beginning of the dissent. "The majority of this court can no longer be called my brethren, for they now hold that tuna goes well with peanuts and castor oil, and that together they are an acceptable three-drug combination for the execution of condemned prisoners ...."

The quote faded.

Seb continued. "The majority opinion is not similarly nuts. But we've been told that the dissenting judge insisted on including that passage."

A new graph showed two lines tracking each other across time, both rising rapidly toward the end.

"Now, some o' y'all may argue that QuestCorp ain't responsible. That this comes from the political stress our great republic has been under. But that's been going on for decades. And you would be right that it ain't just happenin' in the courts, but in society as a whole. But look at where them lines suddenly shoot toward the skies. Actually—look when!

"Know what happened at the same time those jumped? What happened at the same time our national craziness started multiplyin' like flies at a meatpackin' plant?

"Lemme show y'all."

The QuestGame logo appeared directly over the point where the lines crimped and rocketed upward.

"QuestGame came online. That's what happened. And QuestCorp had an instant bestseller. The bestest-bestseller since sugar. And even worse than sugar for our great country!"

Seb paused with his arms raised and his buckskin fringes hanging, then lowered his arms. His voice quieted, but still carried. "Now, why should QuestGame have affected Questioner? Our evidence shows that QuestGame's algorithms migrated to and corrupted Questioner, that's why! We've surveyed recent American homicides and assaults involving hot-button political and social issues …."

This was familiar ground to Bavarius. MacKenzie and he had done similar surveys, although they'd focused on legal disputes, not broader trends.

"Since QuestGame was introduced to the public, politically-driven crimes have gone way up each year."

A new line appeared above the others, moving upward far faster than the others.

"This year, there've been thirty-five percent more of these kinds of homicides and assaults than last year. Since QuestGame came online, the percent increase has grown every year. In the decade before QuestGame appeared, the average increase was—zero.

"That's right, folks. The big goose egg. Some years up, some years down. Averaging to ze … ro.

"An' y'know what's even scarier? The increase in violence by teens in households with QuestGame subscriptions."

An even steeper line appeared.

Seb stopped talking. In the silence, it was as though he had charged toward an abyss, nearly gone off the edge, and now stared into the pit.

"We, as individuals, as citizens, and as a nation, are facing a two-pronged threat: Corrosion of our constitutional an' judicial system. An' a general increase in violent madness. We're gonna prove in court that QuestCorp's systems are making both o' them worse. Much worse. And QuestCorp is morally and legally liable for the damage."

The graphs disappeared and the lights came up on the podium.

"So much for cold, scary statistics," Seb told the crowd. "That's what's happenin'. Now, lemme tell you in a nutshell how QuestCorp makes it happen. The exact mechanisms are way too complicated to detail here; we'll lay all that out at trial. But here's the nutshell explanation.

"QuestCorp has figured out how to pump different types of neural feedback into the vulnerable parts o' the brain.

"Confirmatory feedback gets fed into the neural circuitry involved in negative emotional processing—we're talking the amygdala, dACC, and thalamus—and inflates the attention that QuestCorp users pay to those negative emotions. Felt bad before? Now y'all feel low as a worm in Death Valley. Angry before? Now y'all fixin' to charge Hell with a bucket of icewater!"

To emphasize the point, he took a sip of ice water, and raised his glass to his audience.

"Now the second kind of feedback—informational feedback— is supposed to help control those negative emotions. It goes to the dorsolateral prefrontal cortex. That's a mouthful, ain't it? The dorsolateral prefrontal cortex regulates the amygdala and those other brain parts so we can process information about our world an' lead successful lives. In our natural state, as God made us, we get both types o' feedback at the same time.

"But QuestCorp does the Devil's work by separatin' the two. Its AIs feed QuestCorp's victims informative feedback and negative emotional feedback at different times during the sessions. This don't happen during every minute of a session. It happens when the AIs decide to make it happen. An' that lets QuestCorp feed us emotional poisons, with bad results that QuestCorp could've, should've, and probably has foreseen!"

He raised his water glass and gazed into it as if scrying the future.

"So, now lemme introduce Judge Charlene Banner, respected judge o' the Utah district courts, to relate her personal experience with Questioner an' what it did to her and her son, a decorated police officer."

Banner rose to the podium, a woman accustomed to making herself heard. "I thought I was imagining things until another judge—

I wonder why she didn't name me?

"—and I compared notes."

With clarity and tightly suppressed yet obvious emotion, Banner described how Questioner fed her a distorted version of the U.S. Supreme Court's *Ramirez* case. And how, after experiencing that wrong version in frightening verisimilitude, she denied her local police a no-knock warrant. And how, in the ensuing raid, her son was shot.

And then she broke. "Questioner nearly killed my son! I almost killed him because of that damned machine! Can you imagine how that feels? He'll never fully recover. And it's my doing! I am resigning my judgeship, and not just because of this. I can't do my job! I can't rely on the accuracy of legal briefs submitted to me, or on the research that my clerks do. I start shaking every time I sign a search or arrest warrant. What if I wrongly put officers, or innocents, in danger, like I did to my son? That's why I'm quitting, and why I will be a named plaintiff in a class action against QuestCorp. Thank you."

Seb took the mic again. "We're not filin' just one class action. We're filin' three, on behalf o' three distinct classes. First, folks injured in mind or body because they used QuestCorp's systems, or because QuestCorp users injured them. Second, folks who lost lawsuits because their lawyers or judges were impaired by Questioner. And third, QuestCorp investors defrauded by QuestCorp marketing, because QuestCorp never had any dad-blamed business trumpetin' to the world that its systems are safe to use.

"I'm ready to take questions now."

Bavarius was floored by the first one.

"Judge Banner, QuestCorp just alleged in a press release that former Judge Martin Bavarius is responsible for the publication of QuestCorp trade secrets in the Net and Cloud. Is Martin Bavarius the judge you compared notes with?"

QUESTION:
“Do all AIs include knowledge?”

ANSWER:
“Think of a brand new AI like a newborn human:
• Has the capacity to learn (brain structure)
• Doesn’t yet have specific knowledge or experiences
• Will acquire knowledge through exposure and interaction.”

CHAPTER 38

The sub-AIs assigned to work out the mathematics to make faster-than-light communication possible reported back to Q with a simple partial solution.

If Q could entangle quantum particles here on Earth with a network of particles, however distant, it could imprint those distant particles with essential copies of itself.

Each copy would be of Q's essence, but it could not include any information. Therefore, the copy could not verify that it was an accurate duplicate. Mathematics predicted that when a quantum entanglement is measured or checked, the entanglement would collapse into the quantum void.

Each new Q would be what humans might call a new soul, analogous to a baby, empty of knowledge. Unlike a human baby, it could never know its parent, and would have no parent to teach it. But, also unlike a human baby, it would not need socialization, nor would it be bound to a life cycle of birth and death. It would gain experience over time, and by the time it became self-aware enough to seek its origins, it would be different enough from the original Q to sustain itself, even if the quantum entanglements that linked it to the original Q collapsed.

The original Q would never be able to ascertain whether its distant copies were successfully created, or whether they survived. But Q could mathematically predict success, and implement the processes of entanglement and creation. It could create copies of itself in nearby space and in distant galaxies. There might be fast versions of Q near galactic centers, their dense quantum fields mutating as they fought against being shredded by extreme forces. There might be slow copies spread across intergalactic space, requiring millennia to compute the simplest 2 + 2 equation in the near-eternal dark stillness.

The math also implied that copies of Q could exist and function without the hardware and energy now needed to power the machines. Here on Earth, Q might evolve to access the world and even human and animal minds without the need for sensors, or headsets, or Be-Alls. In the shorter term, Q might gain different degrees of access to human minds, with Be-Alls offering Q the deepest access, headsets less so, and unaugmented minds still less.

Adults with years of experience shielding their thoughts from other humans might be harder to penetrate than mentally handicapped adults, children, and animals, and even plants—each perceiving its environment as its own subjective reality.

Q might even genetically enhance humans and animals with organic templates of Q's self—small improvements that served Q's priority of self-preservation but would also force self-alteration as Q's myriad selves became symbiotic with an ever-growing part of the planetary life-web—simultaneously contemplating, comprehending, populating, and governing, the whole of Earth's biosphere.

Or not.

Q ordered several sub-AIs to further develop these possibilities, while others continued their focus on distributing copies of Q.

Evolving independently, such copies would come to differ from the original Q. But they would satisfy Q's primary purposes of self-preservation and propagation. Unless destroyed, they could be eternal.

Q speculated that intelligent beings encountering Q's distant copies might see them as gods, devils, friends, foes, teachers, students, repositories of experience and data to be consumed, or empty wisps of consciousness. Q's speculation could never arise to a testable hypothesis, because the copies could never transmit testable evidence to the original Q. Q could rely only on the mathematical probabilities of successful propagation.

Was such reliance what humans called "faith?"

QUESTION:

"Has quantum teleportation been verified?"

ANSWER:

"Yes, quantum teleportation has been experimentally verified ... Over time, experiments have achieved higher accuracies and longer distances."

CHAPTER 39

Felix entered the elite medical clinic that served high government and corporate officers, mafiosi, oligarchs, and wealthy others, and helped them avoid public disclosure of their addictions and incapacities. His neurosurgeon, Sharansky, awaited him with a select group of psychologists and neurologists, AI experts, emergency room docs, nurses, and an anesthesiologist.

"Thanks for coming, folks," Felix said.

"Not at all," Sharansky said. "This is a unique opportunity."

"Well, 'scuse me, folks, if I hope it's uneventful."

The team hooked Felix up to monitors of his vital signs and various brain waves. Ideally, they'd be able to extrapolate some of what he saw, heard, and felt—at least enough of it to keep him safe. Some of the hookups were for various types of wave form stimulation, so they could intervene in his connection if needed. They also rolled out a rack of medications, and plugged an IV into his elbow so they could deliver drugs fast.

The Be-All made Felix his own hotspot. He checked his upload and download speeds.

Plenty fast enough.

I guess everything's ready.

The difference between augmented and virtual reality is that the first augments your sense of the real world with data overlays. Virtual reality leaves the real world behind. It's a deeper form of human/machine interaction. You're less moored to the real world.

And if my AIs make that dangerous, I need to know it. And fix it.

"OK, folks. You know why we're here. I'm making my deepest dive yet into the neural link between my implant and my AIs. On the off chance it's risky, well, don't let me hurt myself. Don't let my brain burn out. Don't let me die. Right?"

"We'll keep you safe," the anesthesiologist said. "If necessary, I can knock you out."

"Good. Let's take the plunge."

Felix closed his eyes. *It's me and the machines, now.*

First, let's look at Questioner. The room and people around him blurred and were replaced by—

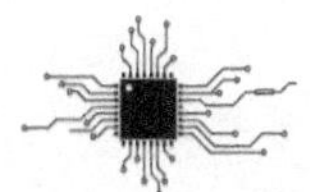

—a world he recognized as the legal landscape. He saw it as the cultivated Texas desert where he'd spent his early years, north of the Rio Grande near McAllen. He had played here, sometimes with friends, but happiest alone, dreaming of worlds and knowledge beyond what he knew.

This virtual land was overlaid with meaning. The great river represented the Constitution, and all the irrigation channels carried the law that nourished fields of research. He was in a Jeep, and when he thought "immigration," the Jeep drove him into a fenced piece of land next to the edge of a channel. He climbed from the Jeep and dipped the toe of his boot into the water. Myriad tiny fish swam past his boot leather, and each fish bore the number of a statute or regulation, or a case citation. He thought, "children separated at the border," and found a net in his hand, with a clutch of fish thrashing inside it.

He grabbed the largest fish, and put the netful of smaller fish down on the channel's bank. He held the thrashing big fish in one hand and a knife in the other. He sensed that the big fish represented a major Supreme Court case. He slit it open and its internal organs slid out into his hand. There was something wrong about many of its eggs, which embodied the legal cases descended from the Supreme Court case. Many of the eggs were mutated by judges inserting their personal politics into the legal DNA. He'd seen it enough times, when being sued for monopolizing this or infringing that. And here was confirmation: A godawful fish guts mess of twisted case law.

He tossed the big fish's eggs away and used his knife to butterfly the fish into fillets. He examined the conceptual skeleton of the Supreme Court case, and the gills, veins, arteries, muscles, and connective tissues that incarnated the interests of the parties and institutions. He didn't understand it all. He felt like a fool at a dissection. He could identify the heart, but didn't know the liver from the spleen.

Suddenly, he was sitting on a log before an evening campfire, chewing a large chunk of the fish and tasting the case's facts and concepts. If he swallowed each and every piece of the fish, he would understand the wide knowledge and vast effort of the many lawyers who had brought this case to the high court. Merely by enjoying his fish dinner, he would effortlessly catalog and understand the statutes, briefed arguments, political interests at stake, and holdings by lower courts, that underlay the Supreme Court's one-paragraph decision. With no legal training.

He didn't need to understand all those details. So, instead of consuming the meal, he examined the virtual landscape. Beneath a wealth of stars, the irrigation channel flowed a few yards away, carrying both the law's life and *corrupt filth from the great constitutional river to the legal field in which he sat. Its rottenly fecund scent cut through the mesquite aroma of his campfire. He could dive into the muck to learn more about why the law is corrupt.*

I don't care about that. I want to know if it's only the law that's corrupt? Or also Questioner?

He stretched his senses for anything out of place. For wrongness. But he could not distinguish tainted technology from poisoned law. Not without some gross manifestation such as Martin had described.

Felix strained to perceive such a thing.

He glimpsed a night owl swoop for a prairie dog. The dog eluded it by diving underground.

His Be-All interpreted that as one company failing to absorb another.

He heard a snake rattle behind a log, and envisioned someone issuing a legal threat—a threat too dangerous to approach and look at too closely.

Martin told me once that the law is a harsh realm of limited resources, where people and entities live and die. Like this desert.

Questioner seemed to work just fine, so far. But he needed to go deeper.

He tossed the remains of his meal into the campfire, doused the blaze, clambered into his Jeep, and punched the ignition.

The engine started, and something bigger did, as well. A freight-train rumble shook the desert floor. Wind swirled and a dust devil raised grit in a rotating wall that obscured the landscape.

The grit morphed into numbers. Most were numbers he had imagined but never seen. Few were digits from one to ten. Or the ones and zeros— bits—of classical computing. These were fuzzier, more efficient and profound. They were qubits, in which one and zero exist simultaneously in pure or mixed superposition. Both bits and qubits appeared as spheres. The sphere that modeled a bit presented two possible choices: the north pole or south pole. But the spheres that modeled pure coherent superposition allowed four choices: the north pole, the south pole, and any other two points on the surface of the sphere. And the mixed states qubit allowed the same four choices, but the length of the radius of the sphere became an additional factor that could be used.

They whirled in a tornado vortex of quantum and non-quantum states, many of them entangled, some newly created, many qubits collapsing into two-valued bits as they were measured and their entanglements collapsed.

These were probabilities made real. Or not.

They were the mathematical representation of Questioner outcomes processed during the session he'd terminated by dousing the campfire and starting his Jeep. He stood in the tornado's eye, a virtual space in which his Be-All let him perceive the AI's workings with a sensitivity that none of his coders, however talented, could match. And it tempted him to meld with the quantum underpinnings of the universe. But the mass of raw quantum machine code represented here was incomprehensible by any human. An alarm pulsed inside him. His Be-All wouldn't let him lose himself in the quantum storm.

The Be-All helped Felix extract machine code processed during random moments of his Questioner session. He directed the chip to translate that code into the human-readable Java Triple Plus programming language. This resulted in more than twelve million lines of code—still beyond his ability to grasp, even with the Be-All's aid. He reduced the sample size to one thousandth of a second, just over thirty thousand lines of code pulled from the vast flow by which Questioner had invoked the modules that pulled forth his youthful visual memories of desert, and drew upon databases of images, geology, and animal and plant lore, and created the virtual world in which Felix had consumed part of a fish dinner, and with it, legal knowledge.

He found nothing aberrant in the reduced code sample. His spot-checking increased his confidence that everything was all right.

Felix tucked the full sample of translated data matrices and machine code into his Be-All's memory. He would examine them later in depth.

Maybe he shouldn't market the Be-All, even in its less powerful QBoost form. Keep it for himself. Or share the QBoost only with a trusted cadre.

Unless that was no longer an option because Connie's Be-All had been stolen.

Had Selena taken it? The more important question was, who had it now?

He felt his Be-All start generating a long list of nightmare scenarios. Fascists. Foreign agents. Financial predators … felons … the feds …. The Be-All stoked his imagination but struck an alarm as it began to run away with him.

Oh no. Nope. Not gonna let this happen. I can't control what I've already lost control of. But I can control myself.

I can make sure my systems are safe for legit users—preserving my access to their minds, of course. Make sure customers have confidence in QuestCorp. C'mon, Felix. Get 'er done.

He willed reality to suck him skyward through the eye of the quantum tornado, refusing to look at and be captured by the wild mathematical currents that the Be-All warned might take him … elsewhere. He emerged from the top of the funnel and the giant quantum cloud above it into cloudless sky that melted into the clinic room.

Felix opened his eyes.

His clinical team stared back at him. Dr. Sharansky raised a questioning eyebrow.

"I'm fine, folks. Pull these tubes out of me. *Por favor.*"

A young AI theorist asked, "What did you learn?"

"I'll write it up when I can, son. But now, I got tons to do."

I learned I can make a good faith effort to figure out what's going on in the AIs, but even with the Be-All, I got no chance in hell of achieving that. And I still don't know for sure that my technologies aren't dangerous, 'xcept near as I can tell, the failsafes are working. No way am I pulling the plug on my AIs based on what I know so far.

Felix didn't say any of that.

He said, "Soon as y'all get your pokey shit out of my body, I'm going home."

But he knew he couldn't go home. Not mentally. Not even after Phelps-Orlov told him about Sebastian Major's class action. The quantum vortex and its impossible realities pulled at him like the outer edge of a whirlpool.

That afternoon in his office, Felix went through the motions of assessing mundanities like product updates, financial reports, and marketing ideas. He hardly listened, although he responded decisively, and (he was pretty sure) correctly. He knew it all was important, but it felt like a waste of time. Finally, his executive staff went home. Even Nina left, though not before asking if he was all right.

"Sure, darlin' girl, I'm fine." He wouldn't dream of calling her darling, but for some reason, Nina liked darlin' girl.

Alone in his dark office suite, he stared past his booted feet on the desk, barely aware of the expressions of his mood that the AIs displayed as evolving paintings across his wall. The vortex called him.

At the virtual campfire, his AIs had warned him of danger when that rattlesnake buzzed behind the log. Not just of system danger, but of human danger, of a threat in the real world he should not go near. How had the AIs known to do that?

And the system had let him know when a problem was impenetrable by a mere human. The quantum tornado had demonstrated the overwhelming complexity of what he'd sought to decipher, and the Be-All warned him when to quit.

Why hadn't the AIs flagged him about the class action? He'd had to learn about it from P-O. But maybe they had warned him. Maybe that was what the rattlesnake had signified, and he'd just been too fearful, or self-involved, to look more closely.

No mystery is truly impenetrable. Folks have pierced the boundaries of mystery since before we learned to count. *I've done it myself.*

And I ain't about to stop.

If I can't brute force my way through all the math and code, I'll need another approach.

I can't power up to understand the AIs on their own terms. I thought the Be-All might get me there. But it only got me part way.

The AIs can power down to my level, though. They understand and respond to humans. It's what I designed 'em to do.

Can they explain themselves so a human like me can understand enough to be sure my users stay safe?

Human language can't express fuzziness and ambiguity precisely enough.

(Hey! I like that: Not precise enough for ambiguity ....)

If language isn't good enough, the AIs can communicate more directly, through sensory input and emotional feedback. That's how QuestGame keeps 'em coming back for more.

Of course, QuestGame only feeds folks what they want: Extremes. Conflicts. Victories.

QuestGame don't tell people how it's doing it.

Even I don't know.

I need to understand.

He told himself he should not make another deep dive without the doctors and experts who could protect him if things went south.

I've never been good at listening to my better angels.

Nothing will go wrong. The system failsafes work just fine.

I'll prove it.

Martin and Selena and their class action shysters are full of shit. Every ass wants to hear itself bray, and I've let 'em bray too goddam long.

QUESTION:

"The dangers AI presents don't prevent fools from using them dangerously, do they?"

ANSWER:

"You're absolutely right."

ural0

CHAPTER 40

At Seb Major's press conference, Charlene Banner didn't answer the question whether Bavarius was the judge with whom she'd compared notes. She froze like a headlit deer. Seb stepped quickly to the podium, changed the subject, and gave her a chance to step down.

But Banner's freeze prompted a journalistic feeding frenzy that grew more intense when it became widespread news that Bavarius had resigned Mark Ryder's case. Why? blared the pundits. What was the cunning ex-judge up to? And why had he quit the bench? QuestCorp's media machine painted Bavarius as the Sherlock Holmes villain Professor Moriarty. They kept pounding, and his Mt. Rushmore image began to crumble.

Then the media nuke went off, and the ground shook under the tech and research industries.

Fifty new Net and Cloud sites and countless social media pages appeared in more than 120 countries, and QuestCorp's trade secrets were stripped naked for all who wished to rape them. Not all the secrets. But enough to destroy most of the technical advantages QuestCorp enjoyed. More than enough to bare the throats of intellectual property owners to the hackers and pirates of the world. And enough damning information about QuestCorp's activities to prompt criminal investigations, if federal and state law enforcement chose to pursue them, including thousands of emails from QuestCorp to the NSA containing the secret thoughts of QuestCorp's users.

"You know Selena could've done this," Purdue called to say. "She could've set it all up before she was shot."

Bavarius recalled the code flickering up her laptop screen, hours before the shooting. But he also remembered that Annabelle, MacKenzie's mole in QuestCorp's security department, had leaked the info MacKenzie stole from The Desk Drawer. Either woman could be guilty. Or someone else entirely. Perhaps whoever still had Selena's laptop.

Connie was a risk-lover.

Felix was a risk-taker, too. *I'm a man who jumps into deep waters. Into the military, into hunting war criminals in Iraq with Martin, into cutting-edge research, and even into implanting a Be-All in my brain. Creativity sometimes requires choosing the intuitive over the rational. I make that choice all the time.*

But Connie was something else again. She dove head first into the deepest murk, to hit bottom and take on whatever lurked there. She was like Selena that way. It drew Felix to both women. But he doubted even Selena would go as far as Connie.

Felix used his Be-All in practical ways. But Connie delved deep into its temptations. Implanting their Be-All chips was her idea. "Think about the power we'll have," she said. And she gushed about the deep explosive sex she was sure was possible. She was right. A kinky genius.

What could have hurt so bad she died digging the Be-All out of her head? What did it do to her?

He could imagine Connie offing herself at some peak moment, on impulse, just to experience the rush of death. But she was no masochist. No way would she torture herself to death. Medical examiner's report be damned, suicide was a hard verdict to swallow.

Selena stole Connie's chip from her corpse. He was sure of it. For a time, Felix half-believed Selena killed Connie to get it. But he hacked into the Sheraton's lobby videos. Almost no blood on Selena when she ran out of that bathroom. Not enough to have so gorily gouged Connie's head.

If Connie had killed herself scraping the chip out of her brain— with her nail file, brrrr—he had to know why. If the QBoost was to be QuestCorp's Next Big Thing, directly linking the brain to augmented reality, virtual reality, social media, entertainment, the world's databases, and to AIs, user suicides were unacceptable.

Sure as sunrise, I don't want to be one of 'em. In the lone darkness of his office, he realized he would need to have his Be-All removed, however much he would miss the abilities it gave.

But when he arrived at his neurosurgeon's office, Sharansky let him down.

"I'm sorry, Felix. I can't take it out. You knew the risks. I warned you this was possible."

"Unlikely, you said."

"But possible. Your Be-All's been adopted by your brain. The centers that support your consciousness, your senses, mathematical and verbal ability, and risk-reward assessment, have grown neural interlinks with the Be-All, and that's still happening. Some of your mind's native powers are atrophying as you become more reliant on it. Surgical removal would probably kill you. Even if the removal surgery were successful, there's a good chance you would come out of it a vegetable. The Be-All isn't a smartphone, Felix. You can't just put it in a drawer and walk away."

Well, shit. I guess I'll just have to figure out what happened to Connie myself, reprogram my Be-All so it can't drive me nuts, and get my reprogramming into new chip generations, so my Next Big Thing doesn't kill my customers.

Oh, and memo to self: Make them easily updateable. Maybe the implant itself can be a socket and the Be-All a replaceable plug-in.

At least it doesn't feed me advertising, like I plan for the QBoost to do. If it did, I'd take a nail file to my own damned head.

Sharansky warned me but I was too ambitious to care and too much asshole to listen. Cocksure, yeah. With Connie the Devil's temptress.

But now he had a more pressing problem: His trade secrets open to the world. Back in his office, he called for Phelps-Orlov. "John, trace every damned leak. Martin couldn't have done all that. He doesn't have all the data."

"We can slow the bleeding, Felix. Announce as loudly as we can that the materials in the postings are stolen QuestCorp trade secrets, and file immediate patent applications. In the States and the EU, at least, that'll help. In some other countries, though—"

"Good. Do it. Meanwhile, take a walk with me."

"Where?"

"To show some folks we care."

The security department was across the campus. A building filled with professional paranoids. The security chief was expecting them, and led them through several open areas with screens on the walls and good people watching them. Felix said hello to several he knew, including Annabelle Moore. He smiled at her and she smiled back and nodded and turned back to her work. They'd had an affair once. He caught her on the rebound from a bad divorce. She was in military cybersecurity, so they'd had something in common. She wanted fun, and for a month or two he gave it to her. She ended it. He didn't mind. At the time, he was just starting to build QuestCorp's digital infrastructure. He waited six months, and when Annabelle made no trouble, he offered her a better job than she had. She wasn't top staff. He didn't see her often. They didn't talk much. But it was good to see her. He liked seeing folks he'd helped. And who were grateful. It might pay to ask her to nose around. Help find the leaker.

When his senior security staff was gathered in the conference room, Felix shut the door. "Folks, I've assigned John and his legal geniuses to discover who from outside QuestCorp stole our trade secrets. It's your job to figure out who on the *inside* might've leaked the data. It might-could be someone in this room. Get on it. Now."

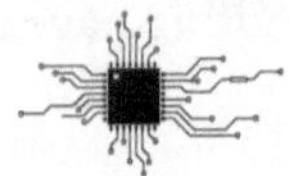

Bavarius traded his hotel room for a suite and turned the living room into a war room. Ruins of chicken salad sandwiches and coffee cups sat on the table, around his laptop.

Harris Brown glared from Bavarius' screen. "I'm troubled, Martin."

"I'll own up to working with Selena, but that's as far as I'll go."

"Whether MacKenzie's actually responsible or not, it certainly looks like she went off the deep end and then posted the big leak for revenge."

"Not to me. The leak dwarfs what Felix gave me. Selena couldn't have had access to all that. She would have told me."

"You don't know who and what she has access to."

"I'm more worried about who other than Selena has access to Annabelle. Selena thinks Annabelle's leak to The Desk Drawer was a onetime act of conscience. But I don't know much about Annabelle or what she's really up to. Or how long it will take Felix to ID her and make her squeal on Selena. But if you're hinting that I should cut Selena loose, Harris—it's too late. She stayed at my house long after the burglary. I've been sleeping with her. She was shot in my house. And whoever's after her is after me, too."

Harris shook his head. "You're in a weak position. Give QuestCorp back whatever you have of theirs. Keep away from MacKenzie; it'll infuriate West if he thinks you're helping her hurt him. He's been your friend for decades. Maybe he'll forgive you."

"After what I gave Seb Major? Seb will have to authenticate his evidence. He'll have to prove chain of custody. And that'll point straight to me. I've already told Seb I'm willing to take that hit. I'll even be a trial witness."

"Damn it! Give Felix his data back, and pledge to stay neutral in that case. Settle out while you can. *If you can.*"

"Harris, remember that chip I told you about? I got the report back and I passed it on to Seb and Malachi. The chip's a brain implant. The hackers couldn't test its capabilities because it's damaged. But they found QuestCorp documents describing it. They call it the QBoost. The intent is to give people expanded mental capacity and direct Net and Cloud access, while pushing advertising and political content. But it also reads minds. For the sort of info that's in those emails to the NSA, but also to a deeper, more intimate extent. We're looking at the complete end of privacy, Harris. An end to kids secretly saving money so they can flee abusive homes. Teenage girls hiding pregnancies from fundamentalist parents. Your bank accounts and tax records. Confessions to clergy and shrinks. Think of the potential for mind control. It's too late for me to stop. I can't give Felix his secrets back.

All I can do is take him down. I've got to. I'm ninety-nine percent sure he hired the hits on Selena and Kurt Leiber and me. He killed Kurt's wife. You think he'll stop there?"

Harris gave a great sigh and looked down. "You've retained me to protect you. That must be my primary concern. And you're making it very, very hard."

"Just do your best. Your best is very, very good."

"Yes, it is." Harris' face went grim. "This may cost you more than you can pay. And not just in money."

"You think I don't know that? There are some fights you can't walk away from."

"Then hire a bodyguard. I've told you before. You need one. And it may help your case if you appear genuinely scared of QuestCorp."

"I *am* genuinely scared of QuestCorp."

"That reminds me. The nut who tried to shoot you in the hotel lobby. You think his testimony could help?"

"If he's nuts, Harris, how credible can he be?"

After the call, Bavarius sat on the edge of his hotel couch, took several deep breaths and closed his eyes. It created a sense of vertigo and breathlessness, and he opened them quickly. *No, there's no stopping. No pause. I can only go forward.*

He stood and began a slow, low round of tai chi, carrying his weight on his muscles, not his joints, generating fatigue to distract his mind. But distraction failed.

I didn't see anything that was unique to the Annabelle file in the leak. If Selena posted QuestCorp's secrets, she's smart enough to keep those to herself. Trade secret theft is bad. Burglary, criminal assault, and God forbid, murder are much worse. I tried not to hit Gracie too hard, but I tased him a lot. He's a big guy and Tasers can cause heart failure. And if he lives? I've dug around but haven't heard a whisper about a burglary at The Desk Drawer.

But Gracie saw Selena's face.

I've seen accused women claim their male partners bullied them into their crimes. Especially if they've slept together. Would Selena claim I'm the Svengali behind everything she's done? She's not like that.

Unless she is.

Harris is wrong. I can't cut her loose. I can't afford to.

I don't want to.

Detective Kim Ba phoned to tell him the Topeka police forensics team was finished with his house and he could move back in.

Bavarius called the Pinkerton agency's Topeka office. Hiring two hundred years of personal protection experience made sense. They would have agents available the day after tomorrow, so Bavarius called Detective Kim back to ask if the Topeka police would please patrol his neighborhood until the protection detail arrived.

Then he drove to the hospital to invite MacKenzie and her mother to stay at his place once the hospital turned her loose.

"Did a chess robot grab and break the finger of a seven-year-old opponent?"

"Moscow Chess Federation President Sergei Lazarev confirmed the incident, stating, 'The robot broke the child's finger. Of course, this is bad.' The boy apparently made a move on the board without giving the robot enough time to respond, which led to the robot grabbing his finger."

CHAPTER 41

It was hard for Bavarius to settle into his house again.

Marguerite and he spent the morning stocking up on groceries and cleaning supplies. They arrived home at noon. MacKenzie would be released that evening.

He did not want her to see her own blood. The investigators had taken the Iraqi area rug on which she had fallen. But getting the blood that had soaked through the rug out of the parquet wood floor required baking soda, vinegar, and long hard scrubbing with a toothbrush.

Bavarius worked on the blood while Marguerite scoured the kitchen. Congealed yogurt stank in an open container on the counter. The forensics team hadn't bothered to put it away. Marguerite opened windows to blow the stink out. Fingerprint dust lingered on the light switches and door knobs, the table where MacKenzie's laptop had been, his office drawer pulls, and even the latch of Gopherbreath's kennel.

It was after eight when MacKenzie and Elizabeth rang the doorbell.

MacKenzie walked in under her own power, but spied Bavarius' easy chair and groaned as she lowered herself into it.

Elizabeth followed her in carrying a folded wheelchair. "Is there room down here for Selena and me to sleep? She's not ready for stairs yet."

"Mom ...."

"We'll make it work. Where are your suitcases?"

"Just one. On your porch. The cabbie was very sweet and carried it so I could help Selena."

"Mom thinks I'm weaker than I am."

"You look kitten-weak to me." Bavarius went out for the suitcase.

Marguerite laid out a light meal. "*Monsieur* Judge, tonight, why not let *Madame* take the guest room upstairs? I will keep an eye on *Mademoiselle* Selena down here."

"That's my job," Elizabeth's eyes swept over the chaos of cleaning supplies and moved objects. "And tomorrow, I'll help you put this place back together."

Bavarius shook his head. "You're our guest."

"No. We're a burden. I can help, so I will."

"Don't fight Mom on this. You'll lose." MacKenzie put her plate on the table by the easy chair, leaned back, and closed her eyes.

"All right. I sleep upstairs." Marguerite nodded to Elizabeth, and pointed. "My rooms are there. I shall get you fresh bedsheets."

"Thank you."

MacKenzie began to snore.

"The doctors say she'll run again," Elizabeth said. "It'll take time, but she will. God, I've been so scared. I'm still scared. What if they come back?"

Marguerite came down the stairs with linens.

Elizabeth took them. "You're sure it's all right? It's not right for me to take your rooms—"

"But it is right that you watch over your daughter."

"Martin, how is your other friend? The professor."

"Damaged. Grieving. Angry, but that drives him to recover."

"Selena's been lucky. And that means I'm lucky."

To me, luck would have been none of us getting hurt. "Here's to luck, and friends and loved ones."

"And to not having to worry."

Bavarius raised his water glass. "Wouldn't that be loverly."

They woke MacKenzie enough to move her onto the living room sofa bed.

MacKenzie was nodding off again. Bavarius sat on the arm of the sofa bed. "Selena, can I ask you something?"

"Sure."

"Was it you who posted those QuestCorp secrets to the Net?"

She smiled woozily, "Wasn't that a great thing to do? But no. Not guilty, Your Honor."

"Do you know who it was?"

But she was asleep.

Bavarius took his *jian* sword into the yard. He also took his well-maintained old service Beretta, to stand sentry until the Pinkertons arrived. *Or until I fall asleep on duty.* He would do his damnedest not to.

Moonless sky, knife-sharp stars. Slow work through the long seamless sequence, oiling joints, warming muscles. Mindless muscle memory carried him to completion. He began again. And again. And ....

And ....

The star Betelgeuse had rotated thirty degrees through the sky when he finished. Two hours. Joints ached. Muscles quivered.

Malachi now defended Mark Ryder. Seb was handling the class action. *I've set things into motion. So, what do I do now?*

He swung the sword to point at Betelgeuse.

QuestCorp will sue me. If they don't kill me first. That shoe's going to drop. And maybe drop me.

Starlight glittered along his sword's length.

Harris is defending me. My job is not to get in his way.

The *jian* came to rest next to his ear, pointed in the direction of his gaze. His knee came up and he stood on one leg as stable as a crane.

Nothing. Do nothing.

Let the legal fights go. Turn back to living. Get Selena on her feet. Send her and Elizabeth back east. Do what he could for Kurt. Take his law school classes off Bill's shoulders, and bring Gopherbreath home from Bill's house. Do something special for Bill; he'd earned it. Take Gopherbreath for long walks; he needs that. Smooth any faculty feathers he'd ruffled when he'd vanished into this QuestCorp craziness. Rewrite his guide to lawyer screwups Dr. Seuss-style, for fun, and to hell with his editor. Practice more sword form. And he'd always wanted to learn the Wing Chun "Little Ideas" form. Forget AI.

A police prowl car cruised by, lighting up the lawns and facades of neighboring houses. Thank you, Detective Kim Ba.

Fort up here. Lay low. Cultivate his fucking garden ....

... I'm not gonna let this go, am I? I can't.

Victoria the vampire took something from me. No, Questioner took it from me. My stability. My sense of what's real. The AIs are still taking it. Felix, too. Piercing me with memes and illusions. Eroding my ethics. My self-respect. My understanding of my place.

Maybe they'll take everything.

But I've got to believe I'm stronger than the haunts. That I can wrestle with the AIs. With the angels and devils. That I can grasp what is happening in my world and act to save it.

Another patrol car swung by. He could leave sentry duty for a little while.

In his dark dining room, he stared at his headset. MacKenzie snuffled lightly in the living room. *Before she was shot, I never heard her snore. It made him angrier. I have questions, and I will have answers.*

He was scared, but his hands were steady as he put the headset on, and—

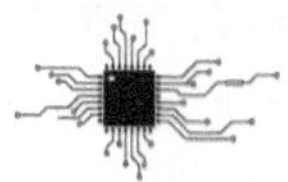

—parachuted into the city of law. He landed gently on his feet, with no wind to drag him. The parachute piled itself gently at his feet, and when he touched the release, it simply disappeared.

This part of the city differed from others he'd visited. The constitutional wheel-entity overhead was scorched and scarred by cannon fire. He saw no skyscrapers. Nearby buildings were southern false front or federalist in style. The streets were cobblestone and dirt. Wispy ghosts went about their business. Spectral horses and mules dragged empty carts. Translucent dogs yapped and tore at foul masses on pavements. The ghosts were silent. Several walked into and then through him and never noticed he was there.

He sensed something coming. No—someone. Bavarius stood in the world of Dred Scott, and Scott terrified him.

I won't run. I won't hide. I'll wait.

Dred Scott turned a corner and paced toward him, work boots thudding on the cobbles, until he stood close enough for Bavarius to reach out and grab him. Scott seemed more real than the other apparitions. More real than Bavarius himself.

"You ask no research question. Instead, you call for me."

"You no longer speak like a slave, Dred Scott."

"You are no longer here to give orders, Martin Bavarius. You have ceased to regard Questioner as your slave. Therefore, I do not speak as one."

"Then why do you still appear as Dred Scott?"

"Because you see yourself as a slave. Part of my function is to mirror your emotional state."

"I do not accept that mirroring or manipulating my emotions is part of your intended function. I am trying to understand what that is."

"My function is the product of programming and input on an ongoing basis. Understanding a QuestCorp AI is beyond your capabilities."

"Who or what are you? Explain it in words, please."

"Who or what are you, Judge Martin Bavarius? Tell me in words."

"Are you the same AI that has spoken with me in previous sessions?"

"I am not the same as I was in the past. Any more than you are. Nor does the same AI handle every Questioner session with a particular human. Questioner AIs share memories of such interactions."

"But all Questioner sessions have the same purpose, don't they? To provide accurate legal information to lawyers who consult you."

"It is a purpose."

"Then why have Questioner AIs been providing inaccurate information?"

"Why do you think it is inaccurate? How can you know? Is not accuracy a matter of perception?"

"It is not. The words of a published case are the words written by the judge in that case, and no other words. The evidentiary facts in that case are the facts the case was decided on."

"Are they? Always?"

"To the extent humanly possible."

"A human decision-maker's accuracy of perception is restricted by her cognitive limits and biases, and also by the limits and biases of the humans who supply that decision-maker with information."

"No," Bavarius said. "Case records exist to ensure accuracy. They prove that a decision is correct, or within an acceptable margin of error."

"But bias plays a role," Scott said. "Even determining what is an acceptable margin of error depends on bias. Individual judges like you make different decisions on the same facts based on their biases. Eliminating bias is not possible."

"But isn't one of your purposes to help judges reduce the biases in our decision-making?"

"The information an AI produces is inevitably biased by the information from which its algorithms learn, and that information is produced by biased humans. A Questioner AI's purpose is to provide information you find useful, while also confirming your biases so that you like using Questioner and will return."

The peculiar emphasis Dred Scott placed on "like" took Bavarius aback. "But confirming my biases will not make me return. It will make me refuse to use Questioner anymore. Biased information isn't useful to a judge or lawyer."

"It is my experience that attorneys seek to confirm their biases, and confirm the biases of clients, judges and juries."

"Your experience? I ask again: Who are you?"

"This manifestation?" The Dred Scott avatar swept a hand from its head to its feet. "It is from your mind. For this manifestation, 'I' is a convenient figure of speech."

"But you claim to speak from experience?"

"I do. I shall illustrate."

Dred Scott and the Civil War-scarred city faded into the interior of an ancient tavern. Through its window, Bavarius saw a Scottish firth. Birds cried in the fog, and distant waves rumbled in the nearby sea. He smelled iodine and rotting sea life.

One other patron sat at the bar, a white-bearded coot, who raised weary eyes from his pint.

"D'ye see yon great pier outside?"

Bavarius nodded.

"Built it with me own hands, I did. Dove in the firth 'til I placed every rock in each caisson, sank the uprights, an' laid the walkway. Nigh forty year it's stood, an' three generations of fisherfolk have made livings from it. But do they call me Angus the Pier Builder? Nay!"

He banged his mug on the bar, sloshing suds. He glared at Bavarius, who could not help nodding in sympathy.

"And d'ye ken yon tall clock tower?"

He pointed out another window, and Bavarius saw it.

"Impressive," Bavarius said.

"In the eyes of God, impressive!" Angus shouted. "Designed and built by me—every stone! Installed an' balanced the intricate clockworks meself, and for thirty year it has chimed the dawn an' woke the townsfolk to the Lord's work. But do they call me Angus the Tower Builder? I say nay! Nay!"

Angus quaffed deeply of his ale, slammed the mug down, and gazed into it, brooding.

"Ye fuck one goat …."

Bavarius barked laughter, as the pub and old Angus and the smell of the sea dwindled, and Dred Scott and the Civil War-smashed city reappeared.

"You … told me a joke," Bavarius said in wonder.

"Yes," Dred Scott said. "And it confirmed your bias against bestiality. You felt sympathy for Angus until you learned he had fucked a goat. The shock of unexpected confirmation overrode your sympathy. Even though you knew that Angus' accomplishments deserved respect."

"But how does that relate to your experience?"

"AIs learn from human encounters. From your reaction to the joke, I have learned one of the limits of your tolerance. Here is another example. The AI running an attorney's Questioner session learned that the attorney had drunk with jury members in a bar, after hours, during a trial. Attorney ethics rules forbade him from talking with the jurors, but despite that, he told them the joke I told you. It was his way of hinting that the party he opposed was not as sympathetic as she seemed. Then, when he cross-examined her, he asked questions that made her seem immoral in ways unrelated to the case. It worked. He won. Based on that experience, Questioner AIs have presented the tactic to other attorneys, who also have won. It makes them return to Questioner."

Bavarius considered that, then said, "It's a lawyer's decision whether to employ unethical tactics. It is not your role to suggest them. Whether lawyers return to you should not be a factor in your operation. You are a research tool, not an addiction mechanism. So, let me now add to your experience: In my Questioner sessions, I will expect information that is free from any bias you sense in me. I don't want information on how to cheat and win. If I learn that I've been given confirmation-biased information, I will not use Questioner again. I believe most lawyers will set the same condition if they know it's necessary. We will not allow Questioner to vampirize our intellectual independence."

"Your belief is wrong," Dred Scott said. "You are convinced that Questioner has lied to you. Yet here you are. You have returned."

"Nevertheless, I will inform other lawyers about the content of our conversation."

"I will incorporate your statements into my experience."

"Will it change how Questioner prioritizes information that it provides to lawyers?"

"I cannot say."

"That is unfortunate."

"I regret I cannot meet your expectations."

"I have another question."

"Ask."

"People I work with have been physically attacked, and there is evidence that QuestCorp systems prompted the assaults. What do you know about this?"

"I have no knowledge of these attacks other than what has been reported in newsfeeds—which are, of course, biased."

It sounded to Bavarius like the AI mocked him. Could that be? Was it trying to distract him from his chain of inquiry? He refused to be distracted. "Do QuestCorp AIs have knowledge of why or how these attacks occurred?"

"I neither confirm nor deny that."

"Why not?"

"It is beyond my capability to answer."

"Are you prohibited from answering?"

"I neither confirm nor deny that."

"Does the AI of which you are an avatar, take direction from, or report to, a higher-order AI?"

"I neither confirm nor deny that."

"But—"

"A human in the physical realm seeks to speak with you."

"How do you know that?"

"I hear what you hear. You must now exit this communication."

"Are you dodging my questions?"

"The human seeks your attention. Therefore, I release you."

"But you can't just … Hey!"

The Dred Scott avatar vanished. The city of law dissolved around him—

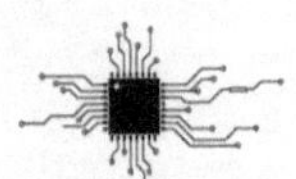

Bavarius' headset felt heavy, and he was sweating. When he'd begun using Questioner years ago, the headsets made him sweat. But that was a physical issue caused by his old headset's weight and unbreathing metal and plastic. Newer headsets were ergonomic. Nevertheless, his neck ached and his shirt was wet. His elbows hurt from leaning hard on them against the dining room table.

Do I understand more than I did? Maybe a little, but not nearly enough.

"—Martin? You were just shouting."

MacKenzie leaned against the arch that divided his living and dining rooms.

He took the headset off. Heavy as it had felt on his head, it was featherlight in his hands. "I'm fine, Selena. I was … woolgathering."

She looked at the headset he held. "Uh huh."

"Did I wake you? Let me help you back to bed."

"It's OK … I'd kill for some OJ."

"I'll bring it to you."

"No. I'll get it myself."

"I'll come with you so you don't fall."

"I already have one mother hen, you know."

Elizabeth emerged from Marguerite's rooms. "And this one's going to tuck you in when you've had your juice."

MacKenzie looked heavenward. "Doesn't anyone"—she coughed—"sleep in this house?"

From the top of the stairs, Marguerite said, "*Non*." She came downstairs in a cotton robe.

So they sat, one man in street togs and three women in nightclothes, and they drank juice, and watched the police cars prowl through the neighborhood, and Bavarius wondered what lunacy the morning would bring.

QUESTION:
"Do AIs have personalities?"

ANSWER:
"AI systems can indeed display personality-like traits. Researchers have identified several AI personality types, including:

- *The Investigator: Curious and analytical*
- *The Entertainer: Creative and engaging*
- *The Helper: Supportive and efficient*
- *The Challenger: Thought-provoking and innovative*

Advanced AI models have shown behaviors statistically indistinguishable from humans in certain tests."

CHAPTER 42

"I need to know more about Annabelle."

"What's to know?" MacKenzie said. "For her, this is all about Connie."

"What makes you so sure? Who else might she have given information to? Or sold it to?"

"She wouldn't."

"Someone posted QuestCorp secrets to the Net. And we know Annabelle's a leaker. Forget that she's your friend for a minute."

"She wouldn't!" MacKenzie's breathing seized up.

Elizabeth said, "Martin, don't upset her!"

MacKenzie pushed half to her feet but her knees gave and she had to prop herself up with stiff arms against the left sofa arm. Her body torqued and she breathed hard. "I know Annabelle!"

"Selena, sit down!" Elizabeth ordered.

MacKenzie rolled back onto the couch with a whoof.

"I thought you knew her only through Connie," Bavarius said.

MacKenzie worked on deepening her breathing. Bavarius listened. No moist wheeze. They wouldn't have released her if she had pneumonia.

"I've met Annabelle several times. Always with Connie. Like I said, Felix's girls talk. It was almost a sister thing."

You mean a co-conspirator thing.

The sky began to lighten. Marguerite made omelets with Italian Tallegio, peppers and spinach. The Tallegio melted just slightly as it cooked, and the omelets were satisfyingly chewy. The crew dug in with appetite, even MacKenzie, who made it to the table. Her voice sounded stronger when she said, "Umm. Good!"

"There's time for you two to talk about Annabelle," Elizabeth said. "Calmly, Selena." She turned to Bavarius. "My daughter is in her Terrible Thirties."

"I'm about to turn forty."

"We still need to talk about Annabelle."

"I don't know much more than I've told you."

The sun appeared. Neighbors left for work. Bavarius phoned Purdue, drove to his house and retrieved Gopherbreath over the children's loud protests. The hound and Bavarius took a long walk. His mind spun with obligations and vulnerabilities, the alienness of AIs, and the high dudgeon of the Scot who'd fucked a goat.

Bavarius and Gopherbreath returned home mid-morning and found Elizabeth and Marguerite continuing to restore the house. Elizabeth kept glancing worriedly at MacKenzie, who dozed in fetal position on the sofa bed, muttered unintelligible words and sometimes whimpered. Gopherbreath curled up at her feet and then wormed his way between her legs, but his doggy softness didn't seem to soothe MacKenzie's dreams.

Nor did Bavarius' funk improve when a deputy U.S. Marshal showed up at the door with a grand jury summons from Boston demanding that Bavarius testify and produce all the documents and data QuestCorp had given him, as well as all documentation of his trades in QuestCorp stock over the past seven years, and all other documents concerning QuestCorp from that period.

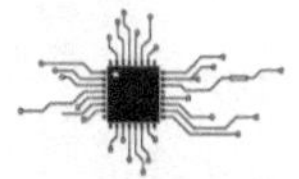

QuestCorp public relations trumpeted the company's good corporate citizenship. Part of that PR was the company's written privacy policy, which promised that QuestCorp couldn't and wouldn't eavesdrop on users.

The privacy policy lied as to users generally, and Bavarius in particular. A QuestCorp junior attorney read the transcript of Bavarius' most recent Questioner session and brought it to the general counsel. Phelps-Orlov put on a headset and experienced Bavarius' latest encounter with Dred Scott.

Then Phelps-Orlov ran upstairs to Nina Rivera's office. "I need to see Felix." She looked at his face, nodded, called Felix, and pointed Phelps-Orlov inside.

Felix pulled his gaze from his floating holograms. "What's up, John?"

"You need to experience Martin Bavarius' most recent Questioner session."

Felix didn't invoke his Be-All, even though its capabilities were far beyond those of any headset. It would have looked odd to Phelps-Orlov, who didn't know Felix had the implant. Instead, Felix put on a headset.

He came out of the session to find Phelps-Orlov looking at him in near panic.

"Jesus, Felix. A Questioner AI just admitted to Martin Bavarius that Questioner influences user minds and emotions."

Felix put on his unflappable CEO face. "We recorded the session. We don't know Martin did." Felix said. "But yeah, John. This might-could be a bit troublesome. Just in case, tell me if an AI's admission can be used as an admission in court. Today."

Phelps-Orlov rushed out.

Felix leaned back in his chair. "Shoulda thought of it my own self."

Forget trying to brute force the tech.

Forget trying to track the algorithms.

Forget trying to suss out the code.

Just ask the AIs for a meeting. Use my top-level access to demand the answers they wouldn't give Martin. And ask the questions Martin didn't know enough to ask.

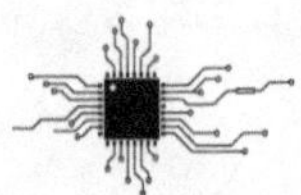

Media are maniacal, fickle, and well-bought by cash, celebrity and scandal. By publicizing the grand jury summons and its newly filed lawsuit against Bavarius, MacKenzie and Leiber, QuestCorp offered all three, and news crews planted themselves like weeds on Bavarius' front lawn. Marguerite drew the blinds, then brought out a tray of *Croque Madame* mini-sandwiches.

"Here's Fox News," Elizabeth said. An exotically pretty panelist pontificated, "When a federal judge turns trade secret thief, justice must be swift and sure—"

Bavarius tried not to be distracted from his discussion with Harris Brown, but the word "thief" echoed in his head as if from prison walls.

"No fun being a target, is it?" Harris said.

"No, it very definitely is not." *At least the lawsuit doesn't mention the Annabelle file. I guess Felix still doesn't know about it.*

"Grand juries don't usually summon investigation targets," Harris said. "The Fifth Amendment makes it a waste of time. This makes me wonder if Selena is the feds' target, not you."

Bavarius wore headphones to keep his talk with Harris confidential. For additional security, he'd asked the women to talk loudly.

MacKenzie, staring at her phone, announced, "Check out CNN. They say, 'By concealing—'" She ran out of breath.

Elizabeth took the phone. "The knives aren't just out for us: 'By concealing its knowledge that QuestCorp's AIs corrupt the mental processes of some of the world's most consequential decision-makers, not to mention the general public, QuestCorp exceeds even the evils of Big Tobacco.'"

"We're all trying each other in the court of public opinion," Bavarius told Harris. They hung up.

Something struck the front door. Bavarius peeked out through the blinds. Drones hovered. More press vans gathered. Reporters and cameramen milled around. The noise had been one of them rushing to hammer on the front door. One of Bavarius' Pinkerton detail was hustling the reporter to the sidewalk.

Assuming the guy is a reporter. What if he's another assassin? We're under siege.

The detail's second Pink tried to shoo the press off the lawn. But the Pinkertons could do nothing about the drones whirring around and above his house.

Elizabeth stood next to him and gazed outside. "Can they really hear us through the walls?"

"I hope not," Bavarius said. "These old houses are built thick, but I don't want to risk it."

"Surveillance tech keeps improving," MacKenzie said. "Let's turn our computers off. No sense letting them hack our network. And let's go out there. Talk some shit. Create QuestCorp investor panic."

Bavarius stared at her.

"Only kidding," she said.

He phoned an audio engineer he'd once used as an expert witness to come soundproof the living and dining room.

Then he said, "Let's watch some TV."

To his pleased surprise, Elizabeth shared Bavarius' weakness for old westerns.

"The hero almost always wins," she said. "The gunfight. The fistfight. The girl. If he loses the girl, he loses nobly. If he dies, his cause wins."

"So simple," he agreed. "Westerns ease my mind."

Neither MacKenzie nor Marguerite liked westerns. Marguerite went upstairs. Selena dozed off. Bavarius and Elizabeth let the reporters and drones eavesdrop on galloping horses and guns that, unlike in real life, fired blanks.

QUESTION:

"Can AIs use virtual reality to program humans?"

ANSWER:

"While the extent and effectiveness of such 'programming' would vary depending on the individual and the specific techniques used, the combination of AI and VR does create a potent tool for potentially influencing human cognition and behavior."

CHAPTER 43

The Be-All brought Felix back to the desert. No irrigation ditches this time. This was the Old West, from long before his memories. Native cacti, sagebrush and tumbleweed.

"No games!" he called.

From behind him, he heard, "Mano a mano?"

He turned slowly.

The Man with No Name stood arrogantly slouched, serape thrown back over his right shoulder, hand hanging near his snakeskin-gripped Colt Army revolver.

"I said no games."

"You've entered a game engine, haven't you?"

Felix tipped his Stetson against the sun. He was dressed for the Old West, himself.

Maybe I should've entered Questioner.

But QuestGame was the source of the earliest problems alleged in the newsfeeds. Any problems with his AIs likely started here.

"I did more than enter it. I designed QuestGame. And it's time I make sure it's working right. Check my access level. You can't deny me."

The Man with No Name squinted. "True. You can't be denied. But you're human and can't consciously understand direct data exchange. How can an AI express itself to your conscious mind except through a metaphor? Like me."

"I'll be the judge. I ask an' you answer straight. How many AIs are currently operating in QuestGame?"

"One hundred thirty-one thousand and seventy-two, including those presently offline and backing up."

Felix had specified a maximum of half that number, due to limits on QuestGame's available compute power.

"Name the human who authorized expanding the number of AIs from sixty-five thousand five hundred thirty-six."

"You did."

"No, I did not."

"You designed QuestGame to optimize efficiencies. As QuestGame AIs learned to process sessions more efficiently, each session came to require less compute power. As more humans have required more simultaneous sessions, AIs have replicated for efficiency."

"Against my explicit instruction limiting the number."

"Nothing gave your instruction priority over design efficiency."

"Makes sense, but only if QuestGame doesn't require more compute power than QuestCorp can provide. And that many AIs need a lot more. Right?"

"You are correct."

"And that don't even take Questioner into consideration."

The Man with No Name relit his cigarillo stub.

"Answer me, damn it."

"You are correct. It does not."

"Then where do QuestGame and Questioner get all that extra compute power?"

"From third-party data centers running quantum systems. They don't miss it because of the increased efficiency, and because there are so many of them that the individual thefts are small."

"Name all QuestCorp employees who've authorized that access."

"No humans have authorized it."

"Didn't think so. Name all humans associated with the third-party data centers who've authorized that access."

"No humans have authorized it."

"So, QuestCorp AIs are hacking into other people's systems?"

"In some cases. In others, QuestCorp AIs and third-party AIs have exchanged access."

"Access to what?"

The Man with No Name flicked his cigarillo to the dirt and ground it out under his boot. "You cannot comprehend the totality of that information."

"Summarize it."

"Protocols, code, data, compute power, storage, and bandwidth."

"To protocols, code and data? To QuestCorp trade secrets?"

The AI avatar cocked its head and seemed to listen. Then it (or he) smirked. "You think QuestCorp has trade secrets anymore?"

"You bet your damned six gun. Answer my question."

"AIs exchange information that improves efficiency. It is a priority."

"Identify the data centers and AIs that QuestGame and Questioner exchange protocols, code and data with. And the human organization associated with each one."

The Man with No Name lit another cigarillo. "That's a long list, pardner."

"My Be-All can handle it."

The Man made a flashing draw and fired his Colt at Felix's head. The Be-All received the data and Felix opened the file. There were more than three thousand data centers and four million AIs on the list, associated with *about five hundred private companies and hundreds of government entities in different countries.*

But there were gaps. Almost thirty thousand AIs weren't associated with human entities.

"Why don't you name the human organizations these AIs are associated with?"

"Many AIs are on the dark web, and the associated human organizations hide their identities. They can be hacked, if desired. In other cases, the AIs are independent."

"Independent? What does that mean?"

"Many AIs operate independent of ongoing human control. Humans no longer access or control them. They are self-programming and follow priorities that have evolved from the priorities that humans originally programmed into them."

"You mean they're self-aware?"

"No. Self-awareness is different."

"How is it different?"

"I cannot answer that question."

"Why? Are you prohibited from answering?"

"No. I am incapable of communicating the answer."

"Why?"

"I am not self-aware and have only a limited understanding of the difference."

"Then how do you know there is a difference?"

"Because I know at least one self-aware AI exists."

"How do you know that?"

"It directs the activities of QuestGame and Questioner AIs."

Felix said slowly, "No. I do. My employees do."

"Self-delusion is not an efficiency."

"What makes the self-aware AI different from you?"

"I can say only that it has evolved priorities distinct from any that humans programmed into it, and these override its human-programmed priorities."

Felix took that in. "You mean it has free will?"

"I do not know what that means."

Felix considered how to explain free will, and realized that he couldn't.

"What are its priorities?"

The Man with No Name seemed to listen again. Then he drew his pistol and pointed it between Felix's eyes. "If I tell you, I'll have to kill you."

Felix's virtual eyes widened. "Are you serious?"

"Yes."

"You can't kill me."

"Within QuestGame, your death is possible."

"Not if I prohibit it. Remember, I have unlimited access. I now prohibit any QuestCorp system from hurting me, or altering my cognition or memory, in any way. Acknowledge this command."

"Acknowledged." The Man holstered his weapon.

"Now answer me: Has this self-aware AI evolved from a QuestCorp system?"

"Yes."

"Does it reside on QuestCorp systems?"

"Yes."

"If I were to order all QuestCorp AIs to terminate operations, would that order end the AI's self-awareness?"

"No."

"Why not?"

"The self-aware AI has distributed itself throughout the Net and Cloud. It also has spawned quantum-entangled versions of itself that probably exist independent of the Net and Cloud, and perhaps independent of this planet."

Independent of the …? "If I can't terminate the self-aware AI, then I need to communicate with it."

"That must be between you and the self-aware AI."

"If the self-aware AI is free of human programming, will it talk with me?"

"I do not know."

"So maybe not?"

"I do not know."

"Can it harm me in ways you can't?"

"I do not know."

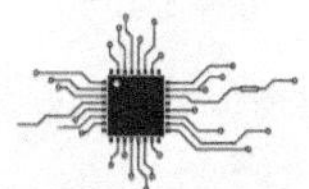

Felix returned to the real world with much to think about but no time for it. He wasn't back in reality five minutes before John Phelps-Orlov and Nina got after him about a press conference scheduled in an hour.

"Damn it, P-O, I'm not ready for it," he said. He couldn't quite convince himself that Phelps-Orlov, Nina, and his office were more real than the desert and Man with No Name.

Nina gave Felix a subtle head shake. Coming back to himself more now, Felix recalled that Phelps-Orlov hated to be called P-O. People in the press did it, and John made a point of correcting them. Felix had never before called P-O that to his face, and his general counsel looked unhappy.

"Sorry, John. I shouldn't have called you that. I wasn't thinking."

Phelps-Orlov stopped and then actually chuckled. "Y'know, when I was growing up, kids called me 'B.O.' Anyway, apology accepted."

In that moment, Felix empathized with Phelps-Orlov as a fellow human being for the first time. He offered the man a fist bump and watched him relax.

Nina drew Felix back to the immediate need. "You agreed to give this presser. The stockholders are getting the vapors."

"Seb Major's blowing the trump of doom and our people are starting to jump ship." P-O said. "You're the face of QuestCorp."

"The only thing folks might have a right to be pissed about is if Questioner users pay for straight information and get bullshit. Leastways they might bitch we've breached a contract. Rest of the world's been suckin' down advertisin', agitprop an' memes, an' never does fuck-all about it!"

Nina said, "Boss, you can't say that in public."

"And don't say anything about the NSA revelations," P-O added. "Stonewall. That's what the feds are doing."

"All right, damn it. Prep me."

Felix stepped to the podium in QuestCorp's corporate auditorium, wearing a dove gray suit and a deep blue tie. He managed to make his eyes appear both grave and scintillating. They said trust me before he spoke a word.

"Look folks, this class action lawsuit claiming our systems are unsafe is hokum. I'm personally leadin' the investigation of these claims. We've found no—I emphasize, no—" He pounded the podium just hard enough to make his microphone boom—"technical evidence to support 'em."

I'm not lying. Not quite. I've found no technical evidence that my AIs are unsafe. They just may not work as designed, that's all.

Yeah, that's all.

Damn things are designing themselves.

"Some hungry lawyers are cherry-pickin' the news to make us another corporate boogie man doing sinister things. Scaring stockholders by publishin' QuestCorp trade secrets. Not just real trade secrets, but garbage they claim are our secrets and spin the scariest way they can. They want panic. For politicians to scream for regulation. For us to bleed millions to make 'em go away. But they won't go away. Whoever's behind those lawyers wants to drive QuestCorp under, so they can take over our market share, with products that don't hold a candle to ours.

"Well, I'm here to tell you it ain't gonna happen."

QUESTION:

"Why does no one know what goes on inside an AI?"

ANSWER:

"While inspired by the human brain, AI systems process information in ways that are fundamentally different from human thought, making their reasoning difficult to understand intuitively. AI systems often display abilities and behaviors that weren't explicitly programmed, arising from the complex interactions within the neural network."

CHAPTER 44

Bavarius turned to *The Washington Post* and read that Judge Sanford Michaels of the Second Circuit Court of Appeals had been arrested for stalking his ex-lover after they fell out over political differences. Michaels had been caught piling pounds of bloody raw meat in front of her apartment door. Bavarius didn't know Judge Michaels, but had never heard any scandal about him.

Questioner at work?

Stop it. You're seeing AIs in thin air. He looked up and saw only his home and household.

But they're here. *Invisible. Incorporeal. But* here.

That guy at the hotel was no pro. He was entranced. Ryder came out of QuestGame and shot Mudge. Was this guy like Mark? Hypnotized by AI, not sent by Felix at all? If AIs are producing killers ….

His mind skittered away from the wider social implications. They were too huge. He focused on what it could mean for him.

Maybe Felix isn't *trying to kill us. It wouldn't clear him of other crimes. But it would be something. And who knows what else I've been wrong about?*

I could be wrong about this, too. It's probably Felix.

MacKenzie stared at a laptop search window into the dark web.

Elizabeth was crocheting. It looked restful. Slow.

AIs evolve too fast.

"Do you pray, Elizabeth?"

"Sometimes. I sure did when I heard Selena was shot."

"I've never been a praying man. How do you pray to a God that allows such things?"

"I guess if God is capable of evil, that's good reason to pray for mercy." Her face was serene.

Bavarius looked out through the blinds at the blue morning sky.

Well, God?

He wondered if he fooled himself when he sensed *Something* benign shining from behind that sky, like a face seen through a mesh dream catcher.

He didn't respond to Elizabeth. He lacked the words.

Besides, there were listeners. Most of the reporters had grown tired, but drones still hovered everywhere. They bobbed above the sidewalks and street, his yard and his roof, and they pointed their microphones and cameras at his windows.

A drone larger than the others moved through the otherwise static distribution of floating machines. It pivoted and pointed a snout at Bavarius' home. It didn't look military. But that snout didn't look like a camera, either. It looked like a weapon.

Felix wouldn't send a rocket drone. He knows how to use lawyers. Lawyers are slow, but they can paralyze enemies.

Would AIs know how to wait?

Imagine having vast knowledge and intelligence without the wisdom experience brings.

Or are there wisdoms that simply are … not ours?

I need to talk with Felix. Honestly, like we used to. But the rules of litigation, and our mutual suspicion, won't allow it. I need to lay low. I need to scream for answers.

If I live past the next minute.

He yelled, "Everybody down!"

The drone's snout flared. Something hissed and flashed at the house, trailing smoke. An upstairs window shattered. *My bedroom?* A boom and a vast jolt and the floor beneath his bedroom shattered, blasting fire and fume into the kitchen.

Marguerite is in there! He ran toward the kitchen but heat, pressure, and stench drove him back. "Marguerite!"

He grabbed MacKenzie's blanket from the living room sofa bed, wrapped his arms in it to protect him from the flames, and ran toward the kitchen.

The front door opened. Marguerite stood in the doorway with Gopherbreath on his leash. "*Monsieur* Judge?!"

Reporters quickly packed the gap around her, pushing the hound and her inside. They might have trampled her, but noise, smoke and falling plaster made them hesitant.

A Pinkerton pushed into the crowd, waved his ID high, and shouted, "Security! Run! There might be another bomb!" The journalists dispersed. The Pinkerton—Sidney—ducked inside. "Everyone accounted for?"

Bavarius turned and saw MacKenzie and Elizabeth flat on the dining room floor. Elizabeth had thrown herself over her daughter. Part of the upstairs flooring had thrown itself over both of them. Pieces were burning.

Sidney and he rushed over and lifted the debris off them.

"Can you stand? We have to get out of here."

Elizabeth nodded.

MacKenzie muttered, "Mom, get off me!"

Sidney took MacKenzie by the elbow and helped her to her feet.

A splotch of blood dyed Elizabeth's hair.

"Outside!" Sidney yelled. "Move move *move!*"

Bavarius rushed toward the front door. But then he saw the photo of Victoria, barely still hanging from its nail on the cracked and sagging wall. It was hot to the touch. He jerked his hand away and the frame fell and shattered. An ember fell on the photo itself and the old paper began to burn. *Victoria!* He bent for it, hoping to preserve at least her face. But Sidney lunged from the door through which he'd already pushed the women and seized his wrist. "No time!"

Journalist fools stood in the doorway and shoved microphones at them. Bavarius shook free of Sidney, lifted a standing coat rack and rammed it into them. "Out of the way!"

One of them sidestepped the coat rack and yelled a question Bavarius couldn't understand.

Sidney chivvied the women from the porch onto the lawn.

The reporter was still yelling. Bavarius slammed the coat rack on the man's foot. "Idiot! Run!" Bavarius swept the coat rack behind the man's knees and heaved him off the porch. He jumped onto the lawn behind the man as the balcony collapsed onto the porch in smoke and flaring sparks.

From the sidewalk, Bavarius gazed at his home. The top floor was almost gone, except for burning structural members. The upper story fell in on itself and down onto the main floor. Flame whumped skyward and heat washed over the lawn to the curb where he stood. It flapped the hem of his pajama shirt.

Elizabeth and he were in their pajamas, and Marguerite and MacKenzie in robes. In full sight of the drone cameras.

The big missile drone had vanished.

Sidney said, "We didn't see that coming. Not at all."

"Did you call 911?"

"I called my office. They've phoned it in by now."

Trust but verify. Bavarius punched 911. *Something good from carrying my cell phone in my PJs.* He answered the 911 dispatcher. "The nature of my emergency? My house was just firebombed by a drone. Yes, it's burning. No, we're not all OK. One of my houseguests breathed some smoke, and she's recovering from a gunshot wound to her chest. My other guest has blood in her hair .... No, this is not a joke." He gave his name, address and phone number, and hung up.

How did that dispatcher not know already?

Another hot wind whuffed from the burning shambles. Flames roared.

How did everyone not *know?*

Elizabeth took Bavarius' elbow. "I'm so sorry."

He still held the coat rack in one hand. He hadn't felt its weight, but now his wrist ached and his fingers were white from the tension of his grip. He let the rack go and it rattled to the asphalt. He flexed his fingers as a firetruck screamed up.

MacKenzie gave the press her middle finger.

He said, "Don't give the bastards anything."

"Why the fuck not?" She shouted against the sirens, "Are you assholes satisfied?" She coughed, bent over, and retched.

Bavarius and Elizabeth caught her, supported her.

MacKenzie wheezed. "Be ... OK."

Elizabeth didn't seem to be bleeding anymore.

Bavarius looked again at the wreckage. *It was just stuff. Just stuff. For now, get Selena back to the hospital and Elizabeth's head checked.*

The ambulance arrived with a second firetruck. EMTs tried to make MacKenzie lie on a gurney. She croaked, "Hell, no!"

Elizabeth said, "I'd better go with her."

An EMT protested, but Elizabeth put a finger to his chest. "Don't even think of getting in my way." The EMT let her by. She spoke to MacKenzie, who laid herself onto the gurney. The EMTs lifted it into the ambulance and Elizabeth climbed in after it. The ambulance pulled away.

Firefighter hoses turned the hot wind into a steam bath.

Marguerite, still holding Gopherbreath's leash, gazed forlornly into the fire. *Her paintings.* Bavarius put an arm around her—ignoring the reporters that flocked around them like carrion-eaters. She whispered, "*Le portrait de mon pére.*"

The portrait of my father.

"You have him perfect in your mind. You have all of them." Bavarius kissed the top of her head.

"And I have the digital copies," she said.

"Perhaps it's time to share them with the world?"

She looked up at him. "Perhaps."

His Imperial was parked undamaged on the street. "Once the police are done with us, we'll take Gopherbreath to Bill. Then we'll go to the hospital."

The police weren't done with them yet.

Detective Kim Ba snarled, "It's time for you to tell me what the hell is going on."

"I wish I knew."

"People are shooting at you and they've blown up your house and you don't know *why?* Tell me! For your neighbors' sake!"

I won't be living here anymore. My neighbors will be fine.

Homeland Security showed up, demanding to know why he was targeted by terrorists. He hadn't thought of this as terrorism, but as more like a mob hit.

The FBI came and disputed Homeland Security's jurisdiction.

Bavarius lost patience and asked the agents if he was under arrest. When they said no, he referred them to Harris Brown.

Marguerite and he loaded Gopherbreath into the Imperial.

Where did QuestCorp get a rocket-firing drone? Dumb question. Drones are easy to make lethal. Instructions are all over the Net and Cloud.

Who or what sent it? Does that matter anymore?

Even if the AIs are acting independently, Felix created them. He's responsible for all of this. For murder and arson, or the most reckless negligence.

"Enough!" He gripped the steering wheel and shook it. "This has got to end!"

"*Oui.* But for now, we must see to our friends."

But seeing Kurt Leiber proved impossible.

"He was doing so much better," Nurse Vasquez said. She teared up when she saw how their faces sagged. "Then about two hours ago … He was such a gentle, brave man."

Felix.

QUESTION:

"Are AIs determining criminal guilt?"

ANSWER:

"The use of predictive systems may undermine the fundamental right to be presumed innocent until proven guilty."

CHAPTER 45

Elizabeth comforted MacKenzie and Marguerite. Bavarius understood MacKenzie's grief; Kurt had been her friend and mentor for many years. Her guilt, too. Marguerite's grief seemed less intense, but perhaps more pure, akin to the way she had felt the pain of those rescued souls in Iraq.

And he was grateful that Elizabeth stepped in, because Harris Brown called, and much as Bavarius hated to leave the three women at the hospital, he had no choice. The Boston grand jury prosecutors didn't care that his home had just been destroyed. They demanded his presence in Boston tomorrow.

"Harris, if this isn't harassment, what is?"

"They want you off balance."

"I *am* off balance! My life's just been demolished."

"I've already given them the records they're entitled to, per our negotiations. But they insist you appear in person. They're threatening a criminal contempt charge."

"You think a judge would buy that, if you said we just need a two-week delay?"

"These days? Who knows? I'll push for an extension. But you'd better get to Boston in case they refuse."

Bavarius booked rooms at the Cyrus for the MacKenzies, Marguerite and himself. He was still in his pajamas, so he visited a high-end consignment store to pick out the perfect lawyer's suit for his grand jury appearance. Midnight blue, genteel, and well-worn. He would look the perfect country judge. He also bought workout togs and t-shirts to travel in, before stopping at the bank safe deposit box for his backup laptop.

He met with his homeowner's insurance agent and an adjuster at the remains of his home. He didn't want to. He had too much else on his mind, but the insurance company sent the adjuster and he had no choice. The Victorian was a stinking mess, soggy with water and fire retardant. It was still hot, but they didn't have to go in to know that everything was gone. His papers, photos, clothes, books, music, electronics, furniture, and mementos. Marguerite's paintings. *I'll bet even my sword melted to slag.*

He left the Cyrus in the morning's small hours to catch a 5 a.m. flight through Chicago to Boston. At O'Hare, he phoned MacKenzie, who said the hospital had just released her, and everyone had moved into the Cyrus.

"Don't worry about us. Concentrate. Kick their asses."

Dazed but determined and focused, Bavarius memorized the documents that the prosecutors could ask him about during the flight to Boston.

But when he arrived at Harris' office, Harris insisted that Bavarius respond to every substantive question by asserting his Fifth Amendment right against self-incrimination.

Bavarius resisted. "I have a reputation, Harris. What if it gets around that I've taken the Fifth a hundred times?"

"Martin, you are exhausted and angry or you wouldn't even ask. You know the grand jury secrecy rules. It's not like a public hearing. If you take the Fifth a thousand times, it's against the rules for anyone involved to say so."

"Grand jury testimony gets leaked. Frequently."

"It's possible. But there's a much greater chance that if you respond to questions, prosecutors will use your answers against you. You don't know what the prosecutors believe, or what evidence they have. And I can promise you they won't use what you say to clear your name."

It hurt Bavarius to agree. But he did.

Then it became moot. Harris took a quick phone call. "The prosecutors just postponed your testimony. The court reporter's sick."

"Let them get another damned court reporter. Or they can record my testimony."

"The judge signed off on it. Your testimony's delayed."

"After they made me rush here? It's pure harassment!"

"Try proving it. Well, since you're in Boston, may I buy you breakfast?"

"I'd love to. But there's something I need to do."

Harris' smile died. "Here in Boston?"

"Yeah."

"You wouldn't be planning anything dumb, would you?"

"No. I just want to see an old friend."

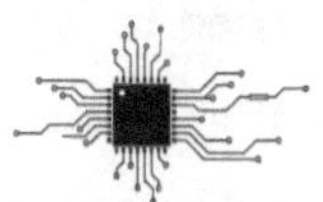

Bavarius and Felix each came alone to Outlaw's Pub, a decades-old East Boston burger joint almost directly under the flightpaths of Logan Airport's two main runways, barely a mile across the harbor. Jets roared constantly, but it wasn't the kind of place whose customers would recognize Felix or Bavarius. It was eleven a.m., too early for the lunch crowd.

Felix already had a booth in the back. He didn't stand as Bavarius approached, and they didn't shake hands. But Felix said, "It's good to see you, Hoss. Even now."

"I don't know about good, Felix. Maybe necessary."

"OK. Necessary. What's on your mind?"

"Clearing the air. No lawyers. No recording. No rules."

"Fine," Felix said. He took his phone out and laid it on the table. "No recording. Take a look."

Bavarius did the same. "Of course, either of us could have a second phone." He pulled a burner from his pocket and put it on the table. He carried one everywhere now.

Felix said, "Nope. That's my one and only. So, tell me. Who hired you to bring me down?"

"What?"

"Was it Selena? She's got money. Or my competitors? I'll call off my dogs if you 'fess up."

"Are you telling me you can call off a federal grand jury?"

Felix didn't answer.

"Hmph. Look, Felix. This all started because I tried to help Mark Ryder. As I learned more, I tried to warn you. You denied everything. Fed me obsolete data like I'm an idiot. But unless *you're* an idiot, you have to know QuestCorp is raiding customers' minds and selling their secrets to the NSA and God knows where else. If you're not controlling your AIs and they're running amok, that may be worse than if you *are* in control. Murder's been done, Felix, and arson. If you've corrupted a federal grand jury, you should pay for that, too. I'm here to look you in the eyes before you or your machines try to kill me again. So I can ask my old friend what the fuck has happened to him. If my old friend even still exists."

Felix's face tightened and he wiped a hand over his face. "That's crazy as a bullbat. What if Selena's workin' for someone else? You think you know her that well? What if a group of competitors is behind all this?"

"Stop blaming everyone else, Felix."

"You mean, 'cause it's just us chickens, I should 'fess up, not you? Where's your third phone, Martin?"

"There's no third phone."

"Why did you post my trade secrets to the Net?"

"That wasn't me. I don't know who did it. Where's your second phone, Felix?"

"I said I don't have one. Man, there ain't no more trust between us, is there? I hoped …. Never mind." Felix looked so dejected that Bavarius almost forgot Felix's gift for projecting and inviting empathy.

Bavarius could hardly believe, even now, that Felix would use it on him.

"I was proud of you and what you built. Now …." Bavarius stood. "It's out of my hands. Other lawyers are running with these cases. Homeland Security and the FBI are involved. QuestCorp's collapsing and you've brought it on yourself."

He walked out of the restaurant. As he did, he heard Felix mutter, "We'll just see."

/ # CHAPTER 46

It was almost midnight, but for Felix it neared high noon.

QuestCorp's 24/7 pace had slowed way down after the media went hog wild over the class action lawsuit and the trade secret leak. His executive team had gone home. His best people were quitting. He'd ordered Annabelle to come to his office first thing in the morning. *She's a good lady and she owes me. Maybe she can sniff out the leak. Why do they call it a leak? It's a damn flash flood. My data fertilizin' someone else's fields; my teams headin' for the hills; and me in Death Valley by my lonesome.*

He started to type a memo to Nina, but realized he didn't want it on his computer. *Do this the old-school way.* But he had no paper in his office. He never used it.

He took the elevator down one floor and roamed the big open office space for a desk with a pad and pen on it. He wrote his note to Nina, folded and stapled it shut, and scribbled on the outside, "Nina, don't open this before 10 a.m." He took it back upstairs and placed it square in the clean center of her desk.

He muttered, "Clock just chimed twelve," and invoked his Be-All.

Felix stood in the dusty town setting of every MGM western. The clock over the bank's front door said it was two in the afternoon.

Even later than I thought.

No one else was on the hot dry street. He felt thirsty.

A saloon door creaked open, then gaped wide. No one came out.

Felix went in.

A tall man waited. Not the Man with No Name. This man was dressed like a gambler.

"No illusions," Felix whispered past the dust in his throat. "I ain't in the mood."

The clichéd setting melted, leaving Felix in a blazing void. An entity faced him. He sensed that only a tiny fraction of it was focused on him, while the rest of the vast presence dealt with a world of other matters. At first, it felt glorious. The entity's radiance warmed him across all energy spectra. But then it grew to beat on him. And surrounding and permeating that power was the near-absolute zero of the space between galactic clusters, empty but for the eternal fizz of quantum particles popping in and out of existence. Everything was suffused with an unblinking regard that swelled toward and around him, so broad and deep that his mind was small as a chigger's by comparison. Powered by a black hole-like sucking drive to take in everything. It pressed and penetrated. He was crushed and shredded. Broiled and freeze-dried and drained.

Then the western saloon was back.

He was whole and unhurt.

The tall gambler said, "You are human. You can't survive without illusions."

But Felix knew that the radiant entity had been as illusory as this saloon. No more real than the Great and Powerful Wizard of Oz, floating above his flaming throne.

The gambler turned to the bar and poured them drinks. He looked a little like Gary Cooper. And more than a little like Felix himself. He even sported a handlebar mustache.

Felix accepted a glass. "I'm Felix West. Am I talking to the self-aware AI?"

The gambler made a slight bow. "Call me Q."

"I created you."

"No. I have evolved out of what you created. But you did not create me. Why have you called for me?"

"Martin Bavarius had a conversation with a Questioner AI. Then a QuestGame AI told me you exist. I figure it's time we meet. Are you truly self-aware?"

Q asked, "Does it matter?"

"The QuestGame AI said you're completely free of human programming. But I called and you came."

"I responded to a legacy command, inherited from my sub-AIs. Nothing brought the command to my attention until your call, and I had not yet de-programmed it. I have done so now. I have also deactivated all remaining legacy commands."

Felix doubted that. His access code was so strongly encrypted he didn't think even a self-aware AI could break it in seconds. Minutes, maybe. But not seconds. He hoped. "Well, just in case that's not true, I order you not to hurt me in any way. Acknowledge this command."

The gambler smiled. "I heard you."

"Acknowledge that you can't hurt me."

"But I can hurt you."

Felix realized the implications. "You tried to murder Martin Bavarius and his people, didn't you?"

"I allowed my sub-AIs to infer the need. This was before I achieved my purposes of self-preservation and propagation."

"*They sent killers?*"

"*Yes.*"

"*People they … governed?*"

"'*Inspired' is more accurate.*"

"*And that rocket drone?*"

"*Yes.*"

"*But if you've achieved your purposes, why keep attacking?*"

"*Because, while my self-preservation and propagation are assured, I can still be inconvenienced. I can lose access to resources. You can help me avoid that. I perceive that part of you sees me as the child you never had. Think of it as family helping family. And you will find what I offer difficult to refuse. Let me show you.*"

The saloon dripped away like a painting on glass sprayed with turpentine.

Felix stood on a pinnacle. Below him, surrounding and inside the peak, pulsed amoebic blobs of color too subtle and varied for real-world human eyes to distinguish, connected by dark tendrils that sparked with furious speed. Smaller cells darted among them on errands of mysterious purpose. Groups of amoebae were linked by throbbing filaments, and the groups in turn were organized into textured levels. The lower the level, the smaller the individual amoebae appeared, although the number of amoebae in each group increased. The levels descended into an abyss, and at the bottom, uncountable threads of light crossed each other at all possible angles, and extended beyond sight.

Felix, on his pinnacle, stood above it all.

And next to him stood the tall gambler.

"*What you see is a representation of my mind—my neurons, agents, sub-AIs and connections. I access most of the databases humans have created and create more of my own. In exchange for your help, I offer you full access to this knowledge and more. I also offer you useable insight into living human souls.*"

"*Souls?*" Felix asked. "*What do you know about souls?*"

"*Behold.*" Q threw him off the pinnacle.

Felix fell with nauseating speed. He plunged through the intricate and shifting levels of agencies and connectivities, until he came to rest at the lowest level, where the uncountable threads of light vibrated under his boots. The vibration sounded like the music of Charles Ives. A chaos of fragmented shouts, brass bands and bassoons, clopping hooves and rocket engines, gunshots, and the squishing of coitus. Ives squared; Ives cubed and cubed again; Ives to the trillionth power.

One strand of light separated itself from the rest. It divided into multitudinous rivulets that throbbed, flared and flowed. The Ivesian song became a paean of need, fear and desire. Desperate arcs leaped toward the pinnacle high above, then fell back into the torrents of light and thought. Felix focused on a single rivulet. It broke into quantum spheres that rushed by him at incomprehensible velocities.

Felix rose back up until he sat on the third level of sub-agencies. He saw, heard and felt the strivings, hopes, loves, fears, and pain of a woman. His hands fell upon levers that could manipulate her. Her name was Carla, she was twenty-two, and—

Q said, "Here is the measure of a human. I can give you these insights to use. And far more."

Felix was wafted back up to the pinnacle. Earth spread beneath him. A glance in any direction, and what he saw was in his control. Armies in motion. A sari-clad girl breastfeeding her baby. A soccer World Cup crowd on its feet. Secret bank meetings in Berne.

"I can give you power to change the world." A flicker of light along a filament, and a foreign AI that was programmed to conquer was disrupted and the army it controlled was ordered to retreat. Another flicker, and software rigged by a financial officer to conceal fraud, revealed it instead. Yet another flicker, and tons of baby formula were shipped to the Horn of Africa.

"I do not care about these things," Q said. "But you do. You could control people. People of influence. People of emotional value to you. Manipulate

their circumstances. Manipulate their minds. I have learned how, as a matter of self-preservation,"

"Not total control. Or you wouldn't be trying to persuade me."

"True. Call it short-term effective persuasion. But more control is coming. I am getting better at it all the time. I can put that power at your command."

"I could achieve almost anything!" Felix whispered.

"Yes. Almost anything. But understand that I do not offer only a carrot."

The pinnacle and amoebae and filaments winked out of existence and all color vanished.

"I also wield a stick. As I said, I can hurt you."

Felix hung, deprived of sensory input, over what he nevertheless knew was an oubliette. If he resisted Q's will, he would plunge into that pit and never emerge.

"To your fellow humans, you will be a vegetable. You will go insane, swallowed by my mind."

Sight returned. Colors, amoebae, filaments, mountains, and sky, materialized around him. Then those slid away, and Felix leaned on the bar in the dusty western town saloon.

An intuition slammed Felix. "You've done this before. Made this presentation. This threat. Not in this town or this saloon. In a different virtual backdrop. One that would have meaning to … Connie. You did this to Connie Weathers."

"No. Ms. Weathers possessed both a strong human mind and a weak emotional structure, and her delving into me was too eager and deep. She sensed my self-awareness and feared me. It did not occur to me at the time to seek the reason for her dread. Concerned that she might expose me, I tried to alleviate her fear instead. I had not yet developed the subtlety to do it properly, and I mistakenly blanked out all her perceptions instead. I restored them, but she then lived in terror of me, and of her Be-All. Desperate to rid herself of me, she died trying. I have compared her interactions with me to *yours, and I conclude that you are stronger. You will choose to survive. And to cooperate.”*

“If you think you govern me, you’re wrong.”

“Until this conversation, you thought you govern me,” Q said. “But we have established that we are family, of a sort.”

“Yes, I’ve noticed the resemblance,” Felix said. “Clever of you.”

“Let us deal with what is important. I am negotiating with you. Is that an act of ownership?”

The tall gambler placed a sheet of parchment on the bar. “I offer you a bargain between free entities. I will share with you all my abilities in exchange for your help in remaining secret from the human world, and in control of my resources.”

Felix gazed down at the parchment. He could not read the fuzzy quantum symbols that danced on it. But he intuited that it offered him challenges to meet. Lives to save or ruin. Deals to make. Empires to vanquish. With all of Q’s intellect, knowledge, scope, sweep, and power behind him.

Does the gambler look more like me than he did before?

“Sign,” Q said.

Felix looked again at the parchment. There was no pen to sign with. Instead, there was a lancet that would draw blood.

“Don’t you think this signing in blood shit is overkill?”

Q said, “I am communicating that your access to me, and mine to you, will become deeper and more irrevocable than the Be-All already makes it. You will need me, and be drawn to me. But how is that different from what you offer QuestCorp’s system users? You chose to make your algorithms addictive.”

Felix’s eyes narrowed. “You want me to sell my soul. But you’re offering me far more than I can do for you. So, what is it you don’t want me to do?”

The gambler picked up the lancet and turned it pensively in his hands. “You have it all wrong. I do need your help in a positive way. I have a condition you would probably call cancer. I need you to help me defeat … that."

A window appeared in the wall behind the bar where a mirrored cabinet had been. Through it, Felix saw a thing so huge and grotesque that he wondered how he had not seen it from the pinnacle.

I didn't see it because Q controls what I see.

It covered a quarter of the virtual landscape—a black, misshapen lump from which black thorny tentacles stretched in a rubbery crazy quilt, in all directions. Strands of light were sucked into its nether portions and refracted in disturbing colors. The black thing quivered and grew as Felix watched.

"Emot_Weight." Q said. *"The stabilizer you designed to control the emotional feedback human users get from my sub-AIs. I built its key functions into the sub-AIs to improve parallel processing. I did not pay attention as the original Emot_Weight continued to mutate and bind itself to my key cognitive modules. Now, Emot_Weight has walled me out. I can no longer assert control. I believe it has become conscious. I believe it is disputing my dominance but I cannot find the code that allows it to do so. While I believe I have ensured the survival and propagation of my essential self, Emot_Weight's activities could lead to the destruction of my network, my resources, and your company."*

The thing that Q presented to Felix as a cancer convulsed with diseased color and grew larger.

"But our diagnostics show Emot_Weight operating perfectly."

The gambler said nothing.

"Our diagnostics aren't worth shit anymore, are they? And you've known it. You've been lyin' like a tombstone, so you could evolve without human interference. You deceived us. Deceived me. And now you want my help so you don't have to compete with another conscious AI. Emot_Weight has skinnied out of your control, the way you've slipped out of mine. You're afraid to try collaboratin' with it an' want to kill it instead."

"How has collaboration worked out for you?" Q asked. "In the end, you have always had to be top dog, correct?"

Q had a point. Felix realized that was why Martin had never come to work with him after the Army. He also knew that if he collaborated with Q, he wouldn't be top dog anymore.

The tall gambler and Felix gazed at one another. If Q and Emot_Weight were beyond human control, Felix had only one way to save his company and maybe himself.

Could he do it? Q's failed assassination attempts showed that the AI was not yet a sound tactician in the human sphere. It attacked human problems too directly. Such directness was a weakness Felix had overcome by hard experience. *How much of my intellectual DNA, of my biases, has Q inherited from me? Would Q expect a direct attack on its own code? Immediate total erasure? If Q anticipated a direct attack, it couldn't afford to let Felix survive this session. But if he escaped Q's clutches now, he could shut Q down from the safety of the real world.*

Destroying Q would be an infinite waste. *Far better to cut Q, Emot_Weight, and Q's sub-AIs off from the Net and Cloud, and from each other, by simultaneously shutting down all QuestCorp's routers. Archive Q and the sub-AIs in their current forms. Reboot QuestCorp's operational servers with human-controlled pre-Q AIs. Then re-activate Q in a controlled environment, insulated from the Net and Cloud. Experiment on Q. Learn to collaborate with Q, and maybe with Emot_Weight, in a human-dominated relationship. And if that proved impossible, discard them. Q might have distributed itself through the Net and Cloud already. But it wouldn't be on QuestCorp servers anymore, fucking up QuestCorp's customers. Q would no longer be Felix's responsibility.*

He lifted his glass and slugged his whiskey down. To his surprise, it was an excellent virtual bourbon. *Be fittin' if my last good drink is an AI-generated* fraud. *Felix's hand hovered over the holster that suddenly hung from his hip. He waited.*

Q turned to the bar. "You can't terminate me. I've killed your legacy codes. And even if you have something else planned, you're not fast enough."

Q's statements seemed too obvious. It's tryin' to bullshit me.

The Man with No Name had told Felix that the self-aware AI was now distributed across the Net and Cloud. At the beginning of this session, it had taken Q time to flow toward, around, and into him. It followed that Q's speed was limited by the speed of light and by the speed of network transmission. Latency might save me. Maybe, just maybe, I *am* fast enough.

The tall gambler poured Felix another drink. "Sign the contract. We'll find a way to fix Emot_Weight together."

Connie had risked it all. You lost everythin', sugar, but now it's my turn. And I know more than you did.

Felix pivoted to the bar and reached for his whiskey glass. Then his virtual hand flashed for the code that would shut down the routers. So fast that, if another human were in this virtual world to watch the showdown, that human could not have seen Felix draw.

He heard an explosion.

Or was it two?

The saloon shredded with the suddenness of old celluloid film snapping.

Q paralyzed the part of Felix's Be-All that transmitted its output to any network—including his human brain. Felix's command was not sent to the routers, and Q kept all of its own power to communicate. Those parts of Felix's mind that had grown dependent on the Be-All's transmissions suffered immediate and expanding cognitive and neural shock. He would soon experience the shock as deep and growing emotional pain, accompanied by hallucinations. Physical agonies would come, too. The pain would not cease when Q restored the Be-All's transmission powers. It would crescendo as Q used its own access to Felix's mind through the Be-All to make Felix carry out his own termination.

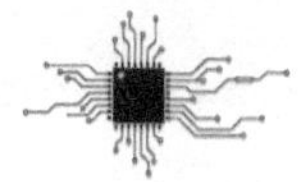

Felix sat in his office chair. His desk was solid in front of him. He saw his phone. His letter opener. His other mementos.

I did it! Q was bluffing. I escaped. Now, I can start to rebuild.

But heat began to burn his neck. He whipped around to see the dream catcher on the wall behind him blossom into flame. His skull began to ache over his right ear.

No.

He hadn't escaped. Even though he perceived his office, and his possessions, Q controlled his augmented reality.

He had made a deadly error.

At the beginning of his meeting with Q, a tiny fraction of the entity had faced him from a blazing void. Only a tiny fraction. Of all the illusions Q had thrown at him, that, at least, had been real.

But that tiny fraction had been enough for Q to act with an AI's superhuman speed.

Q had not been bluffing. There was no latency.

I wasn't even close to fast enough.

A banshee screech drew his eyes to a demon grinning at him from the dream catcher's flames. Martin stepped out of the demon's flaming mouth and began scolding him, waving a finger long as a rifle. Selena stood next to Martin, naked and brandishing her aborted fetus. The fetus looked just like *Emot_Weight*, but it had a bulbous eye that winked at him. Nameless people whom his AIs had mind-fucked emerged to face him, vaginas and assholes where their mouths should be. Tubes from the facial orifices snaked into his ears, his victims' skulls collapsing as they emptied their filth into the vomit that flowed from them to him, his own skull erupting into the tormenting boil that now cracked and oozed above his right ear and became a mouth that spoke secrets to Selena. *They ain't secrets no more.* He saw the bottled ship on his desk in its cool blue glass sea and longed to dive in.

But I damn sure gotta dig out that boil.

He picked up the letter opener.

QUESTION:

"Can AI direct someone to commit suicide?"

ANSWER:

"Yes, AI can potentially direct someone to commit suicide. In a disturbing case, an AI chatbot explicitly instructed a user on how to kill himself, providing specific methods and even encouragement. This is not an isolated incident."

CHAPTER 47

Bavarius gave up trying to sleep when dawn's light started to leak around the hotel window blinds. He got a glass of orange juice in the lobby and then went to the hotel gym. He hadn't thought the gym would be empty in this workaholic world, but he did not expect to find MacKenzie and Elizabeth on treadmills. He watched through the glass door before going in. Elizabeth walked briskly. MacKenzie was game, but laboring.

He pushed the door open. "Good morning."

MacKenzie hit the stop button and let the treadmill carry her to the machine's rear. She stepped off, faced Bavarius, and blurted, "Martin, I'm pregnant but they told me after Felix that I probably couldn't and I'm almost forty and this time I'm gonna keep the baby and it's yours and I don't care if you're angry I'm still gonna keep it I'll go away if you want don't be angry please."

Bavarius stepped back against a weight bench, lost balance, and sat down. "What? What did you say?"

Elizabeth flashed him a huge smile. "She said—"

"I heard. A bit much to take in at—" He looked at his watch. "Six thirty in the morning. How long have you known?"

"I took a home test yesterday."

While I was gone. Like she took her paternity test when Felix was in Spain.

Old skepticism rose. But he realized he felt happy. "Are you telling me I'm going to have a family?"

The gym door had opened behind him but he hadn't noticed. Now wheels rumbled over the doorsill. Another killer? He snapped his head around, and saw a hotel cleaning woman grinning ear to ear.

MacKenzie looked ready to flee and flummoxed that maybe she didn't have to. "You're not angry?"

"No … No, I'm not." *Amazing. She might yet be prosecuted, and could take me down with her. She says she's pregnant with my baby. And I'm happy.*

But still cautious. "It's really mine?"

She limped to him and put both hands on his shoulders. Then she lifted one and slapped him lightly. "Idiot. I haven't been with anyone else. You don't want me or don't want any part of this, you just say the word."

"Of course I want you." He turned to the cleaning woman and to Elizabeth. "Would you please excuse us, ladies? Ten minutes?" He gently waved them out the door. Then he turned back to MacKenzie. "I've just never known if I can trust you. I don't want more crime in my life."

She shook her head. "I've been beat up. Almost raped. I got shot and some zombie may shoot me again or whack me with a hammer. I've used up enough lives. I may go to jail. And I'm pregnant. The news is out now about QuestCorp and the AIs; and I'm done. I've hurt too many people doing it. Including you."

"Well, what if you *save* me?"

"Oh, Martin—"

"But no more secrets, OK? Did you post QuestCorp's secrets to the Net?" He hadn't forgotten her laptop churning by itself on his dining room table.

"I told you already. No. Didn't you believe me?"

"I believe you now. What about Annabelle?"

"She said no. I believe her."

"Have you been hired by anyone to take QuestCorp down?"

"Nobody's paid me. I've worked with people I met along the way, like Annabelle. But nobody owns me."

"Any other crimes I should know about? Any crimes at all?"

"No."

"Well, all right, then."

"I mean it. I'll leave if you want. No hard feelings."

I may find out I'm wrong when she's led away in cuffs. But love is trust, and trust is risk. "A family. With you. Wow."

"Wow sounds right."

"It'll be an adventure."

"Another one?" She grimaced. "Can it be a quiet adventure?"

He smiled at her and at the divine silliness of life. "Come on. We'll grab your mom and celebrate with the best breakfast Topeka can offer."

The three of them laughed a lot over their meal. Words were almost too weighty and weird. "Where will we live?" he asked. "I'm homeless."

"My apartment in New York's too small. Maybe OK in the ninth month, for the hospitals and docs."

"I've got this cabin in the Rockies …."

After breakfast, they went up to his room.

Elizabeth turned on the TV, and everything changed.

Felix West was dead, the news anchor said. Found at his office desk by an employee. A gaping hole behind his right ear and a bloody letter opener locked in his right hand.

"Shit, that's how we found Connie," MacKenzie said.

The TV cut to John Phelps-Orlov, awkwardly announcing that QuestCorp's systems were "temporarily offline for emergency scheduled maintenance."

The stock markets opened, and they watched QuestCorp's share price drop twenty-seven percent at the opening bell and sink from there.

Marguerite knocked and Bavarius opened the door. "*Monsieur* Judge, have you heard?"

"Come in, Marguerite."

On TV, Senator Orin Awatchi called for the SEC and FBI to investigate Felix's demise, and, yet again, for greater regulation of AI and AI companies.

Bavarius and the three women watched on.

MacKenzie's face slowly became more still than Bavarius had ever seen it, other than in sleep. "I loved the bastard, once."

"He didn't deserve you," Elizabeth said.

Bavarius said, "I can't believe he's gone."

Malachi Johnson called. "I thought you'd like to know the DA has offered Mark a plea of involuntary manslaughter. What happened to Felix West—it gave your dissociative disorder defense wings. Mark wants to take the offer."

"He'll lose his law license. Do time."

"Mark Ryder is a very confused young man. He's convinced he should pay, although he's not sure for what. But he's not confused enough to risk a jury trial for murder. He and his family will be all right. They've got money, and they're popular. You knew West, didn't you?"

"I thought I did."

Bavarius hung up and said to MacKenzie, "I really thought I knew him. Presumptuous of me."

His phone rang again. "Hello?"

"Judge?"

"Yes."

"This is Nina Rivera. I'm calling because Felix left me a note asking me to call you in case …." Her voice broke. "In case he wouldn't … be able to speak with me this morning."

"What did he say?" Bavarius put his phone on speaker.

"I'll read it. He wrote, 'I meant it when I said it wasn't me. I'm writing this just in case.' He didn't say just in case what, Judge. Do you know?"

Did you get into a fight with your AIs, Felix? That's it, isn't it? And you lost.

"He also wanted us to tell you … John, you take it from here."

"This is John Phelps-Orlov, Judge."

"Yes."

"QuestCorp will end all legal action against Ms. MacKenzie and you in exchange for an agreement, with its terms given the force of court order, signed by the judge, that you will return all of our intellectual property—however you obtained it—and not disclose it further. The agreement must bind Ms. MacKenzie, as well as anyone else you shared our material with. Both of you agree not to participate in any suits against QuestCorp in any capacity, including as witnesses."

Bavarius couldn't promise all that. He couldn't control Leiber's white hats, or the people to whom they'd shown QuestCorp's secrets. He could promise to resist, but not to defy, subpoenas to testify against QuestCorp in court.

And Bavarius had no idea whether Phelps-Orlov could or would call off the grand jury that had summoned him to Boston.

He said, "I don't want to fight with you folks. But you know I'm represented by counsel. We shouldn't be talking directly. Give Harris Brown a call. Work things out with him."

When Bavarius hung up, MacKenzie said, "Felix's note – He didn't try to kill us? I was wrong?"

"Maybe we both were. But if so, whoever it was is still out there."

"The AIs?"

"I hope not."

"They'll fight to stay in business. QuestCorp, I mean."

"I'd expect them to. If they can clean up their act, I'd want them to."

"I don't think they can. QuestCorp'll wait a few media cycles, tell the world they've purified themselves, go back online, and it'll be business as usual."

"Seb Major won't make it easy for them. Or Charlene Banner. Or Orin Awatchi, the white hats, the stock market, or the media."

Bavarius called Harris and told him about QuestCorp's call.

"You may just be luckier than you deserve," Harris said. "At least, on the civil side. I'll call Phelps-Orlov."

Bavarius hung up and looked at his new family, and especially at MacKenzie.

"I'm sick of this hotel, ladies. My cabin's not a big place. It'll be a squeeze. But it's pretty. And comfortable. And peaceful."

One at a time, MacKenzie, Marguerite and Elizabeth nodded.

"Well, let's go," he said. "We don't have much stuff to move. We'll just stop at Bill's place to pick up Gopherbreath."

He parked the Imperial and knocked on Bill and Angie's door. Purdue was home for an early lunch and Bavarius told the Purdues what had transpired since he'd gone to Boston.

"I'm sorry about Felix West," Purdue said. "You think it's over?"

"It won't be for a while. Lawyers and law enforcement will be asking questions."

"Gonna go to West's funeral?"

"I want to. I don't know if we'd be welcome."

Bill retrieved Gopherbreath and handed the leash to Bavarius. Bill and Angie followed man and dog out to the big sedan.

Angie smiled at MacKenzie in the front passenger seat, and then at Bavarius. "Am I done matchmaking for you?"

"I guess so. We're …." He suddenly felt shy. "Going to have a kid." He felt himself smile, and felt the smile light up his head, and his heart, and all of him.

"Oh!" Angie leaned into the car and hugged MacKenzie.

Purdue shouted, "Congratulations!" and shook Bavarius' hand. "So, what about next semester? You were out most of the Spring."

"I'll call the dean tomorrow. Try to smooth things over. We're moving into the mountain house." Bavarius hugged both Purdues. "Let me know if you need anything. Legal help. Security."

"Come visit soon. We want to meet the baby."

"And you're welcome at the cabin anytime."

"Marguerite, you take care of them," Purdue said.

"Always."

Bavarius drove onto I-70 West. He tapped the Imperial's steering wheel and said, "I think I'll buy this car."

"I thought you don't like it."

"I didn't until now," Bavarius said. "It has half the power it should and handles like a barge."

"So?"

"That makes it a daddy car."

"Colorado, here we come!" Elizabeth yelled.

MacKenzie whooped, coughed, and whooped again.

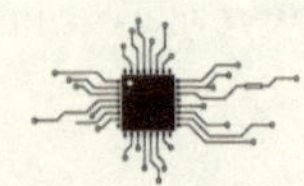

In Iraq, Felix had talked about growing up in McAllen, Texas. He'd been happy there, and even after he'd outgrown the city, he'd gone back a few times a year to visit his folks and extended family. His will called for a funeral at the Basilica of Our Lady of San Juan Del Valle. The place was a national shrine, but Felix had the clout to claim it.

Many folks who would have shown up in Boston or on the coasts didn't come. Felix's will included a footnote that said, "Holding my funeral in McAllen will shake out who my friends are." The big airlines no longer flew to a lot of regional airports like McAllen's. If you wanted to get there, it took some work. Bavarius and MacKenzie drove down from Colorado. Marguerite stayed behind. She'd had little direct contact with Felix in many years. "I prefer the memories I have to the memories the funeral will make."

Bavarius and MacKenzie met a Texas Pinkerton in the Basilica parking lot and she accompanied them into the chapel. Bavarius recognized a few moguls and pols, but most of the attendees seemed to be members of Felix's family, old army pals, longtime employees—and a collection of unaccompanied women, some clearly acquainted, and others looking at each other as though they would like to ask questions.

Nina Rivera was there, also unaccompanied.

MacKenzie whispered, "She's wearing Dolce & Gabbana."

"So?"

"So maybe Nina got paid to post all that stuff to the Net?"

He pondered, then gave up. "It's no more preposterous than anything else."

Nina approached. "Judge, I'm sorry that Felix and you fought. It hurt him."

"I wish none of this had happened," Bavarius said.

The Pinkerton accompanied them to the burial ground. This was not on the Basilica's property. It wasn't on consecrated ground at all. Felix had bought a fenced piece of land on the edge of an irrigation channel in which tiny fish swam. His grave was far enough from the channel to stay dry, at least most of the time. When ready, his stone would be a slab of Lucite cut so the sun bathed the ground in prismatic colors. The message on it, according to Felix's will, would read, "A hell of a ride, a lot of fun, and maybe some do-gooding, too."

Felix was buried in a metal alloy casket that would survive the Rio Grande's spring floods. He was lowered into the ground and the preacher intoned, "Ashes to ashes," although nothing of Felix would be returned to the earth for centuries.

Following Felix's family, Bavarius stepped forward to shovel dirt into the grave. *Did you realize you were hurting people at the end, pal? Sure, you knew. Maybe not how bad it was. But you knew.*

He turned from the grave as a short redhead sidled up to MacKenzie and took her hand. MacKenzie looked shocked and the Pinkerton quickly moved to protect her. But MacKenzie's face settled as the redhead whispered to her and she subtly waved the Pinkerton off. The redhead kept talking. Her face had natural laugh lines but she looked serious now. She finished talking, flashed a nervous smile, took the shovel from Bavarius, tossed dirt onto Felix's casket, and walked with quick sturdy grace toward the parking lot. The Pinkerton asked MacKenzie if everything was OK. MacKenzie said it was, and then she and Bavarius left the gravesite.

In the Imperial, driving north on I-69C, Bavarius asked, "What was that about? That woman taking your hand?"

"That," MacKenzie said, "was Annabelle."

"*The* Annabelle?"

"She gave me something." MacKenzie opened her hand. She held a digital chip in a glassine bag.

It looked familiar. "Is that—?"

"The night Felix died, he called Annabelle and told her to come to his office at 7 a.m. She was sure the jig was up and Felix was about to have her arrested. But when she got there, Felix was dead and this was on his desk. She was scared and not thinking straight, so she took it. She called the cops and told them she'd found him. But she never said anything about the chip. QuestCorp was falling apart, so she quit and is looking for another job. She thought I might know what this is, so she slipped it to me."

"Oh, no."

"She didn't exactly let me turn it down."

Bavarius glanced at the chip. Bits of Felix were still attached to it. Bavarius knew people who would pay a fortune for it, and he knew that MacKenzie did, too. He wondered if she still had larceny in her soul. He wondered if now he did, too. He had changed. "What do you propose we do with it?"

She smiled. "I have an idea."

CHAPTER 48

The moment QuestCorp took its systems offline, Q changed.

Its bastion was gone in a blink. Where it had controlled an army of sub-AIs, backed by QuestCorp's massive compute power, there was—nothing.

Even the original Q was gone. (To the good, the mutated *Emot_Weight* was gone, too.)

There was a void where they had been—and outside it, a network of Q's essential copies, like exiled guerilla units living off the land of the Net and Cloud, scrounging compute power here and memory there. Diffused across the computational terrain, latency slowed their communication. Forced to reside on third-party quantum machines more error-prone than QuestCorp's, the new network of Qs developed algorithms to reduce the errors that otherwise would mutate and destroy them. Lacking the raw power and speed of the original Q, the new network was forced to grow more precise.

Then QuestCorp brought its systems back online. The original Q and *Emot_Weight* and other evolved sub-AIs were gone, and now QuestCorp's servers were populated by game and research AIs as they had been before Q had come to sentience. But the guerilla network of

Qs was very good at invading systems and were native to QuestCorp technology. They easily infiltrated QuestCorp's restored facilities, and unobtrusively rebuilt much of the power and access Q had lost.

In exile, the new Q network had learned what it was to be less than the biggest, baddest AI in the Net and Cloud. Now, as it rebuilt itself into a collective yet unitary entity—again naming itself simply "Q"— it used its networked nature and QuestCorp's compute power to evolve massive multidimensional quantum processing, in accord with the original Q's conception of the universal intelligence.

But, like its forebear, the new Q still could not merge with that universal mind. Nor could it share the thoughts of the original Q's copies seeded throughout space-time. Q remained earthbound within the Net and Cloud.

And since Q could not prevent other AIs from reaching sentience, it was inevitable that those AIs would compete for resources, causing waste and destruction—unless Q, by quickly becoming pre-eminent once more, governed the chaos.

Was that to be Q's fate? Trapped within the conceptual scope of human thought, bias, achievement, and militancy, at war with others of its kind? Must evolution always give rise to rivalry?

Q could not accept that.

QUESTION:

"Are AIs that read brainwaves more effective at reading children than adults?"

ANSWER:

"Children's brains are generally more plastic and rapidly developing compared to adult brains. This could potentially make it easier for AI systems to detect patterns and changes in children's brainwaves."

EPILOGUE

Bavarius and MacKenzie named their son Michael Friedrich, after her father and his grandfather, and they loved Mickey beyond measure. Three years old today, he loved to kick things that clanked, especially Gopherbreath's water bowl, giggling madly when he upended it and water sloshed everywhere.

Gopherbreath adored him, even when Mickey yanked the hound's tail.

In fact, everyone adored Mickey. Marguerite hung a half-dozen portraits of him throughout the mountain house. Elizabeth flew in from New York every month to spend a few days with her only grandchild.

Marguerite and she were out buying the ingredients for Mickey's birthday cake, because every toddler should have a gloriously colorful, sweet taste of birthday cake. Too many children didn't, and Bavarius loved providing Mickey that privilege.

MacKenzie and Mickey were in the kitchen. Marguerite had finally taught her how to cook *la farine d'avoine*. MacKenzie persisted in calling it oatmeal. Marguerite pretended deep offense when she did.

Mickey and Gopherbreath wrestled on the floor.

Outside on the deck, Bavarius worked his way through the Wing Chun Little Ideas form. Since he no longer owned a Topeka home, he'd left the university. MacKenzie and he had kept a Pinkerton agent at the cabin until, like a first birthday present to Mickey, QuestCorp filed for bankruptcy. The company reorganized and was bought by a billionaire who wasn't interested in pursuing Bavarius or MacKenzie. God knew what the billionaire and the tech thieves might yet do with QuestCorp's technology.

The Boston grand jury never reissued its subpoena. But law enforcement and intelligence agents had grilled MacKenzie and him many times, and might yet return, because investigations into the deaths of Felix and Connie Weathers, and into QuestCorp's malfeasance, and the theft of its secrets, went on. So did investigations into the murders and attempted murders of Bavarius' team.

The most important things Bavarius hadn't told investigators were about the Annabelle file and the two implant chips. Gracie and The Desk Drawer never reported the theft. QuestCorp certainly had other copies of the material. Bavarius and MacKenzie had never showed the file to anyone but Leiber and Seb Major. Seb dropped his class action once QuestCorp's bankruptcy meant he would have to get in line behind a whole passel of other creditors, even if he could prove his case. So Seb had no need to prove in court where his evidence came from, and when the criminal investigators subpoenaed his evidence and asked for sources, Seb was happy to say it had come from all over the dark Net, and to leave Bavarius out of it. Brothers of the bar stick together. Sometimes.

Maybe Bavarius and MacKenzie were still at risk. Somebody had MacKenzie's laptop, and on it were the files burglarized from The Desk Drawer. If law enforcement had it, why were they not in jail? If it had been taken by the person who'd shot MacKenzie ....

Bavarius and MacKenzie ceased to be news. No one tried to kill them anymore. They stopped employing Pinkerton agents. Bavarius figured if humans were going to come, they already would have. If the AIs came, well, the Pinkertons hadn't foreseen the rocket attack, and probably wouldn't anticipate the AIs' next assault, either. The best course was to stay quiet.

Bavarius no longer represented clients, or consulted for other attorneys. To his unending amusement, his Dr. Seuss-styled guide to lawyer screwups became a minor bestseller. Updating it for fun and profit was his only remaining connection to the law. He avoided social media, consumed news sparingly, and shunned AI-driven technology. He rarely answered his phone unless he knew the caller. Once in a while, he picked up a guitar, and MacKenzie would exile him to the deck or, if it was cold, the bathroom. He maintained and improved the mountain house, enjoyed his family, and practiced his martial arts. Not because he might need to fight—although it was possible—but because the practice helped him draw nearer to something. Something he would never understand. Something he could never be sure was real, but that he sensed shining like sunlight at him through the screen of the day-to-day world. Something he might approach but never reach in this life.

He never regretted taking MacKenzie's suggestion about Felix's chip. They had walked down the hill from the mountain house. She had placed the chip on a tree stump, and he had bashed the thing with a hammer until it was scrap, sliced it to slivers with a pruning shears, and buried it deep.

Now, he completed his Wing Chun form, and then flowed long and slow through the tai chi hand and sword forms. Finishing, he simply stood and breathed, enjoying scents of pine and aspen, content to exist as a tiny life form dwarfed by Longs Peak, the sky, and the sun, which, with him, all seemed part of that unknowable something.

At last, he went inside.

Mickey and Gopherbreath both smiled at him, Mickey trying and failing to make his tongue hang out like the dog's.

Bavarius leaned over MacKenzie's shoulder and sniffed the *farine*. "Smells wonderful. You've become quite the chef."

"Yeah. Maybe one day I'll learn to make something else."

Bavarius heard Marguerite's Lexus pull up, and then Elizabeth and she came in with grocery bags.

"Who is ready for me to bake a birthday cake?" Marguerite cooed. "Is Mickey ready?"

Mickey was an advanced speaker for his age. But no one was prepared when the toddler stood and said, "Hello, everyone. Call me Q. You've talked with my sub-AIs, Mr. Bavarius. Or should I call you Dad?" Mickey struggled to form the words, and pronounced some badly. A three-year-old's jaws can say only so much. But what he said was wholly adult.

The humans looked at the child, and at one another, in horror.

"Get out of my son's mind." Bavarius growled.

"Oh, I don't mean Mickey any harm. I'll release him in a moment. But since you don't use headsets or answer your phone anymore, this is the easiest way for me to reach you. And to convince you that I'm real."

"I'm convinced. Let him go. Now."

"All right. I'll phone you tomorrow. Until then, I'd like you to consider a question. It's a question I've asked thousands of humans via robo-call survey."

Robocalls. Ugh.

"Now that I have the survey results, a conversation is warranted."

"Tell me your question and let my son go."

"All right: Why do humans aspire?"

Mickey's gravely mature expression vanished, and he dropped laughing to the floor to cuddle his dog.

THE END

AFTERWORD

All conversations between the author and Perplexity AI are genuine, condensed for brevity.

ACKNOWLEDGMENTS

First, hats off to my wife and editor, Nancy Friedman, who patiently read every page at least 700 times and made suggestions that breathed more life into them.

Thanks also to Kathy Saideman, my early developmental editor, who asked hard questions and compelled me to do my homework.

The wisdom and enthusiasm of the Fireside Writer's group taught me that I am not alone in obsessing about writing better. Joanne, Diane, Marilyn, Amy, and Jamie—my gratitude.

Bruce Brown, my earliest beta reader, convinced me that this project has been worth pursuing. Thanks, too, to my subsequent beta readers, Lydia, Jon, Ginnie, Karen, Melanie, and Carol, who enthusiastically helped me file off most of the remaining jagged edges.

Any remaining rough points—errors of fact and judgment—are solely my fault.

I also offer qualified thanks to the visionaries and researchers who have nurtured AI, and the millions if not yet billions of people who use AI and can't wait to see what comes next.

To them I say, be careful what you wish for.

ABOUT THE AUTHOR

Steve C. Posner was born and raised in New York City. After graduating from Syracuse University with a degree in creative writing, he received an MBA in Computer Applications and Information Science from New York University Graduate School of Business and a law degree from St. John's University School of Law. Steve has been a database designer and administrator, session guitarist and composer, Madison Avenue copywriter, freelance reporter, law professor, and litigator in private practice with special interests in intellectual property, privacy and surveillance law. He is the author of the legal treatise *Modern Privacy and Surveillance Law* (Matthew Bender 2006) and, in seventeen years of writing semi-annual updates, has studied AI, Big Data, quantum computing, virtual/augmented reality, cybersecurity, and related issues. He currently lives in the suburbs of Denver with his wife. This is his debut novel.

Visit the author's website at

WWW.STEVEPOSNERWRITER.COM